Popping the Clutch

A CarTubers Manual for Love

Rochelle Bradley

Dedication

For my car enthusiast kiddos and Prince.

Acknowledgments

A shoutout of appreciation to my beta reading, author pals, Aliya DalRae and CJ Warrant. Your insight and suggestions were spot on.

Thank you to my car enthusiast husband and son for helping me with track, engine, and other car details, schematics, and recommendations.

Special thanks to master mechanic Mr. C for reading PTC and double checking to make sure all my car information was spot on.

To the YouTubers who share their love of cars with the world: I appreciate your time and effort to educate and entertain the world. Keep following your passion.

Author's Note

Dear Reader,

Thank you for reading Popping the Clutch.

My prince loves cars and prides himself in problem solving and maintaining our small fleet of family vehicles. He has installed his appreciation of quality engineering and upkeep to our children. He watches endless car influencers on YouTube. So much so, that I've started dreaming about them and thus we have the birth of The CarTubers Manual for Love series.

Ever since my son was a toddler, he loved cars, too. Not planes or trains—cars. Especially the big yellow Hummers. He's now 22 and graduating from UNOH (University of Northwest Ohio) with a business degree focused on—you guessed it—cars. He's part of the racing club and interns as crew chief, and other positions, for Rise Motorsports (car 31) in the ARCA Menards series.

I'm surrounded by car lovers and had to do a lot of research for this one, but I love Callie and Dyson's story, and I hope you will too.

Enjoy and keep sassy,
Rochelle

Prologue
Callie

Filled with high status sports cars, murmuring people, and hot spotlights, the car show overwhelmed my senses. Still, every time I glanced at our entry, a 1986 C4 Corvette with a flawless copper metallic finish, I smiled with pride. My brother Jay and I had successfully rebuilt the crashed Corvette as part of Enzo's Auto Tech's CarTube channel.

My master mechanic father, Alexander Ferenzo, had taken Jay and me under his tutelage as soon as we could hold a wrench. We learned the fundamentals of engine schematics while other children climbed trees and rode bikes. I'm still shit at bike riding.

Jay dubbed himself the stage name *Enzo* for our CarTube show. We had the same dark brown hair and green eyes—not uncommon for siblings, and the ladies found him irresistible even if he rattled on about exhausts or torque.

According to my father, I was the true reason the Corvette ran. I had an eye for troubleshooting and, more importantly, the patience to diagnose correctly.

Jay also agreed I was the reason we finished the restoration in time for the show, except he credited my looks and viewership rather than my skills. He believed my feminine presence on the show drove the views higher, so we made more money, thus allowing us to purchase parts faster. I knew my value, so I usually ignored his comments and just rolled my eyes.

Some of our CarTube viewers had visited our booth to congratulate us on the completion of our project. They wanted pictures of Jay and me with the car.

This auto show wasn't big like SEMA, but one step at a time. It was a tremendous success for Enzo's Auto Tech to be here, at the Kansas City Car Meet—to have come this far in such a short time. I was confident we'd get to the Specialty Equipment Market Association Show in a few years.

My father's ringtone sounded, and I picked up. "Hi, Dad."

"Hello, Calloway Turbo. Are you going full throttle?" Dad greeted me with my nickname, then coughed.

Biting my lip, I ignored his cough and the wheezing that followed. "Did you see the pictures I sent? It's a great turnout. Jay is playing host, and we've visited with some fans of the show."

"Great. I knew you could do this. I'm so proud of you." He coughed again, reminding me of my childhood cat, Mr. Morris Garfield, who hacked up hairballs.

"Dad?"

He cleared his throat. "I'm fine. Just a frog. Have fun and tell Dyson and Corey hello."

"Will do. Love you Daddy." Since his heart attack, I never knew when talking to him would be my last time.

Ending the call, I waited for my brother to return from his hour-long bathroom break.

"Hey," Jay greeted as he sauntered toward me.

I stared at the red and white bag in his hand before meeting his gaze

"I couldn't refuse the smell of popcorn." Jay grinned as he tossed a handful into his mouth.

"It does smell good," I countered. "Did you get me one?"

He held only one bag, and his smile slackened. "Uh. Um."

"It's okay. I'll run and get my own. Be back in a few minutes."

I saluted and turned away before he could swallow. My time browsing exhibits would be based on Jay-minutes. A few equaled thirty to sixty.

I ambled toward the far side of the arena. The aisles of shiny cars in a kaleidoscope of colors could hold my attention for hours. I ventured toward a cherry red Lamborghini Diablo.

Once I reached the car, I walked to the side, admiring the lines. "Classic beauty," I muttered.

"Callie."

My name came from somewhere. I glanced around.

"Callie, in here."

I leaned over and peered into the supercar. Inside, Dyson Gabbard, of the CarTube channel Gabby's Garage, waved.

"Hey, how's it going?"

In my perusal of the car's exterior, I hadn't noticed him behind the wheel. I opened the door and slipped into the passenger seat. "Taking a break?" I asked as he raised the tinted windows.

"Yes. I'm going to sip my water and not talk."

"You're talking to me," I offered with a laugh.

He chuckled. "Yeah, you're different. I don't have to answer the same questions over and over, like I'm on repeat."

I studied him. Dyson, with his boy-next-door charm and sparkling hazel eyes, offered a lopsided grin. His short, spikey hair brushed the headliner and his long legs folded comically in the small space.

"You don't mind talking about your baby," I teased with a smirk. "You love it when they ask you questions."

"I know," he laughed, leaning his head against the headrest, "I just needed to rest my vocal cords for a moment."

Glancing out the windscreen, I noted fans had gathered, snapping pictures of the gorgeous car.

"How's your dad?" Dyson asked softly.

"I just spoke with him. He seemed in good spirits. He was

really bummed about not coming, especially since we're not too far from home, but he has to take care of his health." I couldn't meet Dyson's gaze.

Nearly losing my father, the inspiration for and the originator of both me and my brother's passion for cars, had been devastating.

Dyson patted my arm, bringing me from the brink of dire thoughts. "Thank you for asking. Dad said to say hi."

"I'm glad to hear he's on the mend."

I wasn't sure about that. The inactivity would probably kill him before his bad heart would.

Changing the subject, I turned in my seat to face him. "I wish you could start the Diablo. I'd love to hear it."

"Me too." He gripped the wheel. "I've got an idea." He fished for his phone, then searched in his albums. "Ah, found it."

He tapped the screen, and a clip from his show played, the episode where he started the Lamborghini, then took it on a drive. The short piece had no commentary. He turned the phone volume up and I closed my eyes, imagining the vibrations. I envisioned putting the beast into gear and then down shifting.

When I opened my eyes, Dyson had a strange look on his face. His gaze dropped to my legs.

"What?" I asked, wondering if I'd don something wrong.

"You air shifted and used the clutch."

My face heated. Living out the fantasies in my head meant sometimes I manifested them.

"I do that, too," he shrugged, smiling.

I returned his smile. A funny feeling flared in my chest. Nothing a snack couldn't fix or chase away, I hoped.

"I'm going to grab some popcorn. Jay had some and it smelled just the right buttery." I opened the door and stepped out.

"Callie," Dyson called. I looked back in as he continued, "I like your dad's idea of the competition between Corey, Enzo, and me. Would you have your own car, too?"

"No," I said, even though I was tempted to join them to show my mettle. "I'll help my brother with filming and editing, but nothing else. This would be his baby."

"That's a shame. He'll lose without you." Dyson winked.

The strange sensation returned, and I rubbed my chest.

"Probably, but I'll be there to record all your shenanigans." I waved and left before I was tempted to speculate about the source of the strange sensation.

I munched on my popcorn, returning to the Corvette. The metallic copper paint glimmered under all the overhead lights. It wasn't my favorite color, but it was unique and made a statement.

Jay stood by the front of the Corvette, conversing with a man with beefy arms, a thick neck, and messy hair. The hood was raised, exposing the clean engine. They occasionally leaned over investigating something.

I kept out of earshot but took a few pictures to show my dad how Jay was working it. Jay noticed me, waved, then returned to his conversation.

At a small table, I sat and ate my snack, waiting for a reply from my dad. It was possible he was napping. I sighed, thinking of the energetic, strong man who'd been devastated by a heart attack. Now he appeared frail and helpless. The most mundane tasks caused breathlessness and frustration.

We'd started the Enzo's Auto Tech channel after I'd returned from college with a BS in business management and a minor in film and my brother had breezed through his tech and tuning classes. Our new skills built on what we'd already learned from Dad, and he was there to guide us behind the scenes. I gave thanks for him every day.

"See you, Enzo," the man said, using Jay's show name. The burly man gave me a once-over as he walked away. I shuddered. His expression was unnerving.

Jay joined me, smiling. He smoothed his polo shirt, giving an extra pat to the Enzo's Auto Tech logo embroidered on the left chest. The red shirt with black and yellow lettering had been Dad's idea. The colors popped.

"Who was that?" I asked, pushing aside my lingering unease.

"Jacob Miller, a consultant. While you were off on your hike yesterday, I met him at the bar. We had a beer together." He reached into his jeans' rear pocket and pulled out a business card. "Nice guy. Doesn't really give a hoot about cars. It was fun talking about the business end of things for once."

I gaped at my brother. He was all about the power of the car—the more torque, the better. And about how a sexy car could catch a needy woman. It was rare hearing him speak about the business side of the–well, the business.

Jay enjoyed going big and flashy. We needed to spend money to make it. I kept telling him there are inexpensive ways to gain followers. Other than exploiting my curves.

A TV crew came through and interviewed us for their local newscast, touting Enzo's Auto Tech as an up-and-coming channel and something to watch.

With Jay's ego appropriately stroked, he called Dyson and Corey on FaceTime to brag. "Guess who just pegged Enzo's as the up-and-coming channel?"

I waved to the men over Jay's shoulder, then gave Jay bunny ears. Dyson and Corey laughed. I began recording a video with my phone. Catching the pre-competition sparring would make for fun teasers or extras. After his call ended, we continued talking with car enthusiasts.

All afternoon people ebbed and flowed like waves on a beach. My feet ached by the end of the day.

"Have you heard from Dad?" Jay asked, glancing at his phone.

"Not since earlier. I had a quick chat with him while you were getting popcorn. And I sent him a bunch of photos from when I strolled around."

"Me too." Worry etched Jay's brow. "I'm going to call him." He paced as he waited for Dad to respond.

Corey and Dyson approached. "Hey there. How did you do?" I asked.

Corey held up a trophy. "They gave me this. So, I guess The Car Magician did all right."

"That's awesome, Corey!" Corey smiled as I studied the glimmering gold car on the top of the trophy. "I predict a Kansas City Car Meet episode on The Car Magician's channel coming soon."

"What's Enzo doing?" Dyson's gaze tracked my brother.

"He's calling Dad." I frowned when I heard Jay leaving a message. "He could be napping."

Jay hurried over to me, and I stepped backward, bumping into Dyson. "Sorry."

"I can't reach him. I'm calling Mrs. Covelli."

"She's his neighbor," I said before the others could ask.

Someone rubbed my shoulders as I waited with bated breath for my brother to report. "She's going next door."

Jay paced and paced, then he paused and his shoulders dropped. "She's calling nine one one."

"No," I choked out, blinking back the tears.

Jay froze, his phone glued to his ear as he strained to listen. Minutes ticked away. I chewed my lip, barely breathing.

Jay lifted watery eyes at me. "He's gone."

A solitary tear slid down his cheek. He closed his eyes and inhaled. Jay's face became a mask of stone as he listened to whatever was going on.

Stunned, my chest tightened. Large arms surrounded me. I spun into Dyson's embrace, then the sobs hit me.

I cried, "Daddy."

Chapter One
Callie

Eighteen months later.

"Stop being an asshole, Jay." I smirked at my brother while holding the camera focused on Jay and his two CarTube guests. Since the inception, I'd helped my brother film Enzo's Auto Tech. We upload twice a week—Mondays and Thursdays with the occasional special edition or live broadcast.

His laughter stalled in his throat as he swung around to face me. "Don't call me that," he growled, red-faced.

"Asshole or Jay?" I laughed. When he was angry, he was easy to goad. I continued before he could respond, "Jay is your name." It was really James Allen Ferenzo, but I didn't push my luck.

His nose crinkled, as if he strained to think of some witty retort.

"Come on, Enzo," Dyson Gabbard called my brother his preferred name. "If you keep harassing your sister, she'll quit."

Dyson briefly met my gaze. A sappy grin tipped his lips, reminding me of his goofy CarTube persona.

"If Callie quits, then she can come shoot for me or you, Dyson," Corey Davidson said, rubbing his scruffy beard.

"Oh? What would it pay?" I asked.

With his hands on his hips, Jay's attitude turned playful once more. "She can have cameos on your shoots. It's guaranteed to boost views. I'll share."

Our guests glanced at each other and nodded. I rolled my eyes. I hated being used to gain views and followers on Jay's channel. When it comes to working on cars—or anything, really, I'm methodical and patient and that makes me a better mechanic than my brother. But for the videos we uploaded for our channel, I preferred to be behind the camera, not leaning over a car engine, my butt in the air while I got my hands dirty. Unless I had an idea for my own show, where I'd have complete creative control of the channel, and *then* I would gladly be the star.

"You aren't the CarTube pimp, *Jay*. I'd work with either of these two because they are professionals."

I zoomed in on Dyson and Corey, who were laughing. Like this moment, it was the raw, unscripted footage I loved the best. Real glimpses of the men behind the CarTube personalities.

"That's the first time I've been called a *professional*," Dyson said. "I kinda like the sound of it. Thanks, Callie."

Jay stomped over to his director's chair and climbed into it. He huffed as he crossed his arms. Dyson and Corey went and sat in their chairs. My wiry brother seemed almost child-size next to the lanky Dyson and brawny Corey.

All three of the men's channels had debuted nearly simultaneously, leading to several audience crossovers—and today's filming was one of the shows meant for all three audiences. This time, they planned to discuss—or argue, motor trends and EVs.

As the men waited for me to give the okay, they settled into a conversation about the traffic around their homes. They agreed stupid drivers are everywhere.

I double checked that the static camera on the stand was fully charged and recording. All the microphones passed the checks. The side profile camera was ready to catch all the shenanigans. And tonight my real fun would begin—I'd edit and splice the videos.

I handed each of the men a sheet with questions I'd researched and found trending with other CarTube channels.

"Ready?" I asked Jay, returning to the camera for one last check of the view.

"Let's roll," Jay quipped his CarTube go-phrase and smiled.

"Ugh, not the cheesy grin. You need to be real," I ordered. "Remember, ten-twelve."

Jay's smile morphed into a cat-who-caught-the-canary grin.

Oh shit. I glanced at the screen, tapped settings and hoped he'd let my numbers comment drop.

"What's ten-twelve?" Dyson asked.

My heart flew to my throat. I attempted to swallow it back down.

"I'm so glad you asked. It's an interesting story, Dyson." Jay's Cheshire grin grew evil. "It's all thanks to you. She knows your Gabby's Garage episodes better than mine."

Dyson glanced at me, so I shrugged.

"Come on, Callie. Don't keep your boyfriend waiting," Jay teased.

I narrowed my eyes, hoping my glare would singe Jay's forehead. The other men waited, staring at me.

I set the camera aside and inhaled. "Here's the deal. Sometimes Jay wears a cheesy grin. It's goofy and not authentic, so one day when I was scoping out the competition, I found..." I squeezed my eyes shut, envisioning the scene–such purity of emotion. Dyson behind the wheel of a red Lamborghini, wind blowing his hair, eyes sparkling, and t-shirt pulled tight on his biceps and chest.

"What?" Dyson asked.

I blinked, feeling heat on my face. "I found joy. Such pure joy. And that's what I want Jay to emulate, not give me some fake smile." I inspected my brother. "You're supposed to be living your dream, and you need to sell it."

"But what is ten-twelve?" Corey asked, keeping to the point.

"It's a time marker in an episode in the forties," I said, picking up my camera. "It's an episode with the Diablo. God, I loved that car." A touch of envy gnawed, as I remembered the supercar.

"Episode forty-three," Dyson and I said together.

"Seriously?" Jay wheezed.

I met Dyson's eyes, and warmth blossomed in my chest. He blushed but agreed. "I loved that car, too."

Corey rubbed his hands together. "I know what I'm watching later."

"You'll see the genuineness in it. That's more appealing. Be real and have fun. I know working with Jay isn't the best, but you've got me today." I bowed with a flourish.

Jay pointed a finger at me. "My sister—the magic maker."

"That's The Car Magician's schtick," I quipped.

"Touché," Corey said, cracking a rare smile.

Corey had a dry sense of humor, which often made my brother scratch his head. He reminded me of a thirty-year-old gamer who lived in his parents' basement. Socially awkward and quiet, with random bursts of wisdom. When it came to diagnosing cars of all makes, the guy was a brilliant mechanic.

After filming the day's interview, Jay offered beers and snacks, so we strode over to Jay's house, which was next to Enzo's Auto Tech garage. My brother lived in our childhood home, while I had moved not too far away. Staying in that house, surrounded by reminders of my father and the echoes of our shared past, was unbearable. Plus, I needed time away from Jay and Enzo's Auto Tech.

While in the kitchen relaxing, Corey watched Gabby's Garage episode forty-three but got so into it he passed the timestamp without pausing.

"What's your favorite thing they don't make anymore?" Jay asked Dyson.

"A manual transmission," Dyson said without hesitating. "They're so rare now and..."

"Most use the flappy paddles and not a stick," I offered.

Dyson lifted his beer in salute.

"Callie loves a stick shift. She knows how to work it," Jay teased, waggling his brows.

My brother–the major tool. His attempt at teasing flopped. But I wondered if it was his way of trying to set me up with one of his friends. I played along. "I do like a good long stick shift—one with a ball on the end. Especially when you put it into gear and pop the clutch... " I closed my eyes and hummed. "There's nothing like it."

"So, Enzo, how about those Chiefs?" Dyson asked.

I laughed, walked to the fridge, and pilfered a bottle of water. On my way back to the guys, a flash of turquoise out the window caught my eye.

I gasped, dropping my water. "Tell me you didn't drive here in your limited edition 911 GT3 RS Porsche with under five thousand miles." I whipped my head to peer incredulously at Dyson.

"I did." He stood and ambled to my side, stooped to retrieve my bottle of water, and together we gawked at the gorgeous car–me in awe and, when I chanced a glance at Dyson, him with a prideful smile.

Without thinking, I exited the house and walked straight to the car, Dyson's heat on my back the whole way. The classy fender curves, raw engine torque, and bright color all mesmerized me. Like a moth to a flame, I reached out to touch the shiny car. At the last second, I pulled my hand back. So many guys hated when anything rubbed the paint, because dirt molecules can microscopically scratch the finish.

I hadn't noticed how close Dyson was until his breath fanned my ear when he whispered, "Go ahead, Callie. Touch it."

I shivered, but was it from his nearness or the anticipation of getting up close and personal with a beautiful ride?

"Really?" I asked breathlessly, studying his intense hazel eyes.

"Yes, really,"

"Don't break my heart, Dyson."

"Never, Callie."

"Get a room," Jay hollered from the door.

My gaze swung to Jay. I thumbed over my shoulder toward the car. "If that room contained the work of art on the driveway, I'd get it."

"Oh, yeah?" Jay asked me, then glanced at Dyson, wiggling his brows.

Ignoring my brother, and not meeting Dyson's gaze, I returned my attention to the Porsche. The curving contours of its body tantalized me. "So sexy," I whispered.

Still feeling Dyson's nearness, I strode to stand by the car's front driver's side fender. Holding my index finger a millimeter from the cool metal, I glanced at Dyson, offering one last chance for him to refuse me.

He stood tall, eyes wide and sparkling in the afternoon sun. A grin split his face, and I returned it. "Ten-twelve," he said.

I may have squealed as I rested my palm on the hood. Inhaling, I started my slow perusal of the luscious vehicle, trailing my fingertips over the curves.

I lost myself in the moment, tuning out nature, my brother, Corey, and Dyson. I peeked inside the driver's side window. Intent on scrutinizing the interior–the smooth black leather seats with bright yellow piping and embroidering, the racing harness, the roll bars–I startled when the door lock disengaged.

My hopeful gaze rose to meet Dyson's. With a nod, he grinned.

Touching the door handle, I slid my fingers under, pulled it open and leaned in. Warm air laden with the scent of leather tingled my senses. I inhaled until my gut hurt.

Not wasting another second, I slipped into the driver's seat. Gripping the wheel, my heart thundered as I used the tip of my finger to trace the Porsche emblem on the horn pad before moving my hand to caress the gear shifter, sliding my hand down to the supple leather boot.

The racing harness had yellow accents to match other special details like the brake calipers.

The seat had been positioned to accommodate Dyson's lanky body. I couldn't reach the pedals because he was a six-two giant. And where Dyson's spiky hair rubbed the roof liner of every supercar he acquired, my head was inches short and my line of sight was only just above the dash.

I scooted to the front edge of the seat, stretching to reach the pedals. "How the heck do you drive this thing?"

"I have legs," Dyson teased, as he gripped the roof of the Porsche and then leaned in.

"Ha." I crinkled my nose, trying to ignore his scrumptious scent and the way his position made his biceps bulge.

He reached down and pulled the lever on the side of the seat. It activated and slid forward until I could touch the pedals comfortably. Then he raised the seat height for me. I settled back as the leather conformed to my body. It was comfy, and I closed my eyes while taking the beast on an imaginary road.

"Dyson, why don't you take Callie home?" Jay suggested.

A grin manifested unhampered on my face.

"Would you like that, Callie?" Dyson asked.

"Duh. Yes, of course, I would." I opened my eyes and met his gaze.

Dyson chuckled. He dug in his pocket. Extending his arm until his fist was mere inches from my face, he opened his palm to show me the key fob. "Would you like to drive?"

My heart stalled. "Seriously?" I gasped.

"Yes, ma'am."

"No way," Jay muttered.

I frowned at my brother, catching his gaze through the passenger window, cracked open about two inches. "You're just jelly that he offered."

I snatched the fob from Dyson's hand without even

considering how I'd get back to the garage the next day if I left my Jeep here. Flipping the small object in my palm, I studied the symbols.

I pushed the ignition, and the beast rumbled to life. The throaty engine purred, and I shivered at the sound, gripping the wheel tighter. The engine's vibrations flowed through my body. *I may need to change my panties when I get home.*

"Are you sure?" I glanced at Dyson again.

With hooded eyes and a gleaming smile, he reached in and helped me adjust the harness before closing the door.

Definitely need to change my panties now.

A moment later, Dyson sat next to me as I adjusted the mirrors and lowered the windows all the way. The smile on my face would possibly be tattooed there forever.

Jay leaned into the car, crossing his arms on the window edge. "Wow. Dyson must really like you, Callie." He smirked, then winked at me.

I rolled my eyes. "The word is trust, not like. He trusts me."

Jay's lopsided grin faltered, and he stood. "Are you implying he doesn't trust me?"

I stole a look at Dyson, pressed back against the bucket seat, silent and still, giving me the space to sass Jay.

"Dyson has seen our videos just as much as we've seen his, and he knows I drive better than you."

"What?" Jay shouted.

I grinned and saluted Jay, then pressed the clutch and shifted to first. I punched the gas, shooting away from the house as I smoothly shifted into second and then third. The force of the acceleration pressed Dyson and me into the seats.

"Woo-hoo!" I hollered.

The rear got a little squirrelly and fishtailed as I turned out of the driveway, but I caught the power and straightened it. No way I would take a chance where Dyson demanded I pull over, so he could drive. Not today.

The beast hugged the curves, and I tried to stick to the speed limit. At a four-way stop, I revved the engine while deciding whether to turn left or right. Right was the most direct route. I turned left.

Flooring it on a straight stretch, joy bubbled up, and I laughed. Dyson joined me. The road dipped into a tree-lined curling noodle.

The sports car responded to my every touch. We became one, my senses responding to every nuance of the finely tuned example of German engineering.

After a short hour, I pulled into the driveway of the white Cape Cod-style house my roommate Amber and I rented. Amber had forgotten to close the door to our two-car garage again. I parked behind her nondescript gray Honda sedan and my work-in-progress Crosley Hotshot.

I couldn't bring myself to cut the engine until after I had revved it twice. With a sheepish grin and a shrug, I offered the fob back to Dyson. "Thank you. That was awesome."

"Anytime." He unbuckled the harness while studying the white house with the black shutters that I called home.

"Want to trade?" I nudged him and drew his attention to my cute little car. Quite the history on the Crosley. Conceived in Cincinnati after World War II, you could buy my car in a catalog.

"Do you have two? So I can wear one on each foot?" His gaze swung back to the house. "Someone is watching us."

Amber was peering out the living room window. "She's probably hoping Jay is with me. She totally crushes on that asshole."

"I thought she was gawking at the car."

I pressed my lips together and sighed. "For Amber, a car is exactly four wheels and a gas tank. A thing for getting you from point A to point B. Not a masterpiece of transportation and art."

Dyson covered my hand, which had yet to leave the shift knob. He squeezed, and a shiver ran up my arm. "You appreciate fine art. Jay was right. I like you."

I tipped my head, staring into his fabulous hazel eyes. "Fine art comes in all sizes, mediums, and *speeds*. I like you, too. You have been elevated to one of my favorite people. You want to come in?"

Dyson grinned meeting my gaze. He squeezed once more, then let go. "Sure."

We climbed out of the low-slung car and Dyson followed me to my front door, where Amber stood waiting to greet us. Her face held a note of disappointment covered by a sparkle of curiosity.

I spun, and Dyson almost bumped into me. "A word of warning. Amber is worse than my brother for teasing me about guys. Just so you know, and you're prepared."

"So, no open mouth kisses?" His eyes crinkled in mirth.

Ignoring the warmth in my belly, I poked him in the gut. "Behave."

"You're no fun," he said with a pout.

I couldn't help the giggle. "That's not true, and you know it."

I continued toward the door and hopped up the three steps to my waiting friend. A high, tight ponytail held back Amber's blonde hair. She wore a fuchsia lipstick that matched her designer shirt, and probably her thong, too.

"Hi Callie. And you must be Dyson—hello." She winked at Dyson and turned back to me. "Jay called an hour ago saying to check out the car you were driving." She glanced at the Porsche. "It's a pretty shade of blue." She held the door open, and I entered with Dyson on my heels.

"Jay called, huh?"

Amber's cheeks blossomed red. "He said you have a new boyfriend."

I glanced at Dyson and rolled my eyes. It seemed like I did that a lot when it came to Jay. "As far as Jay's matchmaking ability goes, I could do a lot worse. But no, Dyson isn't my boyfriend. His car might be my new love, though."

Dyson's brows shot heavenward, and he chuckled.

"Ah, geez, you and your cars." Amber threw her hands in the

air. "You're worse than your brother."

"In my opinion, that's a good thing," I chirped, staring out the window at the gorgeous vehicle. I hoped my dreams would be full of flashes of Dyson's blue baby.

I gave Dyson a tour of the small house, which Amber and I rented. Two bedrooms, one full bath, a tiny kitchen, and dining and living rooms. Everything I needed to live, especially since I wasn't home much—I was either filming or editing footage at the shop or studio. When I wasn't working on Enzo's Auto Tech stuff, I tinkered with my Crosley. Progress on its restoration was slow, but I was happy with what I'd done so far.

When we returned to the kitchen, Amber sat at the table, texting. She giggled and glanced up when Dyson said he should go. We moved toward the door.

"Um, Jay says you need to thank Dyson properly," Amber said. Her gaze swung from me to Dyson.

With hands on my hips I said, "Ask my brother this, Amber. How do I thank a man who's already let me finger his stick shift and given me the ride of my life?"

She blinked cow eyes and Dyson busted out laughing. We exited, and I walked him to the car. He was still chuckling.

"My brother is such a nosy asshole," I muttered, without taking my eyes from the sun glinting off the Porsche's hood.

"He likes to tease, but what would happen if Amber reported to him that we kissed?" He stared at the house. I didn't have to turn to know Amber watched us as a willing spy for my brother.

"If she accurately relays my message, he'll be sputtering with the double entendres I offered." I smirked, giddiness and elation bubbling through me.

I faced Dyson. The breeze ruffled his chestnut-colored hair and the sun glinted off the moving strands. When he caught my gaze, I couldn't pull away. Flecks of gold and green sparkled in his eyes.

Gratitude swelled in my heart. He didn't have to let me drive his car, but he had taken a chance. "Thank you for letting me drive your baby," I said, my voice hoarse with emotion as I touched his arm. "It made my year. I don't know how I can ever repay you."

"You're welcome. There's no need to repay..." Dyson glanced away, his gaze distant. "Actually, I might need your help with something."

"What?" I asked, willing to help him, especially with his CarTube episodes.

"Something with my family."

"Oh?" My curiosity was piqued. I knew nothing about his family other than he had a sister who'd made an appearance on Gabby's Garage a few times. To his credit, Dyson hadn't dangled his sister as a piece of juicy meat for his viewers.

"I don't know yet. But I might need a favor."

I smiled at him. My neck started to ache. Any girl who dated Dyson would have to strengthen her neck muscles in order to keep her head tilted so she could look into his beautiful eyes. "Sure, anything. IOU."

"Anything?" His gaze jerked to mine.

I swallowed, then opened my mouth to speak. It snapped shut when he lowered to kiss me. My heart worked overtime, and I found my lung capacity inadequate. His lips lingered on mine for a moment, but the sweet kiss still ended too soon.

He pulled away and walked to his car. I stood speechless, watching him.

"I'll see you later, Callie." He called as he sank into the driver's seat. "Ouch."

I giggled as I heard the seat slide backward and lower. Then the engine rumbled to life and my hand flew to my heart. But instead of closing my eyes and savoring the feeling, I couldn't peel my eyes away from the driver. He winked before sliding on sunglasses. As he pulled onto the street, I began to breathe again.

I could still feel the pressure of Dyson's surprise kiss on my lips. Maybe it was more than the car that turned me on.

Chapter Two
Dyson

Two weeks after Callie's drive and the kiss I'd stolen, memories of her sweet taste had me longing to pull her against me to probe her mouth fully and claim her as mine. That would teach Enzo to tempt fate.

As I coasted my Yukon into Enzo's parking lot, I saw Callie's little yellow Crosley and one of Enzo's project beaters. I couldn't deny him credit for making that deal. I'd bought my Yukon for a song. But to get the thing in operating order, it'd cost more than a song--more along the lines of an opera. Thanks to Corey, though, who really did live up to his channel's name—The Car Magician, the Yukon was Ol' Reliable and my daily ride.

I entered the building and swore I could smell a hint of vanilla and almonds–Callie. Poking my head in the office, I spied Callie staring at a monitor. She chewed her bottom lip as she studied the footage.

She wore a white t-shirt and her long, dark hair was pulled into a braid that landed halfway down her back. If she wore makeup, I couldn't tell. Callie had a classic beauty that appealed to me. Not only me, unfortunately—any red-blooded hetero male. And that's why Enzo liked to stick her in his episodes. Her presence made his ratings rise. Probably because it made other things rise on the viewers.

I hated her being used for her T and A almost as much as Callie did.

"Hello, hello," I called as I knocked on the door frame.

Callie jumped and swiveled in the seat to face me, her hand over her heart. "Geez-Louise, Dyson, you scared the crap out of me." She blew out a breath.

My gaze dropped to her chest. My show's logo embellished the shirt she wore. "Nice shirt," I teased.

"Uh huh, is that all you're looking at?" She crossed her arms, hiding the words. I noticed how her movement pushed up those Ts and my gaze rose to hers. Her brows dipped as a blush blossomed on her face.

Ignoring her comment, I said, "Thanks for pimping my show. That's prime real estate."

Oh shit, did I just say that? My face heated, and I had to be as red as the 1985 Ferrari Testarossa I'd just sold.

Luckily, she giggled and I wouldn't get sued for sexual harassment.

After a beat of silence, she said, "What did you drive today?"

"Kiss me for a drive," I teased.

Her eyes widened. "Ohhh, is it something good?" She leaned back so she could see out of the window. The desk chair accommodated her movement.

How the hell did she not blatantly reject me and shut me down? Had I actually tempted her?

She snapped upright again. "I can't see what it is. It's not the Porsche, is it?"

"No, not today. It's something I actually fit in." I chuckled as she pushed past me, eager to see my ride. I followed her hip-hugging jeans as we exited the building. She stared at the Yukon with a frown.

"That's it?" she groused. "So boring."

I leaned close, where her almonds and vanilla scent was

stronger. "It's fully loaded. Do you know the MSRP?"

She ran a finger down my chest, giving me goosebumps. "Why Dyson, are you going to quote retail, torque, and other seductive stuff to me?" She fluttered her lashes as she tipped her tempting lips toward me.

My heart threatened to leap out of my chest. Her hooded green eyes sparkled a mischievous glint. I wrapped an arm around her waist and tugged her close. She squealed and her eyes widened.

"Dyson," she whispered.

Her phone chimed, and she backed out of my arms. "Time to leave for my hair appointment."

"Are you getting it cut?" I asked, following her into the building.

"I'm getting highlights and a trim," she said over her shoulder. She bypassed the office, going straight toward the work area. "I'm filming Jay troubleshooting and rebuilding the sixties Ford he bought. I want the premium footage for the channel, even though the only thing I like about the truck is its sparkling blue paint."

The large workspace could hold four vehicles with room to spare. A blue truck was up on the lift and Enzo pointed a flashlight at the undercarriage. Cameras encircled him as he worked.

"Look what I found lurking around?" Callie said as she ambled toward her brother.

Enzo glanced over and smiled. "Hiya Dyson. Great timing. I could use a second pair of eyes. I'm looking for a leak." He rubbed his grit-smudged cheek.

I stared up into the space where the light flashed but saw nothing. "Maybe you should take it to the Magician."

"Cheater," Callie whispered.

Enzo chuckled. "My ever-charming sister."

"Jay, I'm leaving for my haircut." Callie met my gaze before turning.

"Have fun, and tell Haley I'd be happy to look at her tires,"

Enzo tossed after Callie.

"I'll do no such thing, jerkwad." Callie offered a one-finger salute, then traipsed toward the door. She paused, turning once more. "See you, Dyson."

"Who's Haley?" I wondered if there was fodder for the tease machine.

"She's Callie's stylist. Haley has a thing for me." Enzo shifted the light, peering in a new area.

"You offered to work on her car?" I hoped I'd kept the surprise out of my tone. Jay Ferenzo wasn't philanthropic.

Enzo shrugged. "All Callie's friends like me. They want me to fix their cars and shit."

"Do they let you do it for the show?"

He lowered the flashlight and met my gaze. "Callie won't let me. She thinks I'll break their hearts. And if they only want me for my mechanic skills, it would serve them right."

Enzo wasn't much taller than Callie and had the same thick, dark brown hair. Italian roots, he'd said. He had swagger, and the ladies seemed to flock around him at events. But he seemed more of a love 'em and leave 'em sort of guy. That is probably the true reason Callie refused to bring her friends around her brother.

"About Callie," I started.

Enzo laughed, "I knew it. You have a thing for her."

My face heated, but I continued. "I need to ask a favor. What's your shooting schedule for June?"

"Why? What's going on in June?" Jay pulled off the black latex gloves he'd been wearing and glanced at the small mirror on the wall. Frowning, he swiped at the grime on his cheek with a microfiber towel.

"I have a family reunion." I studied the shelf with various oils and other fluids.

"And you need Callie to feed your cat or something?" Enzo surmised, still wiping at the streak.

"No. It's in Alaska and I'll be gone for two weeks."

"So, you need Callie to water your plants and check your property."

"No." I glanced at the ceiling lights and sighed. "I wanted to ask you about that."

"Sure. I don't mind but Callie–?"

"I'm trying to tell you," I heaved in exasperation. When he remained quiet, I continued. "I wanted to see if I could borrow Callie for the trip. My mother thinks I have a girlfriend, and I thought Callie would be game to help me out."

Enzo crossed his arms and leaned back against the workbench. "Wow, Dyson. Lying to your mom, and your whole family too. Ouch. What did Callie say?"

Hearing the deception put so bluntly threw me, and I rubbed the back of my neck. "I haven't asked her yet."

"Dyson, my man. Let me save you some time. She'll say no. She hates devious shenanigans." He raised his index finger. "Although, maybe if you promise you'll let her drive the GT3 RS for a month or so, she'll go along with it."

"There's an idea." I rubbed my chin. "I'm pretty sure bribing her wouldn't be the way to go. But I wish I could have asked her while she was here."

"You can ask her," Enzo pointed out. "Just go to the salon." He pulled out his phone and sent me the address. It was only a few miles away.

"Is she not coming back?" Killing time by sorting Enzo's truck issues wasn't what I had in mind for the day.

"Nope. Not today."

"Fine. I'll message her."

"Dyson, you need to show up and ask. This is a personal request for a sensitive topic. And I know my sister. She'll appreciate the face to face." Enzo motioned to follow.

We walked to the office. Large whiteboards canvased one wall. One held a shopping list of car parts and web addresses. Two others seemed to feature lists of upcoming shoots, titles and ideas.

"Have a seat." He tapped on a laptop, opening a digital calendar. "We have stuff in the works, but I'm confident we can work around your..." he coughed, "family emergency."

"Thanks." I relaxed back into the desk chair, swiveling from side to side.

Enzo's eyes sparkled with mischief, much like his sister's did sometimes. Although similar colors, both were framed with long, dark lashes. "You know, it's funny you came to me to ask permission to date my sister."

"I'm not dating–"

"Stuff it, Romeo." He laughed.

I stood, glancing toward the door. "I should go catch Callie before she leaves the salon."

"Alright." Enzo walked me to the door. "Good luck, Dyson. I'm sure I'll have a few questions about the trip later."

Once in my car, I entered the address into the GPS and arrived at the salon. Parking, I noticed a man waiting in a gray sedan with a large ding on the driver's door. *Probably has a wife in there.*

I approached the building's chic exterior. At least, it looked fancy to me. "Salon Forty-Four" was backlit against the brick exterior.

Suddenly nervous, I decided to FaceTime her before going in.

Callie picked up, her face a mask of worry. "Hello?" Her greeting came as more of a question.

"Hi Callie. Do you have a minute?" I asked.

She frowned, glancing to the side. A dark cape covered the Gabby's Garage shirt. Her hair appeared wet and some aluminum foil thingies stuck out of it.

"Actually, I don't. I'm in the middle of getting highlights."

A red-headed woman peered over Callie's shoulder. "Is this him?" she asked.

Callie's cheeks blossomed pink, and she sighed. "Geez, Haley, yes. Dyson, I'll talk to you later."

Haley wiggled her fingers in a wave. "Bye."

"Okay, bye." Before the call ended, I heard Haley say, "You're right. He *is* cute."

Elation coursed through my veins, giving me the courage to enter the building for a face-to-face encounter. As I opened the door, pungent smells assaulted me.

With a slight nod and a small smile, the receptionist acknowledged me. A handset was cradled between her ear and shoulder. She pointed to the phone and gave me a thumbs up. I waited patiently, my gaze sweeping across the unfamiliar space, searching for Callie's beautiful face amongst the workstations.

The young woman hung up and said, "Can I help you?"

"I'm here to visit Callie Ferenzo. She's with Haley." Shifting uneasily, I hoped the woman would lead me to the right place.

She tilted her head, sizing me up. "What do you want?"

"I'd like to ask her out," I replied. It was the truth—from a certain point of view.

A smile broke out on her face, and she sprang from her seat. "Follow me."

I followed her down a hallway and into a large warehouse-like room. Barber shop-like chairs were everywhere, with mirrors and lights. Some of the stations were vacant, but most had clients getting some sort of hair treatment. The rhythmic snip of scissors and the noxious fumes from hair products filled the air.

The further I went into the room, the more the chatter quieted. Toward the far-right side, I met Haley's gaze. She stopped talking mid-sentence, then she swiveled Callie in the chair until she faced me.

I continued forward, aware that all eyes in the room were on me. I was an anomaly, like a virgin in a whorehouse.

Callie's eyes widened, and a blush fanned her face. "Dyson, what the hell?"

"Hello again." I chuckled as her blush intensified.

"Are you here for a cut?" she asked, sizing me up.

"Uh, no," I mumbled.

"He's here to ask you out."

My gaze snapped to the receptionist, who hadn't returned to her post. I shot her daggers as a chorus of *Awww* rose from those within earshot.

"He's what?" Callie asked.

"I've got this, if you don't mind," I told the receptionist firmly.

"Of course," she mumbled, leaving.

"Dyson?"

"Callie." I stood in front of her as my gaze panned the room. As I met each woman's eyes, they looked away. Finally, a measure of privacy.

I liked Callie's dark hair. She didn't need to do anything to make her more beautiful, but I couldn't tell her that. And I definitely couldn't tell her that the pieces of aluminum foil in her hair made her look like she'd stuck her finger in a socket.

Haley began working again.

"I need to ask you something," I started, inhaling to find my courage.

Callie smirked. "I heard. Go for it."

"Thanks for your permission. Remember, I said I might need your help with my family? Well…"

"Oh!" Callie straightened in her seat. "I don't know how I can, but I'll try."

I glanced at my shoes. Getting out of the mess I'd created for myself was as easy as calling my mother and explaining she'd read more into the word "girlfriend" than I'd intended. Although I'd had Callie in mind the first time I'd said it, so it hadn't been an outright lie. The second time Mom asked about the woman I'd been seeing, I'd been at Enzo's that day for a shoot. So, again, I wasn't lying. Not exactly.

Then Callie and I took that drive and we kissed. The last time Mom asked about *that girl,* I answered honestly.

"I have a family reunion in June. It's in Fairbanks, Alaska and lasts a few days." I met her eyes. "My mother believes I have a girlfriend, and I'll be bringing her to the reunion."

Callie's eyebrows rose. "Oh. Alaska. I've always wanted to visit Alaska. Who is she?"

"If you'd like an all-expenses paid trip to Alaska, then *you're* my girlfriend." I smiled, and she blinked. "I talked to your brother about Enzo Auto Tech's shooting and editing schedule. He said it would be fine as long as you're okay with it. What do you say?"

Callie chuckled. The silence stretched, and her expression became thoughtful. "You're not joking."

"No." I shifted as Haley stepped close to work on the other side of Callie's head, dabbing something on her hair.

"And you talked to Jay about the trip?" She managed to draw her eyebrows together, even with all the stuff in her hair. My confidence in a positive outcome waned.

"Yes. He checked Enzo's Auto Tech's shooting schedule and calendar."

"Oh."

"I wanted to ask you face to face, but you left before I finished talking with Enzo." I offered the specific June dates and continued, not giving her time to voice a *No*. "We'll meet my folks and sister in Anchorage and travel to Denali State Park for a day or two. Then we'll head to Fairbanks for the family reunion and a local car show I've been sucked into judging. After that, we'll come home."

"Hmm. Sleeping arrangements?" Callie asked, that pretty blush sweeping across her face again.

"I booked a king size bed at each hotel. Hope you don't mind sharing." My heart raced at the thought of Callie in my bed, even if she was an arm's length away.

"I suppose that would seem appropriate *if* you had a girlfriend going on vacation with you..." Her brow crinkled in thought.

"I'd appreciate your help. I don't want to disappoint my mother. Again." Callie's eyes locked on mine. I offered a lopsided grin. "I'll cash in my IOU and add a week of letting you drive the

GT3."

She jerked to face me. "A whole week? Me with the Porsche..." A dreamy expression crossed her face.

"Don't move," Haley scolded, straightening Callie's head.

Callie rolled her eyes, and I chuckled.

"Dyson, you didn't have to throw in the Porsche. I would have helped you, anyway. But since you have–no take backs."

I gasped at her response. "Really? Awesome. Thank you, Callie. I'll get out of your hair so you can finish."

"Haley, you asked me if I was getting my hair highlighted for a special occasion. Well, it looks like I'm going to Alaska for my fake boyfriend's family reunion."

"Alaska. How romantic," Haley cooed.

The cape moved as Callie lifted her arm, raising her index finger. "*Pretend* romance," she clarified.

"I'm sure you'll have questions. Call me and I'll fill in the details." I turned to go.

Callie called, "Dyson, how long does your mom think we've been dating?"

"A few months," I admitted.

"And you've never mentioned a woman by name?" One of her dainty brows rose in question.

I sighed as I glanced at the ceiling. My mother had expectations. "Mom refers to my girlfriend as *that girl.*"

"So, I'm *that girl?*"

"Now you are." I laughed.

"Okay, I can work with that." She nodded.

I left the salon in wonder at her bravery. I now had a fake girlfriend for my trip. Mom would be pleased.

Maybe my mother was onto something. I thought I had it all–cars, money, and fame. But I didn't have someone to share it with–I didn't have love.

For the rest of the day, my heart sank each time my phone chirped—I dreaded Callie coming to her senses and canceling.

Chapter Three

Callie

As I stowed my carry-on backpack under the seat in front of me, a petite, white-haired woman said, "Pardon me, dear. I'm in the middle seat, next to you."

"Hold on, I'll move out of the way." The row across from ours was empty, so I scooted into the row while the woman got settled.

The older woman struggled to stuff her small bag in the overhead bin. I moved to help, but a stout man with a thick neck blocked my path.

"Hey babe, you're in my seat." His rumpled business suit and disheveled dark hair suggested he had just rolled out of bed after a late-night bender.

"I'm not sitting here. I'm over there." I pointed to my seat. The woman had the suitcase over her head now.

"That's nice." He pushed around me, into his row, brushing his arm against my chest. I hugged myself protectively, but it was a little too late.

Once on the other side of me, he leaned over, rubbing my backside with his bag as he attempted to stuff it under the seat. I mumbled a sarcastic "Excuse you," the tone making my feelings perfectly clear. I didn't like being touched by a stranger, even accidentally in the tight space.

I helped the woman finish shoving her bag into the bin and we both sat. Once we were in the air, the little woman tapped my arm. She motioned me closer and said in my ear, "Do you know that man, dear? He is staring at you." Her breath smelled of peppermint.

"I don't know anyone on the plane."

She patted my hand and nodded. "I'm Dottie. Nice to meet you."

I glanced around, finding the man who'd bumped into me staring unabashedly. When we made eye contact, he smiled wolfishly. My inner voice screamed *Creeper*. The hairs on the back of my neck stood up and an unsettled feeling gnawed at my gut. *I wish Dyson hadn't had to fly out two days ago.*

"I'm Jake."

"Hello." I replied politely.

"You look familiar. Have we met before?" Jake said, tilting his head and studying me. While not unattractive, his bodybuilder's physique was definitely not my type. Nor was his slovenly appearance.

If Jake watched any CarTube videos, he might know Enzo's Auto Tech and have seen me on the show.

"We've never met," I insisted.

"I know I've seen you before. Are you a model?" Jake leaned into the aisle. "Maybe we could get a drink when we land."

"No, thank you. I'm meeting my boyfriend for a long, romantic vacation." Take the hint, buddy.

I glanced at my watch. How long was this flight from Seattle to Anchorage? Too long. I shook my head, pulling out my phone. I studied Dyson's messages. Just before I'd boarded, he'd sent me a selfie. He'd said he was impatiently waiting in the penthouse suite of our hotel. A warmth filled my belly thinking of spending days–and nights–with him.

I tapped on the photo and posted it to Dyson's contact, which I'd named *Sexy Stick Shift* for the trip.

"I know that guy. He's Gabby from Gabby's Garage on CarTube."

I shut my phone off and stowed it in the seat pocket.

"That's it, isn't it? He's awesome. Oh, I know where I know you from. Enzo's Auto Tech, you're Enzo's hot sister. Can I take your picture?" He fished out his phone and snapped a picture before I could say no.

I glanced away as he started bombarding me with personal questions about my brother, my life, and Dyson.

"Dear," the woman beside me said, drawing my attention. "You're meeting your boyfriend?"

"Yes," I smiled.

"Are you sure he's your boyfriend?" Jake questioned, as if he knew my secret.

"Ignore him." The older woman glared ice picks at the repugnant man. She lowered her voice, "If he doesn't stop staring, I'll get the attendant."

"I'm not sure what they can do. It's not like they can chuck him out the window," I groused.

"Have you ever been to Anchorage before?"

I turned my back to Jake and the aisle to get a reprieve from his stare and hopefully mask the conversation somewhat from his prying ears.

"Nope. I've never been to Alaska." With the creeper out of sight, I let a little of my excitement seep through. "I can't wait. Everything I've seen online is beautiful."

"Are you going above the Arctic Circle or to Denali? That's Mount McKinley."

Though my attention was primarily focused on her, I peripherally observed the weirdo across the aisle. "I'm not sure what we are doing the whole time. But I know we are getting together with a bunch of his cousins. I'll leave it to the family's discretion. I'm just along for the ride."

"My son lives outside of Anchorage to the north. It's a pretty area and my grandkids love it. They are all into the outdoors. There's a lot of it there." She chuckled, waving her hand, then leaned over, watching something behind me. "You know, dear, I think it's time. I need to go to the bathroom. When I return, I'd love it if I could stretch my legs in the aisle for a while."

"You'd be willing to change seats?" I smiled with relief.

"Yes, dear. Excuse me." She unbuckled her belt and stood. I backed out of the row and let her out. I scooted back into the row, sitting in my original seat to gather my items.

Jake aimed his phone at me. The man's stalker vibe gave me a shiver. "Are you recording?"

"No, I'm taking a selfie." He replied with a smarmy smile. His dark eyes narrowed on my lips.

My face heated as anger crept to the surface. I tried my best business tone. "You don't have my permission to record me."

"I can do whatever I want." He licked his lips.

The man next to Jake leaned in to see his screen, then met my eyes. "He's focused on your chest." Jake glared at his seatmate and the other passenger's face turned red. He returned his gaze to his magazine.

"Of course, he is," I mumbled, shaking my head and glancing at my attire.

At least my outfit wasn't the low-cut style my brother liked me to wear for shoots. Or my usual jeans or novelty shirt pimping someone's CarTube channel.

I'd tried to look pretty for my pretend boyfriend. I'd worn a comfy dress. It fit more like an oversized t-shirt and came down to my knees. It was turquoise, like Dyson's Porsche. The capped sleeves had a slight ruffle on the edge. Speaking of slight, that described the V neck. It had a lowercase V. No sprawling views of my C cups.

It wasn't about sexiness, it was about comfort.

Now I wish I'd opted for my knee-high boots instead of the sandals. Giving Jake-the-creeper a view of any bare skin gave me the willies. The boots would be better to kick him with, too.

I removed my bag and stuffed it under the middle seat of the row in front of us, then I scooched over to our middle seat. As soon as I buckled the belt, I leaned back with a sigh and closed my eyes.

Sensing movement, I kept my eyes shut, letting Dottie get comfortable. Then a rough hand rubbed my leg, traveling under my dress and up my thigh. My eyes sprung open, and I jerked upright.

"What the hell? Get off me!"

I stood, slapping his hand away and sending his phone sailing across the airplane cabin.

My heart hammered, and I gritted my teeth. Red-faced, Jake loomed over me, his bulk blocking my escape.

But I didn't feel threatened. Instead, a righteous anger, hot and fierce, surged through my veins.

"Is there a problem here?" the blonde attendant asked. As I panned the plane, several people held their cameras, trying to catch footage. Dottie, my flight-friend, met my gaze and nodded. I hoped that indicated she'd dropped the lowdown to the attendant.

"She assaulted me," Jake stated, standing as tall as he could. Someone handed him his phone.

I gasped, then laughed. "In your dreams." When I sobered, Jake vibrated with rage.

Inhaling a calming breath, then blowing it out, I spoke in an even tone. "Yes, there is a problem." I closed my eyes and stomped on my anger. "Please tell this man to stay in his row, stop touching me, and delete all photos or videos he has taken of me. I clearly told him he did not have permission and he still does not."

"He's in my seat," Dottie complained.

"Sir, please return to your seat." The attendant glanced from Jake to me.

While the attendant talked to Jake, she blocked him from my

view. Relieved, I hugged myself and sat down.

Dottie slipped into her seat and sighed. She leaned close. "I told her about that jerk. I suggested they let you out with the others that need assistance." She glanced around to make sure Jake was occupied. "Maybe you should text that man of yours."

"Airplane mode," I said, waving my phone.

"Have your message ready to go once we land." Dottie shrugged. "I hope they help you."

"Once I'm with Dyson, I'll be fine."

I tapped my phone, then showed Dottie the hot selfie Dyson had sent. "This is from this morning. We're staying at the hotel for a few days until his immediate family arrives." I rubbed my cheek. "I've never been to a family reunion before, just small gatherings. Dyson said it happens every five years and everyone comes from everywhere. I wonder if they'll look alike."

"Sometimes. Genetics are strange. Are you worried?" Dottie shifted a little.

"This is the first time I'm meeting his parents and sister." I rubbed my hands together. "Actually, I've never met any of his family before, and I'm a little nervous. He's shown me pictures, but it's not the same. His mom has expectations."

"Oh?" Dottie grinned. "Do you think he'll propose?"

My blood pressure dropped when my heart leapt. I couldn't string words together for a reply.

"I can tell you really like him. And you make a cute match. I have a good feeling about you." Dottie winked and patted my arm.

My ears popped as we began our descent. "Not much longer now."

Once the plane landed, I sent my planned text.

Dyson:

> !!

Dyson:

> I'm at the baggage claim. Do I need to get security?

I alerted him to Dottie's plan. The blonde attendant nodded to us. I pulled my bag onto my lap and glanced out the window. Mid-June in Alaska–the land of the midnight sun–and the evening was as light as midafternoon. If the circumstances weren't so harrowing, I'd lose myself in the scenery. Now I only wanted to run to Dyson's arms.

The passengers all unbuckled their seatbelts when the light went off. People stood and stretched. Dottie stepped into the aisle, blocking Jake, and I slid past and hurried toward the front. I joined a veteran in a wheelchair and a family with a stroller. We all walked up the jetbridge. They moved slowly but once we were in Concourse C, I hurried around them, following the signs toward the baggage claim.

A moving walkway sped up my progress, but once it ended, I heard a familiar but unwanted voice.

"Hey babe. You look thirsty. Let's get a drink." Jake arrived at my side and kept pace.

I wanted to ignore him, but I emphatically said, "No. What part of 'I've got a boyfriend' don't you understand?"

"No. He's not your boyfriend." His furrowed brows became one as they knit together in a V. He was close enough to touch me, so I stepped away. "I'm as much your boyfriend as he is."

I glared defiantly with my hands on my hips. My shoulder ached from the weight of my bag. Even though it was the truth, Jake the Creeper didn't need to know he'd nailed it. My personal life wasn't his business.

I turned on my heel and power walked toward baggage claim. Jake matched my steps, laughing. He grabbed my shoulder, his fingers digging in, but I broke away, spinning.

My phone rang. Dyson's ringtone. With a sigh, I tapped the screen to answer the video call.

Relief flooded me when I looked upon his concerned face. His brow dipped over his expressive hazel eyes. "Callie, where are you?"

I glanced up. Beside me was a lady's room. "I'm going into the bathroom so I can talk privately." I threw Jake a venomous glare, then I hustled into the restroom. Once inside, I set my bag on the ground and heaved a relieved sigh.

"He won't leave me alone. What should I do?" I asked Dyson.

Wincing, I rubbed my shoulder where the loser's grip had dug into my skin.

"Did he hurt you?" he growled with a feral undertone that warmed me inside.

Not now. Stupid hormones.

"I don't want him to touch me," I whispered.

"Stay on the call. I'm coming to get you," Dyson said. He glanced around and strode in a new direction. Behind him, the baggage carousel remained motionless.

Dyson asked to speak to security and was pointed to an office. Time passed and after a few minutes, I hoped the stalker would get bored.

A woman washed her hands. She met my gaze in the mirror and smiled. She left, then returned a moment later. "A man asked me to check on you. Are you okay, hon?" A look of concern fluttered over her face.

"Is he a disheveled businessman?"

"He's a big guy in a black suit."

"I don't know that man. He won't leave me alone."

"This is my boyfriend. He's here to pick me up," I said confidently, showing her Dyson on my phone. "I'll be fine. Thank you."

The woman nodded and left. Maybe I should have left with her. Although Jake was pretty brazen and probably would have followed me, anyway.

"Callie, are you still in the bathroom?" His gaze left the screen. "The turnstile is on. Your fellow passengers are snagging their baggage."

"I'm stuck in the bathroom with him outside. He sent a

woman in to check on me. Can you believe it?"

"What a dick," Dyson growled. "I'm at security. Still waiting to see if they'll let me in."

He mumbled something and a woman's voice replied, but I couldn't make out the words with the din of the background noise. "Oh? Callie, hold on. There's a woman named Dottie who found me at security and verified the story about Jake."

After a moment, Dyson glanced at the phone again. "They won't let me in, so an officer is coming to walk you out. Here she is." He handed his phone to a middle-aged, dark-haired woman.

"Hello Callie, I'm Jenelle Akpik. I'll be there in a moment. Please confirm the bathroom where I can find you."

"The restroom by Concourse C at the end of the human conveyor thingy," I said, "Also there's a thick, thirty-ish year-old man with dark, greasy hair and wearing a black suit standing outside waiting for me."

I closed my eyes as tears of gratitude welled. "Thank you for coming," I whispered.

"I'll be there shortly. Hold on." Jenelle handed the phone to Dyson.

"Thank you, Officer Akpik," Dyson said hoarsely. Once more, he turned his attention to me. "She's on her way. It will all be fine."

"Okay. This isn't how I imagined arriving in Alaska." I leaned against the gray concrete block walls. The bathroom was clean with all the automatic conveniences, but it was my prison.

"Not my idea either," he said. "I'm really sorry."

"You didn't plan the creeper. Don't apologize."

"I owe you."

"Oh?" I couldn't help thinking of the Porsche again.

"Callie?" a woman called as she entered the bathroom. She was barely five feet tall, but wore a navy uniform with the airport's name embroidered on it. "I'm Jenelle Akpik. Dyson sent me to make sure you're alright."

"Oh, thank God," I breathed to Dyson. "She's here."

"I'll hang up now," Dyson said.

"No, please don't," I told him, meeting his gaze. "You will not leave me until I see you face to face."

I held my phone up. "You're going to escort me."

"All the way to my arms," he said with a wink and a grin.

A warmth bloomed in my chest, chasing away the chill, and I returned his smile, feeling a lightness in my heart.

"Are you ready?" Jenelle asked. "You'll be fine. There's another agent out there talking to *the problem*. He won't bother you again."

I nodded and picked up my bag. Feeling achy from the stress of traveling and dealing with the loser, I stepped out of hiding.

Jenelle engaged me in pleasant conversation, but it was hard to focus on anything other than my search for Dyson.

I had one mission: launch myself into Dyson's embrace.

"I see you," he said as I traveled down the escalator. In the sea of faces, I searched until I found him near the security desk. He wasn't hard to find, since he was taller than most. My heart rate skyrocketed, and my chest constricted. How I longed to bury my face in his broad chest and have him hold me until I forgot the horrid creeper.

Behind Dyson, Dottie waved. Her smile broadened as I approached.

At the bottom of the escalator, I ended the call and stuffed the phone into my bag. I ran toward him as he strode across the space. He opened his arms, and I didn't slow.

He absorbed my hit, encapsulating me in his strong arms. I inhaled his spicy scent, reminding me of fresh air and woods. He crushed me to him, but I was already having difficulty breathing due to his nearness.

He nosed my hair and whispered next to my ear. "You're safe now. I've got you."

My arms slithered around his waist, and my bag tugged me to one side.

After my breathing calmed, I lifted my gaze to his and smiled shyly.

"Welcome to Alaska," he said, sporting his CarTube show's greeting tone. "The goofiest state in the union."

His attempt to lighten the mood wasn't lost on me, but I still felt raw. I buried my nose in his chest again. He tried to pull away, but I whimpered, "Not yet."

Rubbing my back with one hand, he tipped my chin, so I met his gaze. "Callie," he said, softly. "We need to get your luggage so we can get out of this place."

His gaze burrowed deep into my soul. Would he kiss me? My attention fell to his lips, and suddenly I wanted nothing more than to taste him. As he lowered, I fisted his shirt and tiptoed at the same time. Our mouths crashed in desperation mixed with longing. I opened with a moan. His gentle probe turned needier with each heartbeat.

We broke apart, and I burrowed my face into his shirt. "That's a much better greeting," I mumbled.

"I agree," Dyson said, turning me toward the luggage conveyor.

Most of the folks had retrieved their suitcases and gone. I spied mine and pointed. "There it is." I moved to get it but froze, staring across the way.

Dyson bumped into me. "What is it?" He followed my gaze to the opposite side of the carousel. Jake stood grinning with his phone raised.

"Why that bastard..." Dyson stepped forward, but I caught his hand.

"He's not worth it." I met Dyson's gaze. "Plus, you're my boyfriend." I added a wink while squeezing his hand.

His grip was firm as he returned the squeeze, then he effortlessly lifted my heavy suitcase, and together we walked toward the exit. When we looked back to where Jake had been, he was no longer there.

"Let's get out of here."

"Are you in a hurry to show me our hotel room?" I teased.

"Are you in a hurry to see it?" he returned.

Our hands laced, we exited the building into the bright day. I blinked while inhaling the fresh air. In the sun, I warmed.

"The car is over there," he pointed to the garage.

Several people waited to be picked up. I spotted Dottie and hurried toward her, pulling Dyson along. When I reached her, she opened her arms. Her grandmotherly embrace enveloped me in a comforting cloud of peppermint.

"Thank you for your help, Dottie," I mumbled.

"You're welcome, dear." She patted my back. "Your young man was so distraught about not being there for you."

I pulled back and glanced from Dyson to Dottie.

"But I had his back," Dottie winked. She leaned in, looked around, then said to us, "I was right, you are a good match. Enjoy Alaska." Dottie waved as she and her family walked toward the car park.

"Nice lady," Dyson said.

A throaty car made its presence known, driving slowly toward the baggage claim pickup area. Dyson shielded his eyes from the sun, then smiled.

"It sounds like a Jaguar F-type," I mused.

"Do you know what year?"

"By the sound, or do you want me to look at the body?" I asked, glancing at my nails.

"Sound? I'd like you to try." A slow grin spread across his face as he considered my challenge.

"It sounds like a supercharged V-8 engine, so it's either a 2019 or 20."

"Well, I'll be damned," he breathed, his eyes wide with astonishment.

"I'm good. What can I tell you?" I laughed at his stunned expression. "Sometimes girls know things about cars." I shrugged, meeting his hooded gaze. I could get lost in the depth of his eyes, trying to figure out if spouting car stats turned him on.

Maybe we had that in common.

Just when I thought he would kiss me again, the Jag honked its horn from beside us. The tinted window lowered, and Jake snapped a picture of us. Laughing, he drove off.

"I didn't see that coming," Dyson mumbled, rubbing his chin.

Surprised and angry, I yelled, "Nice car, asshole!"

Chapter Four
Dyson

Callie remained quiet on the drive from the airport. Neither of us brought up the jerk or the kiss that ignited all kinds of desires. I tried to focus on driving while constantly studying the rental car mirrors.

I planned to let Callie out at the hotel's front door while I parked in the attached garage, thinking it was the boyfriend-y thing to do. But not knowing if Jake might turn up yet again, I opted to park and walk her in.

The thought of that dick, finding Callie again had my gut churning. We'd hear the Jag a mile away, but that didn't mean I wanted to chance him finding her without me.

She gazed around the lobby of the hotel. Was she studying the decor or searching for that pervert?

"Are you all right?" I asked as we stepped into the elevator. Waving the keycard, I punched the top floor.

Callie offered a small smile, then blushed. "I'm fine." She held onto the strap of her bag with a death grip.

On the tenth floor, the elevator opened to wide windows with a panoramic mountain view.

"It's so beautiful," she said with awe. "I could appreciate this view forever."

"It's the same from our room. You can relax on the sofa with a glass of wine and stare outside." I continued forward, tapping the keycard to unlock the door.

Inside, she glanced around at the amenities. Small living room with a sofa, two blue chairs and a coffee table, a kitchenette, and a doorway that led to our bedroom. I swallowed, hoping goodnight kisses would become a thing. I enjoyed her passion for cars and hoped it could also be directed at me.

"The bedroom is in here." I pulled her suitcase into the room.

Setting her bag on the white coverlet, Callie inspected the furniture. She pulled out the drawers and opened the closet, then nodded. "A few nights here, right?"

"Yes." The space between us on the king size bed wouldn't be enough to keep her heat off my mind. She'd only be an arm's length away.

"I'll unpack my things. And get settled." She unzipped the bag and hung her clothing in the closet. She set a pair of shoes on the floor under her clothes.

"Your family is coming tomorrow?" She took a few pairs of socks and put them in an empty drawer.

"No. We have tomorrow to play."

She glanced at me, tilting her head. "Good, that will give us a chance to practice."

I sat down on the edge of the bed while she worked. "Practice what?"

"Touching. Kissing. You know that kind of stuff, so we aren't awkward by the time your family gets here."

"Are we awkward?" I rubbed the back of my head.

"We are supposed to have been dating for a while, right? I don't think we have the boyfriend-girlfriend vibe yet. People in relationships are familiar with their partner's body. Being together is natural. And every time I think about kissing you, this happens." She pointed to her face as her cheeks turned red.

"How often do you think about kissing me? Wait–does that

mean you don't enjoy kissing me?"

Her features pinched, and she looked at me as if I had another head. "Did I act as if I didn't enjoy kissing you?"

"No, but–"

"It's awkward."

"So, we practice?" Something silky caught my eye in her suitcase. "Are we practicing with that?"

Her blush intensified, and she laughed. She partially lifted an emerald-green negligee. It still had the tags. "Do you like it?"

Dear Lord in heaven, how will I keep my hands to myself if Callie wears that scrap of a nightgown? "Hell, yes."

"I brought it in case, for the facade, well, because we're supposed to be boyfriend and girlfriend. It's something couples do, right?" Her cheeks flushed crimson as our eyes met. "They wear these types of things."

"I didn't bring…"

She dropped it in the open drawer. "Don't worry. The gown and a pair of matching boxers came as a his-and-hers set."

"That's cool. Thanks."

Callie handed me a satiny pair of boxers. I held them against my body. "These are the shortest boxers." They wouldn't leave much to the imagination. My junk would hang out.

Callie stared at my groin, probably thinking the same thing. Heat radiated off my face, and I glanced in the mirror. My face was as red as hers. Yeah, we needed practice.

I wouldn't mind trying on the new clothes and practicing.

She snatched the boxers back and something blue and lacy from her suitcase and then tossed them in the drawer with her socks. "I bought some new undies for this trip, too. Gotta love an excuse to update my wardrobe."

"I like your dress. It's the same color as the Porsche."

A smile lit her face, and her eyes glowed. "Right? I had to have it. I rarely wear dresses, but when I saw it, I had to try it on. It would look cute with boots, and I almost wore some." Her face clouded, and she stared out the window. "Should have worn the boots, then maybe he wouldn't have..." She shivered.

God damn that Jake prick.

I reached for her and pulled her into my arms. "Callie, you rock a pair of jeans and car shirts. Gabby's Garage shirts make you especially sexy, but the dress is pretty. Makes me appreciate your legs." Her warmth against me stalled my thoughts.

"Thanks. Are you practicing?" A slight grin tipped her lips, and her cheeks pinked up again.

"You're blushing. Does that mean you're thinking of kissing me?"

Her blush intensified. I leaned in and kissed her nose, earning a giggle. She sighed and relaxed, laying her face against my chest. It was amazing how well we fit together and how good it felt to have her in my arms.

"Did you say something about a glass of wine?" she asked, pulling away.

"Yes, I did. I got a few bottles of my mom's local favorites from Glacier Bear Winery." Gently taking her small hand, I guided her through the doorway into the surprisingly spacious kitchen area. "I think I'm going to like practicing."

"Me too." She blushed.

"There you go, thinking about kissing me again," I teased, tugging on the cork. Once free, I poured her a splash of black currant wine.

She sipped it and hummed. "Tasty."

"Wait until you try the blueberry." I opened the other bottle and poured a little for her.

"Mmm. That's good too. Delicious."

"Which do you like better?" I asked.

Callie glanced at her glass, thinking. "I need to try the first one again to see which I like best."

I chuckled. "They're both my mom's favorites." Once I filled our glasses, I lifted mine in salute. "To practicing."

"To pulling off being a couple," she added, then clinked my glass. We sipped, and we moved to the sofa and sat.

After a few sips, she said, "Dottie, the lady who helped me on the plane, saw your picture on my phone and thought we made a cute couple." Callie kept her gaze on the burgundy liquid.

"We're each adorable on our own. No wonder she thought we were a cute couple." I chuckled at her giggle.

She'd taken a seat on the far side of the sofa. She was too far away. I needed to touch her. "Hey, why don't you come here?" I patted next to me. "Let's practice."

She rolled her eyes but moved over. I sat my wine on the small table, then extended my arm. She leaned back against me.. At first, she was rigid, but after a moment she relaxed with a sigh.

I loved the ability to make her comfortable and content. After the visit's rough start, I was determined to protect Callie, no matter the threat. With her free hand, she reached up and played with my fingers that dangled over her shoulder. The light touches sent sensations up my arm.

I kicked off my shoes, extended my legs, and put my sock-clad feet up on the coffee table. The mountain view, with the green forest and striking blue sky, was our TV. The longer we sat, the more comfortable I became. I leaned over and kissed the top of her head, inhaling almonds and vanilla.

She pulled her feet under her and laid her hand on my chest. "Tomorrow, can we find a park with a trail and go for a walk? I'd like to record something for my show."

"Really? Enzo's Auto Tech in Alaska?"

"No, this would be for *my* channel." She glanced at me with a smile lighting her face.

"Your show? Tell me about it."

Callie's grin grew, and her eyes widened. "Well, I haven't published anything except a thirty-second intro to the channel, which I'm calling End of the Road. Instead of focusing on the journey, it's a show about the destination, about where the road ends. Hiking trails, overlooks—that sort of thing."

"Sounds cool."

"Thanks," she turned reflective and snuggled into me. I stroked her hair. "Ever since we—Dad, Jay and I—started Enzo's, I've itched to do something creative like this."

"Your dad wasn't interested?" I asked, hoping to not bring up her past pain.

"He liked the idea." Callie wrapped an arm around my stomach. "But we all agreed we should grow the main channel first. Then Dad died..." She sighed sadly. "Now if I bring it up, Jay shoots it down. And to be fair, one channel is hard enough."

"But...?" I wanted her smile to return.

"But, End of the Road is my dream. I've been secretly accumulating footage for the past two years. I'm getting close to launching the channel, but having an episode in Alaska would be cool."

"Having Gabby from Gabby's Garage make a cameo could help boost your channel launch," I suggested.

"No, it's not about name dropping. I want to do this on my own." She tried to sit up, but I held on.

"That's fine. When we go to dinner, let's ask the locals for the perfect place."

"Great idea, Dyson."

"I have them occasionally."

She chuckled and settled back against me. "I recorded a short teaser for release during our trip. Nobody needs to know where I am. Ugh. I hope that loser Jake doesn't post anything about us or where we are."

To distract her, I asked about her channel. "Where did you get the idea?"

"For End of the Road? I thought it would be fun to find out what adventures are at the dead ends. It's turned into more about hiking and scenic overlooks, but there are only so many hiking trails in Kansas near us. When I travel to the auto shows, I try to find some *exotic* destination." She chuckled.

"That explains why Enzo is at the bougie dinners, but you're not sometimes." While networking at the auto events was the primary goal of the swanky dinners, I went to see Callie.

Now I'm eager to see the new channel and support her any way I can. Especially if it purges Jake from her mind.

"I have my mic," I offered. Callie's voice is mesmerizing and soothing. She'd be great at narrating. "And I can hold the camera for you."

She lifted her face and met my eyes, wearing a huge smile. "Really? That would be awesome. It's a struggle to capture everything by myself."

"Your brother never helps?"

"No. Besides, I don't want Jay to go. He talks too much."

"Gotcha."

Her stomach growled, and she rubbed it. "Sorry."

"Let's go eat. It's later than you think because of the light."

"Let me go to the bathroom first."

I nodded. While she was in the other room, I texted Enzo about Callie's safe arrival and also about the dick on the plane.

Enzo:

Is she okay?

Me:

She's fine. We're going to dinner. I'll protect her.

When we arrived back at the hotel, we entered the bedroom. I dropped my keys and wallet on the dresser.

Callie yawned. "I'm beat. I'm going to get ready for bed. Which side do you want?"

"You choose." I didn't care. Either side would be torture.

She grabbed some clothes out of the drawer and once she was in the bathroom, she closed the door. I kept envisioning the skimpy negligee she'd held up earlier on her slender body. Would it hug her curves or would it hang loose?

I paced the hotel room, searching for a distraction. There it was—my camouflage-patterned bag of camera gear, bulging with everything I needed for a shoot. I unzipped the sturdy nylon container, revealing the lightweight microphone and its rechargeable battery pack. Checking the battery level, I found them mostly charged. I'd let Callie use them for her on-location shoot at the park tomorrow.

Looking out over the mountains in the distance, I speculated about our next day's adventure. A warmth filled my chest as I imagined Callie retelling the facts we'd learned just a few minutes ago.

The night clerk knew of a little traveled, low-impact trail near Flat Top Mountain. Callie had popped the location into her maps app while we talked to the woman, to be sure we had it right. Hope had shone in Callie's bright eyes as she studied the images.

"Looks beautiful," I had agreed, and she hopped with glee while hugging me.

I loved her body pressed against mine.

The door to the bathroom opened, and Callie padded out of the bedroom.

"Oh my God, you look..." My erection switched off the flow of blood to my brain, and I lost my words. A messy bun held her hair in place and her face had a rosy glow from a fresh washing. Instead of a form-fitting gown, she wore short PJ bottoms and an oversized well-worn Gabby's Garage tee. Much sexier with my brand marking her.

She glanced down at her attire. "Is something wrong?"

"You look stunning."

She threw her head back and laughed. "Yeah right."

"I like you wearing my brand," I admitted, wondering what she'd do if I pointed out how much. My now-tight khakis needed to go.

"Maybe we can work out promo terms," she chuckled. "Seriously though, I thought it was appropriate for our adventure and, honestly, it's my favorite. The cotton is uber-soft."

I approached her, studying the design more closely. The decals were peeling in some places. "Holy shit. This is a first gen logo."

She shrugged. "I got this on sale at a car show because they only had smalls left. I have three." She spun around, modeling in an exaggerated way.

So adorable. I wanted to take her into my arms and kiss her senseless—and more. But we were pretend-dating and getting naked probably didn't qualify as practicing.

"Callie, are you done in the bathroom? I think I'll take a shower now." She didn't need to know my shower would be a cold one.

She pulled back the covers and climbed onto the right side of the bed. "Is this okay?"

"Sure." My shave kit and other toiletries were already in the bathroom. I found my lounge pants and a clean pair of boxer briefs. I took a last glimpse of Callie before closing the door; she was sitting up, covers pulled to her waist, with an open book.

I closed the door and turned on the water. I shucked my clothes and entered the lukewarm stream. As I cleaned my body, I wondered if I would have a perpetual hard on for the next two weeks.

Biting my tongue, I turned the water to cold and refused to move until I had counted to sixty.

I opened the door expecting to meet Callie's gaze, but she was on her side–book still open and light on–but breathing deeply, sound asleep. The three-hour time difference was killer.

Her face was relaxed and sweet. I marked her page and closed the book, setting it aside. Then I pulled the blanket over her arms, tucking her in like a child. She mumbled something but didn't wake.

I turned off the light, but it didn't plunge the room into total darkness. Light seeped in from around the room-darkening blinds. We were in the land of the midnight sun and the sun would rise again soon.

I laid on the bed and closed my eyes, but the almond and vanilla scent reminded me I wasn't alone.

Chapter Five
Callie

I awoke facing a sleeping man. His soft snores made me come fully awake and sit up. Dyson's relaxed state and tousled hair gave me pause.

I needed coffee so I could function. Quietly, I tiptoed out of the room, closing the door softly. I brewed the coffee and took my mug to the window.

Leaning against the wall, I watched people and cars move around the city like a video game. In the distance, clouds clung to the mountains.

Thirty minutes and another cup of coffee later, Dyson wandered out of the bedroom, shirtless. *Yum.* I'd had enough caffeine to get my blood percolating.

He yawned and scratched his chin. Hair, the same pale brown as his head, sprinkled his chest. Would it be soft? To find out, I had to touch it.

"Good morning, sleepy," I said, raising my mug to him.

He grunted and walked over to get coffee. He drew me to him like metal shavings to a magnet. I encircled his waist, pressing my face to his back. My hands gently combed his chest hair.

"Callie." His voice was deeper and rough, primal, and it

triggered desire.

"Hmm?" I hummed against his back.

"Coffee."

I chuckled, letting him go and returned to my spot, staring at the scenery. Dyson Gabbard was a caveman in the morning. One-word sentences and grunts.

Seven a.m. in Anchorage was ten in the morning at home. "The day's a wastin' my dad always used to say," I taunted before turning to face Dyson again.

He made no indication he'd heard me as he shuffled over, raising the mug to his lips. I gawked at his contoured chest and abs and highly tented, plaid pajama bottoms.

Who'd have thought the host of the goofiest show on CarTube would have the hottest body on the platform?

Thank God he was in a pre-caffeinated, zombie-like state and didn't notice my intense stare or blush.

I downed the rest of my coffee and nearly skipped out of the room calling, "I'm going to take a shower."

Once out, I found Dyson dressed in black shorts and a Gabby's Garage shirt. I tried to forget the memory of his luscious body, but the image remained imprinted on my retinas.

Dyson studied me from toes to crown. "I like your pants."

"These leggings are comfortable and perfect for hiking or whatever we're doing today." The lightweight, gray leggings had pockets which held my lip balm and phone.

"I thought we'd get a bite before driving around. We can check out the wharf or museums, too. Let's look at the brochures in the lobby to see if there's anything we definitely have to do before my family gets here."

"Fine. I'm game for everything." I bit my lip, hoping we wouldn't run into Jake anywhere.

As if reading my mind, Dyson rubbed my arms. "Don't worry. You've got me."

I did indeed. For the next two weeks, I had a man to call my own. I leaned against him and sighed when he hugged me.

"I like your hugs," I mumbled, returning it.

We drove slowly through Anchorage until the buildings thinned and the wilderness stretched before us. Dyson turned the rental SUV into a narrow gravel lane.

"If we hadn't been told about the trailhead, I'd think we were on a fire road."

"Do you hear banjos?" Dyson shot me a side glance before laughing at his *Deliverance* joke.

"Let's check." I lowered the window and breathed the fresh air. The pungent aroma of pine assaulted me. Closing my eyes, I relaxed into the seat. "Nope."

"We're here." He stopped before pulling into the parking lot. "I thought you'd like to get footage of your arrival."

"Oh! Great idea." I sat up straight then twisted to start the dash cam, only to find it on. "You've been recording?"

"Yes. I thought you could speed it up and do a time-lapse." He leaned, stuffing his arm in the back and pulled out another camera and the portable mic. Switching it on, he handed it to me.

"Hold it out your window low, but away from the car." Lowering his window, he turned on the other camera. I wrapped the cord around my wrist and dangled the mic outside.

Dyson held the camera up and near the roof. His long arms reached where I couldn't see. "Ready?"

I nodded, grateful for his foresight. He honked the horn, then let off the brake. We edged forward until we parked.

He lowered his arm, cradling the camera, and I set the battery box and mic in my lap. "Thank you for helping me. The horn will make the perfect audio spike to align the clips."

We exited the car, and he came around to fasten the mic to

my shirt. His expression was all business, but his touch at my neck lit a fire, and I exhaled loudly.

His gaze flicked to mine. "Performance anxiety?" A lopsided grin touched his face as his eyes sparkled.

"Maybe a little." I replied honestly, "I usually just use my phone. All this fancy equipment makes me nervous." I bit my bottom lip.

"Don't worry about it. Use your phone like normal. You can consider everything I shoot as bonus footage."

"Okay," I leaned in and hugged him.

Dyson raised the camera and focused it on me. Watching the digital screen, he said, "Maybe we can find a place where we can practice kissing."

My face heated, but I rolled my eyes. "Let's hike."

Every place I visited for my channel, I had tried to capture a couple of different angles of the trailhead sign and map. The Flat Top Mountain trail was only a two-mile loop, but with the time and elevation change, I'd opted for the moderate hike for my first adventure in Alaska. Plus, I sometimes found it hard to breathe around Dyson.

Warnings about poisonous plants and dangerous wildlife cautioned hikers to remain alert. I didn't want to disturb any bears or moose.

We were alone in the parking lot, but the sky was blue, and the day was warm. Others were apt to join the mountaineering club.

At the trailhead, I checked my backpack to make sure I had remembered water and my portable battery charger for my phone, and offered to stow Dyson's key fob.

"I'm good." He slipped a backpack onto his back. "I've got snacks and water."

"Great. Let's roll," I quoted Jay's go-phrase from Enzo's Auto Tech.

Tall, green grass and wildflowers lined the rocky path as we started out, but soon we were trekking through a grove of pines hand in hand. When we emerged from the forest at the crest of a hill, I panned the horizon, catching the spectacular view in the video. Dyson munched on a handful of trail mix.

We passed a large boulder with other hikers stretched out on top.

"That's a great photo op," Dyson pointed out. "Let's get a picture on the way back."

The trail narrowed and became rocky. Dyson insisted I lead the way, and we continued up the hill. Winded, we arrived at the pinnacle. A platform with a bench overlooked Anchorage and beyond.

We sat, catching our breath and enjoying the view. I dropped my backpack on the ground near my feet and Dyson fished in his for more trail mix.

"This day couldn't be more perfect," I said, laying my palm on his thigh, just above his knee.

"Mmhmm," he hummed, then downed the rest of his water.

He put his arm around me, and I snuggled into his side. I laid my head on his shoulder and the minutes ticked away.

White cotton-ball clouds floated lazily across the blue sky. A hawk flew overhead, birds twittered from distant trees. A warm breeze carried earthy and pine scents.

Dyson checked his watch.

"What time is it?" I asked.

"Time to practice," he said evenly.

I lifted my head and met his gaze. Keeping a straight face, I asked, "What do you want to practice?" My hand still rested on his leg. I drummed my fingers, catching his attention before I slid my hand towards his crotch.

His brows spiked, and he caught my hand, holding it mid-thigh. He leaned close, his breath fanning my face. Would he kiss me?

At that moment, I heard voices carrying in the wind. Dyson

heard them, too. He planted a quick peck, then leaned back with a smirk.

Three people came into view, laughing and smiling. One man with short grey hair, a younger man with similar features, and a middle-aged woman.

Dyson sighed, then stood, offering me a hand. "Is there anywhere you'd like to stop on the way back?"

"Maybe where the rocky trail curves around that large boulder. If I climb the rock, then maybe I can get a good shot of the valley."

"Let's do it," he replied.

I took his hand, and we passed the family. "Hello."

"Hi, great day for a walk," the woman said, her ponytail swaying.

When we got to a steep, narrow part of the trail, Dyson walked in front of me, and he offered me a hand a few times. Now I understood why he wanted to walk behind me on my way up, because I had a great view of his nice ass.

With my phone ready to snap pics and record video, I took several of Dyson's legs, arms, and butt.

The way down seemed more treacherous than the way up. We had to watch our footing over the rocky trail. Once I stumbled into Dyson, but thank God he was in front to stop me from falling headfirst and busting my lip, or worse.

We reached a fairly smooth area where Dyson and I could walk side by side. A flock of birds took flight, making us stop and listen, a spooky sensation washed over me—as if unseen eyes watched me through the pines.

"Do you hear anything?" I asked him.

"Shhh," he hushed, glancing from one side of the trail to the other. The sunlight showed through to the forest floor, but we couldn't see far into the dense woods. "I don't think it's anything big because we would hear it approaching."

"You mean like a bear?" I asked.

He met my gaze and nodded. "We should keep moving, just in case."

I didn't like the sound of that. My heart rate increased, and I kept looking behind me and off to the sides. I'd be a bear appetizer because the bear would catch me before it caught Dyson.

About ten minutes later, we reached the boulder. Again, we heard sticks cracking behind us.

"Do you think there is something following us?" I asked, clutching his arm.

"I hope not." He glanced at the enormous granite boulder, about the same height as him. He gave me a boost, and I scrambled up. I reached and lifted his backpack as he climbed to the top.

He handed me his camera and I adjusted the settings. I used the zoom lens to search for grizzlies, moose, or caribou. But I couldn't see anything.

"Callie," Dyson murmured softly. I met his gaze, and he continued, "Let's take a selfie."

If he was trying to distract me from pondering my forest fate, it worked. I leaned close until we were cheek to cheek. He extended his long arm, then I stuck out my tongue while crossing my eyes. He tapped the screen, catching my funny face. We laughed.

"Let's get a few pictures I can send to my mom." He chuckled at my surprised expression. He'd had plenty of time to send a picture or two.

Trying again, I let him take a few of us, just smiling. Then I kissed his cheek and the next time he kissed mine then we kissed each other.

Honestly, I wouldn't mind if we practiced more, but I thought I heard a twig snap in the distance. Instead of looking into the woods, I needed to focus on the picturesque view.

I stood up and spotted a lake glimmering in the sun. First, I filmed a panoramic movie in both vertical and horizontal, then I turned toward Dyson. He lounged on the rock with his eyes closed, his face tipped toward the sun wearing a peaceful expression. He was a thirty-something year old man with the body to match, but his sweet smile gave him a childlike innocence. Until he opened his eyes, which seemed to devour me whole.

Heat rose from my body, and I drank the last of my water.

I was grateful I had secretly snapped a few pictures before he caught me watching.

"Are you ready? I think we should head back."

Dyson helped me off the rock, and we started downhill once more. It was grassy with a few scattered trees. The trail hair-pinned around a small cliff. We paused along a steep grassy knoll where I could see the parking lot in the distance. "I can see the rental."

Suddenly, something nearby shrieked. We couldn't see it because the cliff wall blocked our view. The shrieks and accompanying heavy footfalls drew close.

"Run!" Dyson tugged my arm, helping me unfreeze.

We bolted down the gravel path. My heart raced. Dyson could take one step to my six, yet he didn't outpace me. In fact, he kept me in front of him.

In a full out sprint, I reached a jackknife turn in the trail. I attempted to follow the path, but I couldn't switch directions fast enough. I teetered at the top of the hill and Dyson ran into me.

We toppled off the trail and down the slope. As I rolled, my shoe flew off and air rushed from my lungs. Luckily, we hadn't fallen from high off a rock face.

"Callie, are you okay?" Dyson grabbed my arms, gently shaking me, and made eye contact.

I couldn't breathe. Dry grass poked me in the back.

My chin hurt. I touched my face, and when I pulled my fingers away, they were damp with blood.

"I'm fine, I think." Everything ached, but not horribly, like when I had broken my leg as a kid. I had bumps and bruises, but I'd live. I glanced at him.

"How about you? Are you hurt?"

"No, I'm just roughed up a little. I'm so sorry, Callie. I can't believe I knocked you off a cliff."

With a hoarse laugh, I said, "That will be a story to tell our grandkids." I gasped, surprised by the unexpected words that had tumbled from my lips.

His eyes widened. "What?"

"Don't listen to me, I just bumped my head," I tried to laugh it off. Looking past Dyson toward the top of the hill, I saw an outline. "What's that?"

"What the hell?" Dyson jumped to his feet. A dark silhouette glanced down at us. "Hey, you!"

The thing backed away, out of sight. I trembled, hoping it wouldn't launch itself after us.

Dyson returned his attention to me. He offered me his hands and pulled me to my feet. I found and slipped on my shoe. I stepped warily at first, then with confidence when my legs worked properly.

"Did your camera survive the fall?" I asked.

We gathered our belongings, making sure we had everything, and then tested the electronics. Surprisingly, my phone screen remained unscathed. Dyson's equipment had weathered the fall as well.

I touched my chin again where there was a dull ache. I pulled my finger away with more blood. "Is this bad?" I asked Dyson.

"It doesn't look like more than a scratch. Let's go back to the hotel and clean up." Dyson took my elbow like he was helping an old lady. But we were off-trail on uneven ground, and I appreciated his steadiness.

"This isn't the *practicing* I had in mind," I chuckled.

He offered me a sympathetic smile.

"What do you think chased us?" I asked. "Was it an animal or a person? Is my mind playing tricks on me?"

"It was definitely a person," he growled. "It was a man. I'm ninety-nine percent sure."

"Do you think it was one of those lumberjack people?"

"Lumberjack people? What do you mean?" With a side glance, he studied me.

"You know, those doomsday preppers who live off the land."

"He's doing some pretty illegal shit if he is a doomsday person. This is a state park. I'm sure he's not allowed to build a cabin here."

After a few minutes, we finally found the trail again. With a sigh of relief, we ambled toward the car. Once safe in the rental, I closed my eyes and exhaled.

"Do you think that was Jake the creeper?" I whispered.

Dyson met my gaze with a measure of concern. Looking in the rear-view mirror, he swore under his breath.

I swiveled in the seat and gasped, "Stop!"

Dyson hit the brakes, and I jumped out. I walked over to the black Jaguar. A thick layer of dust and grit coated the exterior. Cupping my hands, I glanced inside the tinted windows. The interior was black leather and posh.

I spun around, searching for the stalking bastard. Balling my trembling hands, I scowled toward the path while biting my lip. "How did he find us?"

"I don't know." Dyson appeared next to me and drew a dick in the dust on the driver's door. "Let's go before he can follow us."

"He's not too smart, is he? Why would you take such a low-profile car on these primitive roads?" I asked.

"I hope he has good insurance," Dyson grumbled. We returned to the car and started back toward the hotel. The entire drive, Dyson kept glancing in his rearview mirror, keeping a watch for the black Jag.

"I was right," I said with a smirk.

"Right about what?" Dyson asked.

"It was a naturally aspirated V8." I leaned back with my Thug Life smile. Dyson laughed, but it didn't reach his eyes. He kept a vigilant watch on the mirrors.

I flipped the sunshade down and turned on the light so I could view my wound in the mirror. It was a short, thin scratch on my jawline. Grime smeared my face and caked my clothes, leaving me desiring a shower. Half my hair had fallen out of my high ponytail, too.

"I'm going to take a shower when we get back, and then I want to comb through the footage to see if we caught Jake." I flipped the visor shut with a new focus.

"Sounds like a plan," Dyson agreed.

We parked, and I mumbled, "Let's hurry. I look crappy."

"I'll leave the equipment for later," Dyson suggested, locking the vehicle. He grasped my hand, leading me into the lobby where crystal chandeliers glittered, making me feel shabby.

"Oh shit," Dyson froze, and I bumped into him. I followed his gaze to the check-in desk. "It's my family. "

Oh, shit is right.

"You said they were coming in a few days," I said, gripping his arm.

"I don't know why, but they're early. There's my mom Judy, dad Tim, and my mom's sister Esther at the desk checking in. Over there is my sister Lucy, and my cousins Asher and Lydia." He pointed to each person as he named them.

"Look, there he is," Mr. Gabbard said, pointing across the lobby at Dyson.

I cringed. "I look like I had a dirt bath. It's not exactly the kind of first impression I wanted to make on your family."

"It will be fine." Dyson glanced at me tenderly. "They'll be fine." He touched my face, and I inhaled deeply.

He took my petite hand in his big one and led me across the lobby toward his family. Their curious gazes scanned us and I felt scrutinized, like a microbe under a microscope.

"What happened to you?" Asher asked. He sized me up from my gym shoes to my unkempt hair.

"Yes, you both look as if you've been rolling around in the hay," Lucy teased with a friendly smile. She wore shorts and a pink tank top, and her eyes sparkled. They were the same color as Dyson's.

"Everyone, this is Callie Ferenzo." Dyson squeezed my hand and smiled gently down at me.

Dyson's mom grabbed me and hugged me until I squeaked. "Welcome to the family, my dear."

I glanced at Dyson in a bit of panic.

Lucy laughed, and Tim said, "Let the poor girl be, Judy."

"You'll scare her away, Mom," Dyson admonished. "Don't I get a hug too?"

The family chatted for a few minutes before Dyson asked, "Why are you early?"

"We're not, son," Tim said.

"Remember? Mom changed the arrival time so we could get to know Callie better?" Lucy grinned at me.

Although Dyson included me in the conversation and the group spoke to me as if I wasn't a stranger, I couldn't help feeling the odd man out. I plastered on a polite smile and nodded when appropriate, but I was self-conscious about my grimy state. Dyson's shirt was filthy, and his hair was a mess. Why do men always look good with messy hair?

I rubbed my arm, brushing the dirt off. People stared at me as they walked by. I looked like a hobo. Eventually, I found my nerve and tugged on Dyson's arm. "Can I have the room key? I'd like to freshen up and change."

"What happened to you two?" his mom asked. Wetting her finger, she attempted to rub the dirt off of Dyson's cheek.

"Mom." Dyson grimaced and leaned away from her hand. "I suppose I need a shower, too."

"We went on a hike. It was really, really beautiful, but on the way back we took a tumble," I said.

"We got a ton of pictures. We can show you later, if you'd like? But we'll need to offload them first," Dyson said.

"Dad and I are on the same floor as you. We'll get settled while you clean up, then I'd love to see your photos," Judy said as she waved her keycard and pressed ten.

"Sounds good." Dyson smiled, rubbing my back.

"We are one level below you," Aunt Esther said, pushing nine. Asher and Lydia followed their mother off the elevator.

"How old are your cousins?" I asked Dyson.

He turned to Judy, who responded, "Lydia is twenty-two and Asher is twenty. Their father left a few years ago and they look up to Dyson. Especially Asher."

The bell rang, and the elevator door slid open. We walked to our room waving to his parents.

Dyson set his keys on the table, and I opened my laptop to share my photos with it. I needed to do a photo dump.

"Do you want to take a shower?" I asked him.

He met my gaze with wide eyes and a lopsided grin.

Did he want to take a shower with me? My body heated at the thought. "You go first. It'll take me a minute to get this going and then I'd like to take a long shower and rub the ache out of my muscles."

"Okay. I'll be quick," Dyson said.

I heard the water turn on. *Had he even closed the bathroom door?* I stuffed the interesting thought of a naked Dyson away, then created a folder, named it Flat Top Mountain, and dumped the photos into the folder. As I waited for the download, the water turned off.

The download was more than halfway done when he came out shirtless but with fresh shorts. I liked him walking around shirtless. I didn't know if I should force him to put on a shirt or keep him like that. Better yet, maybe pants-less too.

"It's my turn," I said, hopping to my feet.

I went into the bedroom, but left the bedroom door open a crack so I could hear when his family arrived. I picked out a cute, summery outfit and laid it on the bed.

In the bathroom, I slid the barn door shut, then leaned to inspect my chin in the mirror. I was lucky. It could have been a lot worse than a couple of bruises and a chin scratch. It was scary and I'm glad I hadn't been alone.

I started the water and since Dyson had just showered it was warm right away. Steam filled the room. The weight of being stalked hit me, and I leaned against the wall. Tears mingled with the hot water cascading over me and flowed down the drain.

Hugging myself, I looked past the last few minutes of the hike and remembered the gorgeous scenery and all the footage I'd gathered for my new channel.

My new channel. Even Jake the creeper couldn't put a damper on my smile.

As I toweled off, I heard women's laughter ringing from the other room. I hurriedly brushed my hair and donned my underwear, all the while trying to decipher the number of voices. His sister and cousins, maybe?

"Oh, no." Like a dummy, I'd forgotten to bring my clean outfit into the bathroom. I wrapped my torso with a towel.

A faint scraping noise met my ears. I slid the barn door open a little so I could peer into the bedroom.

Movement caught my eye... Asher kneeled by my open underwear drawer. My lacy, blue silk nightgown dangled from his fingertips.

"Dyson!" I screamed, startling the boy.

Dyson burst into the room. His gaze met mine, and I pointed. He gave me a once over before his gaze dropped to his cousin who still held my gown.

"What the hell!" With a murderous look, Dyson yanked Asher to his feet. "Drop it and get out," he growled.

Studying his shoes, the young man slunk away. Murmurings

erupted from the living room.

Dyson stalked to my side. "Are you all right?" He checked me over, ending with his hands on my shoulders.

"Why does this happen to me? Why now?" My lip quivered, and I bit it to keep it from trembling.

Dyson pulled me to him in a fierce hug, and part of my brain registered regret that he'd put on a shirt. Still, I found it hard to breathe, but being smothered by his concern helped steady me.

"Why would he do that with you in the other room?" Anger flared to life.

"I will find out," Dyson stated as he strode away, leaving me alone. Seconds later, I could hear the thunder in Dyson's voice as he attempted to get at the truth.

I locked the door, then dropped the towel. As I pulled a green short-sleeve shirt over my head, I tried to breathe deeply. My hands shook as I pulled on my white shorts.

My anger grew with every heartbeat. A fierce urge to shield Dyson from harm overwhelmed me. Asher had disrespected Dyson and me. Why?

I squeezed my eyes shut, and the muscles in my jaw clenched tight as I fought to control my anger.

I opened my eyes and squared my shoulders. Stepping from the dimly lit bedroom into the bright kitchen, I found Dyson standing with his arms crossed, a frown etched on his face. I met his upset apologetic gaze before turning toward his family.

Lucy and his cousins sat on the sofa. Thank God his parents weren't present. Nearest the door, Asher rose and stepped toward me.

I froze, staring warily at the boy. My gaze flicked to Dyson, who nodded.

Before anyone could say or do anything, I snapped and rushed the young man, knocking him flat against the door. I held my forearm against Asher's throat.

His eyes wide with fear, Asher mumbled apologies, his voice

barely a whisper.

Asher wasn't much shorter than Dyson, but the twenty-year-old was a twig. Even so, I'm sure he could have easily broken away, but he didn't. I could see remorse in his features, but it did little to exorcise the anger.

"Why?" I growled, my voice a low, dangerous rumble I didn't recognize.

Asher swallowed. His gaze skittered around the room, settling behind me where I could feel Dyson's heat.

"Why did you do that? Why would you do that to your cousin? You don't know me. You ruined his surprise."

"Answer her," Dyson demanded.

"You are Callie Ferenzo. I just–"

Asher's eyes widened again as I applied more pressure. "Why would you do this to Dyson?" A sheen of sweat appeared on his brow.

"I don't know," he started. His gaze shifted from me to Dyson then back to me. His face flushed crimson, Asher let out a heavy sigh. "I wanted the money."

"Explain," I ordered.

"I will if you back down."

I dropped my arm to my side. A red blotch lined his throat, and he rubbed his neck.

"There was a man who said he'd give me ten thousand dollars for a pair of your underwear." Asher glanced at his hands.

Gasping, I stumbled backward, bumping into Dyson. He turned me toward him and pulled me into his arms. I buried my face against his chest and breathed in his clean scent.

"What did he look like?" Dyson demanded as he sat in the blue armchair and took my hand, pulling me gently onto his lap. I laid my head against his chest and sighed, my anger subsiding some.

Asher sat on the other blue chair and described his meeting with a man suspiciously sounding like Jake.

Dyson tapped on his phone screen, pulling up an image from the airport. "This him?"

Asher glanced at the image then confirmed it was Jake with a nod. "I'm really sorry. Ten thousand dollars is a lot of money." He scrubbed his face. "I wasn't going to take your panties. I just wanted to see what kind you liked so I could buy something and get the money."

"You were going to scam the pervert?" Lydia said, studying her brother.

Asher shrugged. "It's a lot of money. I didn't mean to scare you."

"More like, gross her out. I wouldn't want some strange guy touching my undies. That's just nasty." Lucy scrunched her nose, making a yuck face.

"It's worse. That dick started harassing Callie on her flight to Alaska." Dyson filled his cousins and sister in on what I'd gone through.

"Sorry, I didn't know." Asher uttered.

"I think it's time to go to the cops." Dyson met my gaze and Lucy nodded.

"Why?" I asked, glancing out the window and finding a measure of solace from the panoramic view. "We're leaving this place and it seems like he lives here. We'll never see him again."

Silence stretched.

"Thank goodness your cousin isn't actually a pervert. That would have been awkward," I whispered to Dyson. He rubbed my back.

"What surprise did my stupid brother ruin?" Lydia asked, sitting up and glaring at Asher.

"I wondered that too," Lucy said, nodding. She tugged at a lock of her chestnut-colored hair.

I sighed and turned my head, glancing at Lucy. Did I want to have this conversation? No. But it could seal the deal that Dyson and I are girlfriend and boyfriend.

"The item I caught Asher manhandling was a secret purchase for this trip. Something I had yet to reveal. Something special for Dyson." I covered my face with my hands, hiding the heat.

Would his family buy it?

"I can take you shopping for something else," Dyson said, squeezing my hand.

"I'm sorry," Asher mumbled, avoiding eye contact.

Ignoring Asher, I surveyed Dyson's face. One brow raised slightly. His color had returned to normal and the tension had visibly eased from his shoulders.

"You want to take me intimate apparel shopping?" I teased.

His gaze dropped to my lips, so I licked the corner of my mouth. He inhaled sharply, then a wicked grin formed.

"I could choose my own surprise. I like that idea. What do you think?" He pulled me close until my hip touched his groin.

"Oh." I squeaked, as he pressed his manhood against me. The more I stared into his hazel eyes, the more his erection seemed to grow. "We haven't practiced this," I whispered.

His hooded gaze slowly drank me in, a silent appraisal that sent shivers down my spine. His hazel eyes, shimmering with an inner light, held me completely spellbound and the day's harrowing events fell away.

"I remember when you opened your suitcase and—"

I placed a finger on Dyson's lips, hushing him before he could expose our farce.

He licked my finger, and heat traveled to my core. I didn't know how to respond.

"I think they want to be alone," Lydia observed, standing up. Asher jumped to his feet too.

"I think a better option is to go shopping," Lucy suggested with a clap of her hands. "I know where we can go. The shops are within walking distance *and* there's a lingerie store. You can get him to buy you a new nightie and maybe some other things."

I craned my neck to look at her. "How do you know where

there's an intimate apparel store?"

Lucy grinned at me, then shrugged impishly. "I've been to Anchorage a lot. I know where the boutiques are." She offered me her hand, and when I took it, she pulled me to my feet.

I had a feeling Lucy and I were going to be the best of friends.

"Grab your wallet, Dyson. You're going to need it," Lucy said.

"I want to go grab my purse," Lydia said, pointing to the door.

"We'll meet you in the lobby in ten minutes." Lucy waved Lydia on her way. "I'll tell Mom and Dad we'll meet them for dinner later."

"I guess I'll go chill with my mom," Asher said, staring at his feet.

Dyson clamped a hand on his cousin's shoulder. "Oh no, you don't. You're staying where I can see you. Be down in the lobby, ready to go."

Once the family had left us alone, Dyson tipped my chin, looking at the scratch. "How do you feel? It doesn't look as bad as it did before."

"It's fine." I checked to see if the download was complete, then stuffed my laptop into my bag. "We can show the pictures to your family after dinner."

He pulled me into a hug. "I'm sorry about my loser cousin. I can't believe he would stoop that low."

I clung to Dyson. His comforting warmth spread through me as his strong arms held me close, a feeling of security washing over me. I tilted my head and looked him in the eye. "Please don't leave my side while we're out. What if Jake tries to pay someone else to..."

"I've got you, Callie. Don't worry, I won't leave you." He rubbed circles on my back.

"Okay. Promise?"

"I promise."

Chapter Six
Dyson

My chest ached to give Callie one hundred percent of my attention–to take in every item she examined, every decision she made, and her every excited gasp–but all the time we were out, my head swiveled, searching for anyone spying on us.

The lingerie store, Naughty and Nice, had possibilities, but every person who raised a phone, anyone entering or exiting the store, the staff, strangers, and even random cars driving past weren't beyond suspicion.

I watched as Callie kept throwing glances toward the entry and frowning. My anger boiled. Even in his absence, Jake's incessant harassment of Callie continued,

In the corner, Asher sat scrunched over, playing on his phone or taking selfies. He seemed unassuming, unlikely to cause trouble, much less steal underwear.

I hadn't spent much time with Asher after Aunt Esther dumped her cheating husband. It was easy to imagine, though, how it must have been hard on my cousins. It still didn't excuse Asher's unacceptable behavior.

Perhaps the money would have been used to kick-start Asher's influencer career. But from half-baked trending challenges to the rambling product reviews I'd seen him post, his attempts to go viral on social media lacked any clear focus.

Maybe if I'd spent more time with him... I shook my head.

"Dyson?" Callie met my gaze over a four-way stand. She lifted a turquoise spaghetti strap gown with a lacy neckline. Heat flushed my face, and with a broad smile, I nodded my approval.

Damn. I wonder if I can get her to pose for me next to the Porsche in that skimpy thing.

In a flash, she appeared beside me, a scrap of fabric dangling from a hanger. "Matching boxers for you." She wiggled her brows, and I laughed.

"I tell you what, if you get the gown, I'll get the matching pants. That goes for anything else. I will get the coordinating boxers. Would you like that?"

"Yes," she said breathlessly, her fiery gaze dropped to my bulge. "I can tell you do, too."

I ended up dropping a few hundred dollars at Naughty and Nice, but it was worth the time and money to see Callie smile. Especially if I got to sample the goods.

After shopping with my sister and cousins, we met my parents and aunt for dinner at a restaurant—chosen because it served my mother's favorite wine. We sat at a table on the patio. Birds chirped, and a breeze fanned us as we took in the view overlooking the Cook Inlet.

Mom sat next to Callie. Who knew what interrogation my mother had in mind? Luckily, Lucy sat on Callie's other side.

Callie had set her phone screen-side up on the table, so I texted, "Are you okay?"

The message popped onto Callie's screen and was visible to my mother and sister.

Mom narrowed her eyes. "Of course she is," she said, then tsked at me and returned her attention to my pretend girlfriend. "What's this picture?" she asked, pointing to Callie's phone.

Callie blushed. "Do you like my wallpaper?"

"That's an old photo." Mom appeared perplexed. "Dyson hasn't had that car in over a year."

"What car?" I asked, my curiosity piqued. Callie raised her phone, showing me her wallpaper. "Oh, geez. That *is* old."

It was from the car show almost two years ago. We sat in the Diablo. I was in the driver's seat, Callie in the passenger's seat, and we gazed into one another's eyes. Her smile was beautiful.

We looked at each other across the table and shared the poignant memory. "It was the day my dad died," she said solemnly. "At the Kansas City Car Meet, when I visited Dyson and checked out his car."

"Apparently, that wasn't the only thing you were checking out," Lucy added, elbowing Callie playfully. I recognized my sister's attempt to lighten the mood. I'd thank her later.

"Well..." Callie chuckled with a shrug. "He looked cute in it even though his hair touched the headliner." She glanced at me and winked.

My family chuckled, and I blushed.

Did she really think I was cute?

Callie glanced at her plate for a moment before turning to my mother. "Dyson's a nice man. Later that day, when we learned that Dad had passed, Dyson was there for me. He didn't know me or Jay very well at the time, but he held me and let me cry in his arms."

She met my gaze again, sincerity shining through. "I don't know if I ever told you, but thank you. You were there for me when I needed it the most."

Emotion clogged my throat, and if I had been next to her, I would have pulled her into my arms–hard and tight. But she was across from me. I nodded, slightly irritated that it was such an impersonal response, but something flickered in her eyes.

Suddenly, I had a longing to practice kissing and maybe a whole lot more. I shifted impatiently in my wooden chair. Callie's green eyes fixed on me and a smirk teased her lips.

She winked, then abruptly turned to my mother. "Would you like to see the pictures of our hike?"

"That would be lovely." A wide grin spread across my mother's face, as if she'd just been given a lifetime supply of Glacier Bear wine. Her eyes sparkled with delight as Callie opened her laptop.

On the way back to the hotel, Callie and Lucy walked in front of me. They seemed to get along–it was both nice and disconcerting. Occasionally, Callie would glance back, then giggle. I could only imagine what childhood yarns Lucy spun.

I hung back out of Callie's earshot. With a subtle nod, I motioned to my father, and he silently matched my pace.

"I'm worried," I admitted, then informed him of what had transpired with the stalker, how he followed us, and how Asher had fallen prey to his whims.

"This is serious." My father rubbed his chin. "I think we should talk to the hotel manager once we get everyone settled."

I agreed. Even though it was after ten when we stepped inside the lobby, the twilight made it feel as if it were seven. The only other person around was the night clerk at the desk. She nodded to us as we passed to the elevator.

Callie was having a good time visiting with my family. She would meet scores of my extended relatives at the reunion, and it was heartwarming having her bond with my closest family members beforehand.

I didn't want to cut the night short, but I'd be lying if I didn't admit I wanted to try out my new boxers and check out what other goodies the Naughty and Nice bag held.

We got into the elevator and pushed the buttons for our floors.

"Good night," Aunt Esther called over her shoulder as she exited on the ninth floor. Lydia and Asher waved and followed.

The door slid shut with a gentle hiss, and Callie visibly relaxed, the tension leaving her shoulders. I met my father's eyes in the mirrored wall.

When we arrived on the tenth floor, Callie and I said goodnight to my folks and sister, then proceeded to our room. I waved the keycard and pushed the door open.

I froze, holding Callie back from entering. "We need to call security." Utter chaos met us—the ransacked room suggested that a whirlwind had descended and scattered our belongings.

"Oh my God," Callie gasped, her body trembling as she leaned heavily against me.

"Dad," I called, catching my father before he entered his room. Sensing the urgency in my tone, he jogged to my side. "Call the front desk and get the manager up here."

The waning light cast distorted shadows across the overturned room, amplifying the sense of threat and violation. The kitchen drawers lay open, their contents littered across the floor in a jumbled heap.

"I'll tell them to call the police, too." Dad whipped out his phone and called downstairs. Within a few minutes, the hotel manager arrived, announcing he'd summoned the police.

Lucy and my parents waited with us. My mother held Callie in her arms and caressed her head like a small child. "Poor dear."

"Did they take anything?" Lucy asked, frowning as she peered into the room.

"I don't know yet. This is a shit show," I told my sister. The sight of the upturned furniture sparked a surge of fury, the strewn cushions and tipped chairs mocking my sense of order and control.

"Please, take Callie to your room, Lucy. I'll take care of this."

"But Dyson, I don't want to leave you," Callie said, tears welling.

"You'll be safe with my family." I hugged her, breathing in her scent. Her frantic gaze, wide and desperate, met mine. Embracing her, I breathed, "Give me a few minutes. I'll take care of this. If I need you, I'll call you." I held her until she relaxed in my arms.

Eventually, she nodded, and Lucy led her away. I immediately felt the absence of her special energy, as if the only light in a dark room had been suddenly snuffed out.

A police officer jotted down notes while another inspected the disaster in our room.

"I'm sorry, Mr. Gabbard. I don't know who gained access." The manager, Mr. Hale, wrung his hands.

"That bastard offered my cousin ten thousand dollars for a pair of Callie's underwear. It wouldn't surprise me if he paid one of your employees to let him inside." I seethed, despite trying to keep my cool because the manager wasn't to blame.

"Nothing appears stolen," I said, taking inventory of our belongings. I was grateful I had paid attention when Callie unpacked.

"Why would someone break in and steal nothing?" Mr. Hale asked.

"Unless he stashed cameras around," I speculated, facing Mr. Hale. Gesturing subtly, I guided him into the hallway, my voice dropping to avoid being overheard. "I need your help to keep Callie safe. We need a room no one knows about except you and me—not even my family." I couldn't think of any other way to keep Callie safe. "I don't care what floor or what type of room, just one where no one will disturb us. Can you help?"

Mr. Hale nodded. "We're fully booked, but I'll make it happen somehow."

"We won't use this room again, but I don't want to check out until tomorrow. The police probably need it for a while longer, anyway," I said, rubbing my chest.

My parents waited down the hall, watching the scene. I signaled to them. "Mr. Hale is accommodating Callie and me in a new room. But..."

"What do you need, son?" Dad asked.

I met his gaze and nodded. "I don't want to risk Jake finding Callie again. That's why I think we need to make a clean sweep of our clothes and other items. I'm worried he put some tracking device somewhere along with cameras."

"Really?" my mom squeaked.

"Callie had her phone, her purse and laptop, plus the new purchases from this afternoon, so those aren't contaminated. But we'll need a few items for tonight."

Mom clutched my father's arm. "Do you think we'll be in any danger?"

"We aren't Callie, and we'll be together." Dad covered the hand she had placed on his arm and patted reassuringly.

I made a few more requests to my parents before sending them on the mission.

Mr. Hale and I fielded questions from the police until they were ready for Callie to give her statement.

I sent a group text to my sister and Callie, asking them to return to the room. When they arrived, I was explaining to the officers the incident with Asher and Jake.

As Callie spoke with the cops, I watched from the hallway with Mr. Hale.

"She's a sweet lady," Mr. Hale stated, nodding toward Callie. "It's good she has you to protect her. I'll go grab your new keycards and return shortly."

In full protection mode, I wanted to puff my chest out and beat it, but instead, I inwardly smiled at his words. Callie's protection just had an upgrade, like a car alarm with the lights flashing and horn sounding, alerting everyone to the potential threat. The squad had been notified and GPS tracking engaged.

"Once we've spoken with your cousin, you can go. If we have questions, we will contact you," the officer told me. "Unfortunately, your belongings are a part of the crime scene.

We'll need to process it, checking for fingerprints."

Callie bit her lip as she glanced around our space. It should have been our safe place. But I felt violated.

I rubbed Callie's shoulders. "I've got everything taken care of. I hope."

"Mmm. That feels great. You're hired." She leaned into my hands, her stiff posture relaxing as I massaged.

"Is this the end of it?" she asked in a small voice.

"It is if I have anything to say about it," I growled.

She turned in my arms and hugged me.

"I swear, Callie. I'll keep you safe." As I tilted her chin up, her troubled green gaze met mine. "Trust me. I've got plans for tonight."

Her cheeks flared red, and her lashes fluttered. "Dyson," she gasped, her voice barely above a whisper.

"Not those kind of plans, specifically, although…"

She gently punched me in the shoulder. "Don't get my hopes up, then dash them," she giggled.

"That's right. You've already told me not to break your heart." I hugged her again. Her curvy heat aroused more than my protective instincts.

"Mr. Gabbard, I've got your…" Hale started.

"Not in here," I snapped. "In the hall."

We exited the room. Mr. Hale cleared his throat and tried again. "The suite's key code has been changed. Here are the new keycards. You will have access to the old room until tomorrow morning at eleven."

"And the new room?" I asked.

"What new room?" Callie responded, gazing from me to Hale.

"We aren't staying here tonight. It's a mess, it doesn't feel safe, and the police haven't finished yet. So we've got a secret room planned."

One of her dainty brows rose. "Secret, hmm. We aren't

staying with your family?"

"What? No way. I want to keep you safe, and Mr. Hale has helped me come up with a plan. We're moving to another room where no one, not even my family, knows where we'll be."

"Okay. Let me get my things." She turned toward the room.

"Callie, stop."

She faced me with a quizzical look.

"We're leaving everything here tonight. In case, he bugged–"

A sharp gasp escaped her lips as she grabbed my arm, her fingers digging in. "You don't think he would...?" She paled.

"I don't know. But we're going to take every precaution."

"Yes, I've got a room especially for you," Mr. Hale said. "Come with me."

She shifted the large tote bag that held her laptop. "I'm ready," she said.

We followed Mr. Hale into the elevator.

"What floor are we staying on?" I asked.

"Five," he responded.

"I'm sorry I'm putting you through this, Dyson." Callie reached over and patted my arm.

"You didn't ask for this, Callie. It's not your fault, but I'll do everything I can to make sure you are safe."

"Promise?" She gazed at me with a sweet expression that warmed my insides and made it hard to swallow.

We exited, and Mr. Hale led us to a room with a door tag that read *Do not disturb*.

"This room had a small fire. The guy dropped a cigarette on the floor. The carpet needs to be replaced, so we are waiting for the contractor to come. It is currently off limits to all staff." Mr. Hale opened the door.

The carpet had a giant square cut out of it right in the middle of the room, exposing the concrete and some kind of dried yellow adhesive.

A stale, smoky smell hit us as we entered. The empty flat

screen TV wall bracket and missing dresser made the room seem open. At least the lone queen size bed was neatly made.

"I put the sheets on the bed myself rather than alert housekeeping. No one will bother you here." Mr. Hale picked up the white towels that were on the bed and hung them on the shelf above the toilet and checked to see if there was toilet paper. "If somebody questions you, contact me."

I shook Mr. Hale's hand. "Thank you for understanding and for helping us out."

"Rest easy and try to have a good night," Mr. Hale said, and then he left. I turned the deadbolt and engaged the door's security latch.

Callie sat on the bed cross-legged, then reached in her bag and pulled out her laptop. She opened it and entered her password.

"I'm going to go through our footage from this morning. Maybe I caught that bastard while we were hiking." She offered me a cunning grin, and then her gaze dropped to her screen. The intensity of Callie's hunt for Jake captivated me—her determination evident in her narrowed eyes and pursed lips.

My phone pinged, and I glanced at the screen. "My parents texted. They're in the lobby with some things for us."

"Like what?"

"Toothpaste and toothbrushes. I don't want to leave you, but I don't want them to come here either. Will you be okay if I go to the lobby?" Worry gnawed at me, and I ran my fingers through my hair.

The laptop's light made her skin seem pale, but her eyes shined. "I'll be fine. I won't let anybody inside. Besides, nobody knows we're here."

"I'll only be a few minutes," I promised, holding her gaze. "I will text, then knock when I come back."

"Go. I'll be here. Just be careful."

She bit her lip, then got up and followed me to the door. My heart ached in my chest. I dreaded leaving her. After I closed the door, I heard the reassuring click of the deadbolt sliding into place.

"Good girl, Callie," I breathed.

I walked up a flight to another floor, then pushed the button to call the elevator. Once in the lobby, I spied my parents at the front desk. Before meeting them, I searched the open space for Jake.

"There you are, Dyson," my mother said, spotting me. With a yellow plastic bag at her elbow, she hurried to me. "Since we don't know when the police will release the crime scene or your items, we bought some souvenir clothing. I hope that works. Also, Lucy gave me this sack that Callie left with her. She thought Callie would want it." She handed me a boutique bag with the Naughty and Nice store logo.

"I bought a few candy bars for you to snack on." My father lifted another bag. "How's Callie?"

"She's getting settled." I stymied a yawn. "It's been a long day."

"I hope you have a good night. I love you," Mom said. She kissed me on the cheek, and I hugged her.

"I love you, too. I'm going up to Callie now. Good night."

I entered the elevator and pushed the fourth, sixth, and eighth floor buttons, but got off at the fourth floor, then took the stairs up to the fifth. As I approached the *Do not disturb* room, I heard Callie talking to someone, and my heart dropped. I only heard her voice as I strained my ears.

I texted, "I'm here," then knocked and stood directly in front of the door's peephole.

"Hold on," she said, then hollered, "Coming."

A shadow darkened the room side of the peephole, then the lock disengaged. She cracked the door before smiling and pulling it open wide for me. I strolled in and hugged her. She squeaked.

"He's back, Jay," she said to the phone wedged between her shoulder and ear.

I set the bags of toiletries and clothes on the bathroom counter, then sat on the edge of the bed and watched her pace in front of the window.

"I know, I know," she said. Her glance flicked to me, then she frowned. "Nobody intended for this to happen, but I'm safe. Why do you need to know what room we are in? I don't even know the room number. But we are fine."

She glanced at me again, then rolled her eyes. "Of course, he's right here. Seriously, Jay. Fine." She muted the call and said, "My brother is a little upset. He wants to talk to you."

She unmuted and handed me her phone, and I put it to my ear. "Hello Enzo." Whatever he had to say, I would take it because I deserved it. I should have traveled with Callie to Alaska.

"What have you gotten my sister into? First, yesterday's airplane situation. Now today some creep in the woods, your cousin–and then somebody broke into your hotel room. What's going on? Do you have a crazy fan?"

"Enzo, the guy's not *my* fan—he saw her on *your* show. He's a fan, but he's–"

"He's not a fan," she growled. She stood and stalked to the bathroom, shutting the door.

"I've taken measures to safeguard her tonight. And I will continue to protect her. We're leaving for Denali tomorrow. Hopefully, the dick lives here. If not, the train we're taking is small, so we'll know if he's on it. My family all know what's going on. We will make sure Callie is safe."

"Give me your word," Enzo ordered, then he sighed and continued, "She's my only family. I don't know what I'd do without her."

"No one knows where we're staying tonight, not even my family. Rest easy. I'll have her call you in the morning."

"Fine."

Light filtered in around the blackout shade. A faint hint of musty smoke lingered as the fan kicked on. I turned, setting the phone on the bed.

Callie rushed up to me, waving something in one hand.

"What's the deal, Dyson?" Thrusting a box of condoms in my face, she giggled.

"Oh, shit." Rational words stalled in my throat, and I flared hot as I stared dumbfounded at her.

With a hand on her hip, she asked, "Is this what you ran out to get?"

"My mom got us some clothes for tomorrow and some toiletries from a drugstore." I scrubbed my face.

Flipping the package in her hand, she studied the box, chuckling. "I guess this means that your mom likes me."

"I guess so," I grinned as she handed me the box. "I better see what else Mom bought us."

Callie followed me into the bathroom. An awkward silence settled as I sorted the items from the first bag–toothpaste, toothbrushes, lotion, soap, and other interesting things, like a bath bomb and a container of lube.

I met her gaze, swallowed, then stuck my hand in the second bag. Where I found a razor and shaving cream—definitely my dad's doing.

I dumped another bag containing clothing next to the sink. Callie chose a tie-dye t-shirt with "Anchorage" printed in bold, black letters, and held it against her body as I grabbed a second matching shirt.

"We're going to be twinning it tomorrow," she chuckled, folding the shirt and placing it on the counter. "What's that?" she asked, pointing to a pile of Pepto-Bismol pink fabric.

With my thumb and index finger, I pinched and lifted the material. "These are what Lucy would call booty shorts. Nothing says tourist like having Alaska printed on your ass." I laughed.

"Are those shorts for you?" Callie grinned. "I guess that's one way to show off your nice legs."

I set the shorts aside and leaned against the counter, crossing my ankles. "So, you like my legs?" She blushed and curled a lock of hair around her finger.

"They're about a mile longer than mine."

"I don't believe you answered the question," I pointed out.

"Yes," she shrugged, then yawned.

"My boring legs, huh?" I teased.

"It's not you, it's this day." She yawned again. "It's catching up with me. I need to put on jammies and brush my teeth."

I opened the toothbrushes and toothpaste. While we were brushing, she met my gaze in the mirror.

"Oh, crap," she blinked with wide eyes. "I just remembered I don't have pajamas."

I spit and rinsed my mouth. "Oh well, I guess you'll have to sleep naked then."

She nudged me in the side with her elbow. "Dyson." A pretty blush fanned her cheeks.

"You have your new nightgown, remember?" I wiggled my eyebrows.

"Okay," she breathed, glancing at the Naughty and Nice bag on the counter.

"If you want, you can sleep in my shirt." I pulled it over my head and handed it to her as her gaze traversed my torso. My gut twisted and my blood ignited. With a hint of a grin, she brought the shirt to her nose and inhaled.

"I wouldn't mind wearing this, but look." She held it up against her body. It was wide and hung to her knees like a dress.

"Get comfy, Callie." I left the bathroom, letting her decide what to wear. She could sleep in whatever she wanted. It didn't matter if she wore the sexy turquoise gown or a fireproof racing suit. Regardless, I would find her alluring, and she'd tempt me.

The door to the bathroom opened, and Callie walked out wearing the sexy blue gown.

Oh boy. I rubbed my palms together, then put them between my knees as I sat on the edge of the bed.

"I love that color on you."

"Thanks," she said, a shy smile gracing her lips as a soft blush painted her cheeks. "Can you help adjust the straps? I need to shorten them or I'll fall out." She turned away from me and uncrossed her arms to lift her hair and give me access to the straps.

"That wouldn't be so bad," I whispered against her creamy neck. She shivered as I kissed my way down to her shoulder.

"Not tonight, Dyson. I'm ready to drop and I don't want to be hot and bothered."

Two things: one—I made her hot and bothered, and two— maybe another night. Fire lapped at my veins, and joy simmered in my soul.

I adjusted the straps, and then she climbed into bed. I escaped to the bathroom to splash cold water on my face. More blue fabric dipped from the boutique store bag—my matching boxers. I slipped them on.

The material was silky-soft, and they fit nicely, although I felt exposed. I clicked off the light and found the room dark.

I climbed into bed beside Callie. She faced away from me, and I laid on my back with a hand behind my head. I tried not to think about what Callie was wearing. And I tried not to think about the bastard and what we'd been through.

Callie sniffled, and it cut my heart. I reached, placing a hand on her shoulder.

"Come here," I whispered.

She turned and snuggled against me, wrapping her arm over my chest. "Thank you, Dyson. I don't feel alone when I'm with you."

"You aren't alone." I stroked her hair, trying to soothe her. The satiny feel of her gown as it grazed my skin kept my heart rate high.

She tipped her head and kissed my chin. I responded by brushing my lips against hers. She smiled and then settled back against me. "Good night, Dyson. You're a great fake boyfriend." She yawned and within a minute, her breathing deepened.

I laid in the sweet torture of purgatory. Neither awake nor asleep. Even if I could sleep, I knew my dreams would be equally tormented.

Chapter Seven

Callie

The time was late morning, at least for Kansas. It was early for Anchorage, though. I rolled away from Dyson and stood, and he didn't wake.

Other than the bed, there wasn't any furniture in the room. I commandeered the bathroom for an office, sitting on the toilet with my laptop on the counter. Sifting through the footage from the hike again, I realized I hadn't captured any evidence of the stalker.

I strung the images into a short compilation for my channel—a teaser for a longer episode. I hadn't planned to post anything about this Alaska trip until after I returned to Kansas. That was my usual posting schedule, about a month out. But now, with a stalker around, I especially didn't want anyone privy to my whereabouts.

After an hour hunched over the keyboard, my back ached. I eyed the green bath bomb.

Should I?

I stretched, arching my back. Then I leaned out of the bathroom and peeked at Dyson. Hearing his soft snores, I closed the door and started the water.

In this smaller non-suite room, I could take an actual soak, not like in the tenth floor suite, which only had a spacious mega-shower.

Steam rose from the water. As I dropped the bath bomb in, a fresh floral scent with a hint of eucalyptus bubbled forth. To keep the heat in, I closed the shower curtain.

I disrobed, slipped past the curtain, and slid into the water. Relaxing, I leaned back and sighed. The warmth eased the ache in my back.

A smile of satisfaction rested on my face. I had exciting content to showcase on End of the Road. I spent a few minutes wondering what Jay's response to my deception would be. Technically, I hadn't lied to him, just pursued my dream behind his back–and kept it hidden.

Maybe Dyson and I could take a hike in Denali. I'd love to get him alone for more shoots. *And maybe a little more practice.*

I closed my eyes, envisioning Dyson's sleeping face. Also, his chiseled pecs and abs.

In the middle of a hot daydream, a knock sounded, and I bolted upright, sloshing water.

"It's me," Dyson said, "I need to pee."

"Come in, I'm in the bathtub."

The door creaked open slowly, and he stepped inside. His shadow moved across the shower curtain toward the toilet. He lifted the lid, did his business, then flushed. "Strange doing morning rituals like this," he said. "How's the water?"

"Warm and relaxing." I slunk down so my breasts were under the surface.

"Maybe I should join you?" he hummed. The water at the sink turned on. "Warm and relaxing sounds good." The ch-ch-ch sound of teeth being brushed met my ears.

"I barely fit, and I don't have legs. You wouldn't fit, let alone both of us." My mind went blank, thinking of naked bath Twister with Dyson. "I'd have to sit on your lap, and I would get cold. Although, the suite shower could have accommodated two adults easily."

A beat passed, the sink turned off, then he said, "I was thinking of a hot tub, but I'm glad you've thought our bathing situation through."

"I'm a planner," I said to cover my embarrassment.

"Callie, I need to go."

"Where? And when?" I asked, sitting up again. The floral scent wafted around me.

"I'm not leaving you. Not that type of going, it's just..." He cleared his throat. "Nature is calling."

"Oh," I chuckled. "That's a problem. Let me rinse off." I lifted the stopper, and the water gurgled as it circled the drain.

"You don't have to get out. I'll be quick." His shadow shifted toward the toilet.

"Okay. I've never read about this in a romance book."

"Not very romantic," he admitted.

"I don't know. There's something about a hero willing to trust the heroine and drop his drawers in front of her."

He groaned, and I laughed.

The water had half emptied, and I stood and started the shower. I adjusted the stream until it was the perfect temperature, then stepped into it. I had small trial sizes of body soap, shampoo, and conditioner. As I was rinsing out my conditioner, the toilet flushed. I squeezed out my hair and turned the water off.

Dyson was still in the bathroom, and I heard the faucet running.

"Can you hand me a towel, please?" I asked.

A white towel appeared inside the curtain. "Here you go."

I didn't mind staying inside the curtain to dry off, as it was warmer there. I wrapped my body with the towel and stepped out. The mirror was steamy and Dyson had wiped a spot clear. I met his gaze in the reflection. His chin was white with shaving cream.

"That's a new look," I teased.

"I like yours, too," he shot back.

"The shower is all warmed up for you," I bowed, leaving the room.

After we dressed in our matching shirts and tidied up our meager stash of goods, we used the stairs to head down for breakfast. In the hotel restaurant, Lucy grabbed me, looping her elbow through mine.

She leaned close, glancing around before speaking. "So did you have a good time last night?" Her face blushed, and she wiggled her eyebrows.

Heat flared on my face, and I glanced at Dyson. Fortunately, he was conversing with his father.

"What do you mean?" I played innocent.

She nudged me with her elbow. "How was your new nightgown? Was it comfortable? Did he like it?"

"That's a little personal. Do you really want to know about your brother's sex life?" I tried to remain stoic.

Of course, the men heard "sex life" and now seemed interested in the conversation.

Great, just great.

Was his mother going to come along and ask how many condoms we used?

"If you really want to know what happened after my crazy day, I was mentally exhausted and I crashed. Your brother is a good man who didn't push me or have expectations. I got a full night's sleep, too. I'm rested and ready to take on this bastard if he shows his face again." With a deep breath, I rubbed my hands together as I prepared for the day.

"I don't see the guy," Asher said, inspecting the eating area. "He was old and rich."

I looked around the room. "I don't see him, either."

"I wish he was here." Lucy's tone promised vengeance. "Show us the picture again. Mom and Dad haven't seen it yet and I want to refresh my memory."

The server set a carafe of coffee on the table, and I poured a cup of caffeinated nectar. While she took our order, Dyson scrolled through his phone.

"Here it is. I showed it to the cops last night." Dyson passed his phone to his father, who passed it to Lucy. Then it went around the table until it was finally handed to me, and I forced myself to look at it again.

The photo was taken at the airport when I was being escorted down the escalator. Jake was behind me, with two guards flanking him. His gaze was fixed on my back, a chilling intensity in his eyes.

It wasn't the best photo, but at least it showed them what he looked like. I passed the phone on with a shiver.

I dismissed Jake from my thoughts and picked up my mug. Lost in the swirling steam of my coffee, I inhaled the comforting aroma and smiled, studying Dyson's family.

His parents had stepped in when I needed help. Lucy too. His family was warm and welcoming, and I liked them. Even Asher, his young cousin with the now-tarnished entrepreneurial spirit.

The server brought our food. Around bites, I learned our travel plans. Since I'd never been to Alaska, I was surprised to learn we'd be traveling by train. Perhaps I should have asked Dyson more questions.

"Train?" I leaned close to Lucy.

"Yes. Usually, we go straight to Fairbanks and it takes all day, but Dyson thought you'd like to see Denali, so we're stopping at the state park and visiting that area for a few days."

"He planned the stop for me?" I doubted it, since I'd only known about the trip for a month.

"Yes." Lucy winked. "He's been wanting to spend time with you for a while."

"How long has this trip been in the works?" I glanced at Dyson, who laughed as Lydia threw a salt packet at her mother.

"The big reunion happens every five years, so..." Lucy turned introspective.

"The Denali detour," I clarified.

"Oh. Three months or so."

Dyson couldn't have planned that far ahead in anticipation of me coming with him. Could he?

With breakfast done, we checked with the manager on duty and learned the police had released our room. We went back to the penthouse suite, where we carefully sifted through our belongings, looking for bugs or trackers, and repacked our luggage with the new toiletries, my laptop, and the unopened box of condoms. Then we checked out and returned the rental car.

We boarded the train in a flurry of activity. The double-decker train cars blew my mind. Dyson led me up a narrow flight of stairs to the upper deck. I gasped. The ceiling was practically all windows. The family selected a couple of rows on both sides of the aisle.

As we pulled away from the station, Dyson threaded his fingers with mine. Staring out the window, the panoramic mountain views captivated me. Every half mile, it seemed like a new picture postcard.

"It's so beautiful," I whispered with my nose to the glass.

Lydia and Asher rose and went down to the lower level. "Asher is always hungry," Esther said with a laugh.

I lifted the armrest between Dyson's and my seat. He scooted closer, and I rested against him with a sigh.

"This is absolutely perfect," I breathed, the words catching in my throat. The sun shone down through the skylight, warming me, and Dyson's protective, reassuring presence and touch added to my sense of peace. The gentle sway of the moving train and the restrained murmuring of the occupants had me in a bubble of contentment. I yawned.

"Tired?" Dyson asked, rubbing my arm.

Instantaneously, my body responded to his caress.

"Not particularly," I purred, then cleared my throat. "I guess the time change and other things have worn me out."

"Other things," Lucy laughed, overhearing us.

"I wish," I mumbled. I'd definitely have preferred spicy time in the sheets with Dyson over all the crazed fan bullshit.

"That can be arranged," Dyson teased, his breath ghosting my ear, a playful challenge in his voice.

"If getting naked with you was my only worry, I wouldn't be worried." I laughed at his wide-eyed expression. Then I kissed him–a-pressing-him-back-into-his-seat, clashing tongues and teeth–kiss.

Lucy started clapping. By the time I broke the kiss, Dyson's hands had strayed up under the back of my tie-dyed shirt. His happy, dazed grin tempted me to go at him again, but there were kids on the train and I couldn't guarantee the encore performance would be PG.

"Damn, girl, I can't believe you like this beanpole," Lucy teased, motioning to her brother.

"What's not to like?" I returned to my perch at the window.

"I could make a list," Lucy started.

"So could I..." I said, my gaze never leaving the landscape.

"I'd like to hear your list." Dyson laced his fingers with mine again.

"Which list?" Lucy laughed.

"Callie's, of course," Dyson tugged me against him. I relaxed, feeling his heartbeat against my back.

"Me too," Lucy said.

With a sigh, I shifted my attention from the stunning landscape to Lucy and Dyson. "I'll trade you my list for your juicy childhood stories," I said to Lucy. Dyson groaned.

"Deal. First the cheesy, mushy list of romantic stuff." Lucy's eyes, wide and bright, blinked expectantly at me.

"Well, he's got nice cars and a nice butt."

"I do?" With a subtle shift, Dyson met my gaze, his eyes intense.

"Shh. My list." I began ticking things off on my fingers. "Yes. Nice butt, pretty eyes, you're sweet, and a great friend–"

"You mean boyfriend," he said, poking my side.

"Great friend," I corrected, "Even better boyfriend. Any car talk is sexy, and this guy knows how to start my motor and rev my engine."

Lucy groaned and rolled her eyes. "OMG, you are so made for each other."

"I guess so. He puts up with my car talk too." I bit my lip.

"It's the same for me. I love it when you speak *car*." Dyson waggled his eyebrows at me.

"Oh?" A wave of heat washed over me, and my stomach churned with nervous butterflies. "It's not a turn off because I know things about cars that the average girl doesn't know? I don't intimidate you?" His hazel gaze held me like a tractor beam.

"Hell no. Remember when I gave you a ride in the Porsche? You listed the specs and even educated me on the previous owners. Hot."

I hummed, grasping his thigh.

"See, your reaction is a turn on." His eyes narrowed, focusing intently on my lips; the air crackled with unspoken tension.

"You let me play with your stick shift and drive the beast." I hummed again.

"Holy shit, Callie, I'm going to have to find an empty restroom."

"Yes. Let's go. We can watch the ten-twelve moment."

"Or make our own." He claimed my lips in a fierce kiss. All rational thought abandoned me, and I grabbed the back of his head, holding him to me.

When we broke the kiss, I asked, "How long is the train trip?"

"About four hours," he mumbled against my lips, taking the bottom one in his teeth.

My body hummed like a tuned drift car, powerful, and if I didn't control myself, I might wipe us both out.

"Moose!" someone shouted from the front of the car. I jumped up. Everyone converged on the other side. I leaned over

Dyson's mom to see the large brown animal.

It stood in a grassy field, not paying any attention to the train chugging by. I snapped a few photos and then took a short movie.

Grinning, I turned around to find Dyson missing. "Where'd he go?" I asked Lucy.

She shrugged and then laughed. "Bathroom, I would guess. You *did* get him revved up. Since he's busy, want to go explore?"

"Sure." Getting a snack and mingling with others might settle my raging hormones, at least until Dyson came around again. I picked up my backpack.

"Hey Mom, we're going to look around. We'll be back in a few minutes," Lucy said, waving goodbye to her family as she pulled me away.

We took the narrow stairwell to the bottom deck. "Is this car for dining or is it a club car?" I asked. "I've never been on a train before."

Lucy froze. "Get out. You've never traveled by train?"

I raised my hand. "Car girl, remember? There isn't much call for a train in Kansas."

"You're not in Kansas anymore." Lucy giggled, then motioned to the space. "This is a sightseeing train more than a typical, cross-country Amtrak."

A bar with a bartender served drinks at one end. The walls had windows, but they weren't the focus. Instead of seats arranged like on a bus or plane, one section had booths similar to what you'd see in a restaurant, and a couple of high-top tables with people standing around them. At the far end of the car were plush sofas. Lydia and a young man sat on one and talked. She blushed when we waved.

We each purchased a glass of cabernet and continued exploring.

"Looks like Lydia doesn't want us to bother her," Lucy said as we passed. Heading into the next car, we stayed on the lower deck until we reached a dark, narrow hallway.

"Here's the bathroom if you need to go," she thumbed to a lady's stall. "I'll hold your glass."

"Might as well." We took turns holding each other's wine, then walked all the way to the front of the lower level, finally returning to the bar car.

I'd emptied my glass. "I'm going for a second. Want one?" I asked Lucy.

"No, I'm good." She headed up the stairs to our original seats while I went to the bar. Lydia wasn't there any longer. I sat in a wing-back chair, sipping my cab and staring out the window. The comforting warmth of the alcohol spread through me as the rhythmic chugging of the train and the blurring scenery lulled me into a light sleep.

Dyson, Jay, and Corey stood in Enzo's Auto Tech's garage discussing my show. Dyson and Corey said I needed more views. My channel was about to surpass my brother's, though, and Jay, his face reddening, angrily defended his show with clenched fists.

Dyson rushed to my defense, chewed my brother out, then strode toward me. His grin, a flash of white teeth, sent a wave of warmth washing over me.

I opened my eyes. A dull ache lingered in my heart from Jay's anger. And even though it had only been a dream, I felt an odd urge to apologize to him for deceiving him, albeit through omission rather than an outright lie. I sent my brother one picture of the moose, letting him know I was thinking of him. I sighed and stood.

I trekked up the stairs, and I met Dyson coming down. "There you are. I've been looking for you."

"I fell asleep."

Back in our seats, the sun's warmth, like a comforting blanket, eased away the chill of the bad dream. I hugged myself and the quiet between us lengthened.

"What's wrong?" he finally asked. "It's not about what I said–"

"No." My gaze flicked to his. "I had a bad dream."

"Callie, you are safe." Dyson, the protector, his voice low and primal, had a way of targeting the needy woman in me.

I nodded, believing it. "I know."

He pulled me into his arms, and I snuggled against him, my back to his chest, with a happy sigh.

"Do you want me to talk about the Porsche?" he chuckled, then kissed the top of my head, and tightened his arms around me.

"It's a beautiful car. How did it come on your radar?"

"I wasn't looking to buy a Porsche. But when I saw the listing, I started researching it. The seller made me an offer I couldn't refuse–the second time."

I chuckled, already knowing the tale. Dyson had a way of storytelling that drew you in, so you became invested. That's why Gabby's Garage was such a successful CarTube channel.

Glancing out the windows as we approached Mount Denali, I wondered how much pretending we were actually doing. Feeling eyes on me, my gaze returned to the occupants. I found Judy Gabbard studying us.

As Dyson continued his Porsche story, I listened, but I also felt his breath caressing my ear, his voice vibrating in his chest, his strong heartbeat, and his hand stroking my arm. I nestled even closer, the scent of his cologne calming me as I relaxed in his protective embrace.

It boiled down to trust. I trusted Dyson Gabbard. But did trust equal love?

Chapter Eight

Dyson

"See you later," I waved as my family drove their rental down the driveway and out of sight. I couldn't help but be grateful to finally be alone with Callie.

After arriving in Denali, we'd stopped so Callie and I could grab some groceries—just the basics, including frozen pizza, wine, coffee, and chocolate. My family was staying at a resort near the state park, but once Callie had agreed to be my pretend girlfriend, I thought she might want some time away from them. I hoped she'd want private time with me.

"Wow. Dyson, you picked a great locale," Callie said, standing on the front porch of the lodge-like cabin built into the sloping hillside. Perched high above a valley, she gazed at the view of Denali and the surrounding wilderness.

"It looked like it would suit our needs," I said with a shrug, unlocking the door.

We stepped into the cabin's open floor plan—its kitchen, dining and family room all one large space. A twenty-foot high sloped ceiling soared above a massive stone fireplace, floor to ceiling windows showcasing a breathtaking view, cool stone counters, gleaming stainless steel appliances, and rich, dark wood flooring.

"Wow," Callie said, slowly spinning in the room.

A small hallway off the kitchen led to a bedroom, a full bathroom, and the garage. I carried the luggage upstairs, with Callie following close behind. The carpeted loft overlooked the main living space. A sleeper sofa sat invitingly in one corner, and a door led to a large master bedroom with an ensuite bathroom.

"Wow. I've never seen such an enormous bedroom." She peered inside the master bathroom, then disappeared from view with a gasp.

I'd seen the pictures online when I'd booked the cabin and I'd be lying if I said I hadn't envisioned showering with Callie in there.

She popped out, thumbing over her shoulder at the bathroom. "There's a shower big enough for an orgy."

"Orgy shower. That's exactly how they advertised it," I teased, rolling the suitcases to the large walk in.

Callie followed me. "Wow, this closet is as big as my bedroom in Kansas."

"Did you look out the French doors?"

Her eyes widened, glittering with expectation. "No." She dashed to the doors and yanked them open. A cool breeze, carrying scents of pine and damp earth, fanned my face. "A hot tub. Oh, so that's what you meant this morning."

"Uh, huh."

"Crap," she muttered, wringing her hands

Stepping onto the covered concrete pad beside her, I touched her elbow.

"What's wrong?" Nothing seemed amiss as I glanced around the patio. There were two rockers flanking a small table and the covered hot tub. With dread, my gaze swept the landscape, and I half expected that dick Jake to appear.

"I didn't bring a bathing suit." She frowned, her brow crinkled.

"That's not a problem." I laughed when she slugged my arm

playfully.

"This place is amazing, Dyson." She smiled, then threw her arms around me. Her scent of almonds and vanilla had become familiar. "Let's put away the food and get a glass of wine."

"Sure." As she skipped down the stairs and into the kitchen area, I followed Callie, mesmerized by the sway of her hips.

I put the coffee creamer, milk, and beer in the refrigerator. Unsure of where to put the bread and the box of cereal, I left them on the kitchen counter. I searched in the drawer for a corkscrew for the bottle of wine. Callie found glasses, and I poured us each a glass.

"Are we still practicing? I mean, it feels like we've mastered the *practice* phase. Have we leveled up?" She blinked her green eyes as she took a sip.

"You mean after this morning's bathroom incident?" Heat spread over my face.

"No. I alluded to the, not one, but two, very demonstrative, bordering on obnoxious acts of PDA on the train."

"I enjoyed those public displays of affection, especially if it made my sister so nauseous she forgot all about telling you childhood stories."

Callie leaned against the counter. One dainty brow rose.

I hurried on, not wanting to dwell on her missed opportunity. "I believe we've leveled up. Are we novices or noobs?"

Callie snickered and clinked my glass. "Noobies."

I downed the last of my wine, strategizing how to level up again. Refilling the glass and topping off hers, I came up with a new goal: to reach expert level by the end of the trip.

The TV hung over the mantle and in the corner was an armoire. Callie opened the door. "Wow." She met my gaze. "I'm saying that a lot lately, but you should see how many games are in this closet."

I padded over to the cabinet. It was like un-played Jenga with game boxes instead of blocks. "Damn. We should have no problem finding something to play tonight. And the dining room table is big enough for all of us."

"Right?"

But game night was a few hours away. I had time to coax Callie into the hot tub, minus clothing.

The wine warmed my belly and relaxed me—and I hoped that was true for her, too. Walking to the picture window, I gazed across the hillside and down the long driveway. "We are so isolated here. It's private."

"It's chillier here than Anchorage," Callie said, standing beside me.

"We are at a higher altitude," I reminded her. Reaching for her, I tucked her to my side. A chill radiated from the window, and Callie shivered. "Maybe the hot tub would be nice."

Callie glanced at me. "It will be freezing out on that porch."

"It will make the hot water feel all the better."

She narrowed her eyes. "I think you just want to get me naked."

"I've said it before–not a problem."

She sighed. "Perhaps we should check to see if it's functioning and not a disgusting green pool." She pulled out of my embrace and headed to the kitchen.

I followed her. "The website said it worked."

"We should check." A mischievous spark ignited in her eyes.

I pointed at her. "I think you just want to get me naked," I echoed.

She circled her finger along the edge of her glass, appearing shy. "Well, of course, I do. I don't like double standards." She tilted her head, grinning.

Warmth spread below my belt, and I returned her smile. Topping off our glasses, I killed the wine bottle.

Callie held out her free hand, and I took it. Honestly, I'd take anything she offered. We walked hand in hand up the stairs to the bedroom and through the French doors leading to the hot tub.

With each step, my anticipation built.

She held my glass while I removed the cover. Steam rose from the bubbling water, emitting the pungent smell of chlorine. In these temps, cold water would have steamed too, so I plunged my hand in.

"It's hot." Yearning coursed through my veins as I glanced up at Callie.

With a thoughtful look, Callie surveyed the landscape.

"What's wrong?" I asked. Twilight had settled like an overcast day about to storm. It was as dark as it would get until the sun rose again.

"What if he's out there?" She met my gaze and shivered.

"Then he's freezing his nuts off." I placed a reassuring hand on her shoulder, giving it a gentle squeeze. "First, he'd have to travel here, and then figure out where we are. I'm pretty sure we'd hear him coming. Look at that slope. He'd have to climb boulders to get up here to see your cute ass." I pointed to a copse of deciduous trees. "Or find a way through that."

"I guess." She shifted, then took a sip of her wine.

"Didn't you buy a robe to match your nightgown?" I asked, trying to get her mind to shift from the stalker.

Callie faced me, handing me my goblet of wine. A fine blush crossed her cheeks. "I did."

Setting my wine on the wooden steps, I returned to the master suite. "I thought I saw oversized towels in the bathroom. I'll grab them." There was a cubby where I found rolled towels. I snagged two and returned to the bedroom.

The closet light flicked on. Leaning against the bedroom doorway, I watched as Callie unzipped her suitcase. Searching a pouch, she pulled out a piece of shimmering fabric.

I backed out of the room to give her privacy. Otherwise, we might not have reached the hot tub at all.

Setting the towels next to my wine, I tried the various settings on the control panel, settling for active jets, and a temperature set at a hundred and two degrees. Callie appeared at the door, wrapped in a turquoise robe that barely covered her to mid-thigh. She hugged herself. My gaze traced the bare skin of her feet up to the hem of her robe, then I swallowed hard.

I winked at Callie, then pulled my tie-dyed shirt over my head. It landed at her feet, and she giggled. She picked it up and began folding it. I shucked off my pants and boxers in one move. I heard Callie's quick gasp. The crisp air chilled me, nipping especially hard at my sensitive parts, which are never exposed to the extreme elements. I stepped into the water with a relieved sigh.

"God, this feels good," I moaned, finding a lounge seat on the far side. I submerged myself until only my head was above water.

Callie dipped her toe in, then hesitated, glancing around from me to the horizon. There was no way in hell I wanted to miss the show, but to make her more comfortable, I closed my eyes.

The water splashed, and I opened an eye in time to see her exposing her glorious backside as she removed her robe. She lowered herself and took a last sip of her wine before dropping her shoulders under the water.

A smile lit her face, and she hummed. The sound shot straight to my dick. I couldn't steal my gaze away from her serene features—the curve of her cheek, the creamy skin of her neck, a lock of her dark hair that curled at her temple. And those kissable lips.

Her foot touched mine. "Sorry." Callie smirked as she continued rubbing my calf.

Two could play this game. I sat up and reached underwater, taking hold of her foot. I massaged the ball, then worked back to the heel.

"That's heavenly," she uttered.

"Let me have your other foot," I said.

The bubbling, steaming water surrounded us, occasionally teasing the swell of her breasts.

I moved onto her ankles, then massaged her calves. When I

couldn't reach any further, I pulled her to me.

Shocked, her chin dunked under and she splashed, trying to stay above the water. I kneaded her thighs as she straddled me. I hadn't planned her position, but it excited me.

Her hands on my chest, Callie leaned close. My hands slid over her smooth hips, settling on her narrow waist.

"It's my turn to touch you. The double standard thing, remember?" she asked, holding my gaze. She started at my hands, her touch feather-light as she intertwined her fingers with mine.

As she explored my body, my heart pounded with each caress. Her bright green gaze devoured me, leaving me breathless.

Callie rubbed my forearm, then my biceps. She ran her palms over my shoulders. Then down my pecs to my navel.

Nothing separated us but some churning water and chilled air. I longed to close the distance and press her soft curves to my hardness.

"What's going on between us?" she whispered next to my ear, her warm breath fanning my neck. Her nipples brushed my chest, tickling me, and sending a zap straight to my dick. "Are we pretending anymore?" She ran her fingers through my hair.

A sharp intake of breath escaped my lips as she caught my earlobe between her teeth, her bite surprisingly gentle. I groaned at the sensations that were making me rock hard.

"Leveling up. I hope." I gasped when her hands dived lower. As they stopped at my navel again, I guided her right hand to my shaft, enveloping it with my own.

Her breath hitched when I moved, essentially jerking off with her help. Her fingers circled around me and she took over. I was in heaven as waves of pleasure cascaded through me. Her hooded green eyes held mine captive. Heat so encompassing consumed me, and I thought the water just might evaporate.

"Do you like that, Dyson?" she asked in a low, raspy voice.

I chuckled. "Hell yes," I moaned. My heart pounded, and I knew I was close.

"Hey, hey," Lucy called from out of sight.

"Shit," I groaned, rubbing my face.

"Lucy," Callie called. "Where are you?"

"Down here. We rang the bell, and no one came."

No one's gonna come now, either.

Lucy scrambled up the slope, then arrived on the porch. "Whew, that's a climb." She peered at us, then the clothes pile, and a mischievous grin split her lips. "Sorry to interrupt."

"We thought we had a little more time," Callie said with a sweet smile. She kept pumping me slowly, keeping me hard. "Go through the bedroom and let everyone in. We'll be down in a few moments. I need to rinse off the chlorine."

"Okay. Thanks."

She was halfway through the bedroom when Callie called, "Lucy, check out the game cabinet in the living room."

Once the door shut, Callie turned her attention to me. "That will keep her busy for a few minutes. Shall we finish what you started?" She giggled, stroking me with her right hand while her left explored my sack. I savored her touch.

"Callie," I moaned. The sizzle of no return started at the base of my dick. I threw my head back at the hot white pleasure released by her hand.

She let go and hovered long enough for a sweet kiss. "I'm going to shower."

I nodded. Completely relaxed, I didn't dare stand yet.

Callie turned in the water, then stood, so I saw her beautiful rear. She quickly grabbed the robe and put it on.

Dripping water, she hurried inside. I gave her a moment, but really I was putting to memory the desire I had witnessed in her eyes, her skill at getting me off, and how much I wanted more.

I needed more. And so did she, because I now owed her an orgasm. There would be no double standard here.

She had asked if we were still pretending. How would she react if I told her I never had?

I hesitated outside the open bathroom door, catching sight of the wet tiles and the sound of running water. Callie met my gaze through the glass over the half-wall of the shower. Her hair was damp. The aroma of almonds and vanilla swirled in the air.

God, I love that scent.

I should have grabbed a towel and left so she could shower alone, but my body wanted more. "Ah, hell," I muttered, standing still with a puddle forming on the floor.

"Dyson, should I leave the water on? Are you coming in?" she asked, sounding shy and hopeful.

Words stuck in my throat. I glanced at my semi-hard dick. I'm pretty sure it'd been in some state of arousal since Callie had arrived in Alaska. "You want me–"

"I'll leave it running if you're hopping in." Reaching for the faucet she murmured, "Otherwise I'll turn it off–"

"I'm in." I joined her. "Callie..." Stepping behind her, I encircled her waist, nosing her hair. "Damn, I love the smell of your hair." My fingers slid over the soft skin of her belly.

"We don't have time for this. We have guests," she said with regret.

At that moment, I wanted to forget the planned game night and focus on her. She spun in my arms. Her breasts against my chest. My dick was once more rock-hard. She tiptoed and kissed me. Her tongue plundered my mouth, and I grabbed her ass, pulling her against me.

She broke away with a twinkle in her eye. "Get cleaned up, Dyson. I'll meet you downstairs." She winked and wriggled free.

I wondered how quickly I could get rid of my family.

As I strode down the stairs later, I heard Callie's laughter ring. She sat at the table with my mom, aunt, and cousins. They had set out the board game Clue.

Lucy and my father rummaged through the game cabinet. There were three distinct game stacks.

"What's going on?"

"We are organizing." Lucy said with her hands on her hips.

"Yes. Card games here, traditional board games, then the RPG type of games. While we organized, Callie and Asher wanted to play Clue. It's their favorite childhood game, apparently." Dad pointed to the nearly empty cabinet. "You're just in time."

I laughed and headed to the refrigerator to grab a beer. The cool bottle in my hand helped to keep the heat at bay. Instead of joining the group at the table, I returned to the living space and plopped down on the sofa.

"The fun part is going to be seeing how you put this all back together again." I lifted my beer in a salute.

Lucy nudged my dad in the side. "We could leave it all for him to do."

Dad rubbed his chin. "We could."

"Ah ha! I knew it." Lucy lifted a black box with white letters. "I knew they had to have it."

"What?"

"Cards Against Humanity. I found one card between boxes, but not the game until I got to the bottom of the cabinet."

Clapping came from the dining room. "Congratulations, Callie." She stood and bowed.

"Your girlfriend cheated," Asher teased with a grin. "Seriously, she has mad Clue skills."

A satisfied smile played on Callie's lips as she settled onto the sofa beside me. Deep breaths helped keep my heart rate down. "Whodunit?"

"It was Mrs. Peacock with the lead pipe in the conservatory. I have a method." Callie nodded.

"We're rusty, so I suggested another game without Callie so we can hone our skills," Mom said.

Callie snuggled next to me, wrapping my middle with her arm. Her damp head gave up notes of her familiar scent. I sighed, putting an arm around her.

"You guys make a cute couple." Lucy sat at my left, opening

the game box. "Why didn't you tell us about Callie sooner?"

Callie remained quiet. When we discussed what we'd say about our pretend relationship's beginning, we opted for more truth-based stories than fabricating the whole thing. "We've known each other for years and kinda flirted with each other. One time when I saw her at an event, we had a great time and when I gathered enough nerve to approach her to ask her out, it was the worst timing ever."

Callie sat up and frowned, quizzically. "What event?"

"The Kansas City Car Meet."

She gasped. "You were not."

"It's the God's honest truth."

She leaned forward, elbows on her knees. Chin in her hands. "No way."

I placed a hand on her back, sorry that this would dredge up her father's death. "You can ask Corey. He went with me for moral support. Then when I met up with you..."

"My father had died."

"Wow." Lucy said, shaking her head. "That is poor timing."

"But why didn't you ask me out later?" Callie asked, her green eyes boring into my soul.

"I wanted to, but it never seemed like a good time," I shrugged. "I also didn't want things to get weird."

Callie frowned again, then she placed her small hand over mine. "Thank you for being there the day Dad died."

"You don't have to thank me." I brushed a stray hair away from her face.

"I'll never forget it. You were a pillar of support I didn't know I needed." Her eyes glistened with unspent tears.

My heart yearned for this woman–protecting her from pain, bringing her joy, and pleasuring her had become my new mission in life.

"As far as getting together..." Callie glanced at Lucy. "It just kind of evolved. I always thought he was cute but, you know, he's a friend of my brother."

"How does your brother feel?" Dad asked.

I met Callie's gaze, and she shrugged. "I really don't know. Sometimes he's cool with it, other times he's a jerk. I don't really care. It's not his business."

"His business... He's afraid I'm going to steal you away from the channel," I offered, rubbing my chin.

She studied me for a moment. "The only thing you can steal is my heart. I promised my dad I wouldn't leave Enzo's Auto Tech."

My heart nearly exploded. I became hyper-aware of the little crinkle at the side of her eyes when she smiled and the length and curl of her lashes as she blinked.

God, she was lovely, and she thought I could steal her heart. Did I want to steal it or did I want her to give it to me freely?

"Have you stolen her heart?" my dad asked me.

"I've told him not to break it," Callie replied before I could utter a word, which worked out because I couldn't speak.

She rose and entered the kitchen, refilling her wine. She offered the bottle to my mother and anyone else. I kept my gaze transfixed on her graceful movements.

What I had figured would be a fun couple of weeks with a girl I had liked transformed into something much more. The depth of my emotion had me drowning.

"You really like her," Dad said softly.

Without looking at him, I responded. "What gave me away?"

He chuckled and took a swig of his beer. "She's changed you."

At this I turned. "What do you mean?"

Dad glanced at my mother. "Finding the right woman makes you a better man. She brings out qualities you had but maybe never used much. Like the whole protector thing. When I met your mom, I thought I knew myself. Turns out she helped me learn who I really was. I was so much more."

He turned back to me. "I see that happening with you. You have a new depth to you that I haven't seen before and Callie is bringing it out."

I had my career. I loved what I was doing, but I hadn't realized that something was missing until I started spending time with Callie. Even as a friend, she added a lot to my life. She was someone who got me. She understood my work, the production aspect and my love of all things with wheels. Having someone to share it with was wonderful. The ability to bring her joy–to make sure she's happy and safe, was a new goal.

"I sent my brother a few pics," Callie said, holding her phone. As she sat it on the counter, it immediately pinged.

She snatched up the phone, her eyes widening as she read the text. "Holy cow!" Callie blinked at me and my family, clearly surprised. "Jay's angry. It's three in the morning at home."

She yawned, and my cousins caught it.

I chuckled. "Is he with Amber?"

"My roommate?" Callie gasped, shaking her head. "I don't think so."

"Then why is he still awake?" I asked, crossing my arms.

"Unless he had his phone on silent, it would have pinged each time I sent him a picture. And I sent quite a few. Oops." She smiled. "He's probably pissed because I woke him." She yawned again. Standing, she brought her glass to the sink and rinsed it.

She came to my side and hugged me. "I'm going to go to bed."

The thought of me removing her turquoise gown had me getting hard. I stood to go with her.

"Dyson," Asher whined. "You can't leave, bruh. You were going to tell me about your expensive cars and play a game with me."

"It's fine. You all enjoy yourselves." She kissed me and walked up the stairs.

When I finally made it to bed, Callie's deep breathing deflated my hopes of getting naked. I may have beaten Asher at Monopoly, but I lost tonight's bedroom games with Callie.

Chapter Nine

Callie

The rich aroma of coffee filled the kitchen as it brewed. Sneaking out of the bedroom had been easy, since Dyson hadn't stirred. I loved waking up next to him, the warmth of his body beside me, and I would miss it once we returned to our regular life.

A dull ache settled in my chest, and I tried to rub it away. I hadn't realized how lonely I'd become until I wasn't alone.

With a cup of coffee in hand, I walked outside to enjoy the chilly morning. It was in the forties, but the sunny day promised to be beautiful. According to the weather app, the high should hit the low sixties.

At the end of the parking area, a trailhead called my name. According to an informational plaque, it connected the property to a main path at the national park.

Back in the cabin, I considered filming another quick video for my channel while I refilled my cup. I snuck back up to the loft to grab warmer clothes and my jacket. Dyson never stirred. As I went back downstairs, I wondered what time he'd come to bed.

In a drawer, I found a notepad and a marker.

"Dyson- I've borrowed your stand for a quick shoot." I gave him brief directions and signed it with ❤Callie. I added "P.S.

Enjoy the coffee."

I placed the note next to the mug I'd left out for him.

In my backpack, I stowed the telescoping stand, a water bottle, and a portable battery for my phone. I didn't expect to have any bars because of the vastness of the park, but I wouldn't be calling anyone, just playing photographer and videographer.

With the last drop of my coffee gone, I headed out into the Alaskan wilderness, the biting wind nipping at my cheeks. Probably not my smartest move, but I wasn't going far.

I sat my phone on a stone for a dog's-eye view. As it recorded, I backtracked, then walked down the path. After checking the footage, I moved on.

In the sun, the temperature warmed. To my right, the hillside plunged dramatically, opening to a panoramic view of the valley below. I panned the scene, then stood still, listening to the birdsong. The woodsy, pine-scented air filled my lungs.

I half expected Bigfoot to cross my path.

My phone pinged–Dyson. I FaceTimed him and was surprised when the call connected. His lopsided grin and sleepy hazel eyes warmed my heart. "Good morning, sunshine."

"Mornin'," he grumbled, scratching his scruffy chin.

I changed the direction of the phone camera, offering him the view. "I made you coffee and left you a note explaining everything."

"Mmm, coffee. God, I love you," he rasped sleepily.

I might have responded the same to coffee, but the words in that particular sequence, spoken by this man, stole my breath. I wiped moisture from my eyes, then heard the toilet flush. "You took me to the bathroom with you again. Ugh."

"Nature." He grinned sheepishly, setting the phone down to pull a shirt over his head. His bedhead stood up on the right and was flat on the left. "Do you need any help?"

"I'm almost done. But it's so beautiful. I could stand here forever and never absorb all the details." I inhaled deeply.

"I'll come find you. Need coffee first, though."

After ending the call, loneliness settled for a moment in the stillness of the woods. I sent my brother a few more photos.

I found a rocky outcrop with a great view. The trail crested and swept down and around a stone monolith. The grassy knoll dropped to a valley with a meandering creek and, far in the distance, Mount McKinley.

Next, I turned my attention to setting up the camera to frame the perfect final shoot. I clipped the mic I'd borrowed to my shirt and stuck the battery pack inside the pocket of my light jacket.

The stand held my phone and overlooked me and the valley. "Check. Check," I tested. I dove into the rich history of Denali, recalling President McKinley's role in its preservation. Included some basic stats and the ways it had changed, but nothing too deep. I was listing the types of wildflowers when Dyson crested the hill.

"Hey there, Callie."

"Dyson," I squealed.

With three long strides, he appeared to float down the gentle slope. He opened his arms, and I jumped into his embrace. He twirled me until I giggled.

"Did you miss me?" he asked, setting me on my feet. He studied the valley.

"More than you know." I met his gaze and longing flashed. I motioned to the view with my hand. "This is something that needs to be shared."

He nodded, his hand warm in mine, as we silently drank in the stunning vista and the distant mountain.

"Callie, you scared the shit out of me today when I woke without you." His lips pressed into a thin line.

"I like waking beside you," I admitted in a whisper. "It's nice not being alone. But coffee called me, then the sun was shining..."

His hard expression softened as he turned to face me. He tucked a wayward strand of my hair behind my ear.

His hazel eyes sparkled in the morning light as guilt gnawed at my conscience. "Next time, I'll wake you. But you were sleeping so hard, and I didn't know how late you had stayed up–"

He leaned over and kissed me, effectively shutting me up. My heart rate launched into the stratosphere, taking me to cloud nine.

His phone rang, and we broke apart with a chuckle. "Great reception out here," he mumbled.

"Who'd have thought?" I shrugged.

"It's my Aunt Esther."

The pretty melody continued to play. He took my hands in his and placed them around his neck. His arms encircled my waist, and we swayed to the music. As the instrumental music faded, we continued to dance, staring into one another's eyes. I played with the hair at the back of his neck. With a few steps to the right and then back, we began waltzing.

No music, only the stars in our eyes and laughter. He led me with an internal rhythm that my soul easily aligned with. The sun shone on us and in Dyson's arms I felt whole. I could move forward with him at my side.

Dyson spun me out. When I came toward him, he caught me in his arms and my butt brushed his groin. "I love your pants," he groaned as I rubbed my bum against his growing manhood.

"Soft, aren't they?" I teased, doing it again. "Yoga pants, supple and skintight."

"Oh, so soft," he caressed my tush. "Great at making things hard."

The same song jangled, disturbing the moment. "Again?"

I didn't want the moment to end. "Don't answer it," I appealed as he spun me away. We swayed like that until the song ended and he stopped moving.

"Callie, I have a surprise for you later," Dyson said, fishing his phone out of his back pocket. "My aunt is our ride to lunch."

"I don't want to leave this place," I whispered. "It's magical."

"I know, but you'll love the surprise too." He tapped the

screen.

"Is the surprise more naked hot tub time?" I asked as he pushed the call button.

Dyson's gaze snapped to mine with a ferocity of longing I'd only seen when I held his junk in my hand. He stepped toward me right as Esther picked up.

"Dyson, where are you? We're here to get you and Callie."

"Sorry. We are on the trail not far from the house. We're on our way back now." He motioned for me to follow.

I retrieved my backpack and took my phone off the telescoping stand while he collapsed it to its shortest length. I stuck it in my bag along with the mic which I'd left on. Oops.

Hand in hand, we retreated toward the cabin. Leaving was the last thing I wanted to do. What I really wanted was to continue our dance. Only naked–the horizontal tango.

"I figured it out." I glanced at Dyson. "We're going lingerie shopping again."

He froze and ran his hand through his hair. With a pained expression, he pointed to his tight pants. "Look what you do to me, Callie. I've had a perpetual boner since I let you feel up my car."

I reached for his zipper, fingering the teeth.

"You're going to kill me," he mumbled.

"No double standards," I uttered, dropping my hands to keep from touching him again.

"Meaning..." His eyes widened. "You're just as turned on."

I poked him in the chest. "And I haven't had a release."

We stared at each other, a tense silence hanging in the air. A car honked, making us jump.

"Son of a bitch." He rubbed the top of his head. "Let's eat lunch, deal with my family, and your surprise, then you'll get your release." He moved to take my hand, but I pulled out of his way.

I held up two fingers. "Two releases."

His gaze narrowed, and I allowed him to take my hand. He

winked at me. "Challenge accepted."

We had lunch at the resort, and I was a nervous wreck. I couldn't eat and didn't talk much. I kept zoning off, wondering when I'd get Dyson to myself and when and where he planned to please me.

I blushed every single time I glanced at him.

"She's thinking of kissing me," he told his sister when he'd caught me staring.

To give my face a chance to cool off, I sent my brother a few texts with accompanying pictures.

My phone had two percent battery. "Ugh."

"Can I borrow a cord to charge my phone?" I asked.

"Sure," Esther said. "I've got one in my room. Follow me."

She beckoned me down a hallway to a nicely furnished room with a view out the window. "Here you go," she pointed to the outlet and cord.

"Thanks, Esther."

After lunch, I checked the progress and found my phone had only charged to eighteen percent. Since I'd be with Dyson, I left it to charge longer.

I struggled to keep my distance from him, but it was hard to resist the magnetic pull between us. I soon ended up beside him. Again. And heat threatened to consume me.

"Are you thinking about kissing me?" he asked, inspecting my had-to-be-red face.

"We haven't practiced what I'm thinking about." I whispered to him before walking to the other side of the room. When I looked over my shoulder, I licked the corner of my lips, winked and dropped my gaze to his groin. Snapping his fingers in front of his junk, he broke my trance, making me giggle.

With a glance, I could make him cherry red. Now we were even.

His smile turned wolfish, and he crossed the room, grabbed my hand, and led me to a front porch. He sat and pulled me onto his lap, then it was his turn to whisper. "I'm going to wear boxers that match your nightie."

"And I'll rip them off with ease."

Whatever he said, I one upped him. It was a fun game.

"I get it," he hissed. "You're more worked up than me." Dyson's gaze held a hint of anger.

That's not what I intended.

"Maybe. I was hoping for something mutual, you know?" I shrugged, my stomach churning. "Don't be upset. I was having fun *with* you, not at your expense."

Dyson's intense, hooded gaze fixed on me. I stopped breathing. He squeezed me tightly, knocking what little breath I had out of my lungs. I gasped, and his mouth covered mine, suffocating me with desire. I groaned and his hand dipped, squeezing my butt.

Longing licked at my core. I was going to die of want. I needed him—naked—now. I slipped my hands under his shirt,

His phone rang, playing the 1964 hit "GTO."

He broke the kiss and grabbed his phone. "Son of a bitch." He touched the screen.

"Yeah." He sighed, gazing at me. "I've got the address. We're about twenty minutes away. Okay, see you there."

"You need to turn your ringer off. That's the second time today we've been interrupted." I wasn't angry, but sexually frustrated.

He pushed me off his lap and stood. "Let's go see your surprise, then I promise I'll turn my phone off, and we can do whatever we want."

"Whatever?" I liked the sound of that. "I'll hold you to it." As he turned, I playfully slapped his rear.

I sat in the backseat and Dyson sat shotgun while Esther drove, which was the best option for not getting naked in front of a family member.

"We're going whitewater river rafting tomorrow. You should

come with us," Esther said, glancing at me in the rearview mirror.

"We'll see," Dyson replied.

I couldn't help but stare out at the magnificent view. Every so often, bald eagles perched in tall trees. We eventually exited the wilderness and entered a small town.

"McKinley Village Airstrip?" I asked, reading a sign.

The airstrip was a single strip with several hangars along both sides. I stuck my head between the seats. "Are we taking a flight-seeing tour?" I asked, spying a few Cessnas parked in a row.

Dyson grinned. "You'll see."

"That's what I wondered, Callie." Esther pulled up where Dyson indicated and we exited the SUV. A thick-set man with a thinning combover waved at Dyson.

"I guess we'll see you tomorrow, Aunt Esther." I waved as his aunt left us with a stranger at a giant white airplane hangar. The door was half open, exposing a dark cavernous hole.

"I inspected 'er for you, sir," the man said, stepping forward to shake Dyson's hand. He eyed me up and down, dismissing me.

We walked toward the hangar, into the shadow of the building. The man opened his palm to Dyson. "Here's the fob," he said.

"Fob for what?" My eyes adjusted to the darkness, and I gasped at the sight inside the hangar. It was completely empty except for a turquoise blue Porsche. I pushed between the men and hurried toward the vehicle. It had yellow accents just like Dyson's. How in the world did he find a car–in Alaska of all places–to rent that was just like his custom, totally sexy GT3 RS?

I threw a glance over my shoulder to find my man wearing a smug grin. I giggled and continued forward. When I reached the Porsche, the door was locked. Meeting Dyson's gaze, I pointed to the car. He pushed a button on the fob, and it unlocked with a snick.

I opened the door, and the scent of leather met my nose. The seat was too far back, and I perched on the edge, not able to reach the pedals. I gasped–it was Dyson's car.

This is my surprise.

He'd had his car shipped to Alaska. I glanced up, finding Dyson striding towards me with a wolfish smile. Scrambling out of the car, I shut the door and leaned against it, facing him.

The balding man hesitated for a moment at the entry, then left us alone.

Dyson's footsteps reverberated in the empty hangar until he stopped before me with a look of hunger in his eyes. I could barely breathe.

"Surprised?" His lopsided grin warmed my heart.

My surprise. I beamed. The hows and whys escaped me and the only thing that came out of my mouth was. "Can't put those miles on a custom ride."

"Cars are meant to be driven," he said, coming close, placing a hand on either side of me on the driver's window, caging me in.

"I can't think," I said as he pressed me against the side of the sports car. "I'm sandwiched by my sexy beasts."

Dyson's breath fanned my neck where he started to kiss.

"I'm so turned on I might orgasm if the seam of my panties rubs me the right way."

Dyson pulled away so he could meet my gaze. "What did you say?"

"You heard me." I hoped I didn't sound as needy as I felt. The cool glass and metal balanced the tall, hot body of my man. I fingered the waist of his pants.

"How can I help?" His hooded gaze scanned my body, dropping to my apex.

I growled, a low, needy sound, and he consumed my lips as if I quenched his desire. Then I reached for and peeled his hand away from the glass and, much like he'd done with my hand in the hot tub, I placed his hand on my sweet spot.

He jerked back, meeting my gaze. "Damn, even through the clothes, you are wet. Holy hell, Callie."

"I don't lie. I'm turned on, Dyson. What are you going to do about it? Or am I going to have to–" I gasped as he curled his fingers on me.

Dyson glanced around the large room then leaned on one side, blocking the light coming in and creating a more private dark cave of pleasure. He rubbed between my legs, and I made sounds I'd never made before. I arched my back as the heat built, then exploded.

My breath came in rapid shallow bursts, and with a sated grin I fingered his chest. Hooking his leg, I pulled him against me. "How far away from the cabin are we?"

"Too far," he groaned as I ground against him.

We broke apart. I wobbled. He held my elbow until I steadied, then walked me around the hood. Once on the passenger side, he opened the door for me and I slipped inside.

"Now what?"

"This is a race car," he grinned as he buckled in.

At the push of a button, the beast roared to life. I shivered for another reason.

"Callie," Dyson caught my gaze. "Want to touch my stick shift?" Foot on the brake and clutch, he had the shifter in neutral, moving it slightly back and forth.

My gaze narrowed as I adjusted my harness. "I like your shifter," I winked. "It's time to pop the clutch." I covered his hand with mine.

With a stiff nod, he floored it. We fished-tailed out of the hangar and down the airstrip. Gaining speed, we neared the end of the tarmac. He downshifted, then turned the car. Before I could speak, he floored it. The sudden acceleration threw me back, pressing me against the seat.

The pure joy on his face reminded me of the original ten-twelve moment, and I grinned.

When he wasn't shifting, both hands gripped the wheel, and his gaze fixed on the road, his face etched with a serious expression. Occasionally, he'd give me a side glance.

He was on a mission, and I was his mission. He drove the Porsche with desperation. I wouldn't have driven any other way.

I would have teleported us to the bedroom, arriving without clothes preferably.

We turned onto the winding two-lane road leading toward our rustic cabin. The pines blurred into a green streak as we sped by.

With each mile, my excitement bubbled, a nervous energy humming beneath my skin.

Were we really going to do this? Getting naked with Dyson would change everything.

I wanted him. I wanted us. I just hoped he wouldn't get another phone call.

The car jerked to a stop at the front door.

I fumbled to unbuckle the harness and, by the time I'd managed, Dyson had my door open. He offered me his hand, and I stepped out. Then he scooped me over his shoulder, his strong arms supporting my weight, and carried me to the door. Once inside, he locked it, then carried me carefully up the stairs. With a heave, he tossed me onto the soft bed. I giggled.

He strode to the bedroom door and locked it, then repeated it with the French doors to the porch.

"What are you–?"

"No worrying about anyone." He made a show of turning off the ringer of his phone and placing it on the side table.

Next, he checked the windows, ensuring each blind was pulled closed. Once he'd secured the room, he fixed his ravenous gaze on me.

He had just double checked everything to safeguard my mental health and for our protection, and I loved him for it.

"It's just us now."

"Good," I breathed. "About time."

He took the hem of his shirt and tugged it over his head. I laid back and put my hands behind my head, enjoying the show. I was going to savor every inch of his tan skin, every nuance of his muscles, and the trail of light brown hair that led to his manhood.

He unbuttoned the fly to his jeans, exposing satin boxer briefs. I swallowed, sure his erection wanted to be freed.

But he stopped. I glanced up, meeting his fiery gaze. My lungs froze, and I forgot to breathe. He stood smirking, with his hands on his hips like an adult Peter Pan. He was my kind of gorgeous—boy-next-door cute, mixed with a tad-of-nerdy, and an OMG body.

"Do you need some help?" I asked, but I didn't wait for him to respond. I crawled to the end of the bed, kneeled, and reached for him.

He pulled my shirt over my head, exposing my fancy new bra. He traced the delicate lace edge, making me shiver.

Leaning in, he buried his nose between my breasts and inhaled. "God, I love your scent—almonds and vanilla," he hummed. His warm breath danced on my skin, sending my heart racing.

I gave his shoulders a firm push. He relented and rose to his full height. I got off the bed and stood in front of him. I needed to feel all of him against me. Now.

Hooking my thumbs behind the waistband of his boxers, I bent over and pulled them down. His erection sprang free, and he stepped out of his pants, kicking them to the side. I stood back up, grazing my cheek along his dick as I rose.

Mesmerized, I couldn't look away from his dick.

"Sit." His voice startled me. My eyes snapped to his, and I found it hard to breathe. He pointed to the edge of the bed. I obeyed his command without hesitation.

His fingers instinctively found the waist of my yoga pants. With my palms planted on the bed, I arched my hips upward, giving him easy access to remove my pants. Gently, he slid them, along with my underwear, down my legs and flung them away.

Dyson kneeled, nudging my legs apart. He buried his face there, inhaling heavily. He hummed as he sampled my nectar, and I writhed under his attention to my sensitive area. Fire pooled at my core as he lapped and laved.

I wove my fingers through his hair and tugged, trying to pull him away. I wanted to kiss him. I wanted his lips everywhere on my body. He doubled down, squeezing my knees with his hands as he moved them farther apart and pressed more firmly into my core. His five o'clock shadow rubbed me just the right way, and I squirmed with pleasure.

I tugged his hair a little harder, and he met my gaze. I reached back to unhook my bra. That got his attention.

Dyson popped up and practically jumped on me, covering my mouth with his. I tasted myself on his lips, his tongue, as he consumed me like a fire consumes oxygen. His hands were as busy as his mouth—he finished what I'd started, flinging my bra to the floor.

I rolled him onto his back, pressing my breasts against his chest, wanting to get closer. He grabbed my ass, pulling me tight against him.

He rolled us again, so I was under him, and started nipping and kissing his way down my neck to my breasts. My every nerve was a live wire. With each lick, each caress, each tantalizing taste, my desire intensified. Another few touches, and I'd explode in an earth-shattering orgasm.

"Dyson," I whispered. "I'm ready for you."

Dyson's gaze snapped to mine. "Are you sure?" he asked with a sensual smile.

I trailed my fingers from his lips to his navel, then gripped his shaft. "As sure as you are," I said, pumping him.

His eyes rolled back in his head. Moaning, he reached for the nightstand where I had placed the box of condoms.

He unwrapped and then rolled on a condom. My breath caught as he held my gaze. I opened my arms to him and he smiled.

He returned to my embrace, placing sweet kisses down my jawline, then back to my lips. The innocent kiss turned hot and needy.

He positioned himself. Holding my gaze, he lowered. I arched to meet him.

"Callie, you are so hot."

"I know what I want, when I want it. And I want you. Now."

"Yes, ma'am." His thrusts surged and swelled like the sea, were steady like a spring rain, became harder as his storm drew near.

Sweat beaded on Dyson's forehead. Fused together as one, we raced to our crescendo. I hooked my leg around his hip, pulling him in with each thrust and he moaned my name. His voice, primal and feral, went directly to my core.

"I'm close," I panted. It felt as though liquid fire coursed through my veins.

Dyson's eyes widened for a millisecond. Then he picked up the pace, pounding me until my sweet release hit me. The most surreal sense of pleasure burst through my body with a flash of white.

Dyson matched my release, moaning, "Callie."

He collapsed next to me and pulled me close. We rested for a moment before he got up and went to the bathroom. In a sex fog, I stared at the ceiling, wanting to try other things with my sexy man. He returned to the bed and laid beside me.

Rolling to my side, I propped my head in my hand. "I'm glad we have all afternoon and evening to ourselves. I like being around you, and now I like you being inside me."

He chuckled, laying on his back with one hand behind his head. "I like being in you, too."

"We've got to stay naked because I want to taste all of you." I rolled, so I was partially on his chest and licked my lips, and went for his nipple.

His eyes narrowed with a spark of desire. "I wonder what I

taste like."

"Is that a challenge, I hear?" I touched his thigh. "Tube steak? Hot dog? Pickle? Eggplant?"

"You won't know until you try it." He wiggled his brow.

I leaned on him so my ear was on his chest. His heartbeat was steady and strong. I sighed. "Dyson?"

"Hmm?"

"I like you."

"I like you, too." He stroked my hair.

"I'm done pretending," I admitted.

"Okay." He wrapped his arm around my shoulders and squeezed. "That's good to know because I quit pretending a while ago."

Our gazes locked. My heart leaped at the tender emotion there. "I still wouldn't mind practicing what we just did a little more." Heat flared my face.

"Do you need me to check your oil?"

"Yeah, you've got the perfect dipstick for it," I giggled. "In fact, I think I need a multi-point inspection."

One of Dyson's brows lifted, and a wicked smirk manifested. "I'll start with your horns." He gently squeezed my breast.

I allowed my eyes to whisper shut, completely surrendering to the pleasure and intimacy of his gentle—and sometimes not-so-gentle, caresses.

Chapter Ten
Dyson

Three days we spent at the cabin in Denali. My parents, aunt, and cousins all left via train for Fairbanks on the second day. I opted to miss the first day of the informal reunion gathering.

Three days I spent loving Callie and her body. My dick was sore. So was my back, my legs, and my arms. And it was all from loving Callie.

They were the best three days of my life. We laughed a lot and loved a lot more, only taking a break for the occasional meal with my family at the resort.

At one point, Callie noticed her phone was missing. Luckily, she remembered that she'd left it charging with my aunt. Aunt Esther brought it to us at dinner that night.

I don't know if my family noticed a shift in Callie's and my relationship. But I suspected my mother did.

I loved watching Callie's gentle spirit as she interacted with my cousins, and the way her eyes sparkled with genuine interest as she listened intently to my parents. I tried not to think that each moment spent with her brought us one moment closer to separation, because the thought of separation caused a stab to my heart.

Honestly, I didn't know how I would look Enzo in the eyes again after doing everything I'd done to his sister, but he'd have to get over it. If I knew Callie, she'd chew him out if he didn't get on board with how our relationship unfolds in the future.

Callie and I had leveled up. We'd gone beyond level ten, way before the end of our stay in the cabin. I wasn't near expert level, but I had a definite hankering to become a Callie master.

The drive to Fairbanks was four hours as the crow flies, but we planned to make a day of it by taking the scenic winding roads and stopping at certain tourist traps and trailheads along the way.

Before leaving the cabin, she opened her maps app, and we strategized where to stop to do a few shoots. She could take video of me with my Porsche for Gabby's Garage and I could video her at a few trailheads for End of the Road. Planning came naturally to both of us.

We filled the Porsche's tank on our way out of the Denali State Park area. After an hour, I pulled over at a scenic overlook.

Callie checked her list. She glanced at me. "It's about thirty miles to our first stop. What's up? We didn't plan to stop here." She looked out the window and sighed happily at the panoramic view of the wooded valley and the distant mountains.

"I know." I parked and turned the car off. "Let's stretch our legs and then you can drive for a while."

"Really?" she squealed.

She exited and happy-danced before coming to the driver's side and hugging me.

Hand in hand, we stood, the silence broken only by the gentle rustling of leaves as we took in the expansive view. The serenity and normalcy of sharing this unique moment with Callie, the sunlight warming our faces, the smell of pine in the air, touched my heart.

"I can't wait to see the waterfall," Callie said as we returned to the car. I helped her adjust the harness so it fit her perfectly.

Back on the road, I searched the equipment bag at my feet. I attached the holder to my camera, ready for today's first End of the Road shoot.

Callie drove with a grace that belied the speed. The car responded to her touch as if it had been designed for her.

When we came to the sign pointing to our waterfall side-quest, I started filming. I aimed my camera at Callie, and her bright-eyed, joy-filled expression filled the frame.

"What are you doing?" she said.

"Capturing a ten-twelve moment on the face of the most beautiful woman in the world."

Moisture filled her eyes, but her grin didn't diminish. Neither did her speed. The Porsche hugged the curves through the tall trees, flying past white and yellow wildflowers.

As we approached the isolated parking zone, Callie eased into a wide spot and cut the engine.

"That was a blast." Her petite hand covered mine, and she smiled. "Thank you for letting me drive your baby."

It warmed my heart to make her happy. "You're a skilled driver."

"Thanks." She blushed as she unbuckled. "According to the map, the waterfall is only a half mile up the trail."

Just like at Flat Top Mountain, our vehicle was the only one in the lot. As I grabbed the gear, I hoped we wouldn't see Jake on any of our adventures today. Honestly, I hadn't thought of the dickhead since getting naked with Callie.

She held her phone, taking clips of the trailhead signage and map. As I locked the Porsche, I overheard Callie reading facts from the posted bulletins. I couldn't wait to see how she threaded the clips and photos together to make an episode. She had an artistic eye I appreciated.

A deep breath brought the crisp scent of pine and the musty smell of the forest floor to my nose. The trees resonated with birdsong. The sun warmed the air, chasing away the earlier coolness.

I took Callie's hand, and our arms swung in time with our steps. We walked in amicable silence, absorbing the beauty of our surroundings. I attempted to commit to memory all Callie's effervescence–the surprise at finding mushrooms, the joy of seeing a new wildflower, and the wonder of spotting a bald eagle soaring overhead.

I was in a state of bliss.

The sound of rushing water started as a whisper but grew exponentially noisier as we neared the falls.

"We're close," she said, pulling me forward.

Continuing on the trail, we descended into a shallow creek bed, and as we emerged from the woods, a breathtaking twenty-foot cascading waterfall came into view. A wooden bridge spanned the water. We stopped on the bridge, admiring the falls.

"I think I'll go down there." Callie pointed to a boulder next to the water's edge.

"That's fine. I'll get some footage from this angle for you."

Her gaze softened, and she leaned in and kissed my cheek. "You are the best."

She lithely climbed down the steps to the pool. Callie recorded herself at the water's edge. And I captured everything with my camera, including a rainbow in the mist.

Having completed her task, she removed her shoes and waded ankle deep into the waters of the pool.

"It's freaking freezing," Callie hissed, but didn't get out. She leaned over and stuck her hand into the water.

Curious, I strode to her side. "Probably melted snow."

She pulled out her hand. Two smooth, grey river pebbles rested in her palm. "This would shrink your parts," she giggled, pointing to my junk.

"Giving him attention is making him grow." I unzipped my pants and exposed myself.

"Hmm. It looks like he needs a little cheering up. After three days of freedom, he resents being confined."

She kneeled and took me in her mouth. I moaned as her tongue stroked my shaft. I ran my fingers through her hair, holding her against me. She worked me until I was close to exploding. "Callie," I groaned. That's when we heard voices. "Shit."

Callie fondled my nutsack with her icy fingers, and I gasped, jumping backward. "Your hand is freezing."

She stood upright with a smirk. "That should help you fit back into your jeans a little easier. I'll make it up to you later."

"You know how to make it difficult to walk," I groused, arranging myself and zipping my jeans before the hikers came into view.

We ventured to the next location. With the stunning view as our backdrop, I parallel parked, and we got to work setting up the camera. When a Honda Civic pulled in, the couple frowned at us for hogging three parking spaces.

"Hi. We're shooting a video for a CarTube channel," Callie explained with a wave. The couple came over and watched.

"Action," Callie called, clapping her hands for the sound spike to match the video.

I jumped out from behind the Porsche, using my signature move, an arm gesture that mimicked a baseball player pitcher throwing a ball.

"Welcome to Gabby's Garage, the goofiest channel on all of CarTube. You might notice that I'm not in Kansas anymore. That's because I'm in Alaska and I'm taking State Route three from Denali National Park to Fairbanks. Many people have asked questions about this car," I motioned toward the Porsche, "I'm here to let you know–yes, I am driving it, and no, I didn't drive it here. And it drives like butter."

Callie held the camera on me as I spouted stats about the GT3 RS. Enthusiasts might know the average specs, but not everything about my custom, one of a kind, street legal race car.

I opened the driver's door and sat, then closed it with the window down. I continued to talk, pointing out unique things as Callie focused on me. Instead of my audience, I smiled at her. She made talking to the camera easy instead of awkward. After I'd finished my spiel, she filmed a closeup of the gauges.

We took a few takes from different angles. In some of the scenes, I held my camera, like I usually did, and Callie gathered footage on my phone for me. It would be interesting to compare our perspectives of the clips when we got home.

When we had finished, we took a few pictures together. Her dark hair fluttered in the breeze, giving off notes of her scent. I would have sent a photo to my mom but the cell service was nil.

Our live audience approached us, asking questions. Todd and Brenda weren't much younger than Callie and me. I invited them to the car meet in Fairbanks over the weekend. We snapped a few pictures together before going on our way.

Mesmerized by the vibrant wildflowers and distant mountains, Callie gazed out the window at the scenic view. We'd seen moose, eagles, hawks, and other animals. Her face was always a mask of joy. This trip was one ten-twelve moment after another for her.

It was nice to see her happy. In Kansas, that wasn't always the case. She was more serious at home. I didn't know if it was the stress of the channel and editing her work or a combination of that plus her brother and his attitude. Or maybe it was working where she'd learned everything alongside her father and having the constant reminder of his absence.

Perhaps it was the beauty of this natural wonderland that had her smiling. Or it could've been our relationship deepening and the amazing sex we were having that led to her joy. Whatever made her so happy, it looked great on her.

But I knew why I was happy. It was all because of her. I just hoped she wouldn't lose interest in me, and that we could continue our relationship back in Kansas. I wanted her permanently in my life, and that was something I needed to talk about with Enzo.

As we approached Fairbanks, the temperature spiked to eighty-five and bugs smashed into the windshield.

I glanced at Callie and said, "Fairbanks summers are surprisingly hot, and because the heat doesn't last long, most places don't have air conditioning."

We pulled into a small park alongside the river, outside of town, where there was a short trail. The humid air hung heavy, clinging to my skin as sweat beaded on my brow.

"If we have time, maybe we can hike the path that goes to the hot springs," she said, her eyes sparkling with interest.

"Do you want to go swimming? Remember, we have no bathing suits, so we'd have to skinny dip," I teased.

She blushed.

"Are you thinking about kissing me?"

"No, I'm thinking about getting naked with you." She winked, then glanced at her phone.

"I don't know if the hot springs are too hot to actually bathe in, but maybe the overflow. Hmm. I will find out."

"I love watching you research."

"We don't have to stop if there's a problem. I didn't mean to hog our day doing shoots for my channel." She bit her lip.

"No worries, Callie. If it wasn't for you, I would have driven straight to Fairbanks enjoying the drive, but not the scenery." I cupped her face. "Plus, the blowjob was nice."

She blushed and poked me in the side. "I can't wait until we can put a *Do not disturb* sign on our door."

I chuckled. It was true. She had tried to pleasure me more than once, but each moment was abruptly interrupted.

Callie was wearing those sexy yoga pants I liked and, if I had the opportunity, I would make her feel good another time. Preferably against the car again.

We walked through the shade hand in hand, emerging at a boardwalk running along a clear-water river. Waterfowl, frogs, and bugs serenaded us, joining the symphony of the leaves rustling in the occasional breeze.

Callie spotted a sign about varying species of flora and fauna and another educating the reader about local wildlife. I lifted the camera, and she cleared her throat, then read the signs, giving a synopsis to her viewers. Using her phone, she panned the riverscape, capturing playful ducks.

I enjoyed watching her sneak up close and collect footage of a dragonfly. Her face, alight with wonder, mirrored the beauty of the natural world around her. I loved her childlike expressions, but I also found myself captivated by her alluring, seductive side.

Seeing these new aspects of her intelligence thrilled me. I'd known for a long time that Callie possessed a remarkable aptitude for auto mechanics and could effortlessly recall details about various models and their histories. Her mind was like a safe when it came to cars. It was a treasure trove of information. Some of her knowledge was new to me. Even with the topics I thought I knew she could go into more detail than I had ever learned.

She fascinated me. I don't know many women who could hold a conversation about disc brakes versus drum brakes, but Callie and I had talked about it. While I knew the mechanics, she explained the different manufacturers and where they got the raw materials.

What the hell?

How did she learn everything and what else did she know? I planned to plunder her mind like I plundered her body.

Her laughter drew me from my musings as she collected images of bugs and the grass blowing. She didn't try to avoid having me in the frame like she had before. I had become part of her routine.

"Are you wanting to cross pollinate our channels? It might give you a subscriber boost at the start," I offered.

"I'm not using you to gain views or subs. I'd like to earn my subscribers organically." She glanced toward the opposite side of the river. "You understand, don't you?"

I nodded, believing her. She'd given me no reason to doubt her word.

If it was about the views, she'd go live and try to name-drop. But as far as I could see, she hadn't posted anything on social media from our trip. And the only people she'd sent images to were her brother and her roommate.

"End of the Road is for fun–it's my creative outlet. I've wanted my own channel for a while." She placed her hand on my arm and squeezed.

Her sun-kissed cheeks were pink from the hike, the heat, and—I hoped, thinking about blowing me later.

"I think I've got enough. Thank you for letting me steal the day." Her smile was contagious, and I put an arm around her shoulder, hugging her to me.

Chapter Eleven

Callie

Dyson's immediate family had accepted me as his girlfriend. Hell, even I came to see myself as Dyson's girlfriend. My girly bits were getting worn out by him.

The next morning, we stopped at a grocery to buy potato salad and coleslaw—our assigned contributions to the family shindig. His mother had said she would bring paper plates, napkins, utensils, cups, and everything else needed for a picnic. Dyson bought a couple of twenty-four packs of beer, hard cider for me, and a cooler with ice. At the last minute, he ran back inside to buy a couple of bottles of the blueberry wine that his mother liked.

They scheduled the reunion to start each day at eleven in the morning, continuing until everyone decided to leave in the evening. There were great aunts and uncles, but most people were cousins. Dyson's mother's grandfather was one of thirteen kids. Every year, they had a family reunion. But every five years, there was a big blowout, like this year, where everyone came together.

Judy introduced me to so many people I couldn't keep their names straight. If I wasn't near Dyson because somebody had pulled him away for a game, I tried to stay with his mother and Lucy.

When I saw two guys standing near the GT3 RS. I got excited. That was my cue to go talk *car*. I managed to walk over—rather than run. "Hi! I'm Callie. Do you like the Porsche?"

"I'm Josh and this is Elijah," one man said, pointing to a guy with a handlebar mustache. The men had to be family—their resemblance to the others here gave them away.

Josh was starting to lose his hair and appeared to be in his thirties. "This is Dyson Gabbard's car, right?" he asked me.

"Yes. Isn't she a beauty?" I ogled the curves of the quarter panels.

"It's cool," Josh replied.

"What do you like about it?" Elijah asked me. "Besides the pretty color, that is."

I chuckled at his assumption that I only liked the car because of the turquoise exterior.

"There's a lot to be said about the color," I began with a wink. "The man who ordered this Porsche bought it for his son for the racing circuit. He requested a custom, one-of-a-kind, specially pigmented color. No other car in the world has this exact paint spec. He also ordered custom seats that were hand-tooled from the finest, most supple leather. Unfortunately, before the car was completed, the son had an accident and injured his legs."

The men pressed in close, listening to me. They motioned for others to come, and soon I had a flock of Dyson's family members listening to me ramble on about the history of his Porsche. I happily divulged insider information about the specialty warehouse where the custom pieces had been made.

"What about the engine?" someone in the back called out.

I started comparing regular, off-the-assembly-line Porsches to this custom racing Porsche's schematics.

The questions became vague, because the men didn't really know what they were asking me anymore. I seemed to answer the same thing repeatedly.

At the periphery of the crowd, I spied Dyson, grinning like a fool–his hazel eyes bright with pride. I hoped. Then I glanced at the driver's side car window, remembering how he'd touched me. I warmed in the summer sun.

"Break it up, you lazy bums. Can't a guy enjoy his girlfriend and get away from work for a while?" Dyson teased as he shouldered his way through the crowd.

"She's your girlfriend?" Elijah asked. "How did you find such favor in God's eyes that he sent you an angel?"

I blushed and fell into Dyson's open arms. "Thank you for rescuing me," I whispered.

"Are you hungry?" he asked.

I buried my face against his chest."Depends on what you're offering me."

He laughed. "Hot dog? Pickle? Eggplant?"

"Are you ready to take a break? Maybe a little one-on-one time?" I wiggled my brows, trying to entice him to take a little time away from his family.

Dyson sighed and glanced around at the dispersing group of mostly men. "I probably shouldn't, but that doesn't mean you won't be busy later tonight."

I stuck out my hand, extending my pinkie finger. "Swear it."

He wrapped his pinkie around mine. "I pinkie-promise."

That small touch heated my entire body. No surprise, really, since his touches—any kind, anywhere—had been incinerating my body for days. His sparkling eyes met mine, and they promised oh so much more. And I literally swooned.

Dyson stooped and kissed my nose.

"Callie, dear," Judy called, waving.

I reluctantly walked away from Dyson toward the table where his mother sat with a group of women with fluffy, white hair. Sauntering to Judy's side, I acknowledged her summons. "Yes, Judy."

"I'd like to introduce you to Dyson's aunts." Judy pointed out and named each one. "Callie lives in Kansas near Dyson and she works on a car show similar to Dyson's. He says she's handy around a car."

As Momma Gabbard bragged about my skills, the various white-hairs nodded their heads. Some murmured to each other.

"And will you leave your show and help with Dyson's?" Aunt Betsy from Anchorage asked.

"No. I promised my dad that I wouldn't leave my brother Jay's show." A pang of nostalgia hit as I remembered my family working in the shop together.

"A brother, that's nice. Do you have any other siblings?" another asked.

"No, it's just me and my twin brother. My father passed away, leaving us the garage. We've turned it into a restoration business. And he helped us start the show. Enzo's Auto Tech. I'd never leave my brother high and dry. It's our show."

"A twin. How interesting," Aunt Tina said, smiling at Judy. She wore a blue sweater despite the summer heat.

"I didn't know you were a twin," Judy said with a sweet smile. "That explains a lot."

I nodded, even though I didn't understand what she meant.

Judy hooked her elbow with mine and led me to a group of her cousins. The old timers told funny family tales, making me laugh. I learned the history of her ancestors and how they ended up in Alaska.

The evening wore on, and I leaned against Dyson while sitting at a picnic table. Two men played guitar and a couple of women sang. Others joined in if they knew the ditty.

The sky was a dusky purple, and the air was cool as I stifled a yawn. Eventually, we made it back to the motel and crashed.

The following morning, we relished each other's bodies, losing track of time until we were late to the reunion.

We parked the Porsche and went to find his parents.

"There's Lucy," Dyson pointed.

"Hiya," Lucy waved us over. "Just a warning. Mom is thrilled about having Callie here with you, Dyson. I bet she has plans to brag to every single living relative about her and maybe tell a few of the dead ones, too."

A nervous laugh bubbled up as I glanced at Dyson, his eyes twinkling with amusement.

"Has she dipped into the blueberry wine already?" Dyson chuckled, searching the area for his mother.

He reached for my hand, and I grasped it like a lifeline. I enjoyed his family, but—just like Jay's show, I didn't like being the primary focus. I inhaled deeply and smiled.

"There you are," Judy said, coming up to us with Tim following in her wake. "Everyone was wondering if you were going to come today." She rolled her eyes. "I told them you'd be here. Callie, dear, you really impressed everyone with your knowledge about the car and your dedication to your family business." She patted my arm.

My face heated. "If you get me started talking, especially about cars, sometimes I can't stop. And they asked the right questions to keep me going."

"You were a saint. They don't know shit about cars."

"Dyson!" Judy scolded.

"He's right. But I tried not to let it show." I winked at Dyson. "I didn't want to hurt their feelings."

"You're so nice." Judy beamed.

Lucy made a this-is-what-I'm-talking-about face, giving a slight head nod toward her mother.

Judy hooked my arm and tugged me toward a copse of trees where a group of women sat watching children blow bubbles. "Come on, there are a few more people I'd like you to meet."

I tossed a glance over my shoulder for help from Dyson, Tim, and Lucy, but they remained standing together. Lucy gave me a tiny wave and Dyson blew me a kiss.

After an hour of being shown off as Dyson's girlfriend, we settled near a group of older men and women, including Aunt Betsy and Aunt Tina.

"Do you like Alaska?" Betsy asked.

"It's beautiful here." Looking up, the leaves fluttered in the breeze and danced in the light.

Betsy nodded. "June is the perfect time to visit."

"It's when all the lower forty-eight come. They can't handle the cold," Tina said. "Isn't that right, Bob?"

An old man with leathered skin and white whiskers grunted. "Huh? Who is old?" He'd misheard Tina.

"Honestly, I didn't expect it to be so hot," I admitted. Beads of sweat peppered my brow and trickled down my lower back.

"Humid too. Bet they didn't tell you that on the vacation brochure," Betsy said.

Tina waved a bug away. "And the state bird is the mosquito."

I pulled my shirt away from my body. "Ugh. I'm so sweaty."

"When is the wedding?" Bob asked.

I glanced left, then right, wondering who he was talking to. Finally, I met his gaze and asked, "Whose wedding?"

"Yours, dear," Tina said with a grin.

"Yours and Dyson's wedding, of course," Betsy agreed with a nod. "It will be a big to-do."

My jaw dropped. I'd always daydreamed about getting married and Dyson would be the kind of man I'd consider. But having it thrown in my face so bluntly was a shock.

"We are looking forward to it," Betsy glanced at Tina and smiled. "It will be nice to visit the lower forty-eight again."

"Have it during the winter," Tina said. "We can escape the darkness."

"Yes. We'll be snowbirds. January is perfect." Betsy winked at me.

Tina gazed at her watch, as if it was a calendar. "That's six months to plan the wedding."

"More than enough time, I'd say," Betsy agreed, squaring her shoulders.

My mouth became dry, and I glanced around for an escape. Judy appeared wide-eyed and at a loss for words.

"I'm not getting any younger. So, it's got to be soon." Bob leaned forward and waggled his finger at me.

I chuckled nervously and patted his arm. "He hasn't asked me, but when he does, I'm sure Judy will let you know," I proclaimed loudly so Bob could hear.

My reply brought a smile to Judy's, the aunts', and Bob's faces.

I texted Dyson about my predicament.

Me:

In case you hear... your aunts are planning our wedding for January

Dyson:

!! On my way.

Within minutes, Dyson arrived at my side. He scanned me from head to toe. "Are you okay?"

I nodded, studying my feet. He tipped my chin so our gazes met. I could get lost in those hazel depths. "Really. I'm fine. It's just..." I shrugged. "Awkward."

He inhaled deeply and his gaze swung to his mother.

"Mom, a word, please." They walked out of earshot. Dyson folded his arms, leaning into a serious discussion with Judy. A sense of frustration emanated from his stiff body.

Judy poked him in the chest, and he ran his fingers through his hair as a frown creased his face.

Betsy joined Judy's side and aimed a wagging finger and fierce stares toward Dyson. Several other older women followed Betsy and joined in with Judy.

Poor Dyson was outnumbered. "Looks like I might need to join him to appease Momma Gabbard." I told Uncle Bob. I rose and strode toward Dyson.

"Your mother is only looking out for you. You need to man up. It's time to settle down," Tina said, joining the party.

Dyson's face blazed crimson, his jaw clenched tight as he fought to keep his anger in check. "I was speaking to my mother," he groused. "This isn't a conversation for you all."

"It was loud," Betsy barked, crossing her arms. Tina nodded, humming agreement.

"No one needs this pressure," Dyson said, throwing his arms in the air.

"Come on, Dyson. Your mother is right, young man."

I came up behind the women. He met my gaze and then rubbed his face.

"I just want you to be happy," Judy implored.

One of the aunts turned and saw me. "There she is. Ask her."

"Damn," Dyson muttered.

They all turned toward me. A chorus of *Ask her* met my ears. I stepped closer until I was beside Dyson. He refused to meet my eyes and gave our shoes consideration.

Based on the old biddies' chorus, I had an idea what they were nagging Dyson about. I decided to move things along so we could leave. "Ask me what?"

Dyson let out a long, weary sigh before finally meeting my gaze. He shot a frown at his mother before returning to study me with an apologetic grin. "I can't believe I'm about to s-say this," he stammered, the words catching in his throat, "but they want me to ask you to marry me."

"Marry? You and me?" I gasped. Even though I'd had an idea, hearing it was still a shock. I glanced at the stern-faced women. One smiled and nodded.

I placed a hand on his arm. "Do you mind if I..." I gave him a half smile as I thumbed over toward the busybody squad.

With a one-shoulder shrug, he said, "Have at it."

Irritation or anger, I wasn't sure which, simmered under the surface of my skin. They meant well, didn't they?

I turned so Dyson was behind me, and I took a protective stance. "How dare you force somebody to propose. He'll propose when he's good and ready. You don't need to bully him into doing it. Dyson's a kind man with a heart of gold. Whether it's me or the next girl, whoever he marries will be lucky. So, back off and let him live his life."

"Oh. She's a keeper, Judy." Betsy patted her arm.

Had I just passed some sort of interview? I rubbed my palms on my shorts.

Judy frowned and moved toward her son. "I'm sorry. I shouldn't have butted in. It's just..." She glanced at me and sighed. "The whole twin-thing got me hoping and acting like a fool. Forgive me."

Dyson's expression softened. "Of course, Mom." Then he scrunched his face and asked, "What twin-thing?"

Judy glanced from Dyson to me and back again. "Callie is a twin, honey. Didn't you know?"

Dyson studied me wide-eyed. Was he hoping I'd deny it? I shrugged. "I don't advertise it. Neither does Jay."

"Weird." Dyson rubbed the back of his head. "No wonder they're all worked up."

"Care to explain why I just chewed out your great aunts?"

"Lucy and I are twins."

"Oh." I squeaked. "Weird."

"Right?" he smirked.

"How did I not know this about you?" I asked.

"You've got a lot in common," Judy said with a dreamy smile. "The whole boy-girl twin thing, cars, and CarTube."

I nodded, taking Dyson's hand. "Weird," I repeated.

My phone rang, playing Jay's ringtone. "Speak of the evil twin." I only had one bar, but I answered the video call. Luckily, it connected. I walked away from the group of older folks, and Dyson followed me.

"Hey, Jay," I said, smiling at my brother. His stubble-lined face grinned. Jay, with a dark beard and mustache shadow, reminded me of my father. I sighed, hit with a sudden pang of nostalgia. "What's with the scruff?"

"I don't have you on my case, nagging at me to be clean shaven," Jay teased. "How's Dyson?"

"He's cute naked," I chirped, making my brother gag. Then I turned so Dyson was behind me. He waved to Jay.

"Hey man, Hope everything's good." Jay drew his eyebrows together and squinted—what he thought of as his tough guy face. "You're respecting my sister, right?"

I rolled my eyes. "He does everything I tell him, like a good boy. And he let me drive the Porsche again."

"What?" Jay screeched.

"Can you believe it? He had it transported here, and we drove it. Wait until you see the pictures. God, Jay, it's beautiful here."

"Let me talk to Dyson."

I handed my phone over. Dyson glanced from the screen to me, then shrugged. "What's going on Enzo?"

"Dude, my sister gets to drive the Porsche twice before your best buddy does. What gives?"

Dyson's brow crinkled for a flash, then he smiled, a shit-eating grin that transformed his face. "Callie's a skilled driver, plus it gets her hot and bothered." He handed me the phone before Jay got past his sputtering. I laughed.

"I'll just talk to Jay for a bit." I motioned to a paved trail, and Dyson nodded.

Ahead, Asher shuffled along the path with his face trained on his phone. The sidewalk led into a wooded area and offered a perfect escape from the cluster of manipulative, expectant aunts.

I wandered to a sign showing the different community park trails with colors. Opting for the short yellow trail, I walked to a small pond, where the path opened, exposing the mountains in the distance. I followed the body of water's circumference. A few times along the trail, our spotty connection made Jay's face freeze mid-word.

"How are you doing on the pickup?" I asked, hoping I wouldn't lose the connection again.

Concern flashed in his eyes. "I'm struggling with what to do next. There are parts I need, and I can't seem to find them." He ran his fingers through his dark brown hair, making it stick up.

"Check the folder on my desktop labeled *Parts*. In it is a list of dealers that carry the pickup parts specific to that year."

"Awesome." He moved through the room and set the phone down. I stared at the tiled office ceiling. "Found it."

He hummed an old song Dad used to sing as he tapped on the keyboard. "Wow, this is extensive."

"You never know what we might need. So, when we start a project, I make a list of everything."

"I found the one I need. You're the best." He picked up the phone again. His smile didn't reach his eyes. "I miss you, Callie."

"Miss you, too." I glanced over my shoulder and, finding no reunion attendees, I said, "Did you know Dyson was a twin?"

"No shit." Jay scratched his chin. "Identical? I can't imagine two of them."

"No, like us. He has a sister, Lucy." I sat on a green bench along the path. The sun reflected on the water, rippled by the ducks. With a touch, I switched to the forward camera, wanting to share the beautiful panoramic view with Jay.

"What are the odds?"

"Astronomical. His sister is really nice. I wonder who is older."

"And if they have different birthdays," Jay smiled. "The view's really pretty."

I grinned. "We are a unique phenomenon." Half an hour apart, one at 11:45 at night and the other at 12:17 in the morning the next day. Twins with different birthdays.

We looked similar with our dark brown hair, green eyes, and long eyelashes. In school, everyone knew us as the Ferenzo twins.

"Any thoughts about what car you'd like for the next show?" he asked.

"Me?" I hoped I kept the shock out of my tone.

Across the pond, children laughed and ran to a small deck that overlooked the water. A couple walked hand in hand after them.

"I can't say that I have. What about the truck?" I asked.

"I don't know. I know we aren't limited on parts but..." He hesitated. "Maybe you could check the analytics to see what's getting watched."

I flipped the camera again, so I was eye to eye with him. "You want me to investigate which episodes trigger the algorithms?" I narrowed my gaze. "Why now?"

Jay rarely wanted my metric research. He followed the likes. Of course, it all linked, but what was different this time?

The solitude of working in the large garage must have been wearing on him. Ah, he's alone. Maybe he's imagining a future where I fall in love and leave. I bet he thinks that if I'm more invested in the business, maybe I won't want to leave. I shook my head, clearing it.

Restless, I began pacing near the bench. A knot formed in my stomach as I worried about Jay. My mind's whirlwind of self-reproach for the two-week abandonment collided with a sudden burst of new ideas. "I'll run some reports when I get home, but I'm not wearing a bikini or anything low cut."

"Not even if it drives the views?"

His tone was light, but his eyes held a glint I couldn't decipher, making it hard to tell if he was serious or teasing. "Listen Jay, that creepy guy from the plane recognized me from the show. I might start dying my hair or change my name." It was time to set boundaries. "I will not put myself out there as a piece of visual meat for perverts. My goal is to engage viewers who value our content, not just my boobs."

My neck hairs prickled with a sudden chill, and an overwhelming sense of being watched made my skin crawl. Were they warning bells for real danger, or the lingering PTSD from being stalked—I couldn't tell.

I swept the area, looking for potential threats. My chest tightened. The family still hung out on the deck, throwing bread to the ducks. On the far side of the pond, a bulky, dark-haired man knelt to tie his shoe. I swallowed. A chilling resemblance to Jake sent shivers down my spine.

Get a hold of yourself, Callie.

How many frumpy, dark-haired men are there in every town? A shit ton. That's how many. I inhaled through my nose and exhaled through my mouth.

I'd been away from the safety of Dyson's family shindig long enough. Walking back the way I came, I strolled, trying to appear leisurely. Occasionally, I peered over my shoulder at the family on the dock. I spied the man still following, matching my pace. His hands were shoved deep into the pockets of his shorts, his gaze fixed on my back.

Feeling my unease, Jay, his voice a low, urgent hum, called my name repeatedly before I answered. I'd forgotten about him.

"What's going on?" Jay demanded.

"I've been away from Dyson too long. I strayed pretty far from the reunion, and he'll be worried."

In the distance, Asher crossed a fork in the trail. He still had his nose glued to his phone and didn't look up. A ray of hope shone, and the tension eased.

Swallowing, I wiped sweat off my brow as I power-walked toward Dyson's family gathering, desperate to catch up to Asher. With a shaky hand, I held the phone up. My brother's words were lost as I used the phone to focus behind me. The man had picked up his pace.

Short, shallow breaths escaped my lips, mirroring my racing

heart. This couldn't be happening again.

Paranoid. Paranoid. Paranoid.

Entering the wooded area, I came to a split in the trail. A yellow trail marker pointed the way, and I hurried on.

How had I become a frightened shell of a woman? My brother's voice continued, God only knew what he was talking about, because I sure didn't. My ears were tuned solely to my stalker as I strained to hear his footsteps behind me.

In the wooded area, my call to Jay froze and then reconnected. I nodded, acknowledging Jay's banter about the pickup as I tried to piece together what he said. Walking with the phone raised to converse yet strategically capturing the path behind, I took a screenshot and sent it to Dyson.

If I lost all reception, how would I call Dyson for help?

A wave of distant laughter, like children playing, drifted through the air. I had to be close. Another paved path met the yellow trail. Jay had frozen on the screen again.

"Callie," Dyson called.

A relieved sigh escaped my lips as he and his father, flanked by a contingent of men, walked towards me. I blinked the moisture from my eyes and fought the urge to fling myself into his arms.

"Keep going, Lucy is up around the bend waiting at the water fountain. We'll wait here and see if it is your *fan*."

A dry bark of a laugh escaped my lips, and I nodded as I hurried past, grateful he had my back. He remained hidden at the trail spur and wouldn't be visible until the man walked near enough to be recognized.

I power-walked forward until I saw Lucy. Her bright hazel eyes scanned me from top to bottom. "Are you all right?" she asked gently.

"A little freaked out," I admitted. I hugged her tight.

"Did something happen?" Jay asked, and I glanced at my forgotten phone.

"Oh, sorry, Jay, I met up with Lucy, Dyson's sister."

Lucy waved. "Hi. I love your sister. So does my brother. We might keep her."

Jay's mouth dropped open then snapped shut before he smiled his charming there's-a-new-chick smile. "Thank you for taking her in. She's not the easiest person to get along with."

Lucy batted her eyelashes as she giggled. "That's what my brother would say too."

"And that's why we get along," I chuckled. The mouthwatering scent of grilled meat wafted through the air, making my stomach rumble. I sniffed deeply. "That smells heavenly. I'm hungry again."

"Uncle Bob was putting his famous BBQ chicken on the grill when I started my walk," Lucy said.

Dyson and the others strode toward us. His gaze bored into me, making my heart gallop. "I'll talk to you later, Jay." Ending the call, I stuffed my phone in my back shorts pocket.

As Dyson reached me, I launched myself into his embrace.

"I'm sorry," I sighed. "I didn't mean to go so far. I was talking with Jay and walking, and then I saw him and I freaked."

Dyson hushed me while stroking my hair. "There's no need to apologize. I watched you until you followed a curve in the path, then Dad and some cousins came over to talk to me. When I realized you hadn't come back, we set out to look for you. Then I got your picture—that was smart, by the way. I'm sorry I wasn't there sooner."

I burrowed my face into his chest. His spicy scent enveloped me, calming me. Once more, I was safe.

"He didn't make it to us, so I don't know if it was Jake," Dyson whispered, his breath warm against my ear. Shivers ran down my spine.

"What if it was him?" I murmured, feeling tears prick my eyes. I blew out a long breath. Shaking my head, I said, "What if it wasn't him and I'm just so paranoid now that I see him everywhere? How am I going to deal when I'm alone in Kansas?"

"You don't have to be alone," Dyson said,

Tilting my head, I met his gaze, a flutter of nerves dancing in my stomach as our eyes locked.

"You have your roommate at home. While you're at work, Jay will be there. So you'll never be alone."

Suddenly, my heart felt heavy, and my throat constricted. I glanced away, but everywhere I looked, the curious eyes of his family watched.

His fingers traced my cheek, and I closed my eyes, reveling in the touch. "And you have me, Callie. You'll always have me."

"Always?" I hummed.

"Yes." Dyson kissed my forehead.

Such a public declaration of affection made my heart leap.

"I'm telling Mom," Lucy teased, "Aunt Betsy called it."

Chapter Twelve

Dyson

The thought that Callie's stalker may have tracked her to the reunion had me on high alert. I'd shown all the family the picture of Jake, and everyone was on the lookout for him. And of course, Asher had firsthand experience with the man.

Callie was safe with my family, but the guilt still gnawed at me, a constant reminder of my inadequacy and my inability to always safeguard her. I hadn't been there when she needed me and that cut like a knife to my heart.

I'd followed her visually until she was out of eyesight. I tried not to worry and told myself she probably needed a break from my family. Engrossed in a lively conversation with my father and a few of my cousins, I hadn't noticed the time passing until they'd asked about Callie. We set off on a stroll, following the trail she'd taken. Then she'd sent the photo.

I had learned my lesson. She was the earth, and I was the moon. I could give her distance, but I would always be orbiting. And my family were the other satellites looking for a destructive asteroid.

Back at the family-owned motel, we settled into our room with two queen beds, the air smelling faintly of fresh linen.

I ran a warm bath and let Callie relax in the fragrant water while I lit the vanilla-scented candles I had bought at the market yesterday when I ran back in to get the wine. Then I brought up a romantic playlist on my phone. Quiet music and the relaxing aroma of the candles soon filled the room.

The tub was in a room separate from the sink, so I was able to brush my teeth without disturbing her. Then I put on the pair of boxer briefs she'd said were her favorite, sat on one of the queen beds, and waited.

Despite the mood music and the candles, my mind wandered to today's incident. I scrubbed my face. What if it was Jake? I suspected it was him, but how did he know Callie was there? How did he know the guys and I were waiting for him? Did someone tip him off? It sounded insane. And who would tell him? But one moment we heard the footsteps drawing near, and the next he'd disappeared into thin air. My thoughts spiraled.

My phone rang, and Enzo's number flashed. "Oh, shit." I rubbed my chin, taking the call.

"Hey, Enzo," I greeted, glancing at my watch and realizing how late it was in Kansas. "What's going on?"

"You tell me. My sister has been ignoring my calls and texts. What happened?" Enzo asked, his voice a low growl, laced with worry and barely suppressed fury.

"Her phone died. It's charging now, but she's in the bathroom taking a soak in the tub. I can have her call you," then added, "if she wants."

Enzo sighed. "Can you tell me what happened today? Something really freaked her out."

"What makes you say that?"

"She got really weird on the call. One minute we're talking normally, and the next she stopped paying attention. She had her camera up, so I was looking behind her instead of at her. Then she practically hung up on me."

"I don't get it, Enzo. You were with her when it happened. Didn't you ask what was going on? Didn't you see him behind her?" I found it was strange that he wouldn't know Callie was being followed.

"The video kept freezing, but I could tell she was nervous. She said she needed to get back to you."

"We think it was that dick, Jake. I never saw him, but it doesn't matter who it was, really. Callie was so shaken by what happened that she spent the rest of the day paranoid."

"Son of a bitch. I can't believe it." Enzo's breath hissed as if he was breathing through clenched teeth. "Thank you for being there for her."

He paused, and the silence stretched until he cleared his throat. "I met your sister. She's cute. Does she live in Kansas? Does she have a boyfriend?"

I sat up straight, my head swimming at the sudden shift in topic. "No."

"No, to which question?" he laughed.

"No, to you thinking you can get to know her better. No, to you thinking anything about her."

Enzo continued to laugh, then he sobered. "Now you know how I feel about you and Callie."

I hadn't given it much thought, but that might be true. How would Enzo feel if I continued to see his sister? Because that's what I intended to do.

Enzo changed the subject once again. "How big is the car meet?"

"It's just their annual summer fair. This year coincides with my family reunion. While typically a smaller car event, my role as a judge has led to a significant increase in signups."

"If you're looking to boost views on your channel, you should use Callie to go live and talk it up," Enzo suggested.

I kept my voice low and even. "I don't think she'd want to do that. She likes channels to grow organically."

"Yeah, man, it would organically grow because she's pimping you. Just have her talk about that ten-twelve shit."

I walked to the bathroom door and heard sloshing. Callie still relaxed in the tub. I had a few more moments to talk.

Enzo asked more questions about the event, the cars participating, and the specific judging criteria I'd be using.

Then he dropped the bombshell, his voice tight with worry. "What are you doing to ensure my sister's safety at this event?"

The same thought had been churning in my gut all day, a nauseating loop of worry, and I sighed. "I'm not going to chain her to the bed and post a security detail," I laughed, a nervous timbre in my voice that betrayed forced confidence. "Callie can stay with me if she wants, or she can go with my family. I'm sure Lucy would be thrilled to give her a tour while I'm judging. There's also a carnival going on so they could go play some games and ride rides."

"That's not ensuring her safety." Enzo growled. "Dyson, I can't lose her," he whispered, his voice barely audible.

I had no intention of losing Callie, but I couldn't force her to stay by my side. Not when she had alternatives. "She's a grown ass woman and can decide for herself where she's going and what she's doing. If you have an issue with that, take it up with Callie."

We ended the call with the safety issue unresolved.

Sitting on the edge of the bed, I rubbed my face, wondering how I could protect Callie from a city full of strangers while simultaneously judging a car event. I hoped she would go with my sister, but this was a car meet and Callie Ferenzo loved cars. Hopefully, I'd get lucky and she would want to help me judge.

The bathroom door opened, letting a plume of steam out. Callie stopped in the doorway. "What's all this? Candles? Music?"

"I wanted to make tonight extra special for you."

"Hmm. I like the way you think."

Callie sashayed toward me, her damp hair flowing to her mid-back. Her emerald green, spaghetti strap gown seemed to make her eyes glow. Her beauty was captivating. I couldn't tear my eyes away. When she caught me staring, she smirked and climbed onto my lap, wrapping her legs around my back

I slid my hands up her thighs to her backside and groaned. "No panties."

"I didn't see the point." She slid her finger from my chin down between my pecs to my navel, then to the waist of my boxers, where my erection strained to be free. "Tonight, you are mine," she said.

"Not just tonight," I smiled as I groped her butt cheeks.

"That's right, you said *always*," she murmured. The intensity in her hooded eyes made my breath catch. As her gaze darted between my eyes and lips, fire licked through my veins, and I warmed all over.

My hands traveled up to her lower back, urging her closer to my hungry mouth. "You heard correctly," I whispered.

Her eyes locked on mine in a soul-penetrating gaze. "Don't break my heart, Dyson," she breathed, her minty-fresh breath fanned my face, causing a shiver to run down my spine.

I had no intention of breaking her heart. Just the opposite. I wanted to safeguard it and claim it as mine. I wanted to protect it forever.

Before I could put words to the longing in my own heart, she rocked forward against my erection and claimed my lips. In a matter of moments, we'd stripped off what little clothes we had on and I lay loving her on the bed.

Holding her hands over her head, I drilled her the way she wanted me to–fast and hard.

She nudged me gently, and I rolled over, pulling her on top, her warm body pressed against mine. She sat on me and I filled her completely. Her full breasts swayed with every movement. I watched where we were joined. My heart ached with happiness, and my veins coursed with an intense, exhilarating fire. I couldn't hold out much longer.

I cupped her breasts, thumbing her hard beads. She moaned and arched her back towards me as we swelled to reach our crescendo.

"You're going to make me come," I breathed.

"That's the point." A playful smile tipped her lips, and her eyes gleamed with a mischievous glint.

Callie tossed her hair back and closed her eyes. "This is good," she mewled, as she ground on my dick at a new angle.

"Ride it, baby. Find that sweet spot."

Her back arched. She used me to get herself off, and it was hot as hell. Hypnotized by her swaying breasts, I tried to keep the erotic scene from setting me off. But it felt intensely good–a deep, primal pleasure.

"Dyson," Callie rasped.

"Come," I ordered.

She tightened around me, groaning as her release milked me. I rose to meet her, filling her completely. She gasped, her eyes snapping open to meet mine. A fiery mix of lust and love shone in their depths.

She held my gaze as I pumped into her, finally letting myself go. I cried out her name.

Sated, I rolled us to our sides and took a moment to breathe in the sweet scent of the vanilla candles mingled with the intoxicating fragrance of our love. I went to the bathroom to remove the spent condom, then I returned to Callie's side.

I loved holding this woman and pulling her against me, feeling her skin against mine. Thinking about returning home and sleeping in an empty bed gnawed at me. I'd miss the hint of almonds and vanilla on her skin and in her hair and the sighs she made while she slept.

I didn't want to let her go, but how could I keep her? Our pretend relationship had turned real so fast.

"Dyson." Callie reached for me and pulled my face to hers. She kissed my lips. The sweet kiss built on the longing in my soul. My fingers traced the smooth skin on her arm.

She bit her lip. Her gaze darted away, then her eyes snapped back to mine with a flicker of something unreadable.

I studied her, the silence between us uncertain and her reluctance clear. "Yes, Callie?"

"I think I'm falling for you," she said, a blush rising on her cheeks.

I opened my mouth to speak, but the words caught in my throat as my heart hammered a joyful rhythm against my ribs. I rolled onto my back with an arm behind my head and a huge grin splitting my face. A wave of happiness washed over me. This was a dream come true.

"It's like you read my mind," I managed to say, my tongue feeling thick and clumsy.

Moisture shimmered in her eyes as an angelic smile bloomed across her beautiful face. I reached for her, pulling her close, our warm skin touching, and our hearts beating in unison.

"I'm falling for you, too." I whispered against her forehead. She sighed happily and soon her breaths deepened.

Opening our motel door the next morning, I glanced back over my shoulder. Callie slept on her side with a small foot sticking out of the covers—peaceful and childlike at rest. I smiled. This beautiful woman had me thinking about and planning the future.

As excited as I was about judging this show, a part of me didn't want to leave. Sure, I rationalized that thought as protecting her, but, if I was honest with myself, the urge was also selfish—I didn't want to be alone. I wanted to be with her.

Forcing a spring into my step, I met Asher at the Porsche.

"Are you ready for today?" he asked, handing me a coffee in a paper cup.

"Thanks. As ready as I'll ever be." I sipped the liquid energy, then I started the Porsche and drove us to the street fair.

Asher flipped through a file of papers. "Ahha. It says the car meet is across the road from the carnival grounds." Asher strained to see the space.

"The carnival is in the parking lot of a strip mall."

The top of a Ferris wheel came into view. "There." Asher pointed.

A woman with a severe bun in a neon yellow vest indicated for us to enter a paved area. I followed a lime green Subaru STI with black rims. The Subaru stopped next to a short, mustached man with a clipboard. After a brief conversation, the car moved on and the man motioned for us to come forward.

I rolled down the window and met the man's gaze. A split second later, his eyes widened with recognition. "Mr. Gabbard, welcome to the Fairbanks Summer Car Fair. I'm Gage Hansen. I'm a huge fan of Gabby's Garage."

He whistled, recognizing the car. "This is the GT3 RS. The one from your show. We have you up in front. Come this way," he beckoned us forward.

A walkie-talkie crackled in his hand as he guided the car toward a large, white tent. All along the way volunteers in neon vests stopped, stared, and many followed along in our wake. I smiled, nodded, and waved to them as we crept along.

"Does this happen often?" Asher said, saluting to someone on his side of the car.

"All the time," I said through a forced smile.

"Wow. This is so cool." Asher beamed.

"Meeting car enthusiasts is fun. Being bombarded with fans on your way to the bathroom? Not so much."

He laughed. "I bet."

"Thanks for helping me today."

"I'm glad to help. But why isn't Callie here?" A hint of disbelief and anger edged his tone.

"She didn't sign up to judge with me. Besides, she's having girl time with Lucy and Lydia. They're going to breakfast."

"I would have thought she'd support you." He faced me with an arched brow.

Gage motioned to the spot they'd saved for me, then stuck his baton in the air and twirled it like a disco version of an aircraft marshaller working his handheld beacon.

Sensing his disapproval of Callie, I ignored Asher.

I'd woken her early and gave her the choice of coming with me, but she'd laughed and told me she had a better offer—going to breakfast with the women in my family. She had kissed me and rolled over. In fairness to her, I *had* woken her up in the middle of the night.

The car meet was my deal. I can't blame Callie for wanting to take a backseat to the car show crowds, especially if Jake was hanging around.

"Callie doesn't like to be the center of attention. She prefers being in the background."

"Are you sure?" Asher said, glancing at his phone.

"Absolutely." It was one of the things I knew for certain about Callie Ferenzo.

From my peripheral, I glanced at Asher. Maybe he crushed on Callie and had wanted her to come. Maybe he was more interested in spending time with me. Could he be jealous of Callie?

"Thanks for hanging out today, Asher."

The kid whipped his head around and flashed brilliantly white teeth. A blush crept to his cheeks. "No problem, cuz."

"We'll see how Gage wants to proceed, but I'll probably need your help."

Asher's sappy grin dropped, replaced by a serious expression. "Do you need me to go live or take pictures? Whatever you need, bruh. I'm here for you."

I gripped the wheel, glancing at the space around my car. A dozen pairs of eyes stared at me like I was some sort of car deity. Several people held phones aimed at the GT3 RS. Who knew a CarTube channel about my passion for cars would turn into a lucrative business with a measure of celebrity?

I inhaled deeply, then exhaled out my mouth. "Ready?"

"Heck, yeah." Asher opened his door and popped out like a coiled snake.

I killed the Porsche's engine, pasted on my CarTube smile, and exited. "Hello everyone," I greeted.

After posing for pictures, the excited chatter of my fans faded as Asher and I were ushered toward a large administration tent. Along the way, I snapped pictures of other cars to send to Callie.

I took a seat, gratefully accepting the offered bottle of chilled water. My phone vibrated in my pocket. I pulled it out and checked my notifications. One of my scheduled Gabby's Garage videos had posted that morning. The numbers had skyrocketed, and the comments were in the hundreds already. I smiled, proud to have hit the jackpot on the CarTube algorithm.

I read the leading comment: Will you be adding Callie Ferenzo to your content from now on?

The next one mentioned Callie as well: Great video, but where's Callie?

Odd. How did they tie my account to Callie?

My heart pounded in my chest, and a wave of unease crashed over me, leaving me breathless. Had Jake posted content with Callie and me together? Where would I even start a search?

"Mr. Gabbard, make yourself at home. If you have questions or need anything, you can talk to any of the volunteers and they will contact me. The judging committee will be with you shortly." With a nod and a wave, Gage was gone. A few volunteers came up to me and asked questions about my channel.

Unfortunately, it appeared I wouldn't be able to investigate Jake until I had some time alone. Hopefully, Callie would remain blissfully unaware of the comments about her until I could figure out the mystery.

Asher paced the small space with his gaze glued to the screen of his phone, his thumbs tapping the device at warp speed.

Politely nodding, I let the volunteers ramble on. I leaned back with a sigh.

Soon I'd be moving from car to car, inspecting and judging them. Along the way, I'd interact with fans, taking photos and talking cars. Asher would get a taste of the nonstop CarTube influencer lifestyle. I closed my eyes, enjoying the calm before the storm.

Chapter Thirteen

Callie

A knock sounded on the door. A glimpse through the peephole brought a smile to my lips. I flung open the door.

"Took you long enough," Lucy mockingly groused.

"Whatever," I said, rolling my eyes. "I had to get beautiful for your brother."

"So you can boink him later?" Lucy laughed.

"Gross. TMI," Lydia groaned.

Lucy moved aside, revealing Dyson's mom and Aunt Esther, their amused smiles crinkling the corners of their eyes.

Heat crept to my face. "Let me grab my bag." I hurried and flipped the light switch, then closed the door behind me.

In the parking lot, Great Aunt Betsy waited to ferry us to breakfast. We climbed into her SUV. Not ten minutes later, we arrived at a greasy spoon called Hal's Diner.

"Hal is part of my Rotary club and I've known her forever," Betsy said, her eyes twinkling with affection.

"Hal is a she?" Lucy arched one brow.

"Halena. But everyone calls her Hal," Betsy said.

Stepping inside, the jukebox's nostalgic tunes and the checkered floors made me feel like I'd stepped back in time to a 1950s diner. Chrome stools gleamed at the counter inside, while booths with red vinyl seats lined the outside wall. The scents of bacon and other goodies wafted over us.

"Something smells heavenly," Judy said with a hum.

"And greasy," Lydia mumbled.

"That's why it tastes so good," I said with a shrug.

Esther, Betsy, Judy, and Lydia settled into one booth. Then Lucy and I slid into the one next to them.

After ordering, I glanced at my phone to see if Dyson had messaged me. And, yes, he had texted, but I hadn't noticed because my phone was on silent. I rectified *that* problem. He'd sent me several pictures of cars.

"Why are you grinning like a fool?" Lucy asked, her eyebrows raised as she sipped steaming coffee from a chipped, white mug.

Without glancing up, I said, "Dyson–"

"Are you messaging about boinking?" Lucy asked loudly.

I lowered the phone and kept smiling. "No, but that's a great idea."

"Yuck. Disgusting."

I laughed, then sipped my iced latte. "I'm so hungry. A hearty breakfast is just what I need."

"Doesn't my brother feed you?" Lucy teased.

"Of course. But I've got to keep my strength up for boinkin' time later." I cocked my head to the side and winked.

"Ugh. What have I started?" Lucy groaned, putting her head in her hands.

The server sat our food on the table in front of us. The plate of crispy bacon, fluffy scrambled eggs, and perfectly toasted bread smelled absolutely divine. My stomach growled in appreciation.

Lucy had ordered French toast on brioche bread topped with fruit, and it looked scrumptious. "I'm in heaven," she mumbled, taking a bite.

My phone pinged, its familiar chime sounding softly. With a light tap, I woke the screen.

"Tell my brother to leave you alone," Lucy said around a

mouthful.

"It's not him." I glanced at the screen, perplexed. "It's a CarTube notification." I frowned, confused.

"What's wrong?" Lucy paused, her loaded fork in front of her mouth.

"It's odd." I glanced across the table at her. "It's my new channel. I haven't released anything yet."

"But I thought you made videos while you and Dyson were driving here."

"I recorded things, yes. And I already have a few shorts ready to go, but I planned on releasing them after we returned home." I bit my lip. "I didn't want to give out my location until this mess with Jake ended."

"Probably just a reminder that your scheduled post will be published soon."

I stabbed the eggs with the fork and shoveled in a mouthful while reading the email about logging in. I'd done that, but why would I get a notification now? A knot of worry tightened in my gut.

"I haven't scheduled anything yet. I have a few drafts I need to do final edits on, but..."

"But what?" Lucy leaned over her plate on the table.

"Watch your shirt," I pointed, then refocused on my screen, tapping it and opening the CarTube app. Blinking twice, I studied the feed then switched to my account.

I gasped and dropped the phone as if it were poison. It hit the tabletop with a thud, then ricocheted to the bench seat.

"Callie, what's wrong?" Lucy stood and came to my side. "You're as white as a sheet and you are shaking."

I tried to swallow, but my mouth had gone dry. I lifted my glass of water to my lips, but my shaking hands caused the water to spill, running down my chin in a small stream.

Lucy's hazel gaze, so reminiscent of Dyson's, pierced my soul. She touched my shoulder.

Emotions threatened to overwhelm me–fear, anxiety, confusion, anger. I closed my eyes. Tears slipped out, and I swiped them away with the back of my hand.

"You're scaring me," Lucy whispered, picking my phone up from the seat and sitting next to me.

I scooted in to accommodate her as she wrapped my hand in hers.

"Someone has hacked my account," I uttered. "They've published things. Private things."

"What?" Lucy squeaked.

Judy and Esther turned and stared, and Betsy grimaced. Lydia's eyebrows furrowed as she picked up on our worried tone and downcast expressions. Excusing herself, she moved to our booth and sat opposite us.

"What's up?" Lydia asked.

"Callie thinks someone hacked her new CarTube account," Lucy said.

"I don't think–I know." I rubbed my face, willing my anxiety to go away. It didn't work.

"What's the name of the account?" Lydia tapped her phone screen.

"End of the Road," I offered. My chest felt as if a VW Beetle was parked on it.

Lydia and Lucy both searched the CarTube app. "Is it supposed to be highlighting cars at the end of their life?" Lydia asked as she swiped up.

"No." I shook my head. "It's about the mystery that waits at the journey's end, a place where the road disappears into the unknown. The destinations—parks, trails, overlooks… That kind of thing."

"Sounds interesting," Lucy said, scrolling on her phone screen. Then she stopped. "Oh, no."

I wanted End of the Road to be my baby. Something to call my own where I wouldn't worry about views or subs. It was to be my creative outlet. Not that I didn't have some creative leeway with Enzo's Auto Tech, but it wasn't solely mine. I didn't like the way my brother portrayed me on the show, and I wanted the freedom to shape my own image.

Plus, there weren't many shows that highlighted the kinds of places I wanted to show off. Campgrounds, national parks, exotic expensive hotels—those places got a lot of attention. But there were hardly any channels showcasing the little places at the dead ends.

I stared out the window at nothing. Someone had stolen and perverted my dream. I sucked in a stuttering breath. All that work...

Lucy touched my arm, pulling me from my dour thoughts.

"This is footage from Denali. So, it happened recently."

"This one focusing on your chest was published three days ago," Lydia said. "Who are you dancing with?"

"Wow, there are fifty thousand views already." Lucy glanced at me. "Can you get into your account?"

I picked up my phone and tapped on the screen, attempting to log in. My password was wrong. I tried again. "My password has been changed."

"Oh, no," Lucy lamented, sitting back. "I'm so sorry."

"This doesn't make sense." Lydia glanced from Lucy to me. "You took this movie a few days ago. Who would've had access to your equipment and been able to hack your account without you knowing? It had to be someone close to you. There were a few days between the first and second posting. Almost as if the hacker was testing to see if you'd notice."

We brainstormed suspects and listed family members, the car delivery man, and others from the trip.

"What about the stalker guy?" Lucy shivered.

"I didn't see him in Denali," I said. I chewed my lip. "What if he was watching me the whole time?" *What if he videoed us making love?* Would he post it on the internet?

End of the Road had twenty posts already. They were all five minutes or less. Many had comments and the channel subs had reached over ten thousand. Each subsequent video gained more views than the last, a clear sign of it triggering the algorithm. It was impressive stats for a brand-new channel.

The latest video had the clickbait title: "Meet Dyson Gabbard."

In the short clip it showed us dancing together, then abruptly zoomed in on his hand, grabbing my butt. The views numbered 500,000 and more as I watched. Content like this could get my profile flagged or worse–banned.

Another video showcased large, bold white letters spelling out the word CONTEST. I clicked play. The video showed me sashaying down the trail at Flat Top Mountain. Glancing over my shoulder, I smiled and waved at Dyson who held the camera out of view, then I blew him a kiss. An AI voice said, "If I get fifty thousand subscribers, then I'll share my adult content link with you. You'd like that, wouldn't you? Like and share."

"What the hell!" A wave of horror washed over me, leaving me speechless, unable to blink, and gasping for breath.

The phone slipped from my hand and landed with a dull thud on the wooden table, again.

My hands trembled, and I was unsure whether to throw my phone in frustration or give in to the overwhelming wave of despair that made me want to curl up and cry.

"This is horrible." Lucy said. "Would Dyson do this to you?"

"No." I gasped, kick-starting my breathing again. I rubbed my forehead as the unthinkable thought hit me like a ton of bricks. "He wouldn't–couldn't do this to me." I shook my head vehemently.

Wide-eyed, they stared at me, then looked at each other.

"Why would he?" Lydia finally asked.

"This would grow his channel, too." Lucy suggested quietly. Then she displayed Gabbie's Garage where the newest video showcased my handsome man smiling his patented goofy grin and pointing to an orange car.

"No!" My voice raised as I doubled down. "Dyson would never hurt me. He's not all about the views, not like my brother."

"Your brother." Lucy's eyes narrowed. "Does he have access to your cloud?"

I rubbed my temples. "While my brother would see nothing wrong with these videos, he would put them on the Enzo's Auto Tech channel to grow *those* numbers. Plus, he's an idiot when it comes to splicing videos into cohesive content. This is not his work."

"And he's not in Alaska," Lydia pointed out.

"Last time I checked," I mumbled. Opening my contacts, I quickly searched Jay's location. Unavailable. His phone must be dead. I sighed and set the phone aside. "He's going to be pissed he didn't think of this as a publicity stunt."

Lucy snorted, then covered her face. Lydia began to giggle, and I caught it. Soon we were all laughing until tears streamed down our faces and my gut hurt.

As we sobered, I stared at my phone, wondering where to go next. "I think I need to try to reset my password on the account. If I can't do that, I'll request they remove it."

"Tell me you have two factor ID setup on your CarTube channel." Lucy pulled her coffee to her and took a sip. She signaled to the server to come refresh our mugs.

"Of course, but I haven't gotten any emails or app alerts from CarTube regarding a password change request."

"Try to reset it now," Lydia suggested.

As I attempted to log in again. Lucy and Lydia speculated about Jake and if he was responsible.

I subscribed to End of the Road so I'd get notified of new video releases. The hacker had changed the password, but the backup email hadn't been changed. Luckily, I had a way to contact the channel and contest the password. Searching for CarTube emails, I found creating a new password and account verification emails in the trash bin.

"What the hell," I growled. "Someone has logged in and updated the password and changed the primary email."

"Well, that limits the suspects." Lydia met my eyes.

It felt like I'd swallowed a hundred-pound rock. Dyson would never hurt me. He wouldn't do this, would he?

I squeezed my eyes shut, inhaled through my nose, and exhaled through my mouth.

"I can't believe Dyson would do this. He loves Callie," Lucy said, touching my arm.

"Who else could it be?" Lydia pointed out.

My eyes snapped open, and I frowned.

The server returned with a fresh pot of coffee. She refilled our mugs. I sipped the hot liquid. As the coffee slid down my throat to my gut, it took away some of the chill that had settled there.

Lucy said, staring into the dark liquid. "I don't think we should jump to any conclusions. We should ask Dyson."

"Yes, let's go."

Chapter Fourteen

Dyson

The incessant chatter of the volunteers, my cousin's endless questions, and the agonizing wait for the judging to begin were a maddening combination. I stood, stretching my back.

A man with a handlebar mustache entered the tent. First Gage and now this guy—I wondered if mustaches were a thing in Alaska. "Hey, I'm Arnold. I'm the head of the judging team. Thank you for taking part in the show today."

I strode toward the man and shook his hand. He had a firm shake and a twinkle in his eyes. "You've been doing this for years," I surmised.

"That's right, son," Arnold nodded.

"Great. Just slot me in where you need me." I rubbed my hands, wanting to get the day started so I could push the uneasiness about Callie being mentioned in my comments out of my head.

"Gage says you're going to have the final say today." Arnold's mustache twitched.

"If you need me to judge, then I'd be happy to help, but if you trust your team and want them to do it, then I can present the trophies to the winners. Like I said, I'll do what you need me to do."

"Great. We can get started. I'd like to see what you've got."

Asher and I followed Arnold out of the tent. I'd had it happen before. Many, like Arnold, weren't familiar with my show. They typically quizzed me, but instead, Arnold stopped and an awkward silence formed as he gazed at a classic C1 Corvette.

"Beautiful," I murmured.

"I'm going live," Asher said, glancing at the car's placard with "1956" at the top. He lifted his phone. "It's old."

"Yeah, it's the first gen for the Corvette." I smiled. "This is where it all started."

A man, who'd been seated in a folding chair, stood and approached us. "Is this your car?" I asked.

"Yes. It's been in my family for years. It was my grandfather's." He smiled with pride.

"It's such a historic car." I leaned closer to Asher and pointed. "In 1956, arctic blue was the second rarest paint color. You had the option to get the side cove silver like this one."

Arnold handed me a clipboard with a sheet of paper. The entry's number was scrawled at the top.

I circled the vehicle, making note of the paint's finish, the tires and wheels wear, the engine bay and interior, and the overall cleanliness. In the small comment box, I made a note of the family ownership and original window sticker.

We continued to another Vette. "This one is millennium yellow. Quite a few years in the early 2000s had this as a spec."

After the ninth Corvette, we moved on to a 2005 Ford GT. All the while, my phone vibrated in my pocket. Something had to be blowing up, but I had a job to do.

"These look expensive." Asher made comments and asked questions as we progressed along the line of cars. He kept his phone up continuing to record me. "Why did the older car get better numbers than the newer one?"

"There could be many reasons. OEM parts." Asher stared

blankly. I inhaled.

This is going to be a long day.

"OEM stands for Original Equipment Manufacturer, or in layman's terms: original parts. They are sometimes hard to find. Using original parts, not mere replacements, is crucial for preserving the car's true character and history."

"Oh."

"That one also had swirls in the clear coat. That's easy enough to fix. It's not what you bring to a show if you are serious about winning." I pointed at the panel. "You can see it at an angle."

Asher shifted his position and gasped. "I see it!"

The crowd grew as the morning went on. The carnival officially started, but that didn't stop car enthusiasts from checking out their favorite rides.

Asher greeted the car owners with the energy of an excited puppy. He introduced me as if I were an A-lister Hollywood celebrity. His joy was palpable, although a bit excessive and irritating.

It was getting harder to focus on the cars. I kept getting interrupted by fans, even with Asher running interference. Since more and more folks wanted to chat and get a photo with me, I motioned to Arnold.

As I inspected a '77 Chevelle, a couple of men my age approached, asking to take a picture. Asher spoke with them as they waited for me. When I finished, I handed the clipboard to Arnold.

"Hey man, I love your show. I'm glad you came here," one with a red baseball cap said.

"Nice to meet you," I said, shaking their hands. When I agreed to photos with them, they handed their phones to Asher. I tried not to look too antsy as my phone continued to vibrate in my pocket. Finally done, Asher handed their phones back.

One friend elbowed the other. "Ask him what you really want to ask."

The red baseball cap man blushed. I grinned, wondering what episode or car he wanted more details about.

"Is it true you're with Callie Ferenzo?" he asked.

My mouth dropped open.

"She's hot. Is she here? We want to get photos with her, too." The man glanced around.

"She hasn't arrived yet," Asher admitted, his frown deepening as he checked his watch.

I glared at Asher, my lips pressed into a thin line. Callie wasn't here for the car show.

The man elbowed his buddy again. Both wore hopeful expressions, their eyes bright with anticipation.

"Mr. Gabbard?" a soft, hesitant voice, barely above a whisper, caught my attention.

Grateful for a distraction, I turned to meet a young woman. Her long brown hair was gathered high in a single ponytail. Turning my back on the men's loud conversation, I focused on the shy woman, her eyes downcast.

"Can I help you?"

A blush fanned her cheeks. "Is Callie with you today?" she asked.

"Why do you think she's here?" I couldn't help my question. We purposely hadn't posted or shared about us or her being in Alaska.

My mind raced. Had someone betrayed our confidence and leaked the information? In reality, our relationship was bound to get out.

"I saw it on her CarTube channel. The thumbnail caught my eye." Her dark gaze rose to meet mine.

"Enzo's Auto Tech?" I asked, confused. Callie was deliberately delaying posting to her own channel until after we got back. She wanted to make sure she had time to perfect them. Plus, there was the Jake factor.

"No. Her channel. Do you mind getting a picture?" She

extended her arm, and I smiled as she took the selfie.

Her channel? Had Callie posted something already? No. The woman had to be wrong. She must be thinking of Enzo's Auto Tech.

My phone vibrated in my pocket again. I pulled it out and tapped the screen, opening my notifications.

So many comments on my videos, not just the new episode but older ones as well. Especially my collabs with Enzo's Auto Tech and The Car Magician.

What in the world?

Callie had insisted she wouldn't officially launch her new channel until we returned. Could Jake have posted pictures of Callie and me together? He took photos without permission at the airport and possibly in other locations.

I glanced around, looking for a quiet place to escape so I could investigate the surge in notifications and Callie's so-called channel. The throng of people had intensified since the beginning of the festival. I hurried behind the line of cars to where a row of Porta-Potties stood. Rounding the corner, I had a measure of privacy under a lone tree in the middle of the parking lot.

Using my shadow to see the screen better, I pulled up my CarTube channel. After checking the most recent number of comments on the newest episode, I clicked on the video and scrolled the feed. So many of the messages revolved around Callie.

Some comments were genuinely congratulatory, while others dripped with a resentful jealousy. Like HarryLarry455, who told me to "make sure to probe her junk in the trunk." It might have been funny if it didn't have a host of disgusting comments agreeing with it and egging HarryLarry455 on.

With each new comment, a fresh wave of dread washed over me as I continued my investigation.

"Hey," Asher said, slapping me on the back.

I jumped, nearly dropping my phone, my heart pounding in my chest from the sudden surprise. "You scared me."

"People are looking for you." He pointed toward the car show.

"Sorry. My phone was blowing up. I needed to see what was going on."

"Anything good?" he asked with a sparkle in his eyes.

My gaze narrowed as I glanced at the phone in my hand. "I'm not sure. I've got a record amount of comments–"

"That's great, bruh." Asher clapped me on the back again.

"But they're mostly about Callie." I rubbed my chin, perplexed by the phenomenon.

Had Jake posted a picture of us together? Maybe Enzo mentioned it to get views. I woke my phone and started to type Enzo's Auto Tech.

"Well... it's not surprising after what she's posted on her channel." Asher glanced away.

I lowered my arm and faced Asher. "What channel?"

"The one she was going on and on about: the road, something. She's plastered tons of hot pics online and keeps tagging you everywhere." Asher met my gaze and shrugged. "I'm sorry."

"What?" I gasped, my stomach churning. It couldn't be true. Callie wouldn't have used me to grow her channel. She'd said she wanted it to grow organically and was sick of her brother's use of her T and A to get views.

"Just search her name. Better yet, wait until later. It might make you salty."

Asher pointed towards the toilets. "I need to take a piss." He rounded the green wall and left me to my tornadic thoughts.

Callie had implied she planned to do more editing on the few videos she'd worked on in my presence. And insisted she wasn't ready to launch. Had Callie lied to me?

Raising my phone once more, I swallowed and entered her name in the search bar.

Links to End of the Road content instantly populated my feed. I couldn't blink. The header was a photo of Callie standing with an impish grin, glancing over her shoulder. We'd been on Flat Top, and she'd gifted me with that flirtatious smile. Now she shared it with the world. She wore the skin hugging leggings showing off her luscious curves.

"Holy shit." I uttered, scrubbing my face. She had posted thirty videos and pushed 30,000 subs in three days. Asher was right. Several video titles mentioned my name. I watched until the end where my *pretend girlfriend* offered a contest to drop an adult content link.

Clearly, Callie had lied to me.

A sharp pain, like a fist, slammed into my gut, leaving me breathless.

I'd been duped. Callie had played her part convincingly, and I'd been completely captivated by her charm.

Surprised my heart still beat, I wheeled around and started for the admin tent. I needed solitude. I couldn't people right now. As I strode through the crowd, it parted. My demeanor or my flinty face moved the masses.

Asher called after me, but I kept on. Until I reached my car— its turquoise blue sent memories crashing over me, each one another gut punch, and I stalled. I stood frozen, the moisture blurring my vision as I struggled to comprehend her betrayal.

"Dyson," a feminine voice called through the crowd.

Callie. I winced as if stabbed in the heart.

The tone of her voice–strained and brittle–told me something was wrong. Conflicting emotions scrolled through my head. No matter how much I wanted to flee the scene and ignore the situation, my legs refused to work.

Scanning the sea of faces, I spotted Callie four car lengths away. Wearing a Gabby's Garage t-shirt, her beauty made my breath hitch. Because Callie, the woman whose love I thought would last a lifetime, had shattered my trust. How had she fooled me?

Even now, when our gazes locked, a small smile flitted across her features. Anger churned in my stomach. I narrowed my gaze and fixed her with a glare that made her smile falter and disappear.

A crowd started to gather, their whispers and curious glances making me shift nervously next to my Porsche.

Callie lifted her hand and continued forward. Beside her, Lucy kept in step.

Lucy must suspect something shady.

A slight dip in one of Lucy's brows betrayed the worry hidden beneath her otherwise neutral expression. She'd be pissed when she found out what Callie had done to us–to me. My ears filled and my vision blurred at how much my family already loved her, and the thought of the hurt I'd brought to all of us.

Callie stopped abruptly, her head jerking to the left. A squeal of delight escaped her as she ran toward someone who lifted her effortlessly into the air. I could tell the person was a man by the arms wrapped around her, but the crowd blocked my view, making identifying him impossible. It was clear she welcomed his embrace, though.

A suffocating wave of nausea hit me as I struggled to tear my eyes away from another betrayal. Then, just when I thought I'd found the strength to break away, my sister shook the man's hand.

Et tu, Brute?

Callie waved her hands vigorously as she talked to the man. The more they talked, the more my heart hardened. Then they all faced me.

"Son of a bitch," I muttered.

"Is that Callie's brother? Isn't he always making her do things to gain views?" Asher asked from beside me as Jay Ferenzo saluted me with a smug smile.

"Yes. Why the hell is he here?" I growled.

"Maybe to celebrate the new channel launch," Asher suggested, twisting the knife in my heart a little more.

I bit down on my building anger and hurt, stuffing them behind a dam of indifference.

Callie started toward me again, walking briskly. Her walk turned into a jog. Her face held a radiant smile. When she reached me, she wrapped her arms around me in a tight hug. I kept my arms stiff at my sides, refusing to hug her back. Her scent wafted over me—taunting me, mocking me. I blinked, envisioning our time in Denali.

"That's Callie Ferenzo," someone said, fueling my turmoil.

I leaned so my mouth was next to her ear. "You *lied* to me," I growled low.

She glanced up, her green eyes wide, and shook her head. She stepped back when I didn't embrace her. "But I need your help–"

"Haven't I helped you enough?" I attempted to keep my tone even since many of our fans were recording the interaction. My sister arrived at my side and Enzo met my gaze with a frown.

Callie tried again, "Dyson, I–"

"Don't waste your breath. I don't suffer liars." My tone was immutable.

Her lips pressed together in a firm line and water gathered in her eyes. Clasping her hands to her chest, a single tear spilled down her cheek.

A sudden coldness settled in Callie's eyes as she straightened her shoulders. She swiped at the renegade tear. Without another word, she pivoted, pulling the knife from my heart as she strode away and leaving me to bleed out.

Enzo hurried after Callie. He threw a venomous glare over his shoulder, then the surging crowd closed in, swallowing them.

I towered over most, yet why did I feel as if I were sinking in quicksand?

Lucy slapped my arm, and I recoiled in pain. "Way to go, dipshit. Callie's account has been hacked, and she only wanted your help."

Chapter Fifteen

Callie

Gasping and teary-eyed, I hurried through the line of gleaming cars, hoping to get lost in the crowd. The sting of Dyson's rejection left me reeling. A nauseous wave of despair washed over me. I couldn't bear to stay another moment with someone who thought I was a liar.

Damn Dyson.

He hadn't even given me a chance to explain. Well, screw him. He was on his own.

And so was I, apparently.

I skirted the frozen lemonade line and made it to the parking lot, where I stood under a tree, trying to hold myself together long enough to get my bearings.

"Callie," Jay called.

My brother jogged to my side. I sighed and launched myself into Jay's safe, waiting arms.

"Are you alright?" Jay asked, patting my back.

"No. I just want to go home." I hiccuped a single, shuddering breath, and then the tears started.

"Okay. That's fine." Jay patted my back, holding me until I could breathe again. "Take deep breaths."

I nodded and wiped my eyes again. Jay tapped on his phone.

"Why are you here?" I mumbled through my tears, trying to distract my wounded heart.

"I thought I'd surprise you." He shrugged and took my elbow as he led me toward the parking lot entrance. "Looks like the surprise is on me."

Moments later, a black four-door sedan with a throaty engine pulled up to the curb. Jay opened the back door and helped me inside the leather interior. I started to scoot over so my brother could join me, but he put a hand on my arm to stop me. He leaned inside and made eye contact with the driver. "Take her anywhere she wants."

"Yes, sir," a deep voice replied.

"The Northern Lights Motel." I gazed at my brother. "Aren't you coming with me?"

"No. I'll be along shortly. I want to have words with Dyson first."

I opened my mouth to ask him to stay with me, but Jay shut the door. I twisted in my seat.

The car pulled away from the fair, the sounds of the carnival fading as my brother grew smaller in the distance. I faced forward, then closed my eyes, willing the tears away.

I had to pull my shit together long enough to make flight reservations, pack, and get to the airport. Getting airborne would be pricey, but I had to get away from this suffocating sense of loss. I had to at least try.

The car hit a large pothole, and the impact jarred my teeth. I opened my eyes in time to see us passing the diner where we'd had breakfast. "I think you missed the turn," I said to the driver.

"The festival screwed up the traffic flow. There are road closures. I'm going around the back way," the driver reasoned. His voice sounded familiar, but his head was turned to look out the driver's side window and I couldn't see his face. *Still paranoid.*

I nodded and leaned back, staring at the passing buildings. After two large intersections, unease started to creep in. I opened my maps app and located the Northern Lights Motel.

Just as I suspected, we were moving away. A new worry niggled in my subconscious. Why was he taking me away from my lodging?

"How much further?" I asked, trying to sound bored and not anxious.

"Not too far now," he muttered, gripping the wheel tightly, still turned to look out his side window.

I scooted over to sit behind the driver and looked into the rearview mirror to see his face—and bit my lip to stifle a scream. It was Jake the creeper–my stalker.

Of all the cars Jay could have summoned on his app, it had to be my stalker. But I was numb—the rejection and devastation I felt from the breakup on top of the possibility that Dyson had hacked my channel... No wonder I didn't notice what car I was getting into. Jake's beautiful Jaguar.

I glanced at the map on my screen and took a screenshot of my location. I silenced my phone, then sent the image to Jay and Lucy.

Lucy's showed as delivered. But when no dots started dancing in the bubble, my heart sank. The carnival was loud. She might not see the message for hours.

Jay's message showed his focus was on. *Who knows when he'll see it?*

I could call, but what would I say that Jake wouldn't hear and understand? Fear twisted my gut while a slow burn of anger simmered beneath the surface.

Me to Lucy:

> I'm in the stalker's jag.

I breathed a sigh of relief when the dots started dancing immediately.

Lucy:

> Get out!

Me

But I'm in a car.

Lucy:

At an intersection.

Hide in a public place like a restaurant.

I shared my location with Lucy. The car slowed at an intersection but didn't stop. There were three businesses—a quickie mart on one corner, a bank that was probably closed, and a mom and pop coffee shop on another. The lights were on, winking at me.

"Stop!" I cried. "I think I'm going to be sick." I rubbed my stomach and covered my mouth.

Jake jerked the car to a stop, and I tried the passenger door. It was locked. "Hurry," I hastened.

The lock disengaged, and I quickly exited the car. I bent over, inhaling the fresh air.

Still pretending to be sick, I turned around and saw the coffee shop across the street. Leaving the car door open, I took off behind the Jaguar, weaving through the traffic.

I heard Jake curse, then a car horn honked. I hoofed it down the alley between the coffee shop and the bank, and circled around the back of the coffee shop building.

Hopefully, I'd buy myself some time and he wouldn't look for me in the coffee shop. At least it would give me enough time to hide in the shop's bathroom and get help.

I peeked around the side of the building in time to see Jake drive past the alley. I only had seconds. Running up the sidewalk to a side door, I pulled it open.

It smelled heavenly. On any other day, I'd take my time to order, but today, I strode straight to the cash register.

The young woman behind the counter smiled and said, "How can I help you?"

"There's a man following me. He abducted me and I just escaped from his car. Please, I need a place to hide." I glanced over my shoulder. My phone pinged, and I jumped.

"Come with me." She beckoned me to the small hallway, out of sight of the entry and windows. "Let me get my manager."

"Mary, there's a woman who needs help."

"If she's hungry, you can give her a bagel and a small coffee," a melodious, gentle voice said out of sight.

"No. There's a dude after her. She's being trafficked."

A chair scraped the floor, and the barista and another woman met my gaze. The bell over the entry door rang. My heart froze in my chest. "Help me," I mouthed.

Mary beckoned me inside the small office while the young woman returned to the counter.

"How can I help you today?" I heard the barista say.

"Have you seen this woman?" Jake's irritated, gruff voice turned my blood cold.

Me

I'm at Little Owl Coffee Shop.

Lucy:

Hold tight. I'm on the way.

I breathed easier. Mary offered me her chair and held a finger to her lips as she crossed to the office door, closed it quietly, and locked it.

She pointed to the screen of her desktop computer where security camera footage displayed four different angles. One was a closeup of the cash register.

I gasped, then covered my mouth.

"No sir, I haven't. Can I get you something to drink?" The girl glanced sideways, then back to Jake.

Jake pursed his lips and stomped down toward the bathrooms. He opened one door and glanced inside, then the other. With a huff, he finally jiggled the office door, then returned to the counter.

"I'll have a vanilla latte with an extra shot of espresso," Jake snipped as he continued to look around.

The barista took his money, then started making the drink. As she worked, Jake rapped on the counter and leaned over to get a better look at the kitchen area.

"I have a friend coming to get me," I whispered to Mary. "I don't know why this creep wants me."

Mary took my hand and patted it. "We'll keep you safe. Don't fret. I know the sheriff." She tapped her phone. "Hey ya, Darrel. Could you come visit the Little Owl? We've got a troublemaker."

Tears welled in my eyes.

Hold it together, Ferenzo.

"Thank you," I uttered, not recognizing my voice.

"Hey," Jake hollered. "I hear voices. Who's back there? Are you hiding someone?"

The barista's eyes grew large. "N-no... Just my boss."

"My ass," Jake said before shouting. "Hey, I know you're back there, Callie. I'm coming to get you."

He leaned menacingly over the counter, but Mary decided to intervene. "Stay quiet and no matter what happens, do not come out. Understand, young lady?"

I nodded and zipped my lips.

Mary exited the office. She met my gaze as she closed the door.

I watched on the monitor as she confronted the red-faced Jake.

"What's going on?" She didn't give Jake a moment to answer, but turned straight to the barista. "I was working on the taxes and told you not to bother me."

Clenching her hands, the girl glanced at her feet. "I'm sorry, Mary."

"What's the hubbub?" she asked Jake.

"I'm looking for a friend. She's very paranoid and her family wants her home." Jake smoothed out his shirt.

"Good luck with that," Mary said, then waved him off. She started wiping the counter. The barista handed Jake his latte.

"She came in here," he tried again.

Mary stopped and stared at him as if he was stupid. She looked around her shop. "Is your friend invisible?"

"Well," Jake's face flushed an even deeper shade.

"Kait, is there someone in the bathrooms?"

"No, ma'am."

"Have you served his friend?" Mary motioned to Jake.

"He showed me a picture. Kathy Perkins kinda looks like his friend, but she hasn't come in today."

"Thanks, Kait." Mary pointed to Jake. "Now that you know there's no one here, you can behave or I can call the sheriff."

I leaned back with a sigh.

Jake groused and plopped into a booth, nursing his latte. He faced the back hallway and stared, sipping his drink. He spotted the camera and glanced into it as if he knew where I was hiding.

I swallowed, rubbing the hollow spot in my chest. I'd never felt so alone.

Chapter Sixteen
Dyson

Posing for photographs with fans and plastering on my signature show smile felt strained and inauthentic. Would the masses see through me?

Lucy glared at me, her arms crossed tightly over her chest, her eyes narrowed in anger. She silently judged me from ten feet away.

My mom appeared at her side and Lucy animatedly swept her arm in my direction. My mother frowned and shook her head.

Ah, hell.

"I need a break," I told Asher. "Let's see if we can sneak away."

"Sure, bruh." Asher stepped between the next set of folks and told the line I had to use the restroom.

Maybe I should. I needed time alone to ponder what I'd just done to Callie and us if my sister was speaking the truth.

As I turned to retreat, I stepped on Enzo's foot. "Yo asshat, what did you do to my sister?" He poked me in the chest.

"Do? I didn't *do* anything." I glanced around and lowered my voice. "Let's go someplace where we can talk without a phone in our faces."

"Sure. But you have some explaining to do." He stuck his hands in the pockets of his khaki shorts and walked by my side.

"You have some explaining, too. Like why the hell are you

here?"

My long stride outpaced Enzo's, and he scurried to keep up. We reached the admin tent, and I lifted the flap and held it for Enzo until he entered. The tent was noticeably warmer than when I'd last been inside. It was damn near hot now. And Enzo kept crowding my space.

"Back off, man. I need breathing room."

"I won't until you tell me what you did to my sister. I've not seen her so crushed since Dad died. What happened?"

I plopped into a metal folding chair and buried my head in my hands. "I wish I knew," I lamented.

A waft of cooler air breezed my legs. I glanced up in time to see my mom, Lucy, Asher, and Lydia enter the white tent.

I wished my father hadn't gone on a fishing trip with Uncle Bob. I could use Dad's guidance right now.

"What in God's name happened?" I aimed that demand at my sister. With an angry stride, Lucy approached, her eyes briefly assessing Enzo before focusing on me.

"Callie's personal CarTube account has been hacked. She's worried sick that stalker bastard has more footage of you—especially the more intimate moments. All she wanted was your help to find the culprit."

Lucy stood over me, arms crossed, a stern look on her face, her silence more intimidating than any words. I leaned back, my mistake settling on my shoulders like a lead cloak, and I felt like an ass.

"All the videos I viewed appeared to be clips from Callie's phone or things I sent her. How could he have hacked her phone too?" I said, opening the CarTube app and slowly scrolling through the episode thumbnails. "How could Jake have had access to her phone?"

"He was at the reunion, remember?" Asher pointed out. "He was following her on her walk."

"But Callie was on the phone with me the entire time she was walking," Enzo recalled.

"That's right." Lucy nodded at Enzo.

Encircled by my family and Enzo, I couldn't think. I knew one thing: I needed to find Callie and talk.

My mother sat beside me, a comforting presence in the stifling room. "Do you remember anytime she left her phone or computer by itself?"

"It had to have been after Denali because there were clips of you dancing with her," Lucy said.

I closed my eyes, remembering the weight of Callie in my arms, her effervescent laughter, and her bright eyes as we swayed. Such a sweet memory.

My eyes popped open. "Well, once she left her phone at Aunt Esther's lodge to charge. We picked it up the next day."

Lydia nodded. "I remember seeing it." Her gaze narrowed on her brother.

Asher remained quiet but nodded, rubbing his chin.

"Callie wasn't married to her phone, either. I mean, she left it charging downstairs when we were upstairs..." Could I have jeopardized her safety? "Could someone have broken in and sent themselves the information?"

I met everyone's eyes before glancing at her channel once more.

"There has to be a clue in the content. The episodes were all posted within the last three days. Every clip I see is from our Alaska trip–the Flat Top Mountain hike, the train ride, the lingerie store, us dancing in Denali. None from the road trip or the reunion."

"The lingerie store?" Lydia mumbled, pulling out her phone and checking Callie's channel on the CarTube app.

Enzo shifted his weight, leaning over my phone. "You took the road trip with the Porsche, right?"

I nodded.

He shook his head, his dark hair falling over his eyes. "This isn't right. Callie didn't post these. There's none with that race car. You know how she loved it. She would have had no qualms posting about that beautiful machine."

I sat back. Hope flared. I hadn't thought about that.

"What about the man who delivered the Porsche?" Asher suggested.

"Her phone was with us at our lodge that day, remember?" Lydia corrected, Asher nodded again, and the tips of his ears turned red.

"So, the suspects are the stalker and a car transporter man," Lucy listed.

"What about the schmuck who tried to steal my sister's underwear?" Enzo asked, meeting my gaze.

My gaze slid to Asher. "Want to explain?"

My cousin's shoulders slumped, and his gaze dropped to his scuffed shoes, his face falling. "That Jake guy seemed rich. He told me he'd give me ten thousand dollars to get a pair of Callie's underwear." His gaze snapped to Enzo, who wore a disgusted expression. "I wasn't going to give him her real panties. I was going to buy some and get the money."

Enzo folded his arms over his chest and glared daggers. Poised like a coiled snake ready to strike, he growled, "I have no words."

A phone chimed. Everyone glanced at their devices. "It's me," Lucy waved.

"Where did Callie go?" I asked Enzo while Lucy checked her texts.

"She went to your motel to pack. She's planning on flying home today." Enzo glanced at his watch. "I don't blame her."

Adrenaline surged as I jumped to my feet, ready to sprint to the motel and catch her before it was too late.

I texted Callie a message.

Me:

I'm a dick. We need to talk.

But it bounced back as blocked. "Son of a bitch. She blocked me."

"I would have blocked you too," Lucy said. "And you," she pointed to Enzo. "Why did you send her off with the stalker in his car? He won't take her to the motel." She waved her phone at him. "She's afraid and planning her escape."

"What do you mean? What car?" My heart leapt to my throat. I launched to my sister's side, but Enzo beat me to her. She lifted her screen so we could see the texts.

Enzo spun, running his fingers through his hair. "Oh no. I can't believe it."

Lucy's phone pinged again. This time, a map of Callie's current location popped up. Lucy glanced at my mother. "Come on, Mom. Let's go get Callie and bring her home."

My mom nodded and stood. She placed a hand on my cheek and said, "Don't worry, son. We'll find her."

I started following them toward the exit, but Lucy whirled and held her hand up. "Dyson, after what you pulled today, you wait here. We've got this." Lucy followed Mom without a look back.

Asher's phone chimed. He glanced at the screen, then lifted his head, wearing a smirk.

"What are you doing?" Lydia asked Asher, pointing to his phone.

His smile faltered, and he stuffed his phone away. "Nothing. Just scrolling."

Ignoring Asher's existence, Enzo turned to me. "We need to go after her."

"I know. But where is she?" A wave of helplessness washed over me, leaving me feeling utterly powerless.

"I'm a dumbass," Enzo said, smacking his forehead. He waved his phone. "Callie and I share our locations. Oops, my phone was on airplane mode, but I received the same messages as Lucy."

He pulled up Callie's live location. A blue dot pinpointed her on the map.

"We can't let my sister and mother go alone. Who knows what that dick could do? Let's go," I said, my voice tight with a mix of anxiety and resolve.

With a stiff nod, Enzo said, "I took an Uber from the airport. We'll need a car."

"I've got one. And it's fast." I pulled out the Porsche fob and dangled it in front of him. As if hypnotized, Enzo's gaze followed the swaying fob. I hurried toward the exit but paused.

"Sorry I can't fit you," I said to Asher and Lydia.

"That's okay, you go." Lydia grabbed me in a fierce hug. "I need some quality time with my little brother. We'll just enjoy the festival. Let us know when Callie is safe." She released me and I strode to a volunteer with a walkie.

"I have a family emergency and need to get out of here ASAP," I said, standing at my full height.

He contacted Gage, who understood and released my car.

In the GT3 RS, we each snapped on our harness. The sun had heated the interior, and between the temperature and my stress, I was sweating my balls off. The slight breeze through the open windows did little to stymie the heat while we waited for the volunteer team to maneuver people and vehicles and create a path out for us. I drummed my fingers on the steering wheel, each second feeling like an eternity. The weight of Callie's fate pressed down on me with the delay.

Motorheads pointed to my car and waved at Enzo and I. Gritting my teeth, I donned my CarTube persona and waved back.

"Come on. Come on," Enzo growled as he saluted a fan. "We'll never get out of here."

A large group of people gawked at the Porsche, blocking my progress. A volunteer, shouting over the din of the crowd, attempted to move the throng, but more people continued to filter in.

"Welcome to Gabby's Garage, the goofiest car show on all of

CarTube," I glanced at Enzo and revved the engine. "In today's episode, we'll learn how to part a crowd in thirty seconds." I revved the engine again.

Enzo grinned wickedly. "Let's roll."

Edging the Porsche forward, the crowd parted, and we finally reached the exit. Once on the road unhindered, I glanced over at Enzo. "Which way?"

"Stay straight on this road for a couple miles, then we'll turn right."

"Gotcha." I popped the clutch, shifted it into gear, and stomped on the gas. The quick acceleration pressed us back into the seats. Enzo's mouth tipped in a grin before he fixed his gaze on the blue dot on his phone screen.

Occasionally, Enzo looked up at street signs, but for the most part, he kept tracking Callie.

"Turn right onto Third Street," Enzo ordered, pointing to a street sign.

I jerked the wheel. Thank God for the safety harness.

Callie's face flashed before me. I can't believe I'd thought the worst of her. My actions had practically thrown her into Jake's clutches.

I held the wheel with a death grip. If Jake had harmed her–I'd hunt him down and end the threat.

"Looks like she's at a coffee shop." He leaned back and glanced at the street signs.

"That's good. Hopefully she'll be safe in public," I said, though not at all relieved. I wouldn't relax until I saw with my own eyes that she was safe, and preferably in my arms.

"I know who stole Callie's channel," Enzo admitted, giving me a side eye.

"You do?" I gasped. "Who?"

"Asher."

I rearranged my hold, loosening and tightening my grip. "Why my cousin?"

"Dude, he's total sus. He's the only one who had the opportunity. *And* he pulled the shady shit with my sister's underwear. Pervy bastard."

My blood pressure rose. Could it be true?

"Who knows, maybe he's in cahoots with Jake and he got paid to get into her phone and share stuff. Whatever the hows or whys, he's the one."

"But he's family–"

"You were quick enough to blame my sister–who's *my* family." My mouth dropped open to retort, but Enzo continued, "And I bet your hairy ass she never gave you reason to doubt her. Unlike your sketchy cousin."

My jaw snapped shut. I'd thought Callie had pulled the knife from my chest when she walked away from me earlier, but I must have been wrong. The pain in my chest was back, and this time the knife twisted a quarter turn clockwise. I'd royally screwed up with Callie. I shifted in my seat, determined to make things right, no matter the cost or how long it took.

"At the light, it's on the left," Enzo said, studying the building. "There's a police cruiser in the parking lot."

Jake's Jaguar was parked in a handicapped spot next to the door.

My heart sank. The lump in my throat made it hard to swallow. I whipped the Porsche into a tight turn and parked next to the cruiser and its flashing lights. Enzo and I peered inside the back of the police car but found it empty.

We hustled to the door. Enzo pulled it open, took three steps in, and came to a complete stop. I bumped into his back, then stepped around him. I shot him a *What the hell* look, before turning my attention to the room and its occupants.

The coffee shop had several booths lining the outer wall. Jake sat in a corner booth while an officer leaned over him, talking. Jake glared at me, and I returned it.

Women's voices came from around the corner. I stalked to

the counter, leaned over, and looked into the back room. My mother and sister faced away from me while Callie embraced my mother, holding her tight. Mom stroked her hair, and I suspected she was murmuring words of comfort like she'd done to me as a child.

At that moment, Callie's puffy, red eyes opened. Over my mother's shoulder, her gaze locked onto me with laser precision and fried my soul. I froze in place, savoring her nearness.

Her nose twitched as if she smelled something bad, and she lifted one of her hands, flipping me the bird. Any other time I would have laughed my ass off, but this wasn't one of them.

I hoofed it to the small room, Enzo on my six, and gathered Callie in my embrace, the scent of almonds and vanilla comforting me. Having her in my arms, I felt whole once more. She relaxed against me for a nano-second, then just as quick, she stiffened and pushed away. My heart ached to make things right.

"No, Dyson," Callie whispered as if she hadn't any strength.

Lucy stepped between us and widened the distance. "We're getting ready to leave. I'm taking her to the motel. And don't you follow us." She poked me in the chest.

"Callie?" I tried again.

"Don't, Dyson," Callie cringed as if I'd slapped her. "I can't..."

"Go, son." Mom placed a warm hand on my arm. "We'll take care of her. Don't worry. She's safe now. We'll catch up later."

I nodded and backed out of the room. Not knowing what else to do, I placed an order for an iced coffee. My focus bounced from Callie to the stalker as I paced and sipped.

As the women made their way through the eating area, Lucy attempted to block Jake's view of Callie.

"There's my girl," Jake hummed. The officer stepped between him and the door, effectively blocking his way out.

"Shut up, you," I growled.

"She's a free woman. Now that you F'ed up your relationship," Jake needled.

Blood pounded in my ears and I balled my fists. Enzo grabbed my shirt at my waist and tugged. When I met his eyes, he shook his head.

"When do I get paid, boss?" Jake called with a sneer.

My gaze snapped to Jake, who stared at Enzo. Enzo snorted.

"Ah, come on, boss. Tell your sister the truth. You paid me to come up here and keep an eye on them." He motioned to me and Callie.

"My brother wouldn't do that," Callie growled with wild, feral eyes.

Jake ran his hand through his greasy hair as he leaned back. "Why don't you tell them the truth about how we met, Jay. About how you wanted me to play cupid for Dyson and your sister."

Enzo glared, tight-lipped.

"And tell her how we met at the Kansas City Car Meet..."

Enzo sighed and closed his eyes.

Chapter Seventeen

Callie

"Jay?" I stepped toward my brother. "Jay?"

His shoulders dropped, and a sigh escaped his lips.

"No," I whispered, my voice paper thin.

I didn't mean for any of this to happen. I met Jake at the Kansas City meet. Since then, I thought he was a friend." Jay crossed his arms and glowered at the stalker turned kidnapper.

I shivered and swayed on my feet. Concern etched on his face, Dyson stepped forward, but I backed into Lucy. She hooked her arm with mine.

"Thank you," I whispered to her.

"No problem."

I focused on my twin. "Why?"

"I asked him to look after you, maybe give you and Dyson a little shove together. I didn't expect him to stalk you... Watch after you, yes, but not the stalker bullshit."

"How was he supposed to look after me?" I gasped when it suddenly hit me. "You shared my location with him..." I couldn't keep the disgust from my tone. "Even after all the creepy crap on the plane, the hike, and then the underwear."

"Sorry."

Jake had scooted back against the wall. He'd been watching

the shit hit the proverbial fan since my rescuers and would-be rescuers arrived. I rubbed my forehead.

First the website, then Dyson, then Jake, then my brother.... Men sucked.

"You hacked my CarTube account. What's the password, dickweed?" I yelled to Jake.

He let out a low, throaty laugh that ended in a loud snort. "I didn't hack anything. I didn't need to. Your brother gave me everything I needed."

"Liar," I cried. "He's an asshole, but not that much of one."

"Callie, I didn't give anyone any information about your channel. It was Dyson's cousin Asher who hacked it."

"What?" My knees buckled. Thank God for Lucy. "He what?"

"No, no," Judy groaned. "Not again."

"How much did you offer to pay him this time?" I spat to Jake.

Jake sat up and sneered. "Listen Calloway Turbo–"

"Don't you call her that." Jay lunged at Jake. Dyson and the cop caught him and held him back.

Hearing my dad's nickname for me was like a sucker punch to my gut. My chest tightened, tears blurred my vision, and I groped behind me for the coffee shop's door handle. Someone helped me out of the building, and I inhaled the fresh air, trying to shake off the new wave of PTSD from Dad's death.

I closed my eyes and inhaled through my nose and exhaled through my mouth. Someone rubbed my back. The anxiety slowly dissipated until I heard Dyson say, "Breathe, Callie."

I stiffened and jerked away from his touch. "Don't touch me."

"I royally screwed up. I'm sorry, Callie." He pleaded with his hands out, palms up.

I knew he was sorry. I could hear the regret in his tone, but I couldn't... I just couldn't.

"I told you in the hangar, I'm not a liar," I spoke as one betrayed and not trusting. "I also told you not to break my heart, and..." I closed my eyes and swallowed. When I opened them,

Dyson appeared to have aged and shrunk in size.

"I can't be with anyone who thinks I'm a liar."

"Callie, please."

"No. It's over, Dyson." The remnants of my heart shattered, and the heels of his betrayal ground them to a fine sand.

He took a micro step towards me.

"Don't." I held my hand up, stopping him from getting any closer.

A waft of java floated over the breeze as my brother exited the coffee shop. He spotted me and sauntered over. A determined yet contrite expression, etched with lines of both resolve and regret, crossed his features. "Listen, Callie," Jay started.

"Nope." I shook my head. There was nothing either of these men could say or do to fix anything.

I pointed at my brother. "Don't talk to me unless you get the password to my account." and then I pointed at Dyson. "Don't contact me at all."

His mouth fell open, and his hazel eyes widened. Then his mouth snapped shut.

"Let's go, honey," Judy said. She pulled me into a hug.

"The sheriff said you could go, and you've said your piece to these m…These two persons. Definitely not *men*." Lucy glared at our brothers. "Now, let's get you out of here so you can pack. We'll let the sheriff deal with the jerk."

I nodded. Judy, Lucy, and I climbed into Aunt Betsy's borrowed SUV. As I buckled into the seatbelt, I glanced out the window and noticed the one-of-a-kind GT3 RS. "Odd. I feel nothing."

I closed my eyes and leaned back against the headrest. If that beautiful, sleek beast of a car did nothing to stir my emotions, then I must truly be broken.

Great.

I tried to breathe slowly and deeply, to keep the dam of grief and sorrow at bay. Once on the plane, I hoped I could just sleep the flight away, but I had to pack first.

It seemed like only seconds passed before we were at the motel. I flashed the keycard and unlocked the door. Lucy found my travel case and unzipped it, laying it on the bed. I folded my shirts and pants. When I opened my undergarment drawer, I froze.

"What's wrong?" Lucy asked, placing a hand on my arm.

I glanced up at her, catching my reflection in the mirror. I'd gone pale, as if I'd seen a ghost.

Maybe I had. The memories associated with those items would haunt me. Frozen, I stared with bittersweet longing at the new lingerie. "I can't take these."

I slammed the drawer closed, so hard that it bounced back open an inch.

"Okay. What about the bathroom?" Lucy asked, distracting me.

Like a zombie, I shuffled into the tiny space. I packed my toiletries, ignoring the spent condom wrappers in the trash. I bit my lip to keep it from trembling. Anger was my lifeline, but this grief was a relentless tide—and the combination of emotions threatened to break me. A heavy sigh escaped my lips as I wiped my eyes and blew my nose.

"I don't understand why your brother hired that Jake guy," Lucy stated quietly, a frown furrowing her brow.

"I don't understand either." I tossed my toothbrush into my makeup bag.

I'd purge my items once I got home. Anything related to Dyson Gabbard and the Alaska fiasco was destined for the trash bin.

"I wonder if Jay hired him because he didn't trust Dyson," Lucy mused.

I offered a one-shoulder shrug as I zipped my bag. I couldn't care less at this point. It happened and what could I do to change it?

As I hefted the backpack over my shoulder, I gave a last glance around the room, and then I tossed my room key onto the bed.

I suppose it's better to end it now than become more invested and find out years later I'd made a horrible mistake.

That thought did little to comfort me. And yeah, the hurt was painful, whether now or in the future.

Lucy and I returned to the SUV and then Judy drove me to Fairbanks International Airport. Judy pulled up to the departure area and let me off. Like I was an old lady, Lucy escorted me to the first airline I saw. Tugging my rolling bag, I approached the woman at the check-in counter. Luckily, there was a lull between flights and the terminal was relatively quiet.

The agent glanced up from her phone, a frown furrowing her brow as she noticed us approaching.

"Hi, my day has been a nightmare, culminating in a heartbreaking split with the person I thought was my soulmate. I'm looking to get home to Kansas, so I can crawl into bed and cry for two weeks straight." I inhaled, swiped at a renegade tear, and continued. "Can you help me or can you point me to where I can buy a ticket?"

The woman's countenance softened. "You poor dear. Let's see what we can do." She tapped on her computer keyboard. After a while, she said, "Hmm. Looks like I can get you on a flight to Minneapolis that will get you to the lower forty-eight today. It's in two hours. Otherwise, you'll have to wait until tomorrow."

"No. I can't wait."

The overwhelming need to flee was almost unbearable. Maybe I could breathe easier if I were states away from Dyson. "I'll take the Minneapolis flight. Thanks," I said, slapping my credit card on the counter.

"Let's look for a connecting flight for you," she said, her smile gentle and understanding. "Get you all the way home."

"That would be great." I sighed and offered my airline angel a strained but grateful smile. At least as grateful as I could muster, given the circumstances.

Once I had the tickets in hand, Lucy and I made for a bench. I wished for sleep, a dark, comforting blanket to help me forget. Even if it was only temporary.

"Do you have somebody to pick you up?" Lucy asked.

"Oh. I hadn't thought of that." Great, something else to throw a wrench into the works.

I shot Amber a quick text, asking what her day looked like and if she could swing by the airport to get me.

A minute later she responded:

Amber:
Jay and I can come get you.

Me:
Jay is unavailable. He's in Alaska.

Amber:
Really? I thought that was your thing. Why are you coming home early?

Me:
Long story. Can you pick me up?

Amber:
Sure. Let me know what time.

Me:
Thank you.

I sent her a picture of my boarding bass with the flight number and time, and promised to keep her updated if there were changes.

Judy found Lucy and me and led us to a cafe, where the aroma of freshly brewed coffee filled the air.

"You need to eat something," Judy said.

"I'm fine. I don't think my stomach can handle anything." Nothing sounded good. "You shouldn't have parked. It's going to cost a million dollars."

She waved. "Pffft. it's nothing. Lucy wanted to wait until you were through TSA, and I agreed. We didn't want you to be alone."

Under their persistence, I bought a coffee and sipped and nibbled on an energy bar.

Judy instructed me to keep my eyes open for people with shifty behavior. And described clever crooks she'd read about on a blog.

I knew she was trying to distract me from my dour thoughts. That offering of distraction, like a branch tossed into the raging river of my soul, was welcome, but I remained numb and adrift. I kept slipping in and letting go. I struggled to maintain focus, my broken heart dragging my thoughts down like a heavy stone.

My eyelids felt like sandpaper grating against my eyeballs, a heavy weight pressed on my chest, and my energy had been completely drained. I just wanted to sleep.

As Lucy and Judy talked cheerfully for my benefit, I studied their family resemblance. It was the shape and color of their eyes that reminded me the most of Dyson.

I bit my lip, pulled my coffee closer, and inhaled its dark roasted aroma. Missing Dyson and what we had was inevitable, yet I couldn't bring myself to trust him to not hurt me again.

How could he *think* I'd stoop to using him? He knew from firsthand experience with Enzo's Auto Tech that I chose *not* to be in the limelight. I hated my brother exploiting my physical attributes. If I'd wanted to capitalize on *that* audience, I could have easily done it with Enzo's Auto Tech, using those viewers to launch a new sexy channel.

I didn't want to focus on the views or subscriber count. Sure, the money was nice, but Enzo's Auto Tech was thriving and we had enough to pay the bills and then some. Add in the sale of a car or parts here and there and we made enough to experiment. Sponsorships and ad placement were the main sources of revenue, the essentials keeping the operation going.

Some of our sponsors might drop us, though, if they saw Asher's version of my show. I needed to contact a lawyer to see what our options were in case that happened.

And Jay–how could I trust my brother again? How could I still work with him and keep my promise to my father?

I stared at the font on the cafe menu, pondering how to punish my brother. He'd wanted me to pick the next car… I would. I had a car in mind. A European car, not quite old—but not new, either. One I'd been wanting to fix for a while now.

Yes. That was it. Find the parts, fix the car, then race it. I'd do it all.

Maybe I'd find two similar cars, and Jay and I could compete to restore them. "Hmm." I felt a very tiny flicker of… Hope? Could the way out of this mess be focusing on the business? That would help me keep my promise to Dad.

Business would be business.

"Callie, are you okay?" Lucy asked, her brows pinched with concern.

I sighed but wouldn't lie. "Of course not." I attempted a tiny smile, "But I will be. Ferenzos are tough."

After Mom left us, Dad repeated that phrase to eight-year-old Jay and me. We lived by it until he died.

"I just thought of a new idea for Enzo's Auto Tech. It will keep me busy. And keep me away from my brother." I grinned, itching to get my laptop out and search the car forums for a deal.

"That's great." Lucy leaned toward me. "New car?"

My smile turned full bloom. "Yes, but I'm not going to say more yet. I need to find it first. Maybe two, one for Jay and one for me."

Judy glanced at her watch, then stood. "It's time for Callie to get in line for security."

Lucy hopped to her feet and drew me in for a hug. "You will text me when you land, right? I'm not letting go until you say you will." The taller woman rocked back and forth, making me chuckle.

"Fine. Yes, yes. I will."

She finally let me go, then Judy held me. In a mother's embrace, the dam that'd been holding back my emotion started to crumble. She whispered in my ear, "Dyson loves you, dear. Everyone makes mistakes. He made a really big one, but I hope you can forgive him."

When we pulled apart and our gazes met, her eyes were as watery as mine. She reached for me and touched my cheek. "Be safe."

I inhaled, picked up my bag, and, with a final glance at my new friends–two wonderful ladies who could have been family, I waved.

Chapter Eighteen

Dyson

Enzo gave a statement to the sheriff. Then we went back to the car show. As bad as things were looking for my Gabby's Garage channel, I felt obligated to honor this commitment. We rode back in silence.

After I'd handed out the final car show award, Enzo and I walked around the festival aimlessly. Like Callie, he'd never visited Alaska before.

Enzo planned to return to Kansas on Monday, but until then, he might as well stay with me. We could sulk together, and he'd keep me updated on Callie's location. At least I'd be able to know if she returned home safely.

Mom had texted Dad, urging his immediate return. Once he'd showered off the fishy smell, Lucy, Enzo, Mom, and I went through the whole mess with him. Dad suggested heading to a bar within walking distance of the motel. Enzo and I trailed him into the dimly lit interior. The odor of stale beer hung heavy in the air.

Aunt Esther waved, catching our attention. We maneuvered toward the high-top table where she and my cousins waited. I brought up the rear because I didn't want to be around Asher.

Enzo spotted him and stalked over, looming menacingly in his space. "Listen, man, you're going to give me the password now."

Despite being a few inches shorter than my cousin, Enzo was angry on his sister's behalf, and I'd seen a hint of volatile madness flickering in his vibrant green eyes.

Asher started, "I don't–"

"Why don't we just login and change it now so I know you're out?" Enzo slid onto the stool next to Asher and leaned further into his space.

Not denying the accusation only solidified his guilt. I fisted my hands to keep them from trembling. A burning rage swelled in my chest, and I clenched my jaw in frustrated silence. I sat as far from Asher as I could, trying to avoid him.

"My phone is almost dead," Asher said, staring at the screen.

Enzo's heavy hand dropped on Asher's shoulder and squeezed, his knuckles whitening. "Then you better hurry." My gaze shot to Enzo's face—I'd never heard his voice so low or deadly.

Lydia folded her arms, glaring at her brother. "I recognized the video from the lingerie store. I kept an eye on you while we were there because I thought you might be uncomfortable. So I know where you were standing, and that video was from your point of view. It wasn't that Jake jerk. It was you."

Asher's narrowed gaze flicked to his sister, then his shoulders slumped. He ran his fingers through his hair as his face blazed blotchy-red.

"Son of a bitch." I pounded the table with a fist, realizing he'd captured footage of Callie shopping in Anchorage. "You little asshole," I growled, rising to my feet.

Dad put a hand out and grabbed my arm. Glaring at my cousin, I strained against my father's grasp as I tried to reach Asher.

"Just do it Asher, you don't want Callie to sue you. How would you pay the bill? Or bail?" Lydia asked, handing me a pint.

I took the glass but had to set it on the high-top table so I wouldn't spill it. Beyond mad my hands shook. It's a good thing Enzo worked Asher, because if I *talked* with him I'd definitely regret what I would say. And the *talking* would get physical.

My greedy cousin not only hurt Callie, but he'd ruined my future. It burned that my own flesh and blood could stab me so deeply.

I downed the beer in three gulps, glowering at Asher after each one.

"It's not going to help," my dad said from beside me. He studied the empty glass.

"Nothing will," I muttered, the weight of despair pressing down on me. "I've lost her."

"Only time will help," Dad said, his words barely audible over the ambient din of the music, voices, and TV.

I glanced at my father, who glowered at Asher as well.

"Does the whole family know what Asher has done?" I asked, crossing my arms over my chest.

"Esther had to explain to Great Aunt Betsy why you and Callie won't be there tomorrow. She gave a brief version, but Betsy caught the gist."

"Oh." My brows rose. "Having Aunt Betsy on Asher's case is probably worse than anything I'd do. Especially since she approved of Callie," I admitted.

"She does like to give tongue lashings," Dad agreed, wearing a slightly evil smirk. "And Esther will make sure he sits next to Betsy."

"Almost wish I was going." I raised my empty glass and clinked Dad's bottle. Then downed the dregs.

Enzo hunched over Asher's phone as the two worked on Callie's channel. After about fifteen minutes and Asher saying *Ow* a few times, Enzo joined me and Dad at our side of the table.

"I've changed the password and made the videos private. No one can see anything now except the header page and her original intro video. I turned off the commenting on the video and changed the channel banner to a generic photo of some mountain from her trip. It has a moose in it." Enzo waved his hand, catching the eye of a server.

The train ride to Denali... I recalled Callie's passionate kisses when our pretending began to change to real.

"Did you delete the old videos?" I asked.

"No. She can do that if she wants. It might be therapeutic." He ordered from the server, then rubbed his face. "Man, what a shit show."

I nodded. "Shit show indeed." Meeting the server's eyes, I signaled for another beer.

"Are family reunions always like this?" Enzo asked.

My father barked out a laugh. "No. But there's always some family drama–someone newly divorced or married again–that type of thing." Dad studied his beer for a moment, then looked up. "Haven't you ever been to a reunion?"

Enzo's face pinched, and his gaze swept the room. "Nah. Dad was an only child. His parents were dead before I was born. I never knew my mom's family. She left us when I was eight."

"I'm sorry," Dad said.

"Don't be. Dad instilled in Callie and me our passion for all things cars. It might not have happened like that if my mother had been around. I love what I do." He picked up his glass and held it, staring into the amber liquid. Melancholy leached into his tone. "I hope Callie will stay with Enzo's Auto Tech. We're a team."

I'd hate it if I had facilitated a brother-sister duo break up. Then again, none of this would have happened if it wasn't for Jake—and all of that was on Enzo.

The bar vibrated with life. Laughter, discussions, romance–and I sat numb to it all, like I was in a wind tunnel. I was barely holding on.

My vision of the future had clouded. This morning, I'd seen myself with Callie by my side. Making our CarTube videos and visiting shows and places at the end of the road. Now?

Dad raised his eyes from his phone, then patted my arm. "Your mom is not coming to the bar. Lucy is stopping by, though."

I blinked my dry eyes.

"Son, you just have to give Callie time."

I nodded, staring at the Keno screen, watching numbers bubble up from fish, until the server brought me another beer. "Thanks."

Across from me, Enzo nursed his beer while studying Callie's location. "Looks like she's on the tarmac," he whispered. He set his phone on the high-top table and scrubbed his face.

I had no idea what I'd do now without Callie around. My entire plan, with the exception of the car show, had revolved around showing her Alaska and making this the trip of a lifetime. "So much for becoming a Callie master," I mumbled, lifting the amber brew, hoping it numbed the pain in my head, heart, and gut.

"Huzzah, I've found two assholes," Lucy announced loudly before plopping onto the stool between Enzo and me.

"Lucy," Dad chastised.

"What?" She appeared exasperated. "Tell me it's not true."

"Him, yes," Enzo said, pointing to me, "Me, I don't think so."

Lucy's eyes widened. "You are the biggest asshole here." Her nose crinkled as she inhaled, preparing to rail Enzo. I hugged myself and leaned back, ready to watch him squirm.

Enzo's brow furrowed in a pronounced V. "Right," he said sarcastically.

"Listen dipshit, if it wasn't for you, that stalker wouldn't have harassed Callie. Her anxiety wouldn't have been sky high. And that jerk put it in Asher's head that he could be rich and famous like his derpy cousin, Dyson, if he only listened to the creep's version of the rich and famous. That's all because of you prompting Jake the stalker to come here."

Enzo's jaw dropped, and his face and ears reddened. I couldn't tell if he was angry or mortified. But I was glad Lucy had given voice to my thoughts. She was so much better at tongue lashings than me—if I didn't know better, I'd swear she was Aunt Betsy's daughter.

As I watched Lucy's words sink into Enzo's brain, renewed anger took hold of me, overpowering my pain of loss. "Why the hell *did* you send Jake?"

Enzo's mouth snapped shut. He blinked, then shook his head. "I thought he was my friend. Jake had kept in touch with me since the Kansas City Car Meet. We'd get together every once in a while and grab a beer. He seemed cool. I mean, we'd known each other for nearly two years."

Enzo scrubbed his face and sighed. "When I mentioned to him I was worried about this trip, about Callie being with you–a near stranger, he suggested someone watch you two. I couldn't go. You all would see me. It all sounded good when he offered to do it and report back to me."

"Stranger, my ass. You and Callie have both known me longer than you knew Jake," I scoffed. Fingering the cool glass, I tamped down the urge to wring his neck. "And you shared her location with him."

Enzo's gaze snapped to mine. "She's my sister. I didn't know your true intentions."

I narrowed my eyes. "You could have asked me."

"Would you have told me you wanted to get in her pants?"

I pressed my lips together, fuming. *Did he really think so little of me?*

"Callie is a grown ass woman, Jay." Lucy came to my rescue. "If she didn't trust my brother, she wouldn't have come. And if she didn't want my brother in her pants, she could have said no." She poked Enzo in the shoulder. "It was you she shouldn't have trusted. And I guess now she doesn't trust either of you after what's transpired. And let me remind you that it's all," poke, "your," poke, "fault." Poke.

Lucy glanced at me, then back to Enzo. "When you see how

brokenhearted she is, remember you both did it."

She hopped to her feet, the stool making a horrid scraping noise. "I'm out." Nose in the air, she strode to the door.

My dad had listened without saying a word. He shook his head. "It's a shame. You boys have some groveling to do. Just let her be and when she's ready to talk, she'll let you know."

I studied my father, wondering how he'd spoken so assuredly. How many times over the thirty years of marriage had he screwed up, and what wisdom could I glean from him?

"How will I know she's ready to listen?" I asked, because I wanted to fix things now.

"You'll know." Dad lifted his beer to his lips.

"Very helpful," Enzo mumbled.

I finished my pint and debated having another. Why the hell not? Callie was gone, the event was over, and I wasn't doing diddly shit tomorrow. Raising my hand, I caught the bartender's attention, then indicated two. One for Enzo and one for me.

When we arrived back at my motel room, I noticed the lingering aroma of almonds and vanilla. I'd pounded one too many beers, and now my foggy brain flashed images of Callie every time I turned my head.

Enzo threw his duffle on the chair by the window. "Which bed?" he asked, staring at the two queens.

"Up to you," I replied, not caring.

I sighed, grateful housekeeping had made the beds, straightened the bathroom, and emptied the trash. Seeing the empty hangers and lack of anything Callie had me feeling numb— until I went to close a partially open drawer and discovered that she'd left her lingerie behind.

Could I ever make it up to her? Would she ever forgive me? Time would tell.

Time might be my greatest ally but impatience was my virtue.

Chapter Nineteen

Callie

Two weeks later

I floated through my early morning—coffee, shower, getting dressed—in a fog. Same routine, different day.

Routine fog—it's how I functioned after having my heart and trust shattered. Sometimes I arrived at the garage not remembering getting in the car. This morning was one of those times.

Opening my space, I inhaled the scents of construction—freshly sawn wood, drywall, and paint. I'd built a wall to section off the old detached two-car garage from the warehouse for my own show. "Enzo's Auto Tech Too." I grinned at the name.

Then I'd purchased a crash-damaged Porsche Boxster and worked to bring the convertible back to life. The problem wasn't the damaged panels, but the previous owner's neglectful maintenance.

I shook my head. "Why pay all that money for a car if you're not going to maintain it properly?"

I rubbed my hands. What was bad for the previous owner was good content for me. I'd already recorded examining the engine codes that had lit the dash up like a Christmas tree and changed the black, who-knows-when-it-had-been-changed-last oil.

I filmed close ups of my arms and gloved hands. I dubbed voice-overs in a man's voice. And while I abhorred how I'd been portrayed in Asher's hacked version of my show, I had enough business savvy to use the Callie Ferenzo/Enzo's Auto Tech search hype to my advantage with the new channel.

Already my two videos had garnered record numbers of subs and likes.

People liked the car, my skill, and my humor—which was mostly my sarcasm spilling over.

Luckily, the model I'd picked was somewhat common and it was easy to find parts, both OEM and retooled, if I needed.

"Callie, can you help me with my video?" Jay popped his head into my portion of the shop. He didn't come through the people door I'd built into the new wall—he'd learned that lesson the hard way.

I frowned but didn't stop what I was doing since I was in the middle of recording. I ignored him, but he stood in the doorway, like a hungry stray puppy.

"No. Figure it out," I clipped, focusing back on the oil filter housing.

"But I'm not the one with a degree in videography."

"You don't have a degree in being an asshole either, but that hasn't stopped you from mastering it," I chirped sweetly, then added, "Google it."

Jay huffed and pivoted. His steel-toed boots made a racket as he stomped away. It was high time he learned to appreciate all I'd done for Enzo's Auto Tech. But still guilt gnawed at and threatened to crumble my resolve to distance myself from him after the Alaska fiasco.

I barely spoke to Jay these days. The new wall was a very real representation of the barrier I'd built around my wounded heart.

Even with the wall, though, I could hear him tooling and

sometimes cursing his car. Which always made me smile. I'd run with the idea I'd had in the airport cafe—each of us restoring a car in competition. The only chance I'd given him to interact was the challenge of rebuilding his own Boxster on the original channel.

He'd used the first video featuring his car to gently taunt me and my ability. I say gently because he knows I can work rings around him. He didn't want to incite me into a frenzy.

Plus, his car was pretty much a cakewalk—or he thought so, at least. It had cosmetic damage inside and a scrape down the passenger side. Even Amber could have seen that. But although it looked solid, I could hear the engine. *It has a timing issue.* I smiled, a little evilly, because I was certain Jay hadn't noticed it yet.

And while I itched to get under the hood of his Boxster and check out the mechanics for myself, that would entail forgiving my brother and I wasn't quite ready yet.

I buttoned up what I was doing and cleaned up my space. I dumped the footage into my laptop and charged my devices.

As I snatched my purse and closed the overhead garage door, I heard my brother speaking to someone–a guy. It sounded as if they were trying to keep their voices low. Suspicious, I moved toward the people door in my wall and listened.

Dyson.

I gasped and stumbled away. Hurrying to my father's Jeep, I put it in gear. I reversed out of the drive as if any moment hell would vomit demons after me. I tossed one fleeting glance at Enzo's Garage and saw Jay and Dyson standing next to Dyson's giant, white Yukon.

I sped down the road and when the garage was out of sight, I inhaled deeply and swiped the water out of my eyes. I blew out a deep breath.

"Breathe, Callie. He wasn't there for you," I told myself.

While I tolerated my brother somewhat, he'd tried to insert little comments about how much Dyson still hurt after our separation.

Two things. Number one: how the hell would he know what a broken heart feels like? Jay had never been in love–head over heels, swoon-worthy–love before.

Number two: It was none of his freaking business.

I sighed when I arrived home. Amber peeked out the window and waved. I closed the front door, threw my purse on the table, and refilled my water bottle.

"You're home early," Amber said. Her head tilted to the side, and she studied me as if I had a great secret.

I didn't want to admit I was too chicken to be in the same building with Dyson. I wanted to simultaneously chew him out and run into his arms. It was easier to stay angry from a distance.

"I finished my project early today." I sucked down a long drink of water. Amber sat across the table from me, her laptop open. "Now I have to organize the footage and edit it."

"Ever since your trip to Alaska, you've been home more." Amber blinked her big brown eyes.

I opened my mouth to retort, but she continued, "I like it. It's nice because I see you more. You worked too much, in my opinion."

"You missed me?" I attempted to keep the shock out of my tone.

"Why does that surprise you? We're friends, but we don't do things together anymore." Amber shrugged her shoulders.

"You're home early too." The time on the microwave clock was just before four.

"I took a personal day because I had a dentist appointment." She motioned to her laptop. "I'm catching up with some work emails now."

"You want to go out to dinner tonight? I could use a glass of wine." I rubbed my chin.

A sweet smile blossomed on Amber's lips. "Sounds like a plan."

"Great. I'll go wash the grime away."

"Take your time. I've got a ton to do." She waved me away and focused on her screen.

I reveled in the hot water, trying to think about the parts I needed to order for my Porsche Boxster and not how miserable Dyson had sounded.

I applied makeup and put on a sundress. I wasn't looking for a guy, but I wanted to feel pretty. Having a good time with my friend would distract me from the hole in my heart.

I slipped on a pair of strappy sandals and rounded the corner into the kitchen. The front door was open a crack, and I went to close it, but then heard voices. I pulled it open and froze.

On the front lawn, Amber squared off against Dyson. Although Dyson was a foot taller than her, he looked wilted—almost as if she'd slapped him like a bad puppy.

"You should leave, Dyson. Now is not a good time," Amber warned.

"I know. I just need to talk with her." Dyson said.

"She's not ready to talk. You should leave."

"I know she's not ready today, but I'll wait until *she is* ready." Dyson nodded his head.

Amber pointed to his big car hogging our driveway. "You're not gonna wait here. Go."

"I deserve how she's reacting." His shoulders drooped even further, if that was possible. The dark bags under his eyes were so large I could see them from where I stood, and his beard looked patchy. He wore wrinkled clothes like he'd slept in them or picked them up off the floor.

I bit my lip. My heart attempted to feel every feeling under the Kansas sun. Our separation hurt him as well.

He did this to us. Remember.

I squared my shoulders. "Amber, are you ready to go?" I asked, keeping my gaze on my friend.

Her brows pinched. She tossed one more look at the unwanted guest, then strode toward me. "Sure."

Amber hooked elbows with me and led me inside. She closed and locked the door, then tugged my zombie-like body along to her car in the garage. I managed a silent apology to my Crosley Hotshot as we walked by it—the car hadn't run right since I'd returned home, and I didn't have the heart to work on it.

"Sit and buckle up," Amber ordered.

Without hesitation, I got in her Honda and secured myself. She opened the garage door. I kept my eyes closed until we'd left.

"We're good," Amber said, glancing in the rearview mirror.

"Thank you for sticking up for me." I turned to the window, Dyson's betrayal stinging my heart all over again. "I just can't deal with him right now."

Amber drove silently; the quiet and her competent, steady driving gave my heart time to calm. Cornfields passed by until I sat up and asked, "Where are we going?"

A little smirk teased Amber's lips. "Someplace new. It's near my parent's place about twenty minutes from here."

"Great." I sat on my hands and studied the cotton ball clouds.

"How's your car project coming along?" Amber finally asked.

I glanced at her with a side eye. "Do you really want to know, or did Jay ask you to ask me?" I crossed my arms.

"Me, a spy?" She placed a hand over her heart in mock shock. "How dare you?"

"Well, my brother's a nosy asshole."

Amber giggled. "And yes, he is. He totally asks me to get you to talk about the competition."

"He does?" I gasped, surprised she admitted it.

"Yeah, don't worry. I'm still mad at how he treated you. I know you are going to win. I have a feeling, plus even if I wanted to leak some juicy car techno details, I'd have to know what you're talking about. Hmm. Maybe I *should* pass information because I'm sure to screw it up." She giggled again. "I could be your secret weapon."

I laughed at her logic. "Maybe so. I did a few things today. Just basic maintenance that hadn't been done in forever. It was gross."

Amber frowned. "I don't understand why people won't maintain a car, especially if you spend a good chunk of change for a fancy model."

"Age old question, but it's good for me." I rambled on about the car until we reached the steakhouse.

The meal was fabulous, and we sampled a few wines. I'd almost forgotten about Dyson until we neared our house.

The white Yukon was parked on the street. The Honda's lights panned Dyson as he sat on the front steps. "What the hell?" I mumbled.

"I'll park and get the mail," Amber said, pushing the garage door opener.

"It's okay. I'll get the mail and tell him off. Maybe he'll get the hint and leave me alone."

"Are you sure?" Amber asked with concern in her tone. She paused the car long enough for me to open the door.

"I'll live." It was the truth. All this heartache meant I was alive. *And what doesn't kill you, makes you stronger—right?* "Besides, I've got to interact with him professionally."

I shuffled the mail as I walked back to the house. Amber closed the garage, so I had to take the steps to the front door. That meant I had to walk past Dyson. I took deep breaths, refusing to meet his gaze.

Instead, I watched him wring his hands as I approached. He straightened and stood as I neared.

"Callie, I–"

"Don't," I cut him off. My gaze snapped to his. "Don't you dare say anything to me." Anger coursed through me. My face heated, and I wanted to run inside, jump on my bed and scream into my pillow.

Dyson hung his head and nodded.

I hurried past him and hopped up the steps. Dyson waited until my hand was on the door. "Callie?"

I paused but did not turn.

"I will be here when you want to talk."

My blood ignited. I spun. "I don't *want* you here. Just leave." I retreated inside to my room, where I flopped on my bed and cried into my pillow.

The next morning, I forced myself into the routine fog. I poured my second cup of coffee. Amber worked on her first cup and stared outside into the dawn.

She glanced at me and frowned. "You won't believe what's outside."

"A rainbow?" I asked, then sipped. The warmth filled me and I hummed.

"Not quite." She pressed her lips together and returned to the window.

My curiosity piqued, I ambled to Amber's side and peered out onto the front lawn. "Holy shit." I raised my cup to my lips as I tried to make sense of the scene.

Dyson sat in a camping chair, the kind that folded and had a footrest and cup holders. He had it reclined, his head tipped back and to the side, and he used a light jacket as a blanket. His eyes were closed in sleep and his long legs were stretched to the max, hanging over the end of the footrest.

"That looks uncomfortable," Amber whispered, as if she was trying not to wake Dyson.

"Was he there all night?" I asked.

"It looks like it," Amber said.

"Why would someone do that?"

"He must want to talk to you really badly." She sipped her coffee, staring at our squatter.

I finished my coffee and decided to leave the house via the garage even though the Jeep was in the driveway. Driving my father's Jeep offered a measure of comfort, and I suspected I would need it this morning after seeing Dyson asleep in the yard.

I snuck out to my Jeep, but in my rearview mirror, I saw

Dyson stand and stretch. I instantly recalled his toned body, his happy trail, and how his muscular form felt.

By the time I entered Enzo's Auto Tech Too's garage, I really had my work cut out for me. I had to shake my memories and focus or I'd lose my bet with Jay and potentially screw up the car.

Chapter Twenty
Dyson

Amber cleared her throat behind me as I watched Callie drive away for the third morning in a row. I shifted in my chair, inspecting the woman dressed in white pants and a bright pink blouse. Her gaze was intense as she studied me.

Based on how coldly Amber had received me when I knocked on their door three days ago, I wasn't sure how this conversation would go. She had stood up for her friend and placed herself between Callie and me.

Truthfully, the woman could call the police and report me for trespassing. But she hadn't. Yet, anyway.

"You love her, don't you?" Amber asked from the porch, tilting her head, making her blonde ponytail swish.

"Yes," I answered simply.

Amber sipped her coffee and continued inspecting me.

Callie had yet to say more than a few words to me but, day after day, I had remained in this ass-numbing chair, patiently waiting for her to open up and listen.

"Dyson," Amber finally said. "Would you like coffee?"

Surprised, I stood and walked to the porch. "That would be great."

"Come in for a minute." She beckoned me inside. Once I

stepped over the threshold, she whirled around and poked me in the chest. "Don't you dare tell Callie I let you in or she might give me the same treatment she's giving you."

She filled a mug and handed it to me.

"If you haven't noticed, she's not talking to me, let alone giving me a chance to say anything. Even if I wanted to rat you out, I couldn't." I sipped and hummed. Having something warm and fresh to ingest was awesome and her coffee tasted divine. "Thanks, it's nice to have something not delivered."

Aghast, Amber said, "You don't *stay* out there, do you?"

"Yes. I've been hanging in your front yard for three days and nights." I sipped the coffee again. "I'm really lucky it hasn't rained. And a little surprised your neighbors haven't reported me to the police."

Amber sighed. "Well, I suppose, having a squatter around would scare away any thieves."

I shrugged. "It's a quiet area. The lady with the golden retriever always waves at me. "

Amber lowered her mug to the table. "What do you do for food?"

"I was serious when I said I had it delivered."

"And the bathroom?"

"It's the only time I've left, but I have watered your bushes around the side a few times,"

"Ugh," Amber groaned. "Don't water the bushes. I'll leave the door unlocked so you can come inside."

Grateful for the small luxury, I smiled. "Thank you so much. I won't tell a soul."

"You better not." She stood and refilled her cup. "More?"

I lifted my mug, and she filled it. "Thanks."

"So, what now?" Amber asked, leaning against the counter and staring into her mug.

"Now I wait until Callie is ready to yell at me or hear me out." I sighed. "I'm in it for the long haul."

Amber's gaze lifted and locked onto mine. "Callie is filling her time following her CarTube dream, so she doesn't have to deal with her emotions. She shut down when her dad died but then, at least, she'd talk about him. This time is different. She won't talk about anything other than the show. I suppose, it's safe and its newness brings a measure of excitement to her."

A lump formed in my throat. *I did this to her.* I squeezed my eyes shut, willing the tears not to form. Guilt eroded my mind like salt on an underbody.

As if sensing my emotional crisis, Amber carried on, "She's really good at it–the whole car thing. From the mechanics to the videography."

I opened my eyes and smiled. Even Amber, a non-car person, recognized Callie's prowess. "Yes. She knows her stuff and then some. I don't know how many times she's educated me on details."

Amber nodded. "I wish I could speak *car*, but it's like a foreign language to me. Honestly, I just want the car to go. I really don't care about the hows or whys." She sighed.

"I'm sure she appreciates you listening," I said, hoping to encourage Amber to be there for Callie when I couldn't.

"Even if my eyes glaze over?" Amber asked with a smirk.

I couldn't help but chuckle. "I can watch her newest video and come up with some comments for you."

Amber tilted her head, rubbing her chin as she contemplated my offer. She nodded slowly. "Sure. But it's got to be somewhat generic, so I might be able to understand her reply."

"Fair." I leaned back in the chair. "You could always ask her about how she keeps her nails clean compared to Jay's. Or something like why her videos are consistently twenty-eight minutes long."

"They are?"

"Yeah. Most of them." I lifted my mug and inhaled the rich aroma.

"Huh. There's so much I don't know about your all's business.

And so much more to it than I would have thought." Amber frowned as she crossed her arms.

"Callie is brilliant at what she does in the garage and behind the scenes. Marketing, too. There's not much to my show. I'm just a giant car nerd who doesn't fix a thing myself. Compared to Callie's mechanical knowledge, I'm a struggling infant," I admitted.

Amber considered me for a moment. Heat crept to my face, and I swallowed. Had I admitted too much?

"It's nice that you appreciate her and you aren't intimidated by her." She tilted her head, her focus going soft.

"If men react that way, it's because they think they know it all." I shook my head. "But they don't. She's a walking encyclopedia and then some."

"And then some, huh?" Amber chuckled. "Beauty and brains."

A slow smile formed, and I fingered the handle of the mug. "She's the whole deal. Smart, sweet, sexy, and so much more..."

A Denali memory popped into my mind. Callie sprawled on the bed with her hair fanned over the pillow. "She's gentle, kind, encouraging and, God, is she patient–with me, and she even gave that stupid, asshole-stalker the benefit of the doubt at first."

My body stiffened at the thought of that dick harassing my woman. I stood and placed my mug in the sink.

"Ah ah. Stick it in the dishwasher, if you don't mind." Amber opened the dishwasher, and I placed the mug on the top rack in the back.

"I appreciate the coffee, and thanks for listening to me, Amber."

"No worries." She put her cup in the dishwasher as well. "Dyson, she'll come around. She just needs time."

I nodded. Before returning to my chair outside, I used the restroom, splashing water on my suntanned skin.

Settling in for the day, I moved my chair to the shade of a maple tree. Even this early, the July heat in Kansas was intense.

In her Honda, Amber waved as she pulled away. I returned it, not relishing being alone with my depressing thoughts once more.

With a sigh, I pulled out my phone to scroll through my usual CarTube entertainment, The Car Magician, Enzo's Auto Tech, and a few other channels. I purposely avoided Callie's new channel, waiting until the afternoon when she usually posted. After three twenty-minute videos which I wouldn't be able to summarize to anyone—even Amber, I caved to the pull of watching the older episodes of Enzo's Auto Tech. He used to pull Callie into the frame for a segment all the time back when their dad was living.

In one, she verbally sparred with her father and brother in a friendly debate on oil viscosity. Her laugh rang out, and I paused on Callie's smiling face. And though her likeness magnified her absence and cut my heart, it was as good as I would get until she'd talk to me again.

Staring like a lovesick fool, I sighed, rubbing my chest. It felt as if something was missing. I had a hole in my soul that only my soulmate could fill.

Sweat trickled down my back and I leaned backward and closed my eyes, seeing the image of Callie's beautiful, smiling face comforting and taunting me at the same time.

I relaxed, trying to find solace in the birdsong and the summer breeze.

"Hey." A familiar voice called to me. "Dyson, wake up."

Someone shook my shoulder, and I jumped to my feet, heart pounding. My hands were fisted, ready for a fight.

"That's a fine way to greet me," Lucy said, crossing her arms.

My mind was foggy with sleep. Was I dreaming? I blinked, not believing my eyes. Then I scrubbed my face. Lucy remained before me, her hair pulled into a ponytail and wearing a Gabby's Garage t-shirt and khaki shorts.

"What's going on? Why are you here?" I asked, finally forming words.

"Hello to you too," she huffed.

"Hello," I snorted. "You surprised me."

"Yeah, I got that. Sorry." She glanced around at my setup.

I moved in to give her a hug, but she stepped back with her nose wrinkled. "I don't think so. You stink."

I smelled my underarm. She was correct. "That's what happens when you're in the summer heat all week and you don't shower."

"Gross. How are you going to win Callie back if you smell so bad somebody is going to wonder where the murder victim is hidden?"

"Ha. Ha." Lucy was right, but I wouldn't admit it to her out loud. "I don't want to miss Callie. I just want to show her I'm dedicated and here when she wants to talk."

"I know, Dyson." Lucy sighed and glanced toward the house.

Again, I asked, "Why are you here? Did Mom send you to check on me?"

"Well–" she started.

"Mom sent you to check on Callie."

"We *did* traumatize her." Lucy lamented, then shrugged. "But no. Callie and I have kept in touch, and I offered to come visit and help her with her show."

"Wow." I grinned. "That's really nice of you."

"It's going to be fun." Lucy studied my Yukon before turning to me.

"Are you staying with Callie?" I asked.

"Not if you're hanging here. I don't want to influence your chances with Callie. I can stay at your place, if you don't mind."

"Sure." I fished in my pocket and pulled out my keys. I unhooked the house key from my keyring and handed it to my sister. "Here you go. Lucy." As I handed it to her, I looked around and noticed an unfamiliar car. "Is that a rental?"

"Yup."

"You're welcome to drive any of my fleet. The keys are in the gray cabinet in the kitchen."

Her brows rose. "Are you serious?"

I nodded. "Just don't take the GT3 RS. I think there are too many memories associated with it. I don't want to upset Callie."

"I think I'll drive the yellow convertible if you have it," Lucy said, grinning. Her eyes sparkled. "And because I'm the best sister in the world, I'll bring you some clean, nice smelling clothes."

"You're awesome." I opened my arms like I was going to hug her.

Lucy held her hand up and stepped backward. "No." She wrinkled her nose again.

I took a step toward her. She backed away as I moved forward until I chased her around the yard. Finally, she arrived at her rental car, winded and giggling.

"Thanks for supporting Callie," I said after I'd caught my breath.

"*Somebody* has to fix things," Lucy said, rolling her eyes.

As Lucy drove off, I stood there, tired but smiling. I knew Lucy loved Callie too. With my sister here, Callie had a friend to talk to, and I had an ally.

Chapter Twenty-One
Callie

"Anybody here?" somebody called from the front of the garage. The industrial fan, which I had on in an attempt to keep the summer temps at bay, droned, making it impossible for me to identify the visitor's voice.

Too bad I couldn't see the door, but I was stretched under the car, trying to tighten a nut with a wrench. Contorted in the limited space, I couldn't easily remove myself without whacking my head. Also, I'd strategically positioned the Porsche, so the rear of the car faced the outer wall of the garage, away from the new wall separating me from my brother.

"Over here," I hollered.

"It's me, Lucy," she said, her voice growing louder as she walked closer.

"Welcome to Enzo's Auto Tech–Callie Ferenzo edition." I shimmied myself out, set the tool aside, and stood.

Lucy grinned. She rushed over and hugged me.

"Ack. I'm filthy," I squealed.

Air rushed out of my lungs as she squeezed. "It's so good to see you, Callie." She pulled back and studied me. "How are you doing?"

Emotions clogged my throat, but I opened my mouth to

respond anyway.

"Don't answer that." She stepped back and glanced around my new workspace. "I want to hear about this competition with your nincompoop brother and how you're owning him."

I chuckled and walked to the slop sink, where I pulled off the black disposable gloves, then washed my hands and arms. Lucy followed me, glancing around the walls.

"This used to be a two-car garage that came with the house." I pointed to the new, freshly painted wall. "It was years later that Dad added on the big shop we use for Enzo's Auto Tech."

"And Jay didn't mind you dividing the space?" Lucy asked.

I walked to the people door set into my new wall and peered through its small, square window. "It's not like he had a choice." I laughed dryly, then shrugged. "He was still in Alaska when I started the reno. Plus, I own half of Enzo's and the property. I just made my own *office*."

"I see," she said, glancing through the window at Jay's messy workshop.

"He was pissed, but he's playing along. What else is he going to do? I run everything behind the scenes."

"Brothers are a pain in the butt, especially twin brothers," Lucy said.

I nodded, attempting to forget her twin as his face invaded my thoughts.

"Tell me what you've done and then tell me what I can do to help. I want to watch you work. And I'd be happy to hold the camera or flashlight for you." Lucy smiled.

"Well." I motioned to the room. "This detached garage was built by the original property owners for storage of their yard tools and tractor, but when Dad saw it, he thought it would make a great workshop. That was my dad. He could see the potential in everything–old cars, buildings, furniture, and even people." With a melancholy sigh, I turned to Lucy. "From childhood, Jay was hyper focused on anything with wheels. I, on the other hand, saw how the cars made people feel, both the owners and all those involved in a rebuild. I wanted to know what made them tick. Dad called me our team manager. We all liked to get our hands dirty–so to speak–getting arms deep to diagnose a problem. But Dad said I had the patience for the other businessy stuff while Jay didn't."

I walked up to the Porsche and studied the open front compartment.

"Looking back, I wish I would have insisted Jay take more time to work on the production side of the business."

"I thought you liked putting the shows together," Lucy said.

My gaze flicked to hers, and I grinned. "I do. It's another way to be creative. But I want creative control for the entire project."

"Control freak," Lucy teased, nudging me in the side.

"Wanna be," I giggled.

"I like this color," Lucy pointed to my convertible Boxster. The convertible top was partially down and in service mode.

"It's lapis blue metallic. You should see it in the sun."

Lucy's eyes widened. "Can we take it for a drive?"

"Not yet. It needs a few things sorted first." I circled to the driver's door and pointed to the open engine hatch, where the serpentine belt was visible.

"What year is it?" Lucy asked, leaning in the open window and inspecting the dash.

"2001 with a mid-mounted 3.2 liter flat-six engine."

Lucy glanced up at me. "Mid-mounted?"

"Yeah. It has a trunk and a frunk–a front trunk."

"How the heck do you work on the engine with only that little opening?"

I smiled as if I knew a secret. "A lot easier than my brother," I laughed.

"I've heard of mid-mounted engines, but I don't think I've seen one before."

"You've seen plenty. Maybe not open and on display like this." I beckoned her to follow me to the rear trunk.

"The first middle-type engine was built in 1901. All *mid-mounted* means is that the engine is placed behind the front axle but in front of the rear. This Boxster's engine is closer to the rear axle. I have to open the convertible top slightly, then open the clamshell to the right angle to have access..."

I paused for a moment, wondering if I'd dumped more info than my audience wanted, as I was prone to do, unless it was Jay or Dyson.

To give her credit, Lucy's eyes weren't glazed over. Yet.

"What are you going to work on today?" Lucy asked.

"I have some hoses that need replacing." I picked up one from the pile I had ready to go on the worktable.

"Great." Lucy clapped her hands. "Just tell me what to do."

For the next hour, Lucy worked with me, helping by recording content, fetching tools, and making me laugh. The time passed faster than usual. I was glad for the camaraderie, but it also made me more aware of my self-imposed isolation.

After a quick lunch, we returned to the Boxster. Lucy tried aiming my static cameras at unique angles. She had a good eye. Maybe if my channel took off, I'd make enough on my own to hire her. Assuming I could talk her into moving to Kansas. *I'm certainly not going back to Alaska!*

A knock sounded on the door between the garages.

"It's your brother," Lucy said, glancing at the window.

"Anyone with him?" I asked, worried Dyson might use Lucy as an excuse to see me.

"No. I don't think so."

I frowned, but dusted off my hands. "Let's see what the asshole wants."

I swung the door open with a hand on my hip.

"Hiya, Callie. I remember this beautiful woman." Jay sidestepped me and approached a blushing Lucy.

I rolled my eyes. "What do you want?"

"To see your friend. Why have you kept such beauty hidden?"

He reached out his hand.

With a giggle, Lucy took his hand and shook it.

"Oh, brother," I groaned. "I think you really came to spy."

Still holding Lucy's hand, he leaned close to her and said, "Do you see how she doesn't trust me?"

"I wouldn't trust you either after what you pulled." She jerked her hand away. And he flinched as if she'd hit him.

Jay's shoulders drooped. "I just wanted you to know Haley is stopping by. I suspect she messaged me, thinking it was you."

"Oh, thanks. I completely forgot." I rubbed my forehead and instantly regretted it when I pulled my grimy hands away.

"Well, Lucy. We'll have another shoot for the show." I glanced at the clock on the wall. "Haley asked me to change her oil."

"That's basic," Jay teased.

I slapped his arm. "Nobody asked you."

"I can do it faster," he said as I pushed him toward the door.

"Probably. But you're messier."

"Hey," Jay whined. He held his ground.

"And you'd put in the wrong filter," I teased, once more shoving his solid chest.

"I can read," Jay said with a wink aimed at Lucy.

"That's not what I hear," Lucy said, crossing her arms over her chest.

"That hurts." With his hand over his heart, Jay dramatically stumbled backward out of my shop and into his. I closed the door, shaking my head.

The moment with my brother felt normal. If only things would stay that way.

Minutes later, I heard a car honk–Haley's arrival signal. I motioned her inside.

"Welcome to my shop." I swung my hand, indicating the space. "This is Lucy Gabbard."

"Nice to meet you, Lucy." Haley clasped her hands. "I'm so excited for you, Callie. I tell all my clients to go follow you and share it with their car loving family and friends."

Heat erupted on my face, and I grinned. "Thank you. That's awesome."

"You're welcome. I've told them that Ginny will be on the show and they have to keep watch for her," Haley said.

"Ginny?" Lucy asked.

Haley pointed to her Civic. "Ginny is her name. I've had her for five years."

I had Haley sign a social media release, then I drove the car onto the small portable car lift. When I exited the car, both Lucy and Haley held my cameras.

"This is going to be the most documented oil change ever." I chuckled and shook my head.

After I lifted the car, Lucy filmed the dirty oil spilling into the oil collection container. Luckily, I hadn't forgotten to put the metal drip pan down to catch any splashes. I'd changed the oil in hundreds of vehicles—it was easy. But talking to Lucy and Haley while doing it added a wrinkle.

As I removed the old oil filter, I glanced over at Lucy. Her smiling expression and wide hazel eyes reminded me of Dyson. A piercing ache hit me, and I bit my lip, hoping the pain would distract me from the longing.

I inhaled and closed my eyes momentarily, trying to still my heart. Realization dawned. I missed Dyson–his touch, his laughter, his understanding, and his body.

The anger came crashing back and my lids flew open. I pasted on a smile and finished my task.

While I enjoyed Lucy's friendship, her every cadence reminded me of Dyson and his betrayal. Her charismatic presence was both comforting and stifling.

Chapter Twenty-Two

Dyson

Without using a signal, a royal blue ford pickup pulled into Callie's driveway, drove across the grass, and jerked to a stop next to me in the yard.

I bolted out of my seat, jumping to my feet.

The squared body style belied the vehicle's age. The door creaked as it flew open and Enzo popped out.

Wearing mirrored sunglasses, he glanced at me and grinned. He wore a threadbare, stained white t-shirt with a yellow Camaro decal. His jeans were just as worn, with holes at each knee.

"Howdy," Enzo greeted.

"Hey," I offered before arching my stiff back in an overdue stretch.

"Still squatting on my sister's property, I see." He scanned my camping setup, then his gaze settled on my bare feet.

"To what do I owe the pleasure?" I strode to the Ford and peered in the window. "So, this is finished?" I gestured to the truck.

Enzo shrugged. "Ish."

"Looks good," I admitted, scanning the exterior panels.

"It's getting there. I'm waiting for a few parts. But now I'm in this competition with my sister..." Enzo shook his head, then rubbed his chin.

At the mention of Callie, I faced Enzo. "How's that going?" I could see something weighed on him, but any news of Callie drew me like a magnet.

"Well, truthfully, I don't know." He motioned to the porch, then proceeded to sit on the top step in the shade.

I took a seat one step lower and waited for Enzo to explain his visit. Not that I didn't welcome the company. I checked my watch. It was midafternoon, and he'd normally work in the garage until dinnertime.

"You're off early today," I prompted, leaning back with my elbows on the porch floor.

"Man, you're sunburned." Enzo studied my face a moment before his gaze settled on his hands in his lap.

I waited for him to sort his words. Waiting was the one thing I seemed to get right lately.

Finally, he sighed. "Your sister is helping Callie. Sometimes, I can hear them laughing. It really makes me miss my sister." He glanced up, meeting my gaze.

His eyes had sunk and the surrounding lines had deepened. The conflict with his sister had taken a toll on him.

I attempted to steer us away from the depressing, deep shit and keep it about the cars. "I can't believe Lucy is helping her restore the Boxster. She's not a mechanic."

A slight grin manifested fleetingly on Enzo's lips. "She's not, but she's helping with the cameras and whatever else Callie asks. I like Lucy. She's a real friend for Callie."

I nodded, and he rubbed his scruffy chin.

"What's on your mind?" I asked.

"It's not fair," he mused softly.

The breeze blew and the maple tree leaves rustled, their shadows dancing on the front lawn.

"What isn't? Many things in life aren't fair, but we have to make the most of it or change our perspective."

"She's getting help with her show." Enzo twisted so his body faced me. "I think I should have a helper too. It would even the playing field."

"But you said Lucy isn't helping with the mechanics." I studied the man, hoping to decipher his meaning.

"But I need a helper," he wiggled his eyebrows and grinned what Callie called his cheesy grin.

"Oh." I sat forward, rubbing my palms on my shorts. "You want me to volunteer? I don't think that's a good idea."

As much as I wanted to see Callie and be near her, I didn't want to get involved in the feud she had with Enzo.

"Is that because you don't work on cars yourself?" Enzo teased. "Maybe I should call Corey?"

"He'd say no. He's on Callie's good side and doesn't want to make her salty." I leaned back again. "Besides, that's cheating."

Enzo's jaw dropped, then he nodded. "Having two mechanics would be cheating, I suppose. But you're not a mechanic."

I frowned. While I didn't get my hands dirty on camera, I knew my way around an engine. "I'm not getting involved. This is between you and Callie."

A cooler breeze blew, and I sighed at the momentary relief from the summer heat.

Enzo huffed and stared at the sky. The clouds raced across in lines.

"I just wanted someone to talk to," Enzo finally admitted. He pulled his gaze away from the sky and glanced toward me. "I thought you'd jump at the chance to hang out in the air conditioning. I also thought since Callie had one Gabbard twin, I could have the other for helping with the rebuild."

"The twin-off?" I chuckled.

Honestly, it sounded like something Callie would invent for a shoot. I wouldn't have minded helping if it would have been Callie's idea. But I didn't want to upset her any more than I had or alienate the Ferenzo siblings from each other.

"How's your build going? Lucy's told me some about Callie's."

A sudden gust of wind slammed my folding chair to the ground, knocking over my insulated water bottle. I had an urge to check the forecast, but my phone was charging in the Yukon.

"Really? What has your sister said about it?" Enzo's eyes sparkled with intense interest. His eyes, the same startling green as Callie's, made me have to look away.

I rubbed my chest, attempting to soothe the burning tightness in there.

"Lucy said they'd changed some hoses. She talked more about how she enjoyed being of use and what she filmed."

"See, that's what I mean. You can help me with shooting the Boxster repairs. It would be nice to have someone hold the camera." Enzo's lopsided grin returned. "You don't have to get your dainty hands dirty."

I glanced at my hands, turning them over, palms up. At first, my self-imposed exile had been hard. I missed messing with my vehicles and editing my episodes. But I had filled my time watching other CarTubers' channels and perusing car auction sites shopping for the next purchase. I may have bid on a few. All but one had ended and luck hadn't been on my side.

My focus was on waiting for Callie. She could yell, talk, or throw car parts at me. I didn't care. I only wished for her to communicate with me. Without her, my soul felt a deep, lingering ache, a constant reminder of what was missing.

"You're on your own, Enzo."

"I know." He crossed his arms over his chest and tucked his fingers out of sight. "My Boxster repair is coming along. I've tackled the obvious things from the lack of maintenance, but sometimes it ticks."

"Cold start tick or–"

"No. I think it's the injectors." Enzo glanced at me.

"Maybe."

"I've made an appointment to get the dents removed. They're

a little more than I want to take on right now. After that, I'll see about getting the Porsche painted and then detailed inside and out."

His words suggested he was forming his plans as he spoke, testing them on me. I nodded my approval. "Sounds like it's coming together for you."

Enzo relaxed his arms. He tugged at a string on the knee of his ripped jeans.

"Any word on the stalker?" I asked, watching a gray sedan roll up the street. I'd seen the car a few times since I'd been here waiting for Callie to talk to me.

"No. He hasn't contacted me or shown up at the garage." Enzo kicked at a rogue leaf. "I've added those doorbell cameras and a few security cameras inside too."

"That's good," I said, with relief.

"I wanted to give you a heads up. Callie is having some friends over tonight." His eyes shifted across the yard before returning to me. "I might have eavesdropped and found out about it. Her hair stylist, Lucy, and someone else she called are coming to dinner."

"Thanks for letting me know." Although, what could I do? I was happy she had friends who supported her.

Enzo leaned in and sniffed. His nose wrinkled, and he waved his hand. "You stink. You might want to shower or something."

My jaw dropped, stunned at his bluntness. I leaned my head and sniffed my underarms and grimaced. "And these are fresh clothes Lucy brought me today." I shook my head.

Enzo tipped his head sideways. "You should run home and clean up. You might impress the ladies." He wiggled his eyebrows up and down.

I glanced at my watch. I couldn't leave. Could I?

At that moment, I recognized Amber's Honda as it pulled into the driveway.

Enzo jumped to his feet. "Amber," he whispered under his breath. "She's early." He raised a hand in greeting, but she glared at him in return. Amber parked the car in the garage, then went to check the mail.

I stood and went to upright my chair and pick up the wind-scattered objects.

Amber approached me, but Enzo intercepted her.

"Hey there, Amber," Enzo said in his flirty tone. Although he had his back to me, I'd bet a hundred bucks he wore a debonair smile and the smolder.

"Don't even start." She stepped around him wearing an annoyed expression, as if he was a pest at a picnic. Her face morphed into a smile when her eyes trained on me. "Dyson, follow me. We need to talk." She beckoned with a wave and pivoted toward the house.

I dropped my bag of snacks into the folding chair seat and glanced at Enzo. He stared open-mouthed at Amber, the surprise of rejection clear on his face. When he finally looked at me, I shrugged.

Amber opened the front door and disappeared inside. She reappeared without the mail in her hand. Hands on her hips, she tapped her foot.

"Sorry, man," I said, placing a hand on Enzo's shoulder. "Thanks for coming to visit."

"No problem. I'll see you." His face was as clouded as the sky had become.

I hopped up the steps and asked, "What's up?"

Her gaze flicked toward Enzo once, making her forehead crinkle. Then she motioned for me to follow her inside. Without a second glance at Enzo, she shut the door hard.

"Callie is having a girl's night here this evening."

"Enzo told me. I'm glad she has good friends to hang out with."

Amber blushed but glanced outside as Enzo climbed into his truck.

"Callie is grabbing pizza on the way back here, so there's

plenty of time." She glanced at the clock on the wall.

"Time for what?" I asked.

"Oh. I need to fill you in on our plan," Amber grinned.

"What plan?"

She left the kitchen and opened the door to the garage. Completely confused, I peered into the dim room, smelling faintly of cars and dry grass clippings.

"While we were out the other day, some guy hit on Callie."

My stomach churned with a sickening feeling, and I frowned.

"Don't worry." Amber opened the rear passenger door and leaned inside, retrieving a plastic grocery sack. She straightened and came toward me. "Callie just rolled her eyes. The guy said he knew cars but didn't. She schooled him about hurricanes and toucans."

"Huracáns and Taycans." I chuckled.

"Yes, those. My point is–you are perfect for each other."

Once in the kitchen again, she thrust the bag at me. "Here. This is from Lucy."

"How did you–?"

"I'll tell you. Would you like a lemonade?" Amber asked. I nodded, and she opened the refrigerator, then poured two glasses.

I sat in the offered seat at the table, hanging the bag on the chair back. The tart chilled liquid refreshed me as I sipped. "Now, about that plan."

"I stopped by Callie's garage and met your sister. Another of Callie's friends was there getting her car worked on and they were filming it. I suggested we all get together for dinner and everyone was available." She took a long pull of the lemonade, then continued. "Your sister handed the camera to Haley and pulled me aside under the pretense of finding out what food we have around here. Since I had the afternoon off, Lucy asked me to give you the clean clothes and then asked me to order you to shower and shave."

"Shave?" I rubbed my scruffy chin. I definitely needed a

shower, but why did my sister send a message through Amber? "Why now?"

"Lucy said you weren't replying to her messages. Anyway, you need to get cleaned up. She wants you to look nice for Callie."

"But why?" I hesitated pushing Callie, fearful I'd mess things up worse.

Amber sighed. "You love her and she loves you. Lucy wants you to show Callie what she's missing. Plus, if you're back together, then you'll be out of the yard."

She glanced at the time again. "You have a little over an hour."

Stunned, I nodded. "I'll try anything to get Callie back, and it's not like I couldn't use a shower. My phone is in the car charging. I guess I should respond to my sister before she sends someone else over." I chuckled.

"Dyson." Amber caught my gaze as I opened the front door to get my phone. I paused. "You can shower here. I'll set out a towel for you."

"Thanks, Amber." I strode to my Yukon and unplugged my phone. I called Lucy, putting her on speaker as I scrolled her text messages.

"Well, if it isn't the doofus," Lucy greeted. "It's about time."

"Sorry, Luce. My phone was charging inside the car. Amber told me about your plan. I'm not sure I want to risk alienating Callie more, though."

"Leave it to me. You just get cleaned up and look good."

"I'll try. At least, I'll smell better." I chuckled. Did my sister have a solution? A flutter ignited in my gut at the thought of seeing Callie soon.

Chapter Twenty-Three
Callie

The smell of zesty pizza filled the Jeep as I pulled into my driveway. My stomach rumbled with anticipation. I couldn't wait to share my favorite local eats with Lucy.

Just as I parked the car, a light sprinkle began, the drops barely disturbing the dust on the hood.

The garage door stood open, revealing Amber's Honda and my little Hotshot sitting sadly under a tarp, waiting to get fixed.

I'd neglected it since I came back from Alaska. In the beginning, it was because I was getting my new shop ready and searching for my Boxster, and lately because Dyson was camped out here and I wanted to avoid staying any length of time around him. But now I missed my little car and longed to get it running again.

Ginny the car, and Lucy's borrowed 1997 Porsche 993 Turbo S were on the right side of the driveway.

"Good. Everyone is here already," I said, grabbing the pizza boxes and then expertly closing the car door with my foot.

I glanced over to Dyson's area, where he nodded as I passed. His hair had grown out and curled around his ears. He had a sun-kissed glow on his cheeks.

"That smells good," he said.

"Yes, it does," I agreed softly.

A light drizzle started, and I hurried to the door. I threw Dyson a final glance. Under the tree, he would remain dry for a while.

The door swung open, revealing the smiling faces of my friends and the cheerful sounds of their conversation. Amber took the boxes and whisked them into the kitchen.

"Welcome home," Lucy said, giving me a hug.

"Thanks. I'm going to clean up. I'll be quick."

With a wave, I skirted the group and went to my room for a change of clothes. I slipped on my favorite leggings and a comfy cotton t-shirt.

Stepping into the bathroom, I was hit with heavy, humid air, and a lingering warmth as if someone had recently showered. Strange. I touched my towel, then Amber's, but found them dry. I shrugged it off and scrubbed my hands.

Glancing in the mirror, I studied my face. My complexion was pale from being inside all the time. Dark circles, the result of sadness, sleepless nights, worry, and stress, shadowed my eyes. Strands of hair had escaped my clip. I looked like someone on the brink of madness.

A burst of laughter came from the other room. Maybe my friends were staging an intervention.

"Okay. Let's go for looking alive," I whispered to my reflection.

I splashed water on my face, applied a touch of eye shadow and liner, then added color to my lips. It wasn't perfect, but I now looked as if I belonged to the land of the living.

Next, I unclipped my hair, releasing a cascade of waves that framed my face and fell past my shoulders. I shook my head, softening the look.

Satisfied with my appearance, I added the final touch—a smile. The irony struck me when I realized the expression was exactly the same as Jay's signature cheesy grin.

Muttering "ten-twelve" didn't help. Instead of improving my grin, I had to push aside a wistful pang and the sudden memory of Dyson in the Diablo. I turned away from the mirror.

My stomach growled–dinner and my friends awaited. Following the heavenly scent to the kitchen, I found Amber and Haley staring out the window with their heads together.

"I wish he'd come camp at my place. I wouldn't mind the show," Haley whispered in awe.

"Mmhmm. This is definitely a perk," Amber agreed.

"Do you think she'd mind if I talk to him?" Haley asked.

Amber tsked. "I don't know. It's the whole girl code thing–you don't date your friend's ex. But by God, this man has a big heart and is one helluva hottie."

My gut churned hearing them talk about Dyson. A hot, prickly feeling, anger or jealousy, simmered within me as I quietly moved to their side and peered out the window.

Shirtless, Dyson did pushups on the front lawn. My heart pounded a frantic rhythm as my body involuntarily reacted to the sight of his flexing biceps and triceps.

A wave of heat washed over me. He was beautiful, and I longed to have those strong arms hold me.

But I had no right to him any longer. I'd given him up and refused to be reconciled.

Luckily, the rain had stopped, and the poor guy wouldn't get soaked.

Lucy sat in the folding chair, talking to him while he exercised. Her gaze darted to the house, where we three stood silently at the window, captivated by her brother's every move. She smirked and said something to Dyson.

His head snapped up as he studied the house. His face flushed crimson, and he stopped exercising. Sitting back on his knees, he put his shirt back on as he conversed with his sister.

With the show over, I sighed.

Haley and Amber turned toward me, their eyes wide with

surprise.

I couldn't blame them for admiring Dyson's physique—the sculpted muscles and sharp angles were undeniable—though it stung to see them openly gawking at my man. *My man?*

"Time to eat," I said, directing everyone's attention to the food.

Amber snapped to attention and set the plates on the table. She retrieved the pizza cutter from the utensil drawer. "There's always one that isn't cut all the way through."

"Very true," Haley agreed, opening one box.

Lucy came inside. She met my gaze but didn't say a thing about Dyson. I appreciated her understanding.

Amber offered Haley, Lucy, and me each a glass of red wine. I took a grateful sip and sighed. Its flavor was heavenly and familiar. "This tastes like–"

"It's Glacier Bear wine. I brought you a few bottles." Lucy shrugged.

"It's fabulous," Haley said, lifting her glass. "Thanks for sharing."

Joy bubbled up from deep inside. Surrounded by my friends, my heart filled with warmth. "I'm glad you all were available for this impromptu dinner."

"Thanks for having us," Haley said. She sniffed the air. "Mmm. That smells heavenly. Did you get the blanca?"

I grinned. "You've got a great nose. Yes. I remembered you mentioning it before and thought I'd try it. I also got my all-time favorite–the deluxe–and a pepperoni."

Everyone grabbed a plate and helped themselves.

I glanced outside toward Dyson. The rain had started again.

Pulling my eyes from the window, I met Lucy's gaze–a smirk played on her lips.

"What?" I asked.

"Nothing," she giggled. "Come sit down and eat before your food gets cold."

After dinner, we settled in the living room and chit chatted while finishing a second bottle of wine.

Thunder rumbled, and I glanced outside at Dyson, who remained in his chair, getting soaked by the rain. He stared up at the sky with a frown.

"He'll go home now, won't he?" Haley asked, also staring out the window like the rest of us.

"No," Amber said, tapping her nails on the side of her glass. "He won't leave until he talks with Callie."

"That's ridiculous. He'll get struck by lightning." Lucy stood and folded her arms over her chest with a frown.

On cue, a jagged streak of lightning illuminated the sky, followed by a deafening crack of thunder that shook the windows in their frames. I jumped to my feet, my heart in my throat.

The next thing I knew, I flung open the door and stood on the porch screaming Dyson's name.

In three strides, he reached to my side. His hands, slick and damp, tightened on my arms as his hazel eyes, filled with concern, searched my face. "What's wrong, Callie?"

Water dripped off his chin. The man was drenched, and a puddle formed under his bare feet.

I'd lost the ability to speak as tears stung my eyes. The overwhelming need to protect Dyson had overridden any hesitation or anger.

He closed the distance between us. His familiar warmth threatened to stall my heart and lungs. "Callie?" he whispered.

I opened my mouth futilely.

A blinding flash of light seared my eyes, followed instantly by a booming clap of thunder that sent me jumping backward out of Dyson's arms. I inhaled deeply, attempting to calm my frantic heart.

"That sounded directly above us," Dyson said, watching the angry clouds.

The wind howled, whipping my hair wildly, while the rain

intensified into a deluge. "I know. I am worried you'll get electrocuted if you stay under the tree. You should probably go to your car..."

A barely perceptible sigh escaped his lips as his gaze lowered and his shoulders slumped.

Disappointing him left me with a heavy feeling in my gut. "Or you can stay here on the porch if you want." I gestured towards the wicker chairs with plump cushions on the covered porch. "At least it will offer some shelter."

Dyson nodded, his shoulders straightening as a wave of relief washed over him. "Thanks, Callie."

I fixated on the storm to avoid Dyson's mesmerizing eyes. I'd worked hard to shield my heart. The ache for him was almost unbearable, but I couldn't give in.

The door creaked open and Lucy stepped up to us. "Hey, look at this. This is just the first wave of storms. There's a tornado watch until two in the morning."

Her phone screen displayed the radar. The red storm blobs moved across the screen as the future cast predicted the times when the storms would hit.

"You are going to come home tonight, right?" Lucy asked Dyson.

"I hadn't planned on it," Dyson said. He pulled off his shirt and squeezed the water out.

His rain-wet torso glistened, and I found it hard to look away.

"You're a dummy," Lucy accused with concern. She poked him in the pec. He flicked water at her face.

I turned to find Haley and Amber watching our interactions. They scampered back into the room, out of sight.

As Lucy attempted to talk sense into Dyson, I returned inside. Rummaging in the linen closet, I found a towel and headed back to the porch. Lucy had gone and Dyson stood alone, staring away from the house out into the night. He'd thrown his t-shirt over the arm of the chair and water pooled beneath as it dripped from the fabric.

"Here." I lifted the towel, offering it to Dyson as he faced me. His hand covered mine, lingering as he took it. Our gazes locked, and I froze.

Shadowing those hazel depths was such remorseful longing it stole my breath. As we continued to stand there, though, a spark of hope flickered in them.

"Callie," he murmured so softly I may have imagined it.

Thunder rolled in the distance, breaking the spell. "We'll leave the door unlocked tonight. If the sirens go off, come inside." I pulled my hand away.

The GT3 RS lived. Its headlights winked at me when it came and picked me up. It drove along curving roads and then a circular track, showing off its power and speed. Then I heard sirens and red and blue lights flashed.

I awoke with a start and sat up, my alarm blaring.
It's Saturday.
Sunlight streamed through the split in the curtains. I threw back my covers and hopped to my feet.

"The day's a wastin'." I quoted my father while stretching and smiling.

As I donned a tank top and denim overalls, I planned my work on the Hotshot. My goal was to get the troubleshooting done before Lucy stopped by to pick me up for lunch.

When I entered the kitchen, Amber sat at the table, holding a cup of coffee under her nose. She wore a vibrant pink dress, her lipstick an ideal match, and her hair was styled to perfection. "Good morning," she whispered.

"Mornin'," I returned.

"We have a guest." Amber tipped her head toward the living room.

I froze. A snoozing Dyson lay sprawled across the sofa. The fuzzy throw barely covered his torso. He faced away from us, a decorative pillow supporting his head.

Amber put her empty mug in the dishwasher as I filled a cup. The coffee's rich aroma swirled around me as I stared at the slumbering man. I couldn't help but remember his morning-tousled hair, the way it stuck up at odd angles, and his gruff, caveman-like sentences.

"I hope you don't mind, but I told him to come inside if the rain blew onto the porch." She smiled apologetically. "I'm going to leave now. Remember, I'm staying in the city with friends tonight."

"Gotcha. Have fun." I waved as Amber picked up her purse and keys. With a final wave, she was gone, leaving me alone with the one man I couldn't trust myself around.

I sipped my coffee, watching the rise and fall of Dyson's breathing while contemplating what would fix my little car. Could it be the flywheel or the carburetor?

Placing my empty coffee cup in the dishwasher, I rubbed my hands together, eager to tackle the problem.

I opened the garage door and removed the blue tarp from the car, folding it before I set it aside. The familiar musty scent of the garage mixed with the outside air's clean after-rain smell.

The Hotshot was tiny and lightweight compared to most modern cars. Her pale yellow paint, red interior, and unusual features—a removable windscreen and step-down sides with a detachable half door—made me pause in admiration. I shifted it into neutral and then easily pushed it out onto the sunny driveway. As a precaution, I wedged two sturdy sticks—saved from a storm last year—behind and in front of the rear tire before pulling the hood release. Like many things on the Hotshot, the hood was removable, revealing the engine.

For fun, I tried starting it, but just as I figured, it wouldn't turn over. I'd replaced many parts but had to admit that when a car was almost eighty years old, finding decent used parts was a problem. The unique cast-iron engine, gravity fed fuel tank, and disc brakes weren't the issue.

As I pulled out my toolbox and prepped the space, I turned on my Bluetooth speaker and chose a playlist my father had created. I hummed and sang along with the classic rock songs as I tinkered with the Hotshot.

The morning sun wasn't too warm, but as the day progressed, the temperature continued to rise. I wiped sweat off my dewy forehead.

After half the songs had played, I stood and stretched. What would my father do? He'd tell me to take a break and clear my mind. I slowly walked in circles around the car, listening to a song and breathing deeply.

Stopping short, I swiveled to examine the engine compartment. "Ah ha! Could it be that easy?" It won't start–could it be the starter? It was one thing I hadn't thought of yet.

"Thanks, Dad," I said to the sky.

A memory of my father shaking hands with Dyson popped into my head. They had both been laughing at some of my brother's antics. Dad had liked Dyson. Had he observed our attraction back then?

I caught movement out of the corner of my eye and found Dyson on the porch with a mug. He gave me a tentative once-over, his eyes lingering on my face, and I returned his gaze. Finally, I acknowledged him, offering a small, hesitant wave.

He approached, and with each step, my heart pounded faster. He stopped at the edge of the driveway, and I sighed.

"How much horsepower does the Crosley have?" he asked, his sharp eyes examining the classic car's faded paint.

This was Dyson, the car nerd, the man I knew before the Alaska trip.

I selected a socket wrench and leaned in the open compartment to unbolt the stubborn starter. Grinning, I said, "You can't handle the power. It's a whopping 26 horses."

His eyes widened and brows shot skyward. "Really? That's crazy."

"It's light, but it's hard to believe the Hotshot won races when the speed maxes out at seventy."

I wrestled with the first bolt, its threads rusted tight. "Ugh," I growled. It wouldn't loosen, so I tried the second, hoping for better luck.

I straightened and frowned. I had a new starter at Enzo's Auto Tech. It was tempting to save myself a trip and ask Jay to bring me the part. But it would probably take him longer to find the box than for me to drive over and back. And he'd likely think the gesture would smooth things over, but I wasn't ready to forgive him just yet. Plus, I enjoyed keeping my brother guessing. I decided to get it myself, peeled off my latex gloves, and glanced at the sky. It was deep blue with a few clouds in the distance. It didn't seem like rain, but Kansas weather could change quickly.

"Did you fix it?" Dyson asked.

"No. I think the starter is bad." Before I lost my nerve, I continued on. "Dyson?"

A fleeting expression of surprise crossed his face before he regained his composure. "Yeah, Callie. What's up?"

"Are you going to stay here?" I asked before thinking and then winced.

"Yes." He tilted his head and his piercing eyes studied me.

"Can I ask a favor?" At his nod, I continued. "If it looks like rain, will you cover the Hotshot for me? The tarp is in the corner." I pointed, as if he couldn't see the big, blue square.

His gaze darted to the shadowy garage before settling on my face again. "Sure."

"Thank you. I'm going to run to the shop and get a part. I'll be back in a few." A smile involuntarily spread across my face.

Dyson saluted and grinned.

As I drove away, I glanced at Dyson in my rearview mirror. He'd remained waiting, as he said he would, a constant reminder of his patience and love. I knew one thing–if he decided to walk away, I would be heartbroken all over again.

It was time we talked.

Chapter Twenty-Four
Dyson

Callie's sweet smile and glimmering green eyes as she spoke about the Hotshot gave me hope. She hadn't avoided me; she'd cheerfully chatted about the car and even felt comfortable enough to sing around me.

Once she left on her errand, I paced until I couldn't resist the need to inspect the Hotshot. The micro car had personality with cool retro gauges and large eye-like headlights.

I admired the old sports car. The engine was simplistic compared to modern vehicles. No GPS, sound system, or crazy wiring harness.

Rubbing my chin, I hunted for the part that had frustrated Callie. I doubted my repair skills could compare to hers, but perhaps I could still lend a hand.

She'd gone for a replacement starter, but when I searched around I couldn't find the old part on the workbench.

Leaning in the open compartment, I found the mechanism. It was still in place. Why would she leave it?

On an impulse, I took the socket and fitted it to the bolt. I applied gentle pressure, but the bolt didn't budge. *Guess I know why she hasn't taken it out yet.* After harassing the bolts and working up a sweat, they finally loosened. Instead, I turned them until they were just barely tight. I'd let Callie do her thing.

Satisfied I'd helped, I returned to my shady spot under the tree. My chair had dried out from the storm, and I stretched my legs out, waiting for Callie to return.

The day turned hot and humid and I texted my sister to bring me something cold to drink when she arrived for lunch.

The gray sedan I'd noticed before slowed as it passed by. A dark tint on the windows made it impossible to see who was driving the car. It eventually turned around in a driveway and parked along the curb. It remained far enough away that I couldn't read the license plate.

I glanced at my watch, noting the precise moment when the sedan parked. Whoever was in there was taking their sweet time getting out.

Callie returned. She parked the Jeep and opened its back gate. In the rear were boxes and a dark part laid out on a green towel.

I rose to my feet and sauntered toward her. Once more, I stopped before stepping onto the asphalt. "Would you like some help?"

She glanced over her shoulder and flashed a smile. "I've got it, but thanks. It's not heavy."

"Do you need to remove the old one first?" I asked.

"I do." She nodded, then twisted her hair up and clipped it. She started the music, squared her shoulders, and pulled on her work gloves.

Watching her process was fascinating. I loved her attention to detail. I held my breath as she reached in with the socket wrench to remove the stubborn bolts. She inhaled and focused intently.

Giddy with my secret, I held my breath as she reached under the hood.

"Yes!" she gasped, then smiled. A moment later, the old, rusty bolts and the defunct starter motor lay discarded on the organized workbench.

With hands on her hips, she scrutinized the mess on the table. After a moment, she glanced my way, as if figuring out what I'd done.

I acknowledged her with a slow nod, and her lovely face blossomed with a smile. Warmth penetrated my wounded soul, and hope continued to grow.

She fussed a few more minutes before she sat in the car. I crossed my fingers and lifted my hands for her to see.

Callie closed her eyes and blew out her mouth. Her eyes snapped open, and her look of eager anticipation settled on the dashboard. With a push of the starter, the Hotshot's engine sputtered, then rumbled to life.

"Success!" I yelled, pumping my fist in the air, a triumphant grin on my face.

Over the Hotshot's racket, a dog barked. I turned to see a woman with short gray hair walking a golden retriever. With brisk, purposeful steps, the woman power-walked toward us. I hurried to intercept her, hoping her dog's bark meant a friendly greeting.

The Hotshot's engine fell silent as Callie cut it, the change immediately calming the barking dog.

I waved, and Callie's neighbor slowed to a stop at the end of the driveway. "Hi," I said. "Nice day for a stroll."

"Yes, Reginald likes his morning and afternoon walks," she said with a wide smile.

"Hello, Mrs. Wilson. Hiya Reggie," Callie joined us but kneeled, offering her hand to Reggie. He offered his paw and his tail blurred as it wagged. I needed to borrow Reggie to fan me as I sat under the maple tree. He'd help cool me off.

Callie and Mrs. Wilson made casual conversation about her grandkids and multiple sightings of a skunk in the neighborhood. As the women talked, I stole a glance at the gray car. The running lights glowed faintly.

Reggie sat on my foot, leaned against my leg, and nuzzled my hand. Patting his soft head, I smiled. "Good boy."

"He likes you," Mrs. Wilson said.

"He likes everyone," Callie giggled.

Mrs. Wilson rolled her eyes. "True. He does. But he doesn't sit on everyone's foot. That's special."

Reggie's chocolate brown eyes crinkled at the corners in a doggy grin directed at me. I returned the smile. "He has good taste."

Callie groaned, and Mrs. Wilson chuckled.

A navy Lexus SUV passed, and the women waved. "There go the Cavanaghs and their four kids." Mrs. Wilson leaned in and lowered her voice as if there were others around to overhear her. "I hear she's pregnant again. With twins this time."

Our eyes met—Callie's and mine—a silent acknowledgment of the unique bond we shared with our twins.

"You have a keen eye for what's happening on the street, Mrs. Wilson." An idea popped into my head. It was time for a fishing expedition.

Mrs. Wilson blushed as she smiled.

"That gray sedan, the one with the dented bumper and the lights on, I bet you know who it belongs to." I gestured, presenting the challenge, while Mrs. Wilson narrowed her eyes and focused her gaze down the street. Callie looked around me, then met my eye with a sparkle of curiosity.

"Funny. I don't know it offhand. It's parked in front of the Joneses' house. The parents park in the garage and their kids are too young to drive. The oldest is twelve, I think. No, I don't know the car." She rubbed her chin.

"I've seen it several times this week, driving up and down the street really slow," I offered, trying to keep my tone neutral. I couldn't look at Callie. The last thing I wanted to do was upset her with my suspicions. "Couldn't see the license plate."

"Oh really? Sounds as if they are casing the 'hood. We had a rash of thefts back in the nineties. I hope this bozo isn't up to no good." She glanced down at her pup. "Well, Reginald. Shall we go find out who the hooligan is?"

Hearing his name, the dog stood, tail thumping a happy rhythm against my leg and his tongue lolling out in anticipation.

"Do you think that's safe?" Having an older woman check out a suspicious car and driver didn't sit well with me.

"Perfectly. My sweet Reginald has a fierce, protective side. Let's move out." Mrs. Wilson resumed her brisk walk.

"Have a nice day," Callie called after her.

The intoxicating scent of almonds and vanilla was so close, it made my chest ache. The urge to embrace Callie was overwhelming, but I remained still, my gaze fixed on her neighbor.

Callie's fingers brushed my arm, sending a shiver down my spine, and then our eyes locked. A worried frown accompanied the flash of concern in her green eyes.

"Dyson, is it Jake?" she breathed. The question hung in the air, echoing the same unspoken thought I'd had since noticing the unfamiliar car.

"I don't know, Callie."

The car, with its dark tinted windows and closeness to Callie's house, gave me a stalker vibe, but I lacked concrete evidence that it was Jake.

Mrs. Wilson slowed as she reached the sedan. Her blatant curiosity was evident as she passed the car, her neck craning to examine it. I hoped she glimpsed the driver or the license plate.

With trembling fingers, Callie gripped my forearm, her eyes wide. Whether consciously or subconsciously, I didn't care. I savored her touch.

"What are we going to do?" she said in a hoarse whisper.

I gently covered her hand and squeezed, hoping to instill a sense of comfort and calm. "We'll be vigilant. If it is Jake, he hasn't approached the house at all."

"Probably because you've been here," she admitted.

"Right. I'm not going anywhere either," I squeezed again.

She offered me a slight smile. "Thank you."

Callie and I broke apart as Lucy pulled in, driving one of my Porsches. The arena red metallic paint on this one glimmered in the sunlight.

"It's a good thing you had Corey fix the air cooling system or Lucy would get baked," Callie said.

A warm, fuzzy feeling buzzed in my gut as I grinned, knowing she'd watched the episode when I'd sorted out the 993.

We met Lucy on the driveway. In her floral dress and shades, with her hair flowing in the gentle breeze, she resembled a glamorous movie star.

"Looking good, Luce," I said.

"Thanks." A crimson blush crept over her cheeks and she smiled. "You look rested, even after the storm, and I can't smell you, so that's a good thing."

I laughed. "I slept inside last night."

With a gasp, Lucy's brows shot heavenward, and her gaze darted between Callie and me.

Callie had watched as Mrs. Wilson knocked on the Jones family's front door and had missed my sister's silent question.

The silence stretched. I let Lucy draw her own conclusions even though they were wrong.

"I slept on the sofa," I finally admitted.

"Oh," she exhaled. Lucy offered me a sad nod before looking Callie up and down. "Are you wearing that to lunch, Callie?"

Callie glanced down at her overalls and squeaked, "No. I just got done fixing the Hotshot and I need to change." Meeting my eyes, Callie hesitated.

"It's okay," I murmured, resting my hand gently on her shoulder. "Go do what you need to do, and I'll fill Lucy in on Mrs. Wilson's mission. Then I'll put the Hotshot back in the garage for you."

Callie's face softened, and she nodded. "Be back in a flash."

Once she'd disappeared from sight, Lucy grabbed me in a tight hug. "I'm so glad you guys are talking again."

Patting her back, I said, "Me too. Let's sit on the porch and I'll give you the update."

We relaxed in the wicker chairs, out of the heat of the sun. However, a knot of anxiety began to grow in my stomach. How would I continue to protect Callie? I ran my fingers through my hair.

"Mrs. Wilson is the nosy neighbor of the street." I pointed to where she tapped on the driver's side window of the gray sedan. While explaining my suspicions to Lucy, Mrs. Wilson put her hands on her hips.

Lucy's leg bounced up and down nervously. "Looks like she's talking to the person."

"Or maybe she's talking to the dog," I offered, trying to lighten the mood.

"If it is Jake, how would she know? You didn't tell her about him, did you?"

"No."

"Oh, here she comes," Lucy said, a nervous energy making her straighten in the chair. "I hope she stops."

Nose in the air and hands pumping, Mrs. Wilson briskly strode toward us. Reginald ambled beside her, attempting to sniff the mailboxes along the way. They'd pass Callie's home shortly.

"Be back in a minute." I pushed out of my seat and jogged to meet Mrs. Wilson. Seeing me, Reginald's tail wagged furiously, becoming a furry blur.

Mrs. Wilson stopped walking and inhaled deeply. "I talked to Brie Jones. It's not theirs and she doesn't know whose car it is or why it's there." With a scowl, she glanced over her shoulder at the mystery car. "There's a guy inside with the car running, so I knocked on the window and asked if he needed help. He said he drives for a ride-hailing app and is waiting for his next client. If you ask me, I think he's lying."

I extended my phone for Mrs. Wilson to see. "Is this the guy?"

Her jaw dropped, eyes wide, as she looked at me. "That's him. You know him?"

"Shit." I scrubbed my face. "No ma'am. He stalked Callie and tried to kidnap her in Alaska."

"Oh my, oh my." Her hand flew to her throat. "He's followed her all the way here?" She tsked and shook her head. "I was going to call the police on him for loitering, but now..." She rubbed her hands together.

"Thanks. He's bad news."

"Come on, Reginald." Mrs. Wilson started off without a goodbye. Responding with a bark, the dog trotted alongside, tail held high.

When the older woman was two driveways away. I inhaled, then called Enzo.

"Hello."

"Jake's back."

Chapter Twenty-Five

Callie

A torrential downpour blurred the neighbor's porch light into a faint, hazy glow. I chewed my lip as I stared out the window, worried Jake was lurking out there, watching.

Lucy had left hours ago, and Amber wasn't coming home. Only the occasional rumble of distant thunder disturbed the eerie silence of the house. Loneliness gnawed at me.

Dyson remained outside, stationed on the porch in sentry mode, ready to protect me. All I had to do was open the door for him and he'd come in. I longed for what we had before he had believed the lie about me and betrayed my trust.

My feet remained rooted, refusing to move. My emotions swirled chaotically like the intensifying storm. I loved him, but hated what had happened. A dull, persistent ache in my chest was a constant reminder of my broken heart.

Jay's ringtone sounded from the kitchen where my phone was charging. I studied his photo on the screen and sighed, grateful for the distraction.

"Hello, Jay." I tapped the speaker icon, then poured myself a glass of Glacier Bear blueberry wine and breathed the fruity aroma.

"Hey, how are you doing?" Jay's brotherly concern was clear

in the gentle tone of his voice, tugging at my heart.

I attempted to tamp the urge to forgive him. "I'm okay. It's really raining."

"Do you want to come over and stay with me?" Jay asked.

"No. I'm fine." Tears stung my eyes.

"I can come and stay with you, if you want," he offered.

"Thank you, but there's no need. Dyson is here."

I poured a second glass of wine for Dyson. Balancing the phone and wine, I opened the front door.

Jay kept on about the storm and severe weather watch, describing the angry red blobs on the radar.

Stepping onto the porch, I met Dyson's wide-eyed gaze, his expression a mixture of surprise and concern. His eyes, like lasers, scanned my body from head to toe, zeroing in on the wineglass. As I offered him the glass, his gaze softened and a smile spread across his lips.

"It's supposed to get bad after midnight." My brother appeared to be an amateur meteorologist.

"Thank you, Callie," Dyson mouthed, lifting his glass in a silent toast. He stretched out his long legs, leaning back in the wicker chair.

"Callie, I'm worried. Jake Miller is mental."

"You think?" I scoffed, rolling my eyes. I leaned against the doorjamb.

Dyson's expression had gone flinty.

Humidity hung heavy in the air as the wind whipped my hair around my face. The temperature had dropped to a pleasantly comfortable level.

I squinted my eyes, studying the horizon through the dark, but even with lightning flashing like the paparazzi on an opening night, I couldn't locate Jake's sedan.

"The Jake Miller I hung out with was friendly. I mean, looking back, he asked a lot about you, but he asked businessy questions so I didn't suspect anything. I swear, if I would have thought he'd flip out and do anything to hurt you, I never would have talked to him," Jay continued in a soft voice. "It was just nice having a non-CarTube friend. I thought he was my friend, but he used me. I was a naïve asshole."

Hearing the rawness in Jay's voice, I bit back my "you've got that right" retort, but failed to hold in a snort.

"Did you have fun with Lucy?" Jay asked, changing the topic.

"We had a fabulous day of lunch and shopping. I hadn't tried on so many clothes since shopping with my sorority sisters. Get this–none of my new clothes have cars or channel logos on them." I chuckled, returning inside.

He laughed halfheartedly. "That's nice."

"What?" I sensed he needed to say more.

"What's what?" he asked.

"Out with it. I know you've got something else to say." I sat the phone on the table. Jay cleared his throat, and I sipped my wine.

"After you and Lucy left, Jake drove off, following you."

I gasped. "Really? How do you know this?" My stomach clenched, and dread washed over me.

"Dyson tried to contact you and Lucy, but she didn't pick up and you still have him blocked. So, he called me. The police showed up at your house, and Dyson and your neighbor reported Jake."

"I didn't see him," I whispered.

"I did. Hope you don't mind, but I went to the restaurant and sat in the parking lot after Dyson called me. I didn't call you because I wanted you to have fun with your friend. Somehow, he knew exactly where you were because he arrived twenty minutes after I did. I caught him on camera–so we have proof."

"Oh, no," I sputtered, my heart hammering in my chest. "How in the world did he find me?"

"Maybe that punk cousin of Dyson's shared your location with Jake. Just to be safe, turn off your phone's location services.

Then you can re-share your location with me, Dyson, or whoever, individually." Jay's voice shifted, adopting the firm, businesslike timbre he reserved for explaining rebuild costs on his videos. This *serious* Jay voice commanded my attention, keeping my thoughts from spiraling.

"You need to file a protection from stalking order. Callie, I'm afraid for you. I asked Jake to help you and protect you, not harass you. I can't believe I ever trusted that snake," Jay lamented.

"Me either," I groused.

"I'm the worst brother ever," he fretted.

Trying to lighten the mood, I offered, "I think, to be the worst, you would have had to contract a stalker on purpose."

"There is that. Second-to-worst brother, then." Jay chuckled.

The sharp crack of thunder made me jump, followed by a disconcerting flicker of the lights. Thankfully, the power stayed on.

"Oh crap. The power went out," Jay said.

"It dimmed for a moment here but stayed on. There's a flashlight in the kitchen drawer you can use." Dad had always kept one there. The thing was massive, about a foot long, with a light that could wake the dead.

"I'm in the shop. I've got a battery powered camping lantern around here somewhere," he muttered. A series of muffled thuds and a yelp came from the phone. "Ow."

"Good luck finding it." I couldn't help teasing. "I'm going to light a few candles. According to the weather app, the storms are only going to intensify."

"Wonderful," he muttered. "I can't find it." He cursed under his breath and a door squeaked.

"I'll let you go so you can focus. Goodnight, Jay."

"'Night, Callie. I love you."

A warmth spread through my chest. I could barely speak, but I whispered, "I love you, too," before hanging up.

With the threat of a blackout, I hastily plugged my phone into the charger on the living room side table.

Amber and I had a few candles in an array of aromas, though they served primarily as decoration.

First, I lit the vanilla-scented candle and centered it on the kitchen table for maximum illumination. The citrus three-wick candle I placed on the hearth while strategically setting the lavender one in the bathroom. I hoped the clashing scents wouldn't give me a headache.

I switched off the interior lights, plunging the kitchen into a dim, candlelit glow. I topped off my glass and sipped. The taste brought memories of Dyson to my mind.

With a melancholy sigh, I moved in the shadows to watch the storm. I plopped onto the sofa, sinking into its cushions, and glanced out the large picture window, relieved that Jake couldn't see inside my dark home.

Pulling the throw over my legs, I relaxed and watched Mother Nature's light show. Lightning flashed outside like fireworks on Independence Day.

I grew chilled as I drank the wine, pondering the protective men in my life. And even with the threat of a stalker out there, I remained safe—thanks to them.

Dyson had stood guard over my house and informed the police on my behalf, and Jay had stalked Jake around town. I had a sneaking suspicion my brother recorded the experience with a colorful commentary.

Tomorrow, I would hug them both, thank them for what they've done, and tell them how much I loved them. A warmth spread over me like a toasty blanket as I released the remnants of anger and distrust.

"Tomorrow," I said with a yawn.

I set my empty wineglass down and plucked the phone from the charger. Taking my brother's advice, I tapped settings and turned my location off for everything. Next, I found Dyson's contact, unblocked him, and added *Sexy Stick Shift* to my favorites.

Then I restarted my phone.

I held my phone to me as I laid back and relaxed again. Watching the raging storm, I had a revelation. The tempest within me had ended.

A high-pitched shriek sliced through the silence as my phone vibrated against my chest. I bolted awake from a deep sleep.

Flailing my arms and legs, I slid off the sofa, knocking my head on the coffee table.

"What the hell?" I grabbed the phone and jumped to my feet.

Tapping the screen turned off the alarm, but a startling message made my heart and breath stall.

"Emergency Alert," it read. The National Weather Service issued a tornado warning. "Take shelter now in a basement or an interior room on the lowest floor of a sturdy building. If you are outdoors..."

My heart catapulted to life again. "Oh, God! Dyson." I whirled around and sprinted to the door. Throwing it open, I found him standing with his phone in his hand and a baffled, worried expression on his face.

He met my gaze and held out his hand. I stepped forward, taking it.

The rain and wind had ceased, leaving behind an eerie stillness broken only by an occasional *splotch* when drips from the maple tree hit the ground. In the distance, lightning flashed, but nothing like before.

I read the message again, wondering if it had my location wrong since I had cleared it earlier.

A siren started wailing. The chilling rise and fall of the piercing, high-pitched alarm made me shiver. I swallowed and leaned against Dyson.

"We need to get inside. Look." He pointed between the houses across the street. "You'll see it when it lights up."

Lightning flashed about a mile away, revealing a dark, twisting funnel. I gasped. The horrifyingly magnificent tornado stole my breath, and I froze.

A barely audible sound met my ears, getting louder with each second. A deep, guttural rumble vibrated through the ground as the tornado approached.

A loud explosion a couple of blocks over, coupled with a flash of sparks, made me jump. A sudden gust of wind sent a trash tote tumbling down the street. Then the sky opened and hailstones the size of golf balls rained down, and the accompanying metallic pings of the hail pelting made me groan. "The Yukon."

"It's just a car. It's replaceable. You're not. Let's go."

I hadn't realized Dyson's arm was around my shoulders, but it grounded me. He guided me to the door and into the house. As soon as he shut the door, I snapped out of my shock.

"The basement is over here." I hurried to the hall and opened the door. I reached for the light switch and flicked it. Nothing. I tried again.

"Power's out," I uttered.

"The sparks we saw must have been the transformer blowing. Do you have a flashlight?" Dyson prompted me. He cupped my chin and held my gaze. "Callie, we'll be okay. We're together."

"Okay," I breathed. "I have a few candles already lit."

In the kitchen, I jerked open the junk drawer and found a large flashlight like my father's. I switched it on. The LED lights were blinding after the soft glow of the candles.

Heart pounding, I sprinted to extinguish the living room candle, then I saw Dyson calmly holding the two other candles near the basement door.

The wooden steps creaked under my hurried descent. Dyson closed the door and followed. The flashlight illuminated the one-room basement. The scent was a curious blend of musty basement and fresh laundry.

"Welcome to the dungeon," I said, forcing a laugh. "We don't do much down here except the laundry." I panned the room with the light. A washer, dryer, and shelf sat in one corner, while an old brown sofa and coffee table from my college days occupied the opposite wall. The glossy tan paint on the concrete walls appeared damp and washed out in the LED light.

Dyson set the candles on the washer, then pulled the table and the sofa toward the middle of the room, away from the windows. He retrieved the candles and set them on the table before he sat. He pulled out his phone and called his sister.

"Lucy's not answering," he said, frowning. His thumbs flew over the phone's keyboard as he composed a text. "I let her know we're safe."

I turned off the flashlight to conserve the battery. I tried my brother. "Jay's not picking up either." Biting my lip, I met Dyson's eyes.

He patted the sofa, inviting me to sit. I dropped beside him and exhaled, unable to relieve any tension.

"The power's off so your Wi-Fi doesn't work and we are in the basement, where the signal is not great. Also, cell towers are down."

"And the ones that aren't could be clogged with everyone calling their loved ones," I added.

"Right," Dyson agreed. "Let's not worry."

The wind whistled as it rushed over the window well—that would have been directly above us if Dyson hadn't moved the sofa. I shuddered.

"What if it hits us?" I asked in a small voice.

Dyson wrapped a muscular arm around my shoulder, pulling me against his warm body. His lips brushed my forehead, a tender kiss that sent shivers down my spine.

Suddenly, I was back on the sofa in our Anchorage hotel suite where we *practiced*, and longing and hurt warred within me, threatening to tear my heart in two.

"Callie, I don't want to die, but if these are my last moments, then I'd die happy."

I shifted to meet his gaze. Even in the flickering candlelight, raw emotion—regret, desire, sadness, and hope—shone from his eyes. It stole my breath and my voice.

He ran his hand through his hair, closed his eyes, then exhaled.

His eyes snapped open, revealing the crystal clarity of his thoughts, and his brow furrowed in determination.

"I'm sorry for everything, Callie. I should have listened to my gut and talked to you. My heart knew the truth."

I held my breath, my heart hammering in my chest.

Dyson shook his head, frowning, "I tried to focus on the car show, but all these guys asked about you–us, and Asher kept making snide remarks about your channel. *Asher*." He snarled his cousin's name, his eyes turning hard and icy as he stared at the candles.

Hearing Asher's name sent a cold wave of bitterness through me.

He blinked and met my gaze again. "I looked up your channel, and it was exactly like everyone had told me." A tremor ran through him as he whispered, "My heart said you'd never do that to me. But there it was–your channel with *your* footage. I felt betrayed and brokenhearted. Then the anger set in–and that's when you appeared."

He broke eye contact and stared at his lap. "I lashed out, but instantly regretted it. I can't stand that I hurt you.

"I'm sorry I didn't listen to you. I'm sorry I pushed you away. I'm sorry I listened to my dumbass cousin. My actions ruined everything, and I understand your response. I don't blame you." With a long, weary sigh, Dyson lifted his head. He fixed his gaze on me, his troubled eyes red-rimmed and glistening with unshed tears.

Something inside me broke—or mended, I wasn't sure which. Paradoxical emotions swirled within me, mirroring the storm outside. A weight had lifted from my shoulders, only to settle in my gut. I inhaled a juddering breath.

"I love you, Callie." He stroked my face gently and warmth filled my chest.

Love poured from his eyes, and my heart raced. "Dyson," I breathed. The weight in my stomach turned to fluttering butterflies.

"I've missed you. Your laughter, your smile, the car talk, your very essence, and my life is empty without you in it."

"I've missed you, too," I echoed. Melting against him, I buried my face in his chest, breathing in his unique scent.

Wind and grit buffeted the window well as the sirens continued to wail. Thunder shook the house.

Shrill, urgent weather alerts suddenly blaring from both of our phones made us jump, yet we clung to each other.

We glanced at our phones. He grimaced. "They've extended the warning's time and a second tornado has been observed."

Anxiety gnawed at me. I stood and paced the small space, wringing my hands. "I don't want to spend the rest of my life cowering in fear," I uttered. Whether a tornado or Jake–I needed to let go of the fear that had been my near-constant companion since that flight from Seattle to Anchorage and seize life. And I needed Dyson to live it fully.

Dyson rose to his feet and opened his arms for me. I rushed to him, my decision revealed by the impact of my body on his. I tilted my head, mesmerized by the warm, honey-like depths of his hazel eyes.

He lowered his head to kiss me, a gentle kiss that warmed my soul and woke my desire for him.

Chapter Twenty-Six
Dyson

I'd done it.

Organizing my chaotic thoughts and explaining them coherently had been as challenging as rebuilding an engine blindfolded, but I'd done it and she'd listened.

I'd poured out my heart to Callie, and she hadn't rejected me.

I had feared I would never get the chance to apologize, but my father had been right.

All it took was time—hastened by a deadly storm. But if the supercell that birthed the tornado brought my love back to me, even if we only had hours to live, I'd be grateful.

Her feminine warmth pressed against me, igniting the longing I had hope to rekindle.

With Callie nestled in my arms, I inhaled deeply, her sweet almond and vanilla fragrance soothing my soul, making my heart take flight.

Her green eyes sparkled with moisture and emotions—joy, determination, desire…love. Her beauty stole my breath, and I lowered to taste her kissable mouth. I savored the gentle, warm caress of her lips. I'd craved her touch so much.

She fisted my shirt, keeping me from breaking the kiss. I chuckled against her lips, then took it deeper. It seemed she'd been craving me as much as I'd been her. Our pent-up longing for each other exploded in a furious clash of warring tongues and teeth.

As I lifted her petite form, her legs encircled my waist and her ankles instinctively crossed and locked behind me. Returning to the sofa, I gently lowered her until she lay staring up at me, her arms around my neck, and her hair a silken fan against the cushions.

I scoured her face, looking for any sign of hesitation.

With a mischievous smirk, she ordered, "Don't you dare stop."

"Yes, ma'am." I smiled at her as she pulled me roughly to her again. I pressed my lips to hers. She opened, and I plundered her mouth. She tasted like my Callie.

Fire coursed through my veins as I pressed her body into the sofa. My length lined with her sweet spot. She arched her back, grinding my erection. I moaned into her mouth.

Her hands found the hem of my shirt and tugged. I reluctantly broke the kiss and sat up. In one motion, I pulled the shirt over my head and tossed it onto the coffee table, then groaned when it landed close to the candles. I stood, moved the shirt, and turned to lay back down—but stopped.

I watched Callie's gaze sweep over my body, landing on my obvious bulge in my shorts. She licked her lips, sending a zap straight to my dick, then bolted upright and reached for the waist of my basketball shorts.

I chuckled, catching her hand. "Somebody's eager."

"Hell, yes." She grinned, raking my stomach with her fingers. "You may have the goofiest channel on CarTube, but you have the sexiest body."

Stunned at how she viewed me, my heart lodged in my throat, clogging my airway. My jaw dropped in disbelief, and I rasped, "Really?"

She cocked her head, brow furrowed, and looked at me like I was an idiot. I let go of her hand and it dropped to my dick, fingering my shaft through the fabric.

She kneeled in front of me and skimmed one hand from my knee, up through the leg opening of my shorts, to my balls.

I moaned, enjoying her gentle exploration. "Callie, your touch–" I gasped as she tugged playfully. Jerking upright, I pulled her up and against me for a fierce kiss.

Breathless and flushed, my lungs burning, I broke the kiss.

Pulling my wallet from my pocket, I set it within reach on the coffee table. The wallet held a condom. We'd need it to finish what we'd started.

As the discordant symphony of the wind, rain, and thunder continued, Callie kneeled on the sofa. I pushed down my shorts and boxers, and my erection sprang free.

Wide-eyed, she stared at my dick like a junkie about to get another fix. Grabbing my ass, she pulled me to her and pressed her face into my groin. She inhaled noisily, then sighed. Her tongue darted out, licking my shaft. My breath caught and my dick jerked, and she hummed.

I'd noticed a damp chill permeating the basement when we'd first come down here, but now the excitement thrumming beneath my skin was keeping me warm.

Callie stood on the sofa, both her smirk and her body wobbling a little as she pulled her shirt over her head. I was captivated by a spectacular pair of breasts, now at eye level.

A smile tugged at my lips as I traced the lace edging the swell of her breasts.

Giggling, she spun, and her dark hair flared. Glancing over her shoulder, she winked. "Unhook me."

I shifted her long hair to the side for easier access to her bra. When I leaned in and placed kisses along her neck and shoulders, she shivered. As I continued my barrage of kisses, my fingers found their way under her bra back, unhooking it. She shrugged off the straps, and the bra slipped down her arms and landed on the sofa at her feet.

"Look," she said, hooking her thumbs in the waist of her yoga pants. She shimmied the pants down, exposing lacy bikini panties that matched her bra. "You did this to me. Now when I buy a bra, I get coordinating underwear, too." She shook her hips from side to side.

"Nice," I said, touching the supple material. I couldn't resist dipping my hands under it and squeezing her perfect cheeks. "Even better."

"Just wait."

Bending over, she stuck her glorious ass toward me as she pushed her underwear and pants off. I playfully swatted her bare rear, enjoying the chance to tease her.

"Dyson!" she squealed, spinning into my arms.

I laughed then sobered as my body reacted to our skin-to-skin embrace.

"I've missed you," I said, nuzzling her chest.

She played with my hair and her every touch had my nervous system anticipating more.

A loud noise, like someone throwing gravel against the window, startled us. We looked at the high window to see that water leaked inside and ran in a rivulet down the wall. It caught the reflection of the candlelight until it pooled on the floor.

The wind howled louder and Callie's grip on my shoulders tightened. Her wide eyes reflected her fear as her breathing became panicked and shallow.

I gently cupped her face, forcing her to meet my gaze. "Look at me, Callie. Breathe. That's it." My thumbs caressed her cheeks, and she blinked.

Callie inhaled loudly, and her gaze darted toward the window.

"I'm going to make love to you now."

Her gaze snapped to mine. "Yes, please." She nodded as a smile touched her lips. "I wish we could go upstairs to my bedroom."

We sat on the sofa before I claimed her lips. I pressed her back while her hands skimmed my arms and chest.

Even though I did my best to keep her focus on me, her gaze occasionally drifted to the window. But I had to keep her focus on me. With any luck, though, the storm would soon blow over and we could take our lovemaking upstairs.

Nudging her legs apart, I rubbed her sweet spot. She moaned, writhing against my hand. I slipped a finger into her, pumping her the way I'd learned she liked. She was slick with need.

I nipped, kissed, and sucked her neck, collarbone, and breasts.

Callie yanked my hair, tilting my head so she could claim my mouth. I moaned as she sucked my tongue.

Usually, she'd roll me onto my back and sit on me, teasing me by rubbing her wet folds over my boner. But the sofa wasn't wide enough, and I was glad she didn't try that maneuver tonight because we'd surely land on the floor.

I continued to play between her legs. Callie arched her back and whimpered. She was close, so I withdrew.

"Dyson," she uttered. "Please," she begged.

Her need triggered a primal desire, a lusty response in me. My heart swelled like my dick had.

"Are you ready for me?"

"Yes," she rasped.

I reached for my wallet, removing the condom package. As I rolled it on, Callie's hooded green eyes greedily watched. I had to hold my breath so I wouldn't come.

Once ready, I waited until she stopped staring at my junk and met my gaze. Her smirk matched mine.

She opened her arms to me and I fell into her embrace, lifting my hips to positioned myself.

"What are you waiting for?" Callie asked, lusty impatience in her tone. She gripped my biceps.

"You," I smirked.

Her gaze softened. "You don't have to wait for me anymore." She cupped my face with both hands. "But I'm glad you did."

My chest tightened, constricting my breath as my heart soared with unexpected joy. She pulled me to her and our lips met in a tender kiss, which turned needy. I surged into Callie and we moaned.

I began moving, and she rose to meet me. We worked in tandem, striving toward our mutual climax.

"Dyson," she murmured, as the intensity of her emerald gaze burned into me. "I love you."

Being with Callie, inside my girl, having her arms around me–I'd come home. I was drunk with happiness and I thought my elated heart might just burst from my chest.

Touching forehead to forehead, I slowed but drove in deep. Her breath fanned my face. Her inviting warmth cocooned me and I couldn't hold out much longer.

"Just because I called this basement a dungeon, doesn't mean you can torture me."

With a chuckle, I sucked her neck, branding her as mine. Agonizingly slowly, I pulled almost all the way out, then slid back inside her velvet heat.

Callie groaned and wrapped one leg around my hip. The other was pinned against the sofa back. But she only needed one to tug me in fast and deep.

"Callie, do you want it fast?" I retreated slowly, and she pulled me in again.

"Yes, like my cars," she hummed as I once more leisurely withdrew.

We played the game a few more strokes. But the tease was maddening, driving me to the brink.

"Dyson," Callie whimpered.

"More horsepower?"

"Please," she begged.

I couldn't deny my Callie. "Yes, Ma'am." I quickened my motions, pistoning my rod into her cylinder.

She gasped. My every nerve was a live wire, and I had to focus on her so I wouldn't shoot my wad before she came.

"Dyson." Callie clenched around my dick, finding her release.

I accelerated my movement and joined her. White hot pleasure sizzled through my body.

Still flushed from the sexual afterglow, our ragged breaths mingled. As I nuzzled her dewy neck, the scent of her tantalized my senses.

Callie wrapped her arms around my back. "Let's do that again."

"Only one condom," I mumbled, reluctant to move.

"Well, shit," she groused.

Chuckling, I pushed up to one elbow and studied her. Her forehead crinkled, and her lips pressed into a thin line.

"Callie, I promise you. Tomorrow I'll buy the drugstore's supply of condoms." Her gaze flicked to mine, one dainty brow arched. "Hell, I'll buy condom stock if it will make you happy."

"That would be nice. I like your dick and we have to make up for lost time."

I chuckled again and kissed her nose. Pushing up, I slipped out of her, immediately regretting the loss of intimacy.

"Let's clean up and then we can try to get some sleep."

The dim light from the candles illuminated the basement. The cement floor was cold as I padded to the bathroom. Nothing happened when I pulled the string hanging from the ceiling. *Dummy. The power is still out.*

Carrying a candle, Callie joined me in the small room. "It's amazing how much light a jar candle gives off," I said.

"And it smells better than the musty basement," she nodded.

While I cleaned up, I heard Callie shifting something. "What are you doing?" I called.

"Finding my tote of Christmas linens. I have sheets and a fuzzy blanket we can use tonight."

When I returned, Callie had draped a crisp white sheet with a cheerful snowman print over the back of the sofa and tucked it neatly into the seat cushions. Unfortunately, she now wore my t-shirt hiding the most exquisite pair of breasts in the world.

Following my gaze, she glanced down. "I thought it was smart," she said, tossing my boxer briefs to me. "Put those on. It will help us resist temptation."

She watched as I slipped the briefs over my legs and tucked in my package. My dick liked the attention. I sighed, mentally preparing myself for being in some state of arousal all night long. Smirking, I accepted the challenge.

Callie handed me a blanket and went to the bathroom. I stretched out on the sofa, ascertaining how the both of us would fit. Laying on my back, with Callie on my stomach, might work, but my legs would hang over the sofa arm or bend awkwardly. I needed to protect Callie, and sleeping with her on me wouldn't work if the window blew in. I had to shield her, no matter what happened.

"How do you want to do this?" she asked, stifling a yawn.

"Face the sofa back and I'll spoon you," I replied. She settled as I had suggested.

I snuggled in behind her, bending my legs, and she relaxed against me. I covered us with the blanket and draped my arm over her, and her fingers trailing mine sent shivers down my spine.

"Goodnight, Dyson," Callie whispered, then yawned again.

"I've got you. Sleep tight, Callie." I hugged her, breathing in her scent with a sigh.

My butt hung over the edge, but I'd gladly take the cool breeze to have my love in my arms again.

Chapter Twenty-Seven

Callie

"Callie?"

I opened my eyes to a snowman and blinked.

"Jay," I mumbled, thinking I'd heard his disembodied voice from a dream. Toasty from head to toe, a nagging pain in my shoulder throbbed as I tried to move my arm. It was pinned beneath me.

Where am I?

"Callie?" Jay again. This time, more frantic. A door creaked open, banging on the wall.

With a jolt, I sat upright on the sofa. The harrowing night's events surged into my foggy mind–the storm, taking shelter in the basement, and making love with Dyson.

The overhead light flicked on and someone stomped down the stairs.

With a grunt, Dyson slid off the sofa, tugging the blanket and me along with him. He grunted again when I landed on him.

"Are you okay?" I asked, now straddling him and his morning wood.

"No," he said with a pained expression, his hands on my thighs. I wiggled side to side and Dyson hissed.

"There you are," Jay said, rushing over. He halted, glancing at our state of undress.

Daylight filtered through the window, but I had no idea of the time.

"What's going on?" I asked my brother, wishing he'd leave me to explore my man's body alone.

"Neither of you were answering your phones. Lucy and I were worried. And when you didn't show up for brunch..." Jay stuck his hands in his jeans pockets and shrugged, reminding me of a little boy. His hair stuck up as if he'd forgotten to brush it.

"What time is it?" Dyson asked, sitting up and holding me.

"After noon," Jay said, turning away with a frown.

I hugged Dyson back, grateful we'd lasted the night, and I had another chance with him.

"It's dark down here. We slept in." Dyson nuzzled my neck.

The ceiling creaked as someone walked around upstairs. They came to the basement door and stepped down two steps.

Lucy's face appeared as she bent over. "Hi. The cops are here."

"What? Why?" I slid off Dyson's lap, looking for my underwear and pants.

"Come upstairs and find out," Lucy teased, beckoning with a wave. She disappeared again.

"It probably has something to do with how half your maple tree is blocking the road. Oh man, you should see the Yukon." Jay shook his head, a sigh escaping his lips. He walked to the stairs.

"Uh oh," I gasped.

"It's just a car," Dyson said, but a frown etched his brow.

"See you up there." Jay took the steps two at a time.

Finally alone, Dyson skimmed his hands under the shirt I wore and squeezed my bare bottom. I kissed his neck, and he sighed.

"I wish we were alone," he lamented.

"Me too." I pushed back and met his sultry hazel gaze. "We can look forward to naptime."

He chuckled and released me. We hastily dressed, then

hurried up the stairs. Before going outside, I thumbed over my shoulder. "I'm going to brush my teeth."

In the bathroom, I threw my hair up in a messy bun, scrubbed my face, and then brushed my teeth. A light rap sounded on the door.

"It's me," Dyson said.

I opened the door, letting him in. Opening the cupboard, I found an extra toothbrush and offered it to him.

As he brushed his teeth, I hugged him from behind. His warmth radiated through his shirt, a comforting heat against my cheek as I sighed contentedly.

Brushing our teeth together, the familiar taste of mint, the sound of water running, these small routines wouldn't be taken for granted again.

"Let's go on a long drive today," I suggested, my hands exploring his six-pack under his shirt.

"To the drugstore? And a quick drive back," Dyson said. He caught my hand and dropped it on the front of his shorts. His rigid penis wanted my attention.

"God, Callie," he whispered, a flush covering his cheeks. "This is how my body reacts every time I'm around you."

His light brown hair with its golden highlights, his sun-kissed skin, and his strong jaw edged with scruff had me counting my lucky stars, but it was his mesmerizing hazel eyes framed by dark lashes that held me captive.

"Callie?" Jay called, breaking the hypnotic spell.

"Coming," I called.

A wicked smile flashed across Dyson's lips. I heated at the promise in his hooded eyes.

I followed the sound of Jay's voice to the kitchen. Lucy pushed buttons on the coffee pot and the thing whirred to life. "See, I told you I can do it," she groused at Jay.

"I didn't doubt you. I just thought they wouldn't want it now," Jay said, folding his arms over his chest.

"Who says no to coffee?" I asked, striding into the room. "Thank you, Lucy."

"You missed the police," Jay said, frowning at Dyson.

"What did they want?" I asked, picking mugs for us out of the cabinet.

"They're checking on everyone in the neighborhood. Look in your front yard." Lucy bit her bottom lip.

I hurried to the front door and gasped. Pulling the door open, I stepped outside. The neighborhood looked like a war zone.

Dyson's heat at my back, we walked down the porch steps, glancing around at the destruction. The old maple tree, under which Dyson had often sat, had split, its massive trunk now in three pieces. One-third remained upright while a huge branch had fallen, partially blocking the road and covering the hood of the Yukon. The other branch landed across the driveway, effectively blocking the garage but missing the house.

The storm had scattered pieces of siding, shingles, gutters, and trash everywhere.

Across the street, a shed, or what was left of it, sat where the mailbox used to be.

"That shed used to be in their backyard," I said, pointing.

"Look at the overturned tree in the Joneses' yard," Dyson said, moving more toward the street and his car. "I wonder if Jake got squished?"

I shielded my eyes from the sun and studied the road. My neighbors were out picking up debris. I saw roof damage on two homes and turned to inspect my house. "Where are the wicker chairs?"

"Your chairs are over there," Jay said. With a sweeping gesture toward the far side of the yard, he indicated his blue Ford truck.

Dyson rubbed his face, inspecting the damage to the Yukon. He walked around the vehicle and the branch. Jay lifted his phone, capturing content.

I shook my head.

"It's not horrible," Dyson said. "Mostly front-end body damage."

I picked my way over to him. The Yukon had dents all over it from the hail. The front right panel and hood had the most damage. "Tire's shot," I pointed out, then bent to look under the engine. "There's fluid."

"Shit." Dyson lowered himself to study the undercarriage.

"Hopefully, a branch only punctured a hose," I said. The alternative would cost a lot more.

Jay trained his phone on the puddle under the car. "More content for CarTube. Back to The Car Magician it goes. It'll be like a visit from a long-lost friend."

I chuckled at Dyson, who frowned at Jay's tease. The laughter died in my throat as I realized how normal I felt.

Facing the sun, I closed my eyes and breathed deeply. Though the damage was extensive, a sense of lightness filled my heart.

"Callie, are you okay?" Jay asked, placing a hand on my arm.

I opened my eyes and turned to my twin. His intense gaze combed my face. I offered a warm smile and pulled him into a hug.

"I'm better than fine." Truth bomb. "Thank you for looking after me. I love you." I placed a kiss on his cheek.

His face turned tomato red, and he covered the place where I'd kissed him with his palm.

Lucy appeared next to me, offering a steaming cup of coffee.

"Bless you," I said, taking it and sipping.

"I'm your favorite sister-in-law," she smiled, rocking back on her heels.

"Hey now," Jay started.

"What?" Lucy poked him in the chest. "Do you have a wife picked out?"

Jay's face reddened even more, and he sputtered, glancing my way. "I–uh." I should have taken the opportunity to tease him about Amber, but Lucy continued on.

"Then don't complain." Lucy narrowed her gaze, daring Jay to open his big fat mouth.

I giggled at Lucy's fight for dominance with Jay. It really wasn't much of a struggle, though. She won, hands down.

Smiling, I glanced over at Dyson. He wore a dreamy expression. Yesterday, our future was a dead end. Now it was an open road, bright and full of promise, beckoning us onward. As he caught my gaze, I winked. He grinned and sauntered over to my side.

The coffee's rich aroma filled the air as I offered him my mug. He took a tentative sip before gently putting his arm around my waist, pulling me close.

"Dyson, I think your sister just proposed." Jay tilted his head, studying Lucy.

Dyson and I glanced at each other, then at our twins. "To you?" Dyson asked, one eyebrow close to his hairline.

"No way, numbnuts," Lucy gasped.

"Not to me," Jay scoffed, rolling his eyes. "On Dyson's behalf."

"No, I didn't," Lucy countered with hands on her hips.

"Yes, you did. You said you were going to be Callie's favorite sister-in-law, so you were proposing *for* Dyson."

"I'm pretty sure that's not how it works," I told my brother.

The yes-you-did no-I-didn't argument commenced between Jay and Lucy. Dyson and I had front row seats.

Placing my head on his shoulder, I said, "This will be another story to tell our grandkids."

Dyson's warm breath, smelling faintly of coffee and minty toothpaste, stirred my hair as he whispered. "What did you say?"

"You heard me," I replied. Finishing the coffee, I set the empty mug on the hood of his Yukon. There was no reason to worry about the paint finish now.

Our twins still playfully argued in the yard, while I took Dyson by the hand and strolled the street. Some houses remained unscathed, while others had severe damage.

"We got lucky last night," I said.

"You could say that. I know *I* did." Dyson chuckled when I nudged him in the ribs.

I stopped walking, turned, and took his hands in mine. Staring into his fabulous hazel eyes, and thinking of what I could have lost, had me tearing up.

I tried to speak, but a lump formed in my throat, silencing the words before they could escape.

Dyson regarded me with a worried expression. A pang of guilt hit me. I wondered if he thought I was running away again.

I squeezed his hands, attempting to reassure him. There was no need for him to worry because I had no intention of ever leaving his side.

I cleared my throat and tried again. I inhaled deeply. "Last night, thinking of losing you forever... It hurt. I don't want to lose you. Ever," I whispered, my heart pounding. "I need you, Dyson. With you, I'm whole."

Tears glistened in his eyes as he leaned down, his forehead gently pressing against mine. "You are the gas in my tank, Callie. I don't want to navigate the roads of life without you."

"I love it when you speak *car*." I kissed him. Dropping one hand, I touched the waist of his shorts near his belly button.

He broke the kiss and turned us toward my house. "Same. So that I don't take you right here on the street, how about you tell me about the Boxster?"

With a spring in my step, I began overloading Dyson with every maintenance issue I'd fixed or major repair I'd made. I delved into Lucy's involvement and Jay's spying tactics.

Arriving back at the house, we found Jay and Lucy flinging small twigs at each other. They'd send jibes with the sticks. Peals of laughter met our ears as Dyson and I watched from a safe distance.

"Jay and Amber sitting in a tree," Lucy sang.

Jay tossed a small stick, and it landed in front of her. She giggled and picked it up.

"Thank God you are not arguing about Lucy proposing anymore," I called to Jay.

"She did!" he yelled so Lucy could hear.

She wheeled around and stomped over. "I did not."

"Even if she did, she wouldn't have won the argument because Aunt Betsy and Aunt Tina called it first," Dyson grinned.

Lucy and I glanced at each other, stunned. My heart thumped a rapid beat, and I warmed all over.

"Hey Enzo, can I borrow your truck?" Dyson asked.

"Sure." Jay dangled the keychain for Dyson.

"I'll be back soon. The drugstore isn't too far away." He winked at me, then grabbed the key from Jay.

As Dyson drove off, Lucy and Jay started another argument about Amber. Ignoring their shouts, I watched as my man disappeared down the street, the taillights shrinking in the distance.

I knew he'd return. And he would find me waiting for him at the end of the road.

Epilogue
Callie

Six weeks later.

Leaning against the gray metal rail of the second story mezzanine, I smiled from my perch overlooking the shop. The overhead doors of the giant warehouse-turned-workshop were open. The September breeze blowing through was nice. Fall was in the air, but the distinct smell of the workshop–tires, engines, rubber matting–was a homey aroma.

"What are you thinking?" Jay asked from beside me. He also leaned against the rail but faced the outside wall, watching ARCA race highlights on the giant television screen mounted there.

"I like Corey's workspace," I said, pushing up from the rail. I threaded my arm with Jay's. "It has a magical feel."

Jay smirked, his gaze roaming the warehouse. "It's a spell. He *is* The Car Magician, after all."

"I like all the brand and model signs he has on the walls. It adds a pop of color." From Ferrari to Ford–metal, neon, or wood–the placards lined the walls above the shelving and tools.

"You're right. Otherwise, he'd hold a monopoly on gray." Jay snickered. "He does have a collection. Do you want us to start collecting them?"

Our garage at Enzo's Auto Tech was tiny in comparison to Corey's. More of an airplane hangar than a shop, Corey's space featured lifts on one side and rows of cars in various stages of repair.

Most of the vehicles needing parts were Dyson's auction purchases. My man's auction addiction kept content for The Car Magician and Gabby's Garage constant and fresh.

"Maybe. But only memorabilia of the models we've worked on."

"I like that idea." Jay rubbed his chin.

Today, Jay and I wore our matching red embroidered Enzo's Auto Tech polo shirts, black pants, and shoes. Team Enzo's Auto Tech was ready for today's competition and interview.

Corey's camera team set up the mezzanine for the pre-competition sparring. Four chairs, equally spaced, awaited the competitors: Dyson, Jay, Corey–and me.

I imagined my father glancing down from heaven, shaking his head and saying, "You're going to bruise some egos."

I grinned. "It's about time," I whispered.

"What's about time?" Jay asked, studying me.

"Nothing." I said, turning toward the open bay doors. The loud beep, beep, beep alerted us to a car carrier as it backed into view.

"Are you worried?" I asked Jay.

"About today?" Watching the truck, he frowned a moment before answering. "Not really. I can't wait to run the track."

"Me too."

His gaze rose to mine, and we grinned. I don't know how long I'd dreamed of taking a car on the track and just letting myself go.

That's a lie—I do know. All my adult life.

Today I'd get to take my fully restored Boxster and push it to the limit. I'd get to see how fast it lapped the track. Hopefully, I would outpace my brother's car.

"The Ferenzo showdown awaits," he teased.

"Scared?" I couldn't help teasing my brother.

"Of you? No. Of our antique automobiles, maybe." His forehead creased in worry.

"I have confidence in your ability, even if you don't. Our cars are sorted." I placed a reassuring hand on his shoulder.

He nodded, keeping his head tipped down and staring at his hands. "I just wish…" Jay's voice cracked, and he sighed.

I closed the space and put my head on his shoulder. "I miss him, too," I breathed.

He rested his head against mine. Together, we missed the man who'd taught, encouraged, and created the environment for Jay and me to thrive. My heart ached to have Dad there cheering us on or fueling the competitive nature between us.

Dyson strode past one of the open garage doors, heading to the rear of the carrier, out of sight. The hydraulic ramps lowered.

"I can't believe Dyson is trusting these fools with the GT3 RS," Jay said, watching as the blue sports car was pulled onto the truck. The driver secured the vehicle while Dyson paced, supervising.

I chuckled, since our Boxsters and Corey's 911 would soon be joining Dyson's.

"It's a Porsche-a-palooza." I laughed at Jay's side-eye.

As I watched, my lapis Boxster was loaded behind Dyson's Porsche. The transporter secured my car, then Jay's and Corey's.

Once the vehicles were safely loaded and locked into place, the car carrier pulled away.

The camera crew followed Corey and Dyson into the garage. The men strode through the room, only to pause and wave at Jay and me. I studied my man's trim physique, his long stride, and the genuine smile he flashed.

Footsteps clanged on the metal steps, then the men crested the mezzanine.

Corey appeared first. I'd been so focused on Dyson I hadn't

really looked at Corey. His appearance was so unexpected that it left me stunned.

"Hot damn," Jay mumbled.

"Right?" I met my brother's eyes and grinned.

"Looking good, my man," Jay said to Corey, taking his hand and pulling him in for a bro hug. After a pat on the back, Jay released him.

Corey's face flushed crimson. "Thanks."

He'd traded his usual oversized black t-shirt for a tailored polo shirt. I'd always thought he had a dad bod, but his chest and biceps filled his shirt just right and his stomach was flat. He looked as if he dead-lifted engine blocks for a gym routine.

The dark, loose fitting jeans he usually wore dragged the ground because they were too long. Today he wore khaki pants with a belt showing off his non-dad bod waist. His once bushy beard, now neatly trimmed, revealed a strong jawline. He'd tamed and shaped his thick, wild mane of curls into a stylish cut.

"Cat got your tongue, Callie?" Corey asked, his blue eyes sparkling with mirth.

"I hope not," Dyson said, lowering his head to gaze in my open mouth, which I promptly snapped shut.

Heat flamed my face. "You look nice," I admitted. "You don't usually dress like that."

Corey glanced down at his attire. "No. Not usually." He took a seat in one chair and David, one of his camera crew, clipped a mic onto him.

We all joined him in the chairs. Corey continued, "Usually, I wear dark clothes because they get grimy. I go thrifting and get the majority of my stuff and then if something gets ruined by oil or some other sludge, I don't feel bad tossing it in the trash."

"Great thinking," I said, moving on. "I like your new shop shirt. It's a nice shade of blue."

"Yeah, it makes your eyes pop." Jay winked and a slight flush fanned Corey's cheeks.

In Corey's stoic way, he responded, "That means a lot coming from you, big boy."

Dyson and I tried to suppress our laughter while Jay's mouth dropped open. I could tell he tried to assess if Corey was teasing or serious.

David miked us all and ran the checks. I itched to review the quality of the sound and the angles of the equipment capturing our interview.

"Before we start, I have a surprise," Dyson said. "Show them, David."

The big screen winked to black, then Jay and I appeared back to back with our arms crossed. We glanced over our shoulders toward the viewers, each of us with a constipated expression.

"This is the *battle* face you wanted us to make the other night?" Jay asked, referring to an evening Dyson prompted us to goad each other about today's race.

"It's a fake commercial. I made one for Corey too. We'll share them during the episode." Dyson pointed to the screen, pushing play on a remote.

Epic rock music played, and words spun onto the screen as David said in an exaggerated announcer voice, "The Turbo Twin-Off featuring the Ferenzo twins. Callie and Enzo face off, racing to finish a rebuild first. Who will win? But wait, there's more..."

Dyson and Lucy appeared back to back, both with goofy grins.

Announcer David continued, "The Gabbard twins have come to help–or hinder–the Ferenzos."

I giggled as Dyson wore a name tag with *Boss* written on it and Lucy held up a socket wrench as if it would bite her.

"Vote now to choose which Gabbard twin should help which Ferenzo twin in the Turbo Twin-Off."

The TV screen changed to Corey wearing a blue bowtie, standing under a spotlight in a dark room. He pulled out a magic wand and waved it as if having a lightsaber duel.

The words *The Car Magician* appeared with a flourish of sparkles.

"Oh, ah," Jay said.

Corey rubbed his chin, recalling, "That's what the green screen was for." A small smile tugged at his lips as he watched.

Next, the Magician stood beside a red Fiat. Corey motioned, and a black cloth covered the little car. He waved the sparkling wand again, saying, "Bippity boppity boo, the Italian car switcheroo."

The cover lifted, revealing a Maserati.

The camera zoomed in on Corey's dazzling blue eyes and he winked as the voiceover said, "Your car troubles will disappear like magic. Come see what The Car Magician can do for you.."

The TV faded to black.

"Wow," I said, clapping.

Jay joined me and jumped to his feet. "Bravo."

Dyson grinned and took a bow. "I can't wait to see the whole thing together."

David handed everyone a notecard, and I read the questions. My thoughts revolved around the Boxster rebuild details, the anticipation of the competition, and the collaboration with my fellow automotive CarTubers.

After an hour of recording, answering questions, and jibing each other, the interview ended.

Jay, Corey, and I piled into Dyson's repaired Yukon. Front, rear and side cameras would catch our friendly banter as we drove to the speedway a couple of hours away.

During a lull in the conversation, Jay leaned toward the front passenger seat I'd claimed. "Did you hear they found the gray sedan belonging to Jake a few miles from your house?" Jay asked.

I spun in my seat, eyes wide, and stared at my brother in disbelief.

Dyson clenched his hands on the steering wheel. "No. Tell us," he clipped.

Jay sighed dramatically. "Nothing much to tell. Apparently, a flash flood swept his car away the night of the tornado. They found it weeks later upside down and under debris. His body is unaccounted for, but he's presumed dead."

Horrified, I met Dyson's gaze. He patted my hand. "That's horrible," I muttered, not wishing such a fate on anyone. "Thanks for letting us know."

"It's over then," Dyson said, refocusing on the road. The rhythmic drone of tires on pavement filled the silence.

David and his crew were in a white van, and they followed, passed, and rode alongside us, their cameras capturing every moment of our journey. As the van passed us again, I sighed.

"Are you regretting stepping onto this side of the camera?" Corey asked me as we pulled off the highway.

I glanced directly into the dashcam and said, "I just hope they do it right."

Jay's laughter was like a burst of sunshine, instantly brightening the mood.

"There it is," Corey pointed to the Hanover Speedway. We glimpsed the grandstand as we drove through a grove of trees.

Dyson pulled up to the staging area, the Yukon's tires crunching on the gravel.

"I'm glad Hanover isn't a short track. I'd hate to go around a hundred times on a half mile circle," Jay said, exiting the car after Dyson parked.

"We don't have the right tires for the banked curves," I said.

"I prefer a road course, too." Dyson locked the Yukon, and we all turned to the entry gate. "I can't wait for the straightaways."

CarTube had agreed to sponsor our pilot track day episode with the three channels. Hopefully, the stats would prove fans liked the content and CarTube would sponsor us for another track day.

Beyond the brick entry arch, our four cars sat gleaming under the sun, the paint reflecting in the light. A slew of crew members took pictures and shot footage as we approached.

After a photoshoot with our cars, we finally had the go ahead to race. We changed into fireproof race suits and helmets. Handlers made sure everything fit properly and the helmet communication system functioned. I met each man's eyes before slipping behind the wheel of my convertible Boxster.

The speedway had fourteen turns, three main passing zones, and several stands for spectators. A pace car would lead the way for the first lap and keep Jay from going full throttle.

"Woohoo!" Jay yelled, his excitement palpable. Everyone laughed, catching his joy.

With a pounding heart and fluttering stomach, I gripped the steering wheel tightly, anticipation building as we lined up. The deep rumble of the engines, the sleek, powerful cars, and the once-in-a-lifetime moment had me tearing up. Remembering my father, gratitude swelled.

In my own ten-twelve moment, unable to bite back my excitement, I hollered, "The day's a wastin'. Let's roll."

Did you love Popping the Clutch?

Please leave a review.

Reviews are like virtual hugs for authors.

Bonus Content

Visit this special page to find out more about the characters from *Popping the Clutch* and see which Ferenzo wins the CarTube race.

Romance with Sass & Shenanigans.
Books by Rochelle Bradley

The Double D Ranch Book
Plumb Twisted
More Than a Fantasy
Municipal Liaisons
Here We Go Again
The Playboy's Pretend Fiancée
Cole's New Song
Brad
Canon
Destination Escape
The 24 Hour Bet
Popping the Clutch
Love, Lattes, & Holiday Tales

Desire Hardmann's Short Erotic Romps
Two Cocks in the Hen House
Two Bulls in the Dairy Shed

Books by Rochelle Bradley & CJ Warrant
Boba Book Babe Mysteries

Pandemonium in Peoria
Silenced in San Antonio
Holiday Glamping

Magic. Mystique. Mischief.
Books by Rochelle K. Bradley

Dragonfly Wishes - Dragons of Ellehcor 1
Dragunzel - Dragons of Ellehcor 2
Descended - Secrets of the Fallen 1
Charmed by Murphy - Murphy Bros. 1
Murphy's Paws - Murphy Bros. 2
The Secret Shelf

About the Author

Born and raised in Cincinnati Ohio, Rochelle developed a love of nature and art. She is a Bearcat, a Buckeye, an interior decorator, and fluent in sarcasm. She currently lives in southwest Ohio and shares her home with a black cat, a leash trained orange tabby, and her Prince.

Rochelle co-hosts (with author CJ Warrant) Wednesday Coffee & Books an Instagram Live show where they interview romance authors.

Rochelle is an award winning author including three IHIBRP (Indie Helping Indies Book Review Project) 5-star awards. *Haunted Memories*, a contemporary romance, won a contest from Ellehcor Publishing House. *Against the Laws*, finaled in the Chicago-North's Fire & Ice Contest.

She loves to connect with readers. Scan Rochelle's Linktree (https://linktr.ee/rochellebradley) where you can follow her on TikTok, Facebook, Instagram, and other social media. Visit Rochelle's website to sign up for her newsletter to keep up to date about future novels and book signings: RochelleBradley.com